SCATTER
HER
ASHES

ALSO BY HEINE BAKKEID

I Will Miss You Tomorrow

SCATTER HER ASHES

HEINE BAKKEID

TRANSLATED BY ANNE BRUCE

R A V E N 🐦 B O O K S
LONDON · OXFORD · NEW YORK · NEW DELHI · SYDNEY

RAVEN BOOKS
Bloomsbury Publishing Plc
50 Bedford Square, London, WC1B 3DP, UK

BLOOMSBURY, RAVEN BOOKS and the Raven Books logo are
trademarks of Bloomsbury Publishing Plc

First published in 2018 in Norway as *Møt meg i paradis* by Aschehoug
First published in Great Britain 2020

Published by agreement with Salomonsson Agency

A catalogue record for this book is available from the British Library

ISBN: HB: 978-1-5266-1079-9; TPB: 978-1-5266-1082-9;
eBook: 978-1-5266-1080-5

2 4 6 8 10 9 7 5 3 1

Typeset by Integra Software Services Pvt. Ltd.
Printed and bound in Great Britain by CPI Group (UK) Ltd, Croydon CR0 4YY

To find out more about our authors and books visit www.bloomsbury.com
and sign up for our newsletters

Kripos, Norway's National Criminal Investigation Service, maintains a central register of people reported missing across the country. Around 1,800 new cases are opened each year – in other words, five people are reported missing every single day. In missing person cases, they always work on the basis that there are four different possible outcomes: the person committed suicide; the person simply left; they met with an accident; or they were abducted.

ROBERT RIVERHOLT'S LAST DAY
AT WORK

'Now, what do you think?' Milla Lind sat with her legs pressed together. She was wearing a trouser suit and on that particular day had chosen a hairstyle Robert Riverholt recognised from the dust covers of her books. Her voice was always so gentle and easy on the ear, not assertive and garrulous like the rest of his clientele. Her questions were never mechanical, diverting from the salient points of their conversation. Milla Lind asked because she wanted to know. That was what he liked best about her. That, and her eyes.

'Fine.' Returning the manuscript pages to her, he leaned back in his chair and ran his fingers through his hair as he flashed a smile. 'I'm looking forward to the rest of it.'

'Brilliant!' Milla's Swedish agent, Pelle Rask, nodded enthusiastically from a sofa further inside the loft apartment, though he didn't look up from his iPad as he spoke. Robert guessed that Pelle had copied the look of timeshare salesmen in Gran Canaria, with his glossy, mid-length hair combed straight back and the two top buttons of his skin-tight shirt left undone.

Milla swivelled towards the sofa without a word before turning back to Robert. 'I'd like to end the series with Gjertrud entering August Mugabe's life.' She grabbed a few strands of her hair and began to roll them between her fingers. 'The moment everything changes.'

When Robert had first met Milla, he'd assumed this habit of hers was a sign of insecurity, believing she suffered from an awkward form of self-consciousness that compelled her fingertips to search out these locks of hair in order to make them neat and tidy. Now he knew better. 'That was when his daughter disappeared, wasn't it?'

'Yes,' Milla replied.

Robert let his gaze drift out through one of the roof windows towards the cloudless Oslo sky. 'I do think that would be a suitable conclusion for the project.'

'August reminds me of you.' Milla dropped the strands of hair and put a gold-enamelled pen between her lips. She held it there for several seconds before removing it again and drumming the lid of the pen on her trouser leg while she studied him. 'More and more.'

'Come off it.' Robert forced a hearty laugh. *I let that go on too long*, he thought, as he pressed his facial muscles into submission, refusing to give way. *Far, far too long.*

Milla kept looking at him. 'I don't know if he always has, or if I'm making him like that.'

'Well. Don't tell anyone.' Robert winked and slapped his thigh before getting to his feet. He gave a nod to Pelle on the sofa before heading for the hallway, where he stopped and turned around again. 'See you in Tjøme later on tonight. You've gathered the troops, haven't you?'

'Yes.' Milla approached him with the manuscript pages in her hand. 'They're all coming.' She stopped and took a deep breath. 'Have you discovered anything? Anything new?'

'Tonight, Milla. We'll discuss it tonight.'

Outside, the sun filled the whole sky, radiating down between the buildings to make the streets look absolutely magnificent. Robert Riverholt had been totally captivated by the city once he'd escaped from the rat race and started working for himself. As he walked down the street tonight, he was so enthralled by the architecture and acoustics that he paid no attention to the purposeful, long strides behind him or the shadow that launched itself at him as he rounded the corner into a side street lined with venerable old city trees. All he noticed was the muzzle on the back of his head and the metallic click as the firing pin struck the rimfire ammunition. And then the sun was gone.

PART I

THE ONES WHO GRIEVE

Chapter 1

I've never liked the transition from winter to spring. The trees are crooked and bare, reminiscent of mutated wild crops shooting up from the ground after an atomic war. All of Stavanger drowns in endless rainstorms that colour the city green and grey, like algae.

The job centre in Klubbgata in the middle of Stavanger has more visitors now than before. The sofa in the waiting room is crowded, the faces stiff and suffused with defeatism.

'Thorkild Aske.' Iljana's handshake has not changed since last time. If anything, her grip is even feebler and her touch even colder, like shaking hands with a corpse in a freezer. 'Nice to see you,' she says, entirely without conviction, as she sinks down into a new blue office chair with distinctive back support.

'Yes, really nice,' I reply, taking a seat.

'Do you remember your date of birth and ID number?'

'Of course.' Between us sits the bowl of plastic bananas, just as dismal as ever. I can see that they've been joined by a bunch of red plastic grapes and an artificial pear, though this fails to give the room a more fruitful atmosphere than when the bowl contained nothing but imitation bananas.

'Can you give me them, then?' Slightly irked, she swings back and forth on her chair.

I recite the series of numbers, at last allowing Iljana to turn away from my ruined face to the computer screen.

'So, you no longer wish to claim work assessment allowance, but instead be paid disability benefit?'

'Yes.' I hand her the envelope I've brought with me. 'Following consultation with my support team, I've decided that this is the only real way forward.'

She snatches her glasses from their perch on her nose. 'After what happened when you ...'

'Visited my sister in the north of Norway last autumn, yes.'

'You tried to ...' Iljana looks hesitantly at me, 'take your own life?'

I nod. 'You'll find the records inside that envelope.'

Iljana clears her throat and leafs through the papers. 'Yes. And you were stabbed with a ...' She looks up from the papers. 'Harpoon?'

'The pressure got too great.'

'Pressure from ... us? From the unemployment services?'

I nod again.

Ulf, my psychiatrist and friend, has reached the conclusion that the time is right to go for the grand slam. Full disability benefit. Ulf and my doctor have even collaborated on writing a letter in which they assert that it was pressure from the job centre to accept a post in the Forus call centre that had resulted in two near-death experiences. In one I had jumped into the sea and in the other I had been shot with a harpoon through the hand and chest. We make no mention of the case I'd got mixed up in up north. In fact, Ulf has threatened to cause a media storm if the job centre continues to make demands of his brain-damaged, extremely suicidal patient in need of nursing care.

'I see.' Iljana continues to riffle through the documents. 'Well, I think we have everything we need to progress matters on our side.' She gathers up the papers and returns them to the envelope before folding her hands on her lap.

'What happens now?' I rub my fingers over the scar on the back of my hand, still sore where the harpoon went in, especially on the rainiest of days. And in Stavanger there are plenty of those.

'So,' she sighs, putting her thumbs together. 'The next step is a neuropsychological investigation.'

'What does that involve?'

She tilts her head slightly in my direction, without meeting my eye. 'That consists of a series of cognitive tests. You'll be called in sometime in the spring.'

'Thanks,' I say, getting to my feet.

Iljana smiles a practised smile that doesn't include her eyes, before leaning forward towards the bowl of plastic fruit. 'Live a quiet life, Aske. Respect your limitations. No more travelling while you're under investigation.'

'Never again,' I tell her. 'Nothing but tranquil nights in my bedsit spent in deep contemplation of the cunning wiles of life and job centres.'

Iljana shakes her head a little and pivots back to her computer screen as I turn and leave.

My mobile rings before I've even left the job centre.

'All done?' Ulf's voice sounds tense and in the background I can hear the thrum of an engine as Arja Saijonmaa sings 'I Want to Thank Life'.

'All done.'

'And?'

'I'll be called in for a neuropsychological investigation sometime in the spring.'

'Good, good,' Ulf says. 'That means we're on the move. Excellent, excellent.' This is followed by a pause, and I can hear him switch on his indicators as he hums along and chews desperately on yet another piece of nicotine gum.

When I came home from Tromsø, Ulf took my medicines from me, and in order to set a good example, gave up his Marlboros at the same time. This has resulted in a massive overuse of nicotine patches and chewing gum. It soon became clear to us both that Ulf had landed himself in a real predicament by this decision. Now he can't possibly give in to his craving without also reconsidering my new medicine regime. It has all developed into unspoken trench warfare, with me biding my time and him chewing.

'By the way, have you packed for tomorrow?' Ulf asks before I have the chance to hang up.

'Sure, all set.'

'No coffee machine or any other unnecessary nonsense, like last time? You can't afford to make a mess of this for your own sake, Thorkild.'

'Only clothes and good intentions. No nonsense this time.'

'This chance with Milla Lind that has come about might be the last one you get.'

'I promise.'

'By the way, Doris is looking forward to meeting you. She's never met an Icelander before.'

'Half,' I answer. 'I'm half-Icelandic, as you well know, and I haven't been there for more than twenty years.'

'No bloody difference. The point is, she's looking forward to it.'

'Ulf,' I begin, screwing up my eyes against the sharp spring sunshine that pushes its way through the rain clouds above the job centre building in the middle of Stavanger city centre, 'about that dinner.'

'Forget it. I issue the invitation, you turn up. No excuses this time … Yes, as a matter of fact,' Ulf goes on in between snippets of his duet with Arja. 'You need to buy some chervil.'

'What?'

'Chervil. You have to bring along some chervil.'

'What's chervil?'

'Chervil,' he barks. His jaw muscles are working in top gear. 'It's a kind of parsley. Pop into a supermarket before you come. They'll have it there.'

'Must I?'

'Yes, I insist,' Ulf concludes as he rings off.

Chapter 2

'Ulf says you're impotent?' Doris looks at me quizzically as we sit at the kitchen table in Ulf's villa in Eiganes. His new girlfriend is a fifty-seven-year-old German sexologist and columnist with her own blog, whom he met at a conference in Bergen.

'No! Believes!' Ulf chops chervil within an inch of its life on a kitchen island nearby. He is wearing a loose, sleeveless tunic, and I can see three nicotine patches on one of his upper arms.

Doris tears a bread roll with her fingers and places the chunks on a plate beside her soup bowl. Soon Ulf arrives with a handful of chopped chervil to sprinkle over her soup. Picking up one of the pieces of bread, she uses it to submerge the chervil leaves in the cloudy liquid before dropping it in her mouth and chewing vigorously. 'Tell me, do you often masturbate?'

I stare intently down into my soup bowl and pretend I didn't catch her question.

'Thorkild doesn't masturbate,' Ulf interjects helpfully as he pours wine into our glasses before sitting down between us.

Doris sinks another morsel into the chervil broth, all the while studying me through narrowed eyes. 'So, how do you know that?'

'That's the whole point.' Ulf licks the green residue from his fingertips. 'He doesn't know. He creates these obstacles, insuperable barriers so that he can avoid engaging with the world beyond his bedsit. Aske is on the run from everything that might be called interpersonal interaction.'

'The modern hermit,' I add, in a desperate attempt to appear cheerful in the midst of this nightmare of a social get-together. I grab my glass and drain the contents. Doris folds her hands under her chin. Her red hair is cropped and spiky, sticking out in all directions in a contemporary hairstyle that reminds me of a flower arrangement designed by a manic depressive. Her thin lips are dark red and her pale complexion hangs loosely in folds without making her seem plump or bloated, but more as if she has lost weight and her skin hasn't had enough time to adjust. She looks content, both with herself and with the plunging neckline on the outfit she's chosen for the evening's interrogation.

'Have you tried to place yourself in a sexual scenario, imagined situations, people who normally would arouse a sexual reaction, to bring about an erection?'

'I don't know,' I reply in a strained voice, and once again let my gaze fall upon the soup bowl in front of me. The sweet aroma and the green, oily liquid bring to mind algae-infested, brackish water. 'What I can say …'

Doris fishes out a cigarette from her handbag once she has finished eating and lights it while Ulf stares, angry and yearning, at the glowing end of her fag. 'You must dare to fantasise,' Doris tells me. 'Let your desires run free again.' Leaning forward, she blows a cloud of smoke up towards the ceiling. 'Sometimes you store them away, believing they're no longer accessible. Sexual repression is not only a

13

feminine concept. Nor is it necessarily forced upon you by others.' She inhales more cigarette smoke and contentedly exhales it again. 'I can give you some exercises that might be worth trying when you're on your own.'

'Thanks,' I mumble as I stir my spoon aimlessly around in my soup. 'You're too kind.'

Ulf turns away in annoyance from Doris and her cigarette and runs a hand over the patches on his upper arm. Then he fixes his eyes on me. 'Maybe we should have one final run through of what awaits you in Oslo tomorrow?'

'OK,' I answer, pleased at last to be able to change the subject and to watch Ulf suffering as much as I am.

'I love her books,' Doris purrs happily. 'Few writers have created a better antagonist than Gjertrud, August Mugabe's wife. By the way, have you read any of Milla's books?'

I shake my head.

'Well,' Doris continues, now using her soup bowl as an ashtray. 'Milla Lind is not only the undisputed queen of crime in Scandinavia, she's big in Germany too.'

Ulf follows her every word as he slurps his soup and then adds: 'She's written twelve books in the series about the melancholy local police officer with the juicy name August Mugabe, whose wife has tried to murder him on two occasions.'

'Three,' Doris contradicts him.

'What?' Ulf drops his spoon, gazing at her and her cigarette with obvious irritation. 'No, it's two. The first …'

'Mugabe's wife has tried to kill him three times.' Doris refills her wine glass. 'In the first book she poisons him, in the fourth she sets fire to the cabin while he is lying in the loft drugged with sleeping tablets, and in the eighth—'

'No, no, not at all,' Ulf breaks in. 'In the eighth book, the hired killer who tries to dispose of him is quite clearly following orders from Mugabe's corrupt boss, Brandt. He says so himself just before he shoots, that this is a greeting from an old friend. If it had been Gjertrud who had hired him, he would have said that the greeting came from someone August loved.'

Ulf looks at me, nodding fiercely, as if to persuade me to confirm his thesis. I refuse to accept any theory from the man who stands between me and my pills, so I ignore him and turn my attention back to Doris.

'It's precisely because he says that,' Doris parries, 'that we know it's Gjertrud who's behind the hired killer. By saying it's from an old friend, it's simply one last insult from the almost seventy-year-old woman who is so filled with contempt for the man who refused to give her a child. Just the same as with the cold potatoes she always serves him for dinner. Powerful symbolism from a childless woman suffused with sadness and bitter regret.'

Ulf smacks his lips as he chews. 'Hm, well, maybe you're right.' He turns to me again. 'As you know, Milla's last consultant, Robert Riverholt, was shot dead in broad daylight by his ex-wife six months ago. Milla Lind took it very hard, and hasn't worked since then. It was through a course in grief therapy at Fornebu that I came in contact with her psychiatrist. Milla and her previous consultant had just started on the research work when he died, and she needs help in completing it before she embarks on her final, concluding book about August Mugabe. Readers around the world are waiting for this book, Aske.'

'And this is where I come in?' I round off. 'As a crime consultant, whatever that is.'

'Ten days in the company of the greatest crime writer in the country, for 3,500 kroner a day,' Ulf adds, raising his glass in a silent toast.

'Rather that than making candles in a sheltered workshop in Auglendsmyrå run by the unemployment services,' I reply.

'It'll be a few weeks before you're called in for that neuropsychological examination anyway, and this is as safe and sound as anything can be. Travelling around with no less a person than Milla Lind – that's not a prescription I can write for all my patients.'

'Thanks,' I respond tersely, and drain my wine glass. 'I need money.'

'Bloody hell, of course we'll see to that,' Ulf says, going on to address Doris: 'You know, I think Gjertrud will make one last attempt on August Mugabe's life in the final book. And the series will end with her succeeding. Eh? Wouldn't that be something?'

'Absolutely,' Doris agrees, taking another cigarette. 'I expect nothing less.'

Ulf leans back demonstratively in his chair, holding the soup bowl in his hands, and drinks the rest straight from the bowl. 'You've to meet them tomorrow at one o'clock at the Bristol Hotel,' he goes on once he has finished. Digging out a blister pack of nicotine chewing gum from his trouser pocket, he snaps out two or three tabs and puts them in his mouth. 'The flight to Oslo leaves at half past eight, so be a good boy and set your alarm. I'll call you anyway to make sure you're ready. Also, we can go through your list of medicines if you like, in case there's anything you want to discuss.'

'You know what I want,' I tell him coldly as I put down my glass.

'That time is over,' Ulf replies as he cleans the side of his mouth with his tongue and drums his fingertips on the porcelain. 'For both of us.' Then he gets up and starts to clear the table. 'You made sure of that up there in Tromsø. But if you're not ready for this, I can respect that; after all it's less than six months since you were in the line of fire, and we can easily—'

'No, I want to do it,' I say. 'I just thought it might be a good idea to have something in reserve, maybe a blister pack of Oxy-Norm at the very least, or …'

'Forget it. Neurontin, Risperdal and Cipralex for anxiety. No Sobril, no oxies. That's the deal.'

'Cipralex is for kittens.'

Ulf pulls a face and spits the chewing gum into the sink before pressing out another two tabs. 'Well, what the hell do you think these are?' He holds the chewing gum out to me in the palm of his hand. 'We've both chosen to sacrifice something for the good of our health. If I can manage it, then so can you.'

'And if I can't sleep?'

'Then drink a cup of camomile tea and write a poem about it.'

Doris places her glowing cigarette in the soup bowl. 'Is it not a bit dodgy, Ulf, to send him there with nothing but Cipralex?'

Fuming, Ulf tosses the chewing gum into his mouth. 'Certainly not. It's exactly because of what happened last time that he's not getting any of the pills he wants.'

I shake my head despondently and get up to leave. Doris approaches me and places a hand on my shoulder. 'About what we were saying earlier. Maybe you should use the time to see if you can find your way back to your own sexuality while you're on the road. See if you have the courage to be curious, to fantasise and reflect on that.' She stops for a moment and looks at me with a half-smile before asking: 'Do you think you'd like to do that?'

'Ulf says that fantasies are dangerous for me,' I reply.

'Well.' As she tenses her lips, the folds at the corners of her mouth pucker slightly. 'You should always reflect on where your fantasies take you, and not least on which fantasies to indulge in. But you're allowed to keep them to yourself, deep down inside, you know. As long as you feel that they give you something, and they don't harm either you or anyone else.'

'You're right.' I give her a smile of some kind and a brief handshake. 'As long as they're not harmful, then.'

CHAPTER 3

The number 9 bus to Tananger is empty apart from the driver and me. It's dark outside, yellow streetlights hurtle past the windows, and the bus rocks from side to side as if it were a ship scudding through the mild spring evening. The trees have new leaves now, and coltsfoot flowers sprout between the asphalt verge and the pavement as we roll westwards out of the city.

I alight at the bus stop just outside the old chapel to find the car park deserted. Pinpoints of light shine between the hedges behind the buildings.

As soon as I reach the path leading into the graveyard, I come to a halt. In front of me I see new brown heaps of earth decked with flowers, gravestones with golden lettering, angels and birds faintly lit up by glass lamps and torches. In the moonless night sky, grey-black clouds flit in from the sea. I've been here many times since I returned from Tromsø. The first time I just stood here without venturing into the graveyard itself.

I keep to the outer edge, following the path between the plots until I reach the right side. A gentle breeze brings me to a stop when I catch sight of her gravestone. It lies fourth from the path, with a lamp on either side, though only one lamp is lit. I stand motionless, staring at the black stone.

'It looks best in the dark,' a voice suddenly says behind me.

'What?' I turn abruptly and gaze into the narrow eyes of an elderly man in a brown overcoat and hat who is standing several paces behind me, with a scruffy dog on a lead. 'Sorry, what did you say?'

'The graveyard,' he answers gently. 'I prefer to come here in the evenings too. It doesn't feel so bare when it's dark. Besides, I think the lights make it look really nice, even when it's raining and windy.'

'Yes.' I pull my jacket collar more snugly around my neck. 'They're lovely.'

'Do you have family here?'

'No, she ...' I begin, but stop.

'My wife.' The man nods in the direction of one of the rows of gravestones on the other side. 'I've been a widower for nearly seven years now. My daughter suggested that I should get a dog,' he says, smiling at the mutt at his feet. 'For company. It's good to have something to fill the emptiness, until the day we meet again.' He looks at me with a gaze strengthened by solemn conviction. 'In paradise.'

I nod faintly.

'Do you have a dog?'

'What?'

'A dog, do you ...'

'No. I take happy pills.'

'Oh? Do they help?'

'I don't really know,' I mumble, while my eyes search out Frei's grave.

'Ah, well,' the man says as his dog tugs on the lead. Then they disappear into the darkness.

20

I wait for a while before taking a step forward on to the soft grass. All at once the ground feels colder, as if winter has not really yielded here, and I retreat to the path again. I rush out of the graveyard, back to the car park.

CHAPTER 4

In Oslo it is wet, and the spring air here is colder than at home in Stavanger, where the smell of cow dung from the fields of Jæren has already begun to creep across the city. In the restaurant at the Bristol Hotel, I'm directed to the cloakroom where a woman takes my jacket and hands me a ticket before I make my way back to the entrance. The Vinterhaven restaurant and Bibliotek bar are almost full of people, piano music is playing, and there is a strong aroma of ground coffee beans mingled with hamburgers and fried onions. I let my eyes roam over the crowds until I catch sight of a woman and two men at a table, partly hidden behind a row of large potted plants. The woman smiles and waves in my direction while the two men regard me with measured curiosity.

I wave back awkwardly and set off in their direction.

'You must be Aske,' the woman says, getting to her feet as I approach their table. 'We've been expecting you.'

I nod and shake hands.

'Eva,' the woman says. 'I'm Milla's editor at the publishing company.'

'Thorkild Aske.'

'Pelle Rask,' the younger of the two men says, without standing up. 'I'm Milla's agent, at Gustavsson. We look after the foreign rights.'

'Halvdan,' the other man says, rising to his feet to shake hands. 'Head of the publishing company.'

'You'll be travelling on to Tjøme after this?' Eva asks when we're all seated again.

'Sure,' I answer. 'That's the plan.'

'Brilliant.' Halvdan picks up his fork and launches into a two-storey-high slice of millefeuille. 'It'll all go well, you'll see.'

'I think she's looking forward to meeting you,' Eva says. 'But all the same we thought it best for the four of us to meet you first to go over a few things.'

A waiter arrives with a small pot of coffee and a cup that he sets down in front of me.

'So,' Halvdan begins between mouthfuls. 'You're a former head of interrogations in Internal Affairs in the police force.' He holds his fork loosely in the air and looks at me under bushy eyebrows, waiting for me to pass comment.

'That's right. But not any more,' I add. All three of them scrutinise me as they nod approvingly. They've obviously been brought up to speed on my history. 'I was deprived of my post by court judgment following an episode a few years ago and had to serve a sentence of just over three years at Stavanger prison.'

'And now you're freelance,' the head of the publishing company concludes before getting to grips with the cake again, taking another mouthful and then pointing his fork at Eva. 'Wasn't it Viknes-Eik who wrote an essay about having to atone for one's sins?'

'Yes. "Fall from Grace", it was called,' Eva answers, sipping from her glass of wine. 'Poignant.'

'"Fall from Grace", yes. A harrowing read.' He swings the fork like a sceptre between us. 'Have you read it?'

I shake my head. I could have said that I know one or two things about falling flat on your face and destroying both your career and your spiritual life, that I have a psychiatrist at home in Stavanger who occasionally believes that I'm still falling, but I'm not in the mood to be so humourless on a first date, and nor do I consider the Vinterhaven restaurant or the Bibliotek bar to be the place for incisive honesty under the guise of witty conversation.

The head of the publishing company twirls his fork around slowly and closes his eyes. 'He shows his fundamental distrust of punishment and atonement, romanticising a society in which the idea of punishment comes from within.'

'It's in my eyes that you shall see my boundaries,' Eva goes on to say, evidently quoting the essay.

'Yes, yes,' the head of the publishing company says. 'You've got it, exactly.'

'You'll have to sign a non-disclosure agreement,' Milla's Swedish agent insists. 'That includes not only complete confidentiality about everything you learn about Milla's next book and its contents, but also whatever information you discover about her and her private life.'

I nod. 'Tell me about Robert Riverholt,' I say, taking a gulp of coffee. 'Milla's previous consultant. I understand that he—'

'Was shot,' the publishing boss interjects. 'Dreadful affair. Affected all of us.'

'Riverholt was an ex-policeman with a troubled personal life.' Pelle runs a finger over the handle of his coffee cup. 'His wife was ill, and she shot him on the street in broad daylight before driving off and taking her own life in a car park beside the lake at Maridalsvannet.'

Eva touches my hand lightly. 'The tragedy had nothing to do with the publishing company or with Milla. But I can understand your concern. It affected Milla as well. She hasn't written a single ...'

'Well,' Pelle Rask clears his throat and picks up a bundle of papers that he pushes across the table, 'if you'd just look through these and sign before we continue.'

I lift the papers and start reading as the head of the publishing company nods to a group of men passing by.

'In the first instance we're talking about one week,' Pelle tells me when I've finished. He hands me a pen. 'We'll pay half of your fee in advance, and the rest when the contract period is over. If there are any delays, or if Milla needs you for longer, we'll continue under the same conditions, if that's acceptable to you. Travel expenses will also be covered, so hold on to your receipts.'

'So.' The head of the publishing company puts his fork down on his plate once I've signed and returned the non-disclosure agreement. 'You must be anxious to learn what this is all really about?'

I nod again. In fact, I'm anxious about what it is that this Milla Lind actually expects me to help her with. But most of all I'm anxious about what I hope will happen when the job is done. Do I really believe that Ulf will meet me at the airport with wide-open arms and a back pocket full of prescriptions and say: *Yes, that's my Thorkild, what a smart boy, and here's your Sobril and oxies back, knock off now, say hello to Frei and your bedsit, see you on the other side.* That's the only reason I can find for agreeing to leave my own space behind: because I believe that this will change something.

'Are you familiar with the books about August Mugabe?'

'No, not really.'

'Well, Milla Lind is one of our bestselling authors, her books are published in more than thirty countries, and she has sold more than ten million books around the globe. In connection with the launch of her last book, *Swallow Heart*, we, the publishing company, issued a press release to the effect that Milla had started work on the final book in the series about August Mugabe. They'd only just started on the project when Robert died.'

'She hasn't written anything since,' Eva says. 'Milla went into a deep depression, and it's only recently that she's felt strong enough to pick up the project again.'

'Milla and Robert had dug up a real missing person case,' Pelle tells me. 'They were going to use it as the background to the book.'

'What case is that?' I ask.

'Two fifteen-year-old girls disappeared last autumn from a residential children's home outside Hønefoss. They got into a car outside the children's home one morning, and since then no one has seen them. The police think they intended to go to Ibiza, the same place they had run away to the previous year.'

'It's really pretty neat,' the head of the publishing company laughs. 'It actually turns out that the case in Milla's book is directly linked to the plot between August Mugabe and his wife, who has of course tried to kill him at least twice.'

'Isn't it three times?' I ask.

'Then you *have* read them,' the publishing boss says, followed by a loud burst of laughter. 'You know, Milla herself refuses to confirm or deny that his wife was behind the pistol shot in *A Bed of Violets*.'

'Everything's been put on ice since Robert was murdered,' Eva says to turn the conversation back on track, 'and it's important for Milla to return to work again.'

'That's where you come in,' Pelle adds. 'You'll take Robert's place. It's a matter of interpreting police reports, helping with technical details, and so on. It's crucial to emphasise that this isn't an investigation as such, but simply research work with a view to assisting with Milla's book.'

'That sounds really thrilling,' I lie.

'Yes, isn't it?' they all answer in chorus before the publishing boss gets to his feet. 'Pelle, Eva, you see to the rest of it. I've got a meeting coming up at two o'clock.' He leans across the table. 'Aske, good luck.' He rounds things off and gives me a firm handshake before striding away.

CHAPTER 5

The bus journey to Tjøme takes two and a half hours. The arrangement is that I should be picked up and accompanied to Milla Lind's summer house nestled somewhere amongst the smooth coastal rocks of the archipelago at the far southern edge of the western coast of the Oslo Fjord. I spend the time on the bus reading one of Milla Lind's books. It's called *Octopus Arms* and is about the deeply melancholic, retired investigator August Mugabe and his wife, who loves to hate him.

I'm more than halfway through the book when we arrive at Tjøme town centre, and have already developed some kind of attachment to the shabby and stooped police detective who roams the streets of wooden houses in Sandefjord, hunting down the man who has seduced and abducted a shipowner's only daughter.

'Hello there!' says a man with a Swedish accent as soon as I alight from the bus. In one hand he is clutching two bulging carrier bags from the off-licence. He bares two rows of brilliant white veneers that contrast sharply with his suntanned, Botox-treated complexion. 'Is it ... Thorkild? The policeman?'

'Ex-policeman.' I grasp his free hand and give it a limp squeeze. 'Pleasure.'

'Joachim,' the man announces enthusiastically. 'Joachim Börlund. Milla's partner.'

We stand looking at each other for a few seconds, he still sparkling and smiling, while my face is locked in the accommodating half-smile I've been practising.

'Well,' Joachim begins before he comes to an abrupt halt, as if he has suddenly run out of steam. 'It'll be only us,' he continues when he has finally regained his enthusiasm. 'Unfortunately, it's too early to set out crab pots, you get mostly water and slops before midsummer, but we've got some good, meaty specimens from the local shop.' He nods in the direction of a nearby Spar supermarket. 'After all, you can't be out at a summer house without eating crab and drinking white wine, can you?'

'Unheard of,' I mutter.

Joachim hoists the bags between us, and is about to say something amusing about alcohol, but changes his mind and gives a strained smile before wheeling around to point at his car, a red Volvo SUV with gleaming wheel trims and radiant paintwork.

'It's only a short drive to Verdens Ende,' Joachim tells me once we are ensconced inside the vehicle.

'Sorry?' I turn to face him. 'What did you say?'

'Verdens Ende,' Joachim repeats, as he presses a button to start the car. 'The house is situated at the southern tip of Tjøme. The place is called Verdens Ende.'

'Are you joking?' I ask, taken aback at the irony: the name means The World's End.

'No.' Joachim looks as if he is holding his breath while giving an exaggerated smile and clutching and letting go of the steering wheel with his fingers. It seems as though he's constantly uncomfortable, or perhaps this happens only in my company. 'It's called Verdens Ende, I promise you,' he adds emphatically.

'Odd name,' I say, turning again to face the front.

'Yes, maybe so.' Joachim exhales loudly, releasing the steering wheel with one hand as he puts the car in gear before driving carefully out of the car park.

'What's your line of business?' I ask as we pass a golf course on the right side of the road. The grass on the greens is emerald, as are the surrounding trees. It looks as if summer arrived in this part of the country some time ago.

'Me?' He casts a glance in my direction before answering. 'These days it's mostly helping with the management of Milla's career. Interviews, press tours, readings, trips, emails from fans throughout the world and a whole lot of other thankless tasks. Previously, I ran a travel agency in Stockholm. Package tours to Asia and South Africa. It was on one of those trips that I met Milla five years ago.'

'Love at first sight?'

'Absolutely. Milla's the best thing that ever happened to me.' He nods vigorously, as if to emphasise what he's just said.

'Tell me about my predecessor, Robert Riverholt,' I ask just as Joachim brakes and flicks on the indicators. He brings to mind a grandmother in a car that's so big she has to hold on tight whenever she's driving.

'Milla took losing Robert really hard,' Joachim says. The car lurches forward when he stamps his foot on the accelerator. 'She hasn't managed to write or do anything at all since then, and I've been the one who's had to work hard to keep the show on the road.' He takes a deep breath. 'But now you're here. Now we're back in business.'

The summer house is a massive Swiss-style villa encircled by an extensive garden and tall trees all around. Through the foliage I can make out the sea and sloping rocks.

'Come on,' Joachim says when I stop in front of the stone steps leading up to the main entrance. 'Let's see if we can find Milla.'

The floor is laid with flagstones and the walls are half-panelled. Further inside I catch sight of several more rooms, all flooded with light from the grand windows. The furnishings are either new and white or old and untreated; every room breathes of the rustic idyll that can only be bought with lots of money and assembled by an interior designer.

I follow Joachim through the living room with its dining table, fireplace and glass doors all the way into the kitchen, which has its own exit to the rear of the villa. He deposits the bags of shopping and sets aside the batch of wine bottles.

'Oh, it's you,' a subdued voice says behind me. I turn to the door that leads out to the garden and look into the face of a woman of my own age, slim, attractive, with recently coloured hair in various shades of blonde. There's something about her gaze, her eyes, that doesn't match the rest of her appearance. She looks straight at me, without seeming to notice me at all.

'Yes.' Joachim moves across and takes her hand in his. 'This is Thorkild Aske.' He leads her cautiously in my direction.

'Hello, Thorkild,' she says. Then she turns to the bottles of white wine, picks one up and reads the label. 'Everyone's waiting for a book,' she says as she studies the bottle. 'But I haven't been well for a long time now and I just can't find the strength to do anything at all.'

'I know what you mean,' I reply.

Milla looks at me inquisitively. 'Do you?'

I nod. 'Sometimes things happen that make time pass more slowly, or stop completely, and it can be difficult to know what it will take to make the clocks start ticking again.'

Shaking her head ever so slightly, she continues to look at me. 'So what do *you* do then?'

I shrug. 'Find some way of enduring the waiting time.' I notice how the taste of gelatine spreads over my tongue at the mere thought of the pills I once had. I could have added that there are few things better suited to making the waiting time easier to handle than prescription meds, but the tiny pupils, the slightly lethargic muscle movements and the tone of her voice all tell me that she already knows this.

'I understand you've been ill,' Milla says, putting down the bottle of wine and leaning on the kitchen island, 'because of a woman, who died?'

'Yes.'

'Maybe they think it will be different with you. Two wrongs will make a right, eh? Or what do you think?'

I'm about to say something, but Milla Lind has already turned away. She points at one of the wine bottles and says to Joachim: 'You can just take this one back. It's no use.' She turns to me again, grabs me by the arm and leads me through the glass door out on to a spacious terrace. 'All these people going around waiting for a book to find out what happens in the end to a character I've invented. In the meantime, Robert is lying in a graveyard, no more than half a metre away from the woman who killed him. Nobody understands,' she says before relinquishing my arm.

'But I'll give them what they're waiting for,' she goes on. 'I'll finish the job, complete the book. And then, after that …' She stops for a moment as her eyes wander past the tall trees to the choppy water in the distance. 'Is that enough?'

Milla walks towards an annexe adjoining the main house. Her eyes are wide open now. As if the brief stroll has blown away whatever it was that lay between us a short time ago. 'Come here,' she says. 'And I'll tell you what Robert and I were working on.'

CHAPTER 6

Milla slides the glass doors aside and shows me into her office in the annexe. 'The study is my personal space.' She closes the doors, sits down at the desk and uses one hand to tidy her hair while switching on the computer with the other. 'Robert and I had just made a start on research for the new book,' she says. As she leans forward to key in her password, the light from the screen flickers over her face. 'We had found a true-life missing person case that we were going to use as background to the book.'

'Is there anything special about that particular case?'

Milla shakes her head fleetingly without looking up from the screen.

'It was in the media and the girls have still not been found. It concerns two young girls who ran away from a children's home outside Hønefoss seven months ago. It seemed to stand out somehow when Robert and I went through real cases looking for something to use in our research. Because the girls were so young, only fifteen years old.'

'And how can I help you with that?'

'We're going to talk to the relatives and the police, and at the same time you'll help me by explaining and clarify-ing the mechanics of such a case. I know you used to work as head of interrogations, and I think that could be really useful with regard to the psychological aspects.'

'What do the relatives have to say about talking to us?'

'Robert met the relatives of one of the missing girls and they were grateful for all the help they could get and pleased that the case hasn't been forgotten.'

'And what about the other girl?'

Milla shakes her head. 'She has no relatives.'

'None?'

'No. By the way, I have a folder for you.' Her face disappears behind the screen, and I can hear her rummaging about in one of the desk drawers before reappearing. After a moment's hesitation, she slides the folder across to me.

'Why did she kill him?' I ask, picking up the folder marked *Robert Riverholt*. 'Robert's wife. Why did she shoot him?'

Milla is about to say something but shakes her head instead. She rolls some strands of hair between her fingertips. 'Camilla was unwell,' she says finally.

'Unwell?'

'Motor neurone disease, a degenerative illness that affects the nerves in the spine and the brain. She was given the diagnosis when Robert was still working in the police. Robert told me they were already drifting apart by then, but he chose to stay for as long as he could. In the end he couldn't put up with any more.'

'So she killed him because he was leaving her?'

'Yes,' Milla replies tersely before turning slightly away from me, towards the books on the bookshelf on the wall. 'She couldn't live without him.'

'Why do the police believe that the missing girls went to Ibiza?' I quiz her as I leaf through Robert's folder about the missing persons case.

'The girls had run away before.' Milla clears her throat when we make eye contact at last. 'They travelled to Ibiza that time.'

'OK.' I continue to peruse the papers. 'So, what's the plan?'

'Tomorrow you and I will go to Hønefoss to visit the children's home and the mother of Siv, one of the two girls. They're expecting us.'

'Why?' I put the folder down on the desk between us.

'What?'

'I mean, if we're not going to do any investigation, if all we're going to do is to root around in what people have to say about these two girls, why do you actually need me, or Robert before me, for that matter? Isn't that something a writer can do for herself here in her study?'

Milla looks at me for a long time, until in the end she nods in the direction of the scar on my face. It runs from my eye all the way down to the cavity between my jawbone and my cheekbone, where it lingers before it comes to an end on a split upper lip that never quite meets my lower lip, even when my mouth is closed. 'Where did you get that?'

'It's from the car crash.' I turn the disfigured side away from her. 'Ulf says I no longer need to talk about it.'

'Is it painful?'

'Just when I'm on my own. Or with other people.'

Finally, she smiles. 'You're right,' she says, leaning back in her chair. 'In fact I could have written all that from in here. Read up about missing person cases on the internet and then plucked out some suitable shadows from my subconscious and given them names, faces and backstories. But this case is different.' She is about to say something more, but instead she takes a deep breath and turns to face one of the windows, where the treetops outside are swaying gently in the wind that sweeps in from the sea.

'In what way is it different?'

'It just is,' Milla tells me, blinking hard several times. 'Anyway, Joachim has made things ready for you in the boathouse,' she goes on, pointing at the woods below the study, where I can make out the contours of a white building down beside the rocky shore. 'We'll start work early tomorrow morning.'

Chapter 7

The living room in the boathouse comprises a set of wicker furniture arranged around a vast panoramic window overlooking the ocean. The only pieces of nautical equipment evident in here are a few maritime treasures suspended on the white-painted walls or from the bare roof beams. I've found a place for myself on one of the wicker chairs, where I sit browsing through the folder I got from Milla. It contains a number of newspaper cuttings, pictures of the missing girls and some case documents.

Siv and Olivia were both fifteen when they disappeared from a residential children's home outside Hønefoss on 16 September last year. They were last seen getting into an unknown vehicle at the bus stop just beside the children's home. The police thought they had travelled to Ibiza because the girls had run away there once before, and on that occasion they'd been brought home by the police and child welfare authorities one week later. But this time no trace of them has been recorded since they got into that car on the morning they went missing.

I pick up the photographs of the two missing girls. Siv has shoulder-length blonde hair and a narrow face with too much make-up, while Olivia has cropped, thick raven-black hair, pronounced cheekbones and pretty eyes emphasised by a thick layer of eyeliner. All the photos of Siv and Olivia are almost identical: two teenage girls masked by far too much face paint and a fuck-you attitude that turns them into static imitations of icons with the obligatory pouting lips and wide-open doll's eyes.

It simply adds insult to injury to know that we won't even investigate the case, and that I've now been downgraded to poking around in the fates of fellow human beings in order to dig up a good story. It strikes me that this is all this week with Milla Lind will bring to the table: a spinning out of the series of losses.

I return the photographs to the table and sink deeper into the chair. Frei never came back, not even after I'd been discharged from hospital in Tromsø and went home to Stavanger. Ulf says it's a sign that the brain injury in my amygdala has not deteriorated, and that her rightful place is in her memorial tomb, rather than an ice-cold slab of meat I could conjure up with oxycodone and benzodiazepines. He thinks the absence of pills and of Frei has made me lonely, and that I am rusting away for lack of human interaction. I could have spoken up and said I'm alone rather than lonely, that there is a difference, but we both know this is not the real problem.

As I shift position in my chair, my eye falls once again on the photos of Siv and Olivia on the table. 'Where were they heading that day?' I mumble before turning away and closing my eyes.

CHAPTER 8

This is the day I've waited for since I was three years old. Siv is restless; she's standing beside me, smoking and squeezing the empty cigarette packet while talking nineteen to the dozen. The sun is already up, and it's melting the frost that clings to the grass in the fields below the bus shelter. Soon it will reach the car park on the other side of the road, where the night warden's car is parked beneath the windows of the common room.

I open my almost-empty bag. Siv has filled hers with teddies, make-up and clothes, but I have next to nothing in mine, because I know that when the sun goes down tonight, all the old shit won't mean anything any longer. This autumn day is the only thing that means anything, because it's the first and last at one and the same time.

'There.' Siv stubs out her cigarette on the bus shelter wall just as a black car comes gliding around the bend, driving towards us. She tosses away the empty cigarette packet and picks up her bag. 'Are you ready?'

'Sure,' I say, sending one last look in the direction of the building on the other side of the road. 'I'm ready.'

CHAPTER 9

I must have fallen asleep in the chair. When I wake, the sun is gone. The surface of the sea consists of uneven lines rolling in towards the sloping rocks. The tree branches creak and rustle. I'm cold, depressed and am missing Stavanger and my bedsit there.

I put on my shoes and go outside, moving towards the main building. I am at the edge of the clump of trees between the boathouse and the main garden when I suddenly catch sight of Milla in the study annexe, leaning face down over the desk with her arms stretched forward. Her eyes are wide open and her mouth is opening and closing as if she is having some kind of seizure.

Just as I emerge from the trees, I see the shadow behind her. He pulls her up by the hair into an upright position, holds her for a few seconds and then propels her forward towards the desk. Milla's facial expression seems to alternate between acute terror and ecstasy. As he hauls her up again, her blouse tears open, exposing one breast. Joachim grabs it with one hand and squeezes hard.

All at once it is as if Milla is looking straight at me. Joachim lets go of her breast and moves his hand up to her throat. Milla opens her mouth and her body tenses. Immediately before she appears to faint, Joachim releases his grip around her neck, instead holding her hair tightly with his other hand so that Milla hovers in mid-air, leaning over the desk.

Only now do I understand that she is not looking at me, but straight through me to the background of darkness. Soon Joachim lets go of her hair and she falls back heavily against the desk, while Joachim retreats into the shadows.

I stand there for some time until, in the end, I start to move towards the house. Through the glass door leading into the study, I again catch a glimpse of Milla. She is buttoning her blouse and turns away when she sees me.

'Do you need anything?' Joachim rakes his fingers through his thin, newly bleached hair when he appears in the doorway.

'My suitcase,' I answer. 'I left it in the hallway.'

'Wait here.' He disappears inside, through the kitchen door to the main house.

I take a step towards the study annexe, but stop when I see Milla at the glass door. She pulls down the venetian blinds and I hear the door being locked. Soon Joachim returns with my suitcase.

'Apologies,' I say. 'I didn't mean to ...'

'You lot don't understand what she's like,' Joachim tells me. 'What she needs.'

'What does she need?' I ask when we reach the woods between the main building and the boathouse.

Joachim stops in front of me to stand on a tussock of grass that makes him almost as tall as me. As he smiles, his teeth glint in the twilight. 'To lose control.'

He shakes his head when I make no response, then steps down from the tussock and walks on. 'People like

Milla need a certain kind of person. A certain kind of man, not ...'

'Yes, I've realised that,' I reply. 'Not someone like me.'

Joachim continues on through the trees without answering.

'Or Robert,' I round off.

'What?' He stops. This time he can't find a grassy mound to stand on, but he takes an extra step away, as if to equalise the difference in height. '*What did you say?*'

'You said, "you lot",' I answer. '"You lot don't understand what she's like." I expect you meant the likes of Robert and me?'

'I saw at once what kind of guy Robert was. Saw right through him.'

'In other words, you're an expert judge of character?'

'You won't be staying here long enough to find out, pal. Here.' Joachim sets the suitcase down on the ground between us. 'You can sort out the rest for yourself,' he says as he heads back up towards the house.

CHAPTER 10

Joachim and I don't exchange a single word during breakfast next morning – only brief looks and a handshake in the
hallway when Milla and I are about to leave.

'And now there's just the two of us,' Milla says as we
settle into her car in preparation for the drive to Hønefoss.

'Yes.' I grip the steering wheel. I haven't driven a car
since my licence was taken from me more than three years
ago, but I couldn't bring myself to tell Milla that when she
handed me the keys after breakfast.

'I used to love travelling.' She turns to me with a smile.
'For book festivals around the world, shopping trips and
city breaks.'

'Tell me about your book.' I've already decided that I
like listening to Milla's voice. It's subdued and mature, and
doesn't dominate the conversation. Milla doesn't strike me
as the kind of person who demands your total attention
when she is speaking. It's as if it's good enough that you're
there, listening, in your own fashion.

'It's going to be about August Mugabe's younger days,'
she begins. The stretch of asphalt ahead twists and turns
through old forests and bare cornfields beneath a grey,
cloudy sky. 'I want to show my readers the man he was
before he met Gjertrud, at the time when he was together

44

with the woman who bore his child, but who didn't want him. She took the child with her and left him before he had a chance to ask her to marry him.'

'Interesting,' I mutter.

'I think I want to make him a bit like you.' Milla turns to face me, her smile lingering as she studies the damaged side of my face, anticipating a reaction.

'Oh?' I ask without taking my eyes off the road.

'A younger version, though.' Milla laughs softly. 'Short hair and with eyes just as grey as the rain clouds out there.' She giggles. 'The way I imagine yours once were. Before seriousness took hold.'

'Before the scars?'

Her gaze has stopped on the jagged furrows of my face. 'I like scars,' she says, reaching out her hand so that her fingertips can lightly touch the line of my wound. 'Both the ones everybody can see, and the ones on the inside.'

'I'd really prefer to do without some of them,' I reply brusquely.

'Oh?' She pulls back her hand. 'Which ones?'

'Camilla, Robert's wife,' I venture, watching Milla's eyes harden as she recoils from my face. 'Did you know her?'

'A little.' Milla turns to gaze out of the side window. 'We met Camilla a few times, Robert brought her with him to the summer house in Tjøme, but I didn't really know her.'

'You said she couldn't live without him.'

'Yes. Robert had only just moved out. Found himself an apartment. He was a good man, not the sort that just takes off when his wife gets ill. You mustn't believe that. He tried for as long as he could. In the end he couldn't bear it any longer. He said he couldn't stay there just waiting for her to die. It wasn't fair on either of them.' Her head slides closer to the window, as if she's trying to find something else to focus on between the trees.

'She wanted to take him with her over to the other side. Playing cards and drinking tea with the spirits?'

'Don't say that.' I can see that her mouth has acquired a lopsided, turned-down curve.

'Sorry,' I say as we pass a small industrial area where the verges are wet and the grass covered in a grey coating of asphalt dust.

'Robert and I used to play a game,' Milla says, leaning her head on the side window. Extensive fields and newly sown acres appear on our right, flanked by sporadic farms with barns, outhouses, agricultural machinery, silos and the occasional burst plastic silage bale tucked away on the fringes with the contents leaking out. 'The "what-if game", we called it. We went through the information and turned it this way and that to find something we could use in the plot of my book.'

'Is August Mugabe also searching for two missing care-home girls?'

'No. He's looking for his daughter. She disappeared when she was seventeen, around the time that August met Gjertrud. August didn't know her, since her mother had refused to let him have anything to do with her, but August had followed her progress from a distance without ever daring to make contact. And when he was finally ready to take the step and meet her, she vanished. The final book will operate on two levels, one when August was younger, around the time when his daughter went missing, and the other in the present, twenty years later, when he starts to search again.'

'Does he find her?' The scent of spring and newly turned earth seeps in through the car's ventilation system.

Milla turns to me and gives a smile of sorts. 'I haven't decided how the book will end,' she replies.

'The fact that no one has heard from these girls for almost seven months,' I begin, turning down the air conditioning. 'That's not promising.'

'So you think they're dead?' Her voice immediately takes on a grating undertone.

'Does it matter?'

She looks at me again. 'Yes, it really does.'

'Why?'

She dwells on the furrows and network of scars on the damaged side of my face. 'Tell me about her, about the woman you killed in a car accident. Did you love her?'

I shake my head. 'I don't think about her any more,' I answer even though that's the mother of all lies. It's been six months since I tried to go over to Frei's side, and failed, six long months since I saw, touched or somehow felt her chill against my skin, but it doesn't mean I've stopped thinking about her. Time passes, not because the yearning fades, but because wanting to die is painful, and you need medicines to alleviate the pain while you work your way down the spiral. There have been days, late nights alone in my bedsit when I've fantasised, struggling to find the entrance to the spiral without arriving there in time before the morning light has started to press against the wool blanket that hangs at the living-room window. Ulf calls it yet another sign that I'm getting better, even though I believe it's a matter of lacking the right motivation.

'I don't believe you,' Milla tells me warily, leaning closer. 'I know what it's like, Robert ...'

'I'm not Robert Riverholt,' I reply coldly, placing my hand higher on the steering wheel so that my shoulder hides my scars.

Milla observes me for a long time. 'No,' she says softly while her gaze slides slowly out of the side window. 'You're not.'

Part II

THE ONES WHO LIE

CHAPTER 11

'Why have they gone along with the idea of talking to us?' I ask, turning on my indicators as soon as I spot the sign marked Åkermyr, the name of the residential children's home. We've hardly spoken to each other during the final stage of the journey. Milla seems tense, restless, though not because of our earlier conversation. It's something else, and I notice that I'm becoming increasingly frustrated with each kilometre we put behind us, not only because she answers my questions with questions of her own, about me, but because there's something about this assignment, this trip, that bothers me, that doesn't add up, and I find it annoying that I can't work out what it is.

'Because they think they can help,' she replies while I park the car in front of the main entrance and switch off the ignition. 'It's a way of keeping the case alive, a way of refusing to give up hope.'

'What do the investigating officers have to say about it?'

Milla unfastens her seat belt and takes hold of the door handle. 'They think it's fine,' she says.

'Sure? Police, at least the ones I know, aren't particularly happy about that kind of interference.'

'These ones are.'

I shake my head in despair at Milla's reluctance to tell me anything at all. 'Will we have a chance to speak to them too during this trip?'

'Maybe,' she replies as she leaves the car.

Åkermyr youth centre is a low single-storey building at the end of a driveway off route 7 to Veme and Sokna. We are met at the steps by a tall, slim woman of around fifty whose name is Karin. She has brown smoker's wrinkles on her face and a nicotine-yellow bob hairstyle that makes her face look too long and her eyes appear to sit too close together. 'You are … Milla Lind, aren't you?' Karin asks, holding out her hand tentatively towards Milla.

When Milla smiles, Karin's wrinkles stretch out into a smile. 'Come in, come in,' she says, ushering us into the building. 'We'll go to the common room – no one uses that during school hours.'

'Do many young people live here?' I ask as we walk along a wide corridor, passing an activities room as well as a music room – according to the door signs, at least.

'We have a care unit and an acute unit.' Karin stops at a door that is slightly ajar. 'Right now, six of the rooms are occupied.' She breathes in through her nose and opens the door wide. 'This is our common room. Come on in.'

Inside, there is a kitchenette with a gurgling coffee machine on the worktop opposite a dining table and seating area comprising brown leather sofas on either side of an IKEA coffee table. The room is furnished in a modern style, but all the same there is something about the smell that reminds me of prison, of psychiatric units, and, come to think of it, even my bedsit in Stavanger is imbued with that same odour. I think it's the absence of some ingredient or other that means it always smells the same in places where too many transitory people pass in and out of the same doors.

'Were you working here when the girls went missing?' I ask once we're settled in the seating area, with Karin on one side and Milla and me on the other.

'Yes. I was the one in charge here then too,' Karin tells us. 'Would you like some coffee, by the way? I think there's a fresh pot.'

I nod but Milla declines. Karin gets to her feet and crosses to the kitchenette, where she selects two bright yellow mugs and pours coffee into them.

'What can you tell us about the girls?' I ask, smiling as she hands me one of the mugs before sitting down again.

Karin's gaze lingers on Milla, leaning her elbows on her knees with the mug in front of her so that the steam from the coffee appears to drift up into her nostrils. 'Siv and Olivia became good friends when they met here. Siv came later, right enough; she was here for respite and stayed part-time at home with her parents in Hønefoss.'

'They'd run off once before, hadn't they,' I go on, 'to Ibiza?'

'That's right. The previous year. But at that time they phoned home after a week. I think they got scared of the whole business. In any case, they were happy when we went down there to collect them.'

'Can you tell us what you remember from the day they disappeared?' I ask, tasting the coffee. 'I'm thinking of the last time they went, last autumn.'

'We didn't realise they'd gone until the afternoon when they didn't come home from school,' Karin says. 'Later we found out they'd been spotted getting into a car just outside here at the bus stop. One of the boys saw them.'

'Had they packed? Taken things with them, other than what they needed for a normal school day?' I cast a glance at Milla: it doesn't look as if she's listening, she's just sitting there motionless on the sofa beside me without uttering a word as she stares at the windows behind Karin and the increasingly blue, increasingly bright, sky outside.

'Just a few bits and pieces of clothing and personal belongings,' Karin tells me, 'but not as much as they'd taken the last time they disappeared.'

'What did you do when you realised they were gone?'

'Well, we called the police, of course.'

'This boy who saw them,' I add. 'Does he still live here?'

It dawns on me that my questions are all at sixes and sevens: they lack sequence, and are too limited. I'm continually expecting Milla to join in, to ask questions and talk about what she needs for her book, but she doesn't say anything, just sits there wearing an expression that alternates between scared stiff and head in the clouds – she is present, but there's something keeping her at a distance from us.

'Yes,' Karin replies. She looks across at Milla before placing her mug down on the table between us. 'But he's at school,' she adds. She too seems to have noticed how ill at ease Milla seems.

Since Milla makes no move to participate in the conversation, I make up my mind to continue asking questions, if for no other reason than to satisfy my own curiosity.

'You said you spoke to Milla's previous consultant, Robert Riverholt?' I say. 'Just after the girls went missing?'

'Yes, it was no more than a few days after they left. He said there might be a TV programme about the girls' disappearance, and that no less a person than Milla Lind would …' She clears her throat, taking hold of her coffee mug again and lifting it to her face. 'I mean, it was really awful to hear what happened to him. I'd only met him that one time before—'

'Do you still have any of her belongings?' Milla suddenly interrupts. Her wrinkles stretch like dry riverbeds across her face. It's as if her skin lacks moisture, and has somehow contracted during the past few minutes.

'Whose belongings?' Karin asks, taken aback.

'Olivia's.'

'Er, I think so, but—'

'Can I see her room?'

'I …' Karin takes a deep breath and tilts her head to one side. 'Why? Kenny gave the impression that this was just …'

'Who's Kenny?' I ask sceptically, turning to face Karin.

'Sorry,' Milla sniffles, suddenly rising from the sofa. 'I can't do this.' She rushes to the exit and hurries through the door.

'What's going on?' I demand when I finally catch up with her at the car outside in the yard. 'Are we investigating this case after all?'

'No.' Milla wheels around to face me. Her face is grey, her eyes wet and brimming with tears. 'But if we *were* … if we …' Milla bites her bottom lip while her eyes drift away from mine towards the bus stop.

'Then I'd have said that this is very strange,' I answer in the end.

'What?' Milla stands staring at the bus stop, her hands clutched to her chest as if there's something down there that only she can see, something that terrifies her. 'What's so strange?'

'That two fifteen-year-old girls get into an unknown car and simply disappear. That they could have headed for Spain without as much as a single trace en route down there. That their mobiles haven't been used since they went missing.' I hesitate before adding: 'And that this is just a research assignment that you and Robert were working on for a book.'

Milla is about to say something, but changes her mind. 'Come on,' she finally tells me. 'We have to talk to Siv's mother before it gets too late.' Then she rushes to the car and sits down in the passenger seat.

The spring sunshine lights up the spruce trees and fields below the road. I take a deep breath of air down into my lungs, feeling how it glides through my system without making any impression, before I move to the car and clamber inside. Milla is obviously keeping something hidden from me, and I've no idea how long I can stand to continue with this charade before I jump on a plane and go back home. At the same time, I don't like the idea of pulling out before I know what it is I'm actually leaving behind.

CHAPTER 12

Siv is sitting behind me in the car, leaning in to the middle. I can see her in the rear-view mirror, staring intently at her phone while cars, buses, caravans, delivery vans, commuters and anxious parents, hurrying to drop off children before heading for work, all pack the road in both directions. I don't really like travelling. It makes me think of livestock being transported in dark trailers without knowing what awaits them at the other end. But this time everything is different. This time I know what's waiting for me when we reach our destination.

'Are you excited?' Siv asks, glancing up from her mobile.

'Yes,' I reply as we speed past a bus lay-by where a camper van is parked, with the driver crouched down, peering in between the wheels.

I can still remember my first journey, the most difficult one of them all. We were sitting at the kitchen table, the sun was shining in through the window, and it was so hot in the whole apartment. I could see from her face that something was wrong. She was so far away, even though she was sitting right beside me. She was left standing on the steps when the man led me away to the car. It was as if her face, her brown eyes and her warm hands were all drowning in the sunshine. Mum, I never got to ask you: were you smiling because you were sad, or because you were happy?

Chapter 13

Siv's parents live in a red-painted house from the eighties with a hipped roof and a basement partially raised from ground level. We're met at the door by Siv's mother, who has short, spiky hair, dyed black. She makes me think of Liz, though she has none of my sister's characteristic fear when she sees a strange man at the door.

'Hello, my name's Synnøve,' she greets us, shaking Milla's hand, her eyes glowing with recognition.

'Thorkild Aske,' I introduce myself when her gaze finally drifts away from Milla.

'Yes, yes, welcome both of you,' Synnøve says, nodding her head. 'Close your eyes to the mess. My husband's at work and the coffee's ready. And water for tea,' she adds. 'He insisted that we must serve tea because artists generally prefer it to black coffee. I bought a lot of different kinds.' She presses her hands to her chest as she stands in the doorway between the hall and the living room.

'Thanks, that sounds wonderful,' Milla says, once she has finally hung up her coat and is able to follow Synnøve to a coffee table set around an enormous glass bowl filled to the brim with teabags of every glorious colour under the sun. In the middle of the room there's a tub overflowing with dirty washing, and even more is draped over the chairs around the nearby dining table. The entire living room stinks of a mixture of fresh lemon and grungy clothes.

'Siv's my eldest, of course.' Synnøve pours boiling water into our cups and nods in the direction of a plate of lemon slices once she has finished. 'She was an only child until she started at nursery, and then the twins came along.' Hesitating for a second or two, dropping her gaze as she ponders this. Then she looks up again, directly at Milla this time. 'That was when she began to change. To get difficult, angry.'

'What do you mean?' I probe. Once again, Milla has that pale glimmer in her eyes, searching for something to focus on, as if she's struggling to retain control of the impressions bombarding her senses.

'She couldn't stand the boys,' Synnøve goes on. 'Refused to play with them, got riled and jealous whenever I was breastfeeding them. Later it just grew worse. Her behaviour was wild, not only with the boys, but also at school, and in the end we had to look for help. She was diagnosed with a behaviour disorder when she was seven. By the time she started Year 3 we couldn't take any more. The child welfare service arranged a respite place at Åkermyr, so she lived there on weekdays and came home to us at weekends.' She takes a deep breath. 'There was no improvement, but we couldn't cope with her at home full-time, we just couldn't do it ... the boys were scared when she was at home, and ... and ...'

Synnøve gives another deep sigh. Her mouth has formed into a lopsided line. 'It's not the way it should be,' she says, 'with your own child. You must both think I'm a terrible mother for not even managing to take care of my own daughter, but ... That anger of hers is something my husband and I have never been able to understand, we just don't know where it comes from. What we've done to make her always so furious with us.'

Milla shakes her head. 'It can't have been easy,' she says.

'Do you have children?' Synnøve tilts her head again.

'No,' Milla whispers in response, almost inaudibly, and all at once I feel afraid that she's going to storm out and leave me sitting here like a fool again.

'Just a minute.' Synnøve gets to her feet and disappears out into the kitchen where we can hear a phone ringing.

'What's wrong with you?' I ask, leaning towards Milla while Synnøve talks on the phone in the kitchen. Now and again she pops her head around the door, as if to ensure we don't take off.

Milla clasps her hands on her lap and takes a deep breath before turning to face me. 'I'm sorry,' she says, squeezing and rubbing her fingers on her knee. 'I'll pull myself together.'

'Pull yourself together? I don't understand what—'

'It was my husband.' Synnøve has appeared again in the doorway. 'He just wanted to know if Milla had actually turned up today. I told him she was sitting here, in our living room, drinking tea. Good God,' she gasps, holding her phone like a trophy in the air. 'It's almost unbelievable.'

Milla blinks hard, time after time, before forcing a crooked smile and turning to Synnøve. 'I hope you passed on our best wishes,' she says.

'Do you and your husband believe that the girls are in Spain?' I ask when Synnøve has resumed her seat in the armchair.

Synnøve nods energetically and smiles. 'She'll phone when she's ready to come home again. I'm sure of that. She did that last time, you see. She got scared then, and rang home to Mum and Dad in tears, asking us to come and get her.' The smile is there again – it makes me think of a mask you might put on to hide whatever is playing havoc under the skin on your face. 'She needed us then. Just give her time, and she'll phone. We keep our mobiles switched on, both Jens and I, all the time, day and night. She'll call us in the end, just wait and see.'

'I understand you spoke to Milla's previous consultant, Robert Riverholt, after Siv went missing,' I say when the conversation seems to have petered out.

Synnøve pours more water into her teacup and presses six times on the sweetener dispenser before stirring her tea. 'He dropped in, nice man. But then I didn't hear anything further.'

'Robert died,' Milla tells her. She changes position, straightens up and reaches out for her teacup that has sat untouched on the table. I can see that the skin on her hands is white where she has been pressing her fingers and nails into it.

'My goodness,' Synnøve says, gripping her own cup, but pushing it away from her and turning up her nose. 'But I should really have realised that something had happened to him when that policeman came to the door.'

'A policeman?' I ask inquisitively.

'We'd just come home from Bulgaria. The holiday had already been booked before the girls disappeared, so we couldn't really ... But we had our mobile phones with us,' she adds, as if that might justify travelling on holiday while their daughter was reported missing. 'Anyway,' she goes on, 'the policeman was standing at the door one day, saying that he knew I'd spoken to Robert after the girls disappeared, and wanting to know what we'd talked about.'

'Do you remember his name?'

'No, sorry.'

'And you?' I turn to Milla. 'Do you know who that policeman was?'

She shakes her head without meeting my eye. 'It was probably someone making enquiries in connection with his murder,' she suggests. 'After all, Robert was shot while we were working on this story.'

'Was he shot?' Synnøve asks, wide-eyed. 'That's dreadful!'

'Yes,' I reply. 'By his ex-wife. Open-and-shut case, apparently.' I shake my head, aware that Milla is avoiding my eye, and turn to Synnøve again. 'Do you recall anything in particular from the time when the girls went missing? Anything unusual?'

'We'd decided to try the weekend visits again. Agreed that Siv could live here at home every second weekend, just as we'd done before. We'd already tried a couple of times, and she was fine then, kind even, but the rest of the week she was with that girl, Olivia.' Her eyes harden all of a sudden. 'I told them up there when she came home that first time, that my Siv shouldn't spend time with her. That she was nothing but trouble, but they wouldn't listen.'

'Did you meet her?' Milla asks eagerly. It's as if something has aroused her curiosity all of a sudden. 'Olivia?'

Synnøve nods. 'Siv brought her here a few times. They came begging for money, or food if they were skipping school. We had to phone up there and ask them to come and pick them up. I didn't like her. I saw the kind of girl she was.'

Milla shifts restlessly in her seat. 'What was it you didn't like about her?'

Synnøve heaves a sigh. 'Siv told us that her mother had given her up when she was little, poor soul. She had no one to guide and help her the way we could with Siv, seemingly. But she was easy to see through. I told Siv that too, told her that girl would just cause problems. But she wouldn't listen, wouldn't learn, and now, now …' She gasps for air. 'I'll tell her that when she calls; this time she'll really have to listen.'

'Listen to what?' I ask, astounded.

'That if she stops hanging around with that girl, she'll be allowed to come home again.'

CHAPTER 14

'I've made up my mind,' I say as we walk from Siv's mother's house to our car. Cold air from the Ådalselva River gusts over the railway tracks and up to the residential area where we are. 'I'm going home to Stavanger.'

'What?' Milla slows down and draws her cardigan more snugly around her. 'We've only just begun, surely?'

'How can I help you when I don't even know what the hell we're doing?'

'We're conducting research,' she says without conviction when we reach the car. 'For a book.'

'Listen here, my bullshit detector has been howling and flashing ever since I first met you. This trip, Robert Riverholt, the whole caboodle, there's something you're not telling me.'

Milla shakes her head, discouraged. 'I don't know why you're so fixated on Robert. What happened to him has nothing to do with what we're doing.'

'This "what-if game" you talked about, that's something police officers do to put into words things that are bothering them, things that don't make sense. If Robert was here now in spirit, and we played that same game with him about his own murder, what do you think he would have to tell us about his own death?'

'Don't,' Milla whispers. Her eyes are lacklustre, like two candles on the verge of burning out. 'Please ...'

I no longer have any time for her objections. I'm fed up waiting, poking around in the fates of other people for no good reason, tired of being taken for a fool. 'I think he'd wonder why Camilla killed him without even looking him in the eye. He'd have said that shooting someone in the back of the head in broad daylight is just about as cold-blooded as it's possible to be. A cold, impersonal execution.'

'OK then.' Leaning against the passenger side of the car, Milla folds her arms across her chest. 'What would you, the expert, have done with Robert if you were Camilla?'

I shake my head at her facial expression, so hard and steeped in contempt. 'I'd have confronted him, said everything I had to say, everything he had to hear, in my car, in his apartment, at home where we'd once shared something worthwhile, and afterwards I'd have crept as close to her as I could, put the gun in her mouth and pulled the trigger. Bang! Together for always.'

'Her?'

'What?'

'You said "her".'

'Whatever, fuck it. If I were to guess, I'd say it was your agent, Pelle, and maybe even your publisher, who've arranged this trip for you. They're willing to do whatever it takes for you to get started on this book of yours again. But you, Milla, I think you're here for a completely different reason.'

'It's not what you think.' Milla turns her back on me. Somewhere behind the trees at the rear of the property we can hear a voice announce over the loudspeaker that the train to Bergen will leave from platform five in one minute.

'What do I think?'

'That we're searching for Robert's killer,' she says softly.

'Who are "*we*"?'

'Me, Kenny and Iver, we ...'

'Are they police officers?'

'Yes.'

'Was it one of them who came here after Robert died?'

'Yes.'

'And it wasn't to investigate Robert's death?'

She shakes her head.

'So why? What is it you're up to?'

At last she turns round. 'Come with me to Drammen.'

'What's in Drammen?'

'Just come with me,' she says softly.

There's something about situations in which the people around me insist that we're all playing for the same team, but at the same time keep their secrets close to the chest. When every single exchange of words becomes a battle. It triggers something in me, makes me curious and makes me want to know why it has to be like that. It's a game I used to love playing before I ended up all on my own in that bedsit beneath the city bridge in Stavanger. I cast a glance at the house we've just left, just as the train speeds along the tracks on the other side of the woods. Siv's mother is standing at one of the windows, smoking a cigarette and holding an ashtray in her other hand. 'OK, then, Milla Lind,' I finally sigh, opening the car door for her. 'Let's go to Drammen.'

CHAPTER 15

We park outside the police station in Drammen and head for the main entrance where we see a police officer in the foyer inside. He's about five foot ten, slim, and moves like a cat burglar, swaying his arms and taking unnaturally long steps as he paces to and fro in there until he catches sight of us and approaches the door.

'Nice to see you again, Milla,' he says once he has opened the door and let us in. His hair is grey, short back and sides, and sticks out on one side, just like the police station roof, but his face is narrow and his complexion pale, almost pink. His mouth is unusually small, with full lips, like the ones on a kissing fish.

'Iver Isaksen,' he says, stretching out his hand. 'I'm second in charge here at the station,' he adds, shaking my hand firmly.

'A pleasure,' I reply.

'Well, I'm second in command in name only, now that Søndre Buskerud has been merged with the main south-east district headquartered in Tønsberg, but we in senior management here have at least been allowed to keep our ranks following the shake-up.' He smiles broadly at his own reflection and squeezes my hand even harder. Iver Isaksen brings to mind a building surrounded by many other buildings. He strikes me as one of those cossetted policemen who only leave their offices when the place is on fire, a politician, a paper tiger who issues parking tickets to himself and always observes the Sabbath.

'So you're the one who's taken over from Robert,' Iver says as he ushers us to the lift.

'Did you know him?' I ask inquisitively.

'Yes. After all, he worked here.'

'Oh, when was that?'

'He arrived here from Kripos and stayed with us until about 2011, when he applied for a transfer to the criminal investigation department at Grønlandsleiret in Oslo.'

We take the lift up a few floors and follow Iver into an office at the end of a wide corridor.

'When did you speak to him last?' I quiz him once we're seated in his office. The books on the bookshelves, the items on his desk, the old campaign posters on the walls along with photos of colleagues in uniform, are all arranged in the room with an eye for extreme precision.

'Well.' Iver plumps down on his chair, twiddling his thumbs as he gazes at me with narrowed eyes. 'I think it must have been around the time he died, but I can't remember exactly off the top of my head.'

'There's nothing on the top of your head.'

'Eh?' He stops twiddling his thumbs. 'What are you talking about?'

'You said you couldn't remember off the top of your head. There's nothing on the top of your head. Policemen with memory problems ...' I leave the rest of the sentence hanging in the air.

Smiling, Iver leans back into the chair. 'What about them?' he challenges me. It suddenly dawns on me that Iver might turn out to be more than a stickler with a cushy number, as I'd first thought.

'They don't exist,' I answer before going on to add: 'Who's Kenny?'

Iver glances fleetingly at Milla who is sitting by my side. She seems anxious, restless. 'Kenny will join us shortly. He was hungry and popped out for something to eat.'

'Doughnuts?'

'What? No, I think ...'

'Just spit it out,' Milla whispers, moving her head slightly without looking up from her lap. 'Tell him everything.'

Iver shifts in his chair. 'But ...'

'He knows,' Milla replies. Once again she makes that movement with her head without looking at either of us.

'OK, OK.' Iver sits up straight and clears his throat. 'What I'm about to tell you comes under the non-disclosure agreement you signed when you took on this job, understand?'

'Yes, yes.'

'Milla and Robert weren't only working on the background material for Milla's book. That wasn't the real reason she hired him.'

'I thought that.'

'He was hired to find someone.'

'The two girls who ran away from the children's home,' I conclude. 'Why?'

'Olivia,' Milla says in a faint voice. 'She's my daughter. Robert was going to find her for me.'

'What?'

'She's mine,' Milla repeats. It's as if she is saying this just as much to herself as to the man with tunnel vision at her side. 'I have a daughter. No,' she says, 'I *had* a daughter. Then I had to give her away.' Something about her face has changed, lines and furrows have appeared around her eyes and lips, just below the thin layer of make-up. Maybe they were there all the time, and it was just that I didn't take the time to notice them.

'Sixteen years ago, I was raped. I got pregnant, and I tried to be a mother to her, tried for as long as I could, but in the end … in the end I gave her up.'

'And the rape, what …'

'It was just something that happened …' Milla wrings her hands, 'one night when I was on my way home from a trip to the city with a few workmates. Last autumn I made up my mind to try to find her at last. I, or we, hired Robert to help me, and he found her, but before I was able to talk to her, tell her who I was, she disappeared.'

'So you didn't engage Robert to find her *because* she was missing?' I ask, taken aback.

'No. Because she's my daughter. We're not really allowed to do it – it's only the child who has the right to ask the identity of their parents, once they've reached the age of eighteen. But I couldn't bear to wait any longer, so I told Iver, and he put me in touch with Robert.'

I shake my head, making eye contact with Iver. 'And you, how do you know Milla?'

'I was the one who dealt with her rape case, and was first on the crime scene. A few years later, Milla contacted me; she'd moved to Oslo and told me she'd started to write. She asked me if I could help her with questions about police procedure, for her book. Eventually, as the years went by, and there were more and more books about August Mugabe ...' he gives Milla an affectionate look, 'we got to know each other better, didn't we, Milla?'

Milla returns his look, smiling and nodding her head.

'Did you know that the rape had resulted in a child?'

'Not until later,' Iver admits. 'And when she told me, and said that she wanted to find Olivia and tell her about ... well, I tried to help her as best I could, but as you know, we who're still on active service, aren't really allowed to ...'

'The last member of this triumvirate, this Kenny,' I say after a lengthy pause. 'Where does he come into the picture?'

At that very moment, there's a noise in the corridor and the door is opened gingerly.

'You can ask him yourself,' Iver says as he gets to his feet.

CHAPTER 16

'Hello there,' says the man who appears in the doorway and approaches us. 'Kenneth Abrahamsen.' In his mid-forties, he has greying, curly hair, deep wrinkles and a forest of chest hairs protruding from the neck of his overly tight sweater. He reminds me of a Greek Adonis in police uniform, thirty years after the beach party has ended. 'Or Kenny, to my friends.'

'Thorkild Aske,' I reciprocate, shaking hands. 'Before we go any further, before I agree to anything whatsoever, let's start at the very beginning. Iver, what *is* the beginning?'

'Milla hired Robert to search for Olivia in September of last year,' he tells me. 'That's the beginning.'

'OK,' I turn to face Milla. 'When did Robert discover your daughter's location?'

'Ten days later,' she replies.

'And one week after you'd found her, she disappeared?'

'Yes.'

'Why?'

Milla shakes her head. 'We've no idea.'

'Did she know you were searching for her?'

'No. Robert and I visited her school and Robert pointed her out during the break. I went back to the school a few days after that, on my own. I just wanted to see her again while we planned our next move, but she wasn't there. Nor the next day either. Then Iver phoned and told me that she … that she was gone.'

'OK. And why couldn't you just have told the truth in the first place?'

'I'm sorry,' she says. It looks as if she's feeling cold, sitting there with her arms wrapped around herself. Her eyes are filled with the same empty darkness as the time when I'd stood out there between the trees, watching her with Joachim in the study.

'But now you know all about me, Thorkild,' she finally says.

'Not everything,' I answer. 'But it's a beginning, at least.'

'So, are you in?' Iver puts on a smile. 'You've taken the bait too?'

In fact, I'd already decided how this day was going to end when I woke up in Milla's boathouse this morning. Research for a book and true-life missing person cases weren't my thing. After our visits to Åkermyr and to Siv's mother, all that was left for me to do was to say thanks but no thanks and, despite Ulf's threats about the job centre sending me to work making candles in a sheltered workshop, take the first plane back to Stavanger.

The air inside Iver's office starts to feel clammy, making it difficult to breathe – I'm not used to being with other people in such a confined office space, apart from my doctor, job centre employees or Ulf. Deep inside, I try to put into words what it is that prevents me from boarding the next flight home as soon as possible, and it occurs to me that it's not because this is now an investigation, or because it's Milla's daughter we're now looking for, but because there is still something that grates.

'There are things we still haven't talked about,' I begin after I've completed my train of thought and feel satisfied with the conclusion. 'Robert Riverholt. He was shot dead in broad daylight while working on this case—'

'By his ex-wife,' Kenny breaks in before adding: 'She was ill, you see.'

'As we've said, Aske,' Iver finally speaks up, 'there's nothing to suggest that Robert's death had anything to do with this. We might have feared that it did, for a moment or two, but the investigation carried out by Oslo police and our own enquiries showed categorically that that theory could be excluded. He was killed by his ex-wife, and that's been established without a shred of doubt.'

'I understand.' I run my fingers over the scar on my face to test whether it's still painful. 'Only in films and books do people die while knee-deep in a case. You know what happens to the guy who takes over, as soon as he starts digging around in other people's muck, don't you?'

'We're working on this too,' Kenny interjects querulously.

'That's small comfort,' I reply, rubbing the rough skin more vigorously.

'So,' Iver says, about to get up from his chair. 'Any more questions?'

'A whole lot, actually,' I tell him, removing my hand from my face and folding my hands on my lap. 'A whole bloody lot, in fact. What were you doing at the time Robert was shot? What have you found out to date about the disappearance? Does anyone, apart from us in this room, know what you've been up to? And, last but not least, what is it you actually believe I can accomplish six months later that you haven't already done?'

Taking a deep breath, Iver sinks back into his chair again. 'As far as Robert is concerned, I understand that you're worried, now that you find yourself filling his shoes, if I can put it like that.'

'Yes, you can,' I reply.

'But there's absolutely no reason to think that his death had anything to do with this. His wife was ill; he had a troubled private life that had a tragic outcome. All three of us knew Robert, and we were all upset by what happened. But I'd like to emphasise yet again that what happened was between him and his wife. A tragic incident. Nothing more, nothing less.'

'With respect to what we were doing at the time,' Kenny says, 'Robert, Milla and I had just come home from Spain the week before Robert died, from Ibiza, where we had been searching for Olivia and Siv without finding anything. We were all pretty depressed about it, and intended to take a few days off to gather our strength before starting up again. In fact, we'd arranged for us all to meet that afternoon at Milla's house in Tjøme to discuss our next steps, when Robert was shot.'

'And what about since then? What have the three of you done or discovered since that time?'

'We're stuck,' Iver admits with a sigh.

I turn to Kenny. 'You've spoken to Siv's mother?'

Kenny nods.

'And?'

'What kind of mother takes her husband and children off on holiday while her daughter is reported missing?' he comments testily before glancing briefly at Milla. 'Sorry, Milla. I didn't mean ...' He presses his lips tightly together.

'Who knows you're working on this?'

'Nobody,' Kenny answers.

'Well,' Iver darts a glance across at Kenny, 'that's not entirely correct.'

'What do you mean?' I ask.

'You see, Milla gave a TV interview before they went to Spain,' Iver points out, 'in which she mentioned that the next August Mugabe book would deal with misper cases, as we call them, and that she planned to use the example of Siv and Olivia in her writing. It was a good cover story for the real task of searching for her daughter.'

'So what specific action do you all think I can take here?'

'We want you to help us find Olivia,' Milla tells me. 'To find out what has happened to her, and bring her home.'

'Home?' I stare in confusion at each of them in turn. 'Aren't you listening to what you're saying? The girls have been missing for more than six months now without a single sign of life. You haven't found out anything at all.'

'Thorkild,' Milla says in a whisper. 'Please. I need your help. She can't just disappear forever. It can't end like this.'

As Milla dries her eyes, she reaches out a hand to me, while Iver rocks back and forth in his chair and Kenny glares in my direction.

'OK,' I say with a sigh, grasping her hand. 'I'm in.'

'Brilliant!' Iver springs out of his seat. 'Let's say all four of us meet again after work tomorrow, maybe in your apartment, Milla? Then we can have more discussion about the way forward, eh?'

'No,' I tell him.

'What?' Iver is shrugging on his jacket and switching off his computer in the same movement. He looks at me in surprise.

'We have to go back to the children's home. I have to talk to the witness, the boy who saw the girls down there at the bus stop the morning they went missing. What's more, I'll also need to have a police officer with me, with an official badge.'

'Kenny?' Iver looks quizzically at his subordinate. 'Can you do that?'

'I'll stay here,' Milla interjects. 'I don't want to go back there, I'm tired and …'

With a sigh, Kenny fishes out his car keys. 'OK, then, let's go.'

It's not just the ache in my diaphragm and lack of fresh air that are bothering me when I finally rise to leave. Iver and Kenny are both police officers who've investigated a case in cahoots with the mother of one of the missing girls and her private investigator, and they must have known that this would lead them deep into a grey area well beyond what can be regarded as normal police work. Apart from their burning desire to help Milla to put her past to rights, I can't think of a single good reason for them going along with her also involving someone like me, with a background in Internal Affairs, in this undertaking. And the more I think about it as I follow Kenny out of the office and along to the lift, the surer I feel that I should have said thanks all the same and gone home while I still had the chance.

Chapter 17

Outside, it is growing dark, the streetlights are on, and they blend in with the city lights, lending the horizon a whitish shade of blue that grows softer and deeper above the skyline. The atmosphere in the car is already as cheerful as at a family mediation meeting. 'How do you know Milla?' I venture when Kenny stops at traffic lights.

'Iver and I were first on the scene,' Kenny replies, drumming his fingers on the steering wheel as we wait for the traffic lights to change, 'when she was raped.'

'And after that?'

'We met her again a few years later. She had started writing by then.'

'Did you ever meet her daughter? Before she gave her away?'

He shakes his head.

'Never?'

'No.' Kenny accelerates as soon as it's safe to drive on. 'Milla moved to Oslo. She didn't mention that she'd got pregnant and given birth to a daughter until a long time afterwards.'

'Why didn't *you* help her to find her daughter?'

He looks at me with a smile. 'We're not allowed.'

'Did she ask?'

'About what?'

'For help?'

'Yes.'

'And instead you introduced her to a former colleague working as a private investigator, who found Olivia, even pointed her out to Milla in the school yard, and then she simply disappeared.'

Kenny shifts uncomfortably in the driver's seat. 'Correct.'

Police personnel don't enjoy answering questions; they prefer to ask them, and Kenny is no exception.

'When did you learn that Robert had found her?'

'A few days before she disappeared.'

'And then what? What happened?'

'I work with the community police, and as soon as the girls were reported missing, we drove out there and spoke to youngsters in the Drammen area.'

'Did you discover anything?'

'The girls had been peripherally involved in the drugs scene in Drammen, but no one there had seen or heard anything of them for a while.'

'OK. By the way, did you know Robert earlier?'

'Not personally. We both worked here in Drammen at the same time, but Robert was higher up the ranks than me, in a different section.'

'In other words, you're one of the foot soldiers?' We pass a petrol station where a group of teenagers are sitting on the bonnets of their cars in T-shirts and jeans, blowing cigarette smoke up into the increasingly cold evening sky. 'The ones who do the spadework.'

Once again Kenny tries to find a more comfortable sitting position. 'Call it what you like,' he grunts.

'Why the community police?'

'I like to get out among people.'

'Not a careerist, in other words?'

Kenny smiles to himself. 'Weren't you once one of the big fish? One of the boys from Internal Affairs in fancy suits and ties, running around making life difficult for the rest of us?'

'Not you, though,' I say, blinking. We've already left the city centre, and are now surrounded by clusters of houses and commercial properties, soon replaced by extensive areas of newly ploughed fields, green and dusty grey, with only the occasional residential pockets in between. 'Just the crooked police officers. The flies in the police soup.'

'The flies in the police soup.' He laughs as he flicks his headlights on to full beam. 'Is that what you call us?'

'Exclusively bluebottles and spiders,' I reply before adding: 'But only the nasty ones, as I said.'

He looks at me again. 'Did you like it? Ruining the careers of your colleagues? Poking around in procedural errors and minor misconduct matters instead of doing real police work?'

'Loved it,' I answer. 'The least little thing we could catch you out in, was a red letter day in Internal Affairs, western section.'

'Christ,' Kenny groans, dipping his headlights as a convoy of heavy lorries approaches in the oncoming lane. 'Bloody hell, you're more like Robert than you realise.'

CHAPTER 18

We meet Karin at the door again once we've parked in front of the Åkermyr children's home entrance.

'Hello, Kenny,' she says, smiling broadly. 'What brings you here?'

'Aske wants to speak to André,' he replies. We follow Karin into her office.

'He's doing his homework just now,' she tells us. 'But we can go and see what he says.'

'Excellent!' Kenny says, rolling his car keys around in his fingers. 'Let's do that.'

'On my own,' I say. 'Could I speak to him on my own?'

'Well, I suppose so.' Kenny looks at Karin. 'Karin? It's OK with me.'

'I don't know,' Karin replies. 'Last time you were here, I didn't quite catch what you actually have to do with all this?'

'Aske's an interrogation specialist,' Kenny breaks in. 'He's helping us.'

'Oh,' Karin says. 'Well, I guess so, then.'

Kenny winks at me as Karin and I leave him in the office. Karin accompanies me down a long corridor to a door with a sign on the wall beside it. She knocks carefully before opening.

'André?' She pokes her head into the room. 'There's a man here. From the police. He wants to talk to you for a minute about Siv and Olivia. Is that OK?'

I can hear the boy mumble something in reply before Karin steps aside and shows me in. 'I'll be just outside the door when you've finished.'

I walk into the room and stand by the door until it closes behind me. The room is a typical boy's bedroom and the boy who sits at the desk with a pile of books open in front of him has mid-length brown hair. His face is slim and his features handsome. He sits with his back partly turned towards me while he fiddles with a pencil and pretends to read one of the books.

'What subject?' I ask without leaving my post at the door.

'Maths,' he answers without moving a muscle.

'Oh,' I reply, scanning the room. 'Why don't you have any posters on the walls? Rock bands, girls in bikinis, maths formulae or something fun like that?'

He gives a faint smile. 'We're not allowed.'

'Well, my bedroom was covered in posters of female rock stars with big ...' I pause theatrically before continuing, 'voices. Samantha Fox, Sabrina, Sandra, come to think of it, most of them had names starting with S.'

Again the lopsided smile appears, just a second before it vanishes once more.

'Have you heard any of them sing?'

'No.'

'Well, that's a shame. All I have to say is ... you'll go a long way to find such big ... voices.'

This time he can't keep the smile from breaking out in full force. 'I know who they are,' he says, shaking his head. 'Dad told me about them.'

'Have you seen the pictures I'm talking about too?'

'No,' he says unconvincingly.

'God-given gifts,' I tell him. 'Their voices, of course,' I laugh when we finally make eye contact.

He turns back to his maths book, but I can see the smile still lingering on his lips.

'Are you police?'

'I was.'

'Was?'

'Got fired.'

Again our eyes meet. This time the contact lasts longer. 'Why?'

'I killed a woman in a car crash while under the influence of GHB.'

'Did you have to go to jail?'

'Three years and six months.'

'What was it like, in prison?' André has finally forgotten his maths book and has turned round to face me.

'Boring. The same thing day in, day out.'

'Sounds much like here,' he says, flicking a finger at the rubber on top of his pencil.

'Well,' I lean back against the door, 'when you're young, everything's boring.'

'What happened to your face?' He uses the pencil to point at the scar that runs from my eye to my mouth.

'The car smash.'

'Did it hurt?'

'I don't remember,' I say, crossing to his bed to perch on the edge.

'Who was she?' André persists, following me with his gaze before once again resting on my eyes. 'The woman you killed?'

'Someone I loved.'

'Do you miss her?'

'Every second.'

André leans forward with his elbows on his thighs, twiddling the pencil between his fingers. His room makes me think of another one: my own, at Police Internal Affairs in Bergen. It's in rooms like these that you can really hear yourself think, everything is condensed down to the two of us, to a conversation with a unique driving force. Everything else evaporates, wiped away by the water surrounding us. All of a sudden it strikes me how much I've missed that room, that part of myself.

'Did you know them well?' I ask finally, leaning forward.

'Not really,' he answers, interrupting his pencil juggle for a brief moment before continuing: 'We were in the same class, but ...'

'Men are from Mars and women from Venus?'

He gives a burst of nervous laughter. 'Something like that.'

'Tell me about the day they disappeared, as seen from your point of view. What did you do that day?'

'I got up, had breakfast and went back to my room again. We had a test that day.' While he speaks, I fish out a little notebook and jot down a few points.

'What subject?'

'Maths.'

'Did Siv and Olivia also have a maths test that day?'

'Yes. But they … they didn't bother much about school.'

'What did they bother about?'

André shrugs. 'I don't know.'

'Boys?'

'Probably.'

'Anyone special?'

'Don't think so.'

'OK. What happened next?'

'I like to go to the bus stop in plenty of time. The others usually arrive after me, right before the bus comes. I packed my schoolbag and went to the laundry to pick up my gym kit. That was when I saw them through the window.'

'Where were they?'

'Down there,' he points. 'At the bus stop. They had already gone down there.'

'Were Siv and Olivia in the habit of going early to the bus stop?'

'No. They were the slowest of all,' he laughs. 'Often one of the staff members had to drive them to school because they'd missed the bus.'

'But that day they were out early?'

'Yes.'

'Do you remember what they were doing down there?'

'Standing beside a car. The passenger door was open, and they were talking to the driver.' He sighs audibly and squeezes the pencil. 'Then they got in, and the car drove off.'

'What kind of car was it?'

Breathing more heavily now, he has started to play with his pencil again. 'I don't know much about cars.'

'Do you remember the colour?'

'It looked new. At least, it was really clean.'

'Did you see the driver?'

He shakes his head.

'But you're sure it was Siv and Olivia?'

'Yes.'

'You're good at casting your mind back, André,' I tell him. 'By the way, did one of them get into the front?'

'Yes, Olivia. Siv sat in the back.'

'So the car had four doors?'

'Yes.'

'Do you know the difference between an SUV and an estate car?'

'It was an estate car.'

'Are you sure?'

'Yes. The police showed me pictures of different cars.'

'Aha,' I say, smiling. 'What did you do after you saw them drive off?'

'I finished packing my gym bag and then went down for the bus. That was the last time I saw them.'

'Weren't you worried?'

'They used to thumb a lift when they wanted to travel somewhere and didn't have the money for the bus fare.'

'OK. Was there anything out of the ordinary that happened that morning, apart from them being out early?'

André shakes his head.

'Or the night before?'

'We watched a film in the TV room.'

'Who did?'

'Me, Siv and Olivia.'

'Was there anything unusual then that you can think of?'

'Noooo.' He sounds hesitant.

'Anything at all? When you think back to that night, what's the first thing that strikes you?'

'Olivia was in a good mood.'

'OK. Better than usual?'

'Yes.'

'In what way?'

'No, just … I don't know. She wasn't so bitchy.' He shrugs before adding: 'She was laughing.'

'Why do you think she was in such a good mood?'

'I don't know,' he replies.

'Thanks for your help, André.' I stuff the notebook and pen back into my jacket pocket. 'By the way,' I say, standing in front of him, 'where do you think they are?'

André swings on his chair as he looks at me. 'In Spain, I suppose,' he says in the end.

'In Ibiza?'

He shrugs again. 'Where else?' Then he turns back to his desk.

Before I leave the room I think about how good it really feels to talk to other people, about other people, and take a rest from your own self. When I was still married to Ann-Mari, that had also been the cure when she became ill – I could find refuge in the interrogations after a tiresome evening and night at home, or days spent with her at the hospital. The tumours in her womb vanished out of sight when the door of the interview room slammed behind me. After the doctors had told her that she would never have a child, after the operation and the divorce, I went to the USA for a year to get even further away, and when I finally returned, the same room had turned into a prison. By the time I leave

André's room, I've made up my mind that helping Milla to find Siv and Olivia can offer me a way out, if only for a short period.

'Everybody needs an exit route,' I mutter to myself before gripping the door handle, opening the door and stepping outside.

CHAPTER 19

'You've got shadows under your eyes,' Siv says, poking at her ice cream with a spoon. We're sitting in a café not far from the River Drammen. Outside, a crowd of teenagers pass by on their way to high school. I like this café, even though I've never been inside it before. I think that's because I've sometimes walked past and seen the faces of people on this side of the glass, watched them sitting close to one another around the small tables. 'Dark shadows like an exhausted whore,' Siv adds, laughing.

'Thanks,' I reply, pulling a face at her. She surveys the café and makes a face back at me.

'Do you think she's rich?' Siv darts a glance in the direction of the toilets. 'As rich as Jo Nesbø, even?'

With a shrug, I push the ice-cream dish away. Siv stretches her spoon out and lifts the last half-scoop of ice cream over into her own dish.

'I think she's a bitch,' she says. 'She must be, to have given you away. I mean, who does that?'

'She's searching for me, though.'

'Are you sure?' Siv looks towards the toilets in the corner of the café again while licking ice cream from her spoon. One of the doors opens and a man emerges. He smiles at the women behind the counter as he heads for our table.

'Yes,' I reply, moving closer to the window. 'He said so.'

Chapter 20

'Did it go well?' Karin looks up when I return to the corridor where she has been waiting.

'Smart boy,' I reply.

When we return to her office, I give a sign to Kenny that we can leave.

The sun has vanished, making space for a glimmering twilight that bears down on the fields and spruce trees. Stopping in the middle of the yard, I gaze across at the bus lay-by where Olivia and Siv were last seen by André more than six months ago.

'They were out early that day,' I say when Kenny arrives to stand beside me. 'Got into a car, travelled to Ibiza, and since then no one has heard a peep from them. I take it that's the theory we're working from?'

'Yes,' Kenny answers.

'The day Robert was killed,' I continue, 'did you speak to him?'

'No, the day before.'

'What did he say?'

'He wanted us all to meet up at Milla's house in Tjøme the following afternoon.'

'Why?'

'Maybe he wanted us to put the Ibiza theory to bed and examine other possibilities.'

I nod. 'In misper cases you work from four scenarios, don't you? The ones who leave of their own free will, the ones who take their own lives, the ones who meet with an accident and cases where some kind of crime is suspected.'

'I don't suppose you're thinking of talking about an accident or suicide now,' Kenny bristles, kicking the gravel at his feet.

I shake my head.

'A crime, though.'

'You said it yourself: Robert would probably have knocked the Ibiza theory on the head. And with every criminal act, there has to be one or several perpetrators. In cases like this, we can put these into two separate categories—'

'For God's sake, Thorkild, I know this stuff, I know—'

'So we're either talking about a chance meeting,' I go on without paying any heed to Kenny's objections, 'or someone who knew them or they'd met before. In Olivia's case, this definition can also be watered down a tad to also refer to people who knew her mother, and who knew that Milla had hired Robert to find her daughter.'

'Do you really think so?' He is standing so close that I can feel his hot breath on my cheek, but this doesn't make me turn away. 'Are you still so keen to ruin police careers that you really believe that Iver or I might have …'

'All I'm saying,' and I finally turn round so that we're standing face to face, 'is it seems to me you've chosen to ignore every other possibility except that the girls went to the Med of their own free will, when the only thing we really know is that they walked out of the door behind us and along the path we're standing on now, down to that spot,' and now I point at the bus stop ahead of us, 'and got into a car. We don't know if they knew the driver, or if they were thumbing a lift and a random person picked them up. But we do know that less than a month later, Robert gets a bullet in the back of the head on the same day that he's called all the involved parties in to a meeting to discuss the case and a possible change of direction.'

'Robert's death has nothing to do with this.'

I take a final look in the direction of the bus stop. 'No,' I sigh as I stride across to the car. 'So you say, all of you, every time I ask.'

CHAPTER 21

An hour and a half later we park outside Iver's home, a semi-detached house in a residential area south-west of Drammen where Milla and Iver are waiting for us. When Kenny marches straight in and kicks off his shoes in the hallway, I follow suit.

Iver is standing in the kitchen with his back to the fridge, while Milla sits at the table. They both scrutinise us expectantly when we come in.

'Thorkild has something he wants to say.' Kenny flops into one of the chairs opposite Milla.

'Oh?' Iver looks at me inquisitively. 'Did you find out something? Something we can use to progress the case?'

'The girls had planned to leave,' I begin, taking a seat at the kitchen table, while Iver remains on his feet beside the fridge. 'I buy that part. Either they were waiting for the car or else they were thumbing a lift, but they'd no intention of going to school that day, I think we can establish that. The boy I spoke to told me Olivia was in a good mood the night before, an unusually good mood. That also fits in with the scenario you've been working from. But ...' I add.

'But?' Milla asks, sounding anxious, and reaching out for my hand.

'If they were thumbing a lift, where's the driver who picked them up? Why hasn't he come forward? That forces us to consider all possibilities, including that the person in question might well be the reason they're missing. In other words, an abduction that, worst case scenario, ends up as a murder. Another dead cert is that you've been searching at the wrong end.'

'What?' Iver asks in a loud voice, before crossing his arms over his chest and dropping his voice to a more authoritative tone. 'What do you mean?'

'All trace of them ends at that bus lay-by. Even though they went to Ibiza once before, you've started with an assumption, and that's never a good idea.'

'We didn't start with Ibiza,' Iver insists, stamping his foot in irritation. 'We followed the leads, and regarded that scenario as the most likely.'

'Robert said the same thing after we came home,' Milla breaks in. 'That it was time to start looking at other alternatives – I think that was why he'd called that meeting the day he died. To start afresh.'

'Did he say why?' I ask.

'No.' She squeezes my hand. 'He never had time.'

'I think Robert was on to something,' I tell them. 'At best, Siv and Olivia had packed for a short trip, a day trip or at least a trip they intended to return from. That conflicts with the idea that they went to Ibiza with the intention of staying there for good.'

'So, what do you want us to do?' Kenny asks. He's been following the conversation closely without saying a word. 'What's the plan?'

'I want to follow that lead and start looking at a scenario in which that wasn't what they'd planned. To find out where they are now, we first of all have to find out where they were heading, what changed, and last but not least: was this change a voluntary one or were other forces behind it?'

Iver nods at the floor, and then lifts his gaze to make eye contact with Milla. 'What do you say to all four of us meeting again tomorrow after work so that we can talk a bit more about the way forward?'

'Will you come to my apartment in Oslo, then?' Milla asks. 'I've a meeting at the publishers and can't face going back to Tjøme tonight.'

Iver nods again. 'Does that sound like a plan?'

'Fine.' I get up to leave. 'Then we'll do that.'

I'd been shattered. That's what runs through my head as Milla and I stand in the hallway putting on our coats: I'd been completely crushed, both physically and mentally, when I returned to Norway just over four years ago following the time I'd spent with Dr Ohlenborg when we interviewed criminal police officers in American prisons. It's vital, now I can feel my policeman's brain sparking to life again, that I don't forget what took place when I came home, what happens when I get too involved in a case, and the consequences that can bring for me and the people in my immediate circle.

CHAPTER 22

It's evening when we park the car in front of Milla's apartment in St Hanshaugen, just beside Alexander Kiellands Plass. It feels as if it's going to rain soon. I can see black shadows moving in the trees at the end of the street, in between the newly sprouted leaves, and I hear the beating wings of tiny birds as they settle down for the night.

'Was it here?' I ask once we've removed our belongings from the car. 'Was this where Robert died?'

'Over there.' Milla deposits a bag on the ground and starts to walk along the pavement to the street corner where the birds are chattering in the twilight. She comes to a standstill with her arms dangling ponderously at her sides, her eyes fixed on the ground.

I approach and stand by her side. 'Was this where you found him?'

'The moment I heard the bang, I thought of Robert. I don't know why, it was just a bang, it could have been anything at all, but all the same the noise cut right into my heart. When we came out, people had already started to gather around him. He was lying face down with his hands beneath him.' She takes a deep breath through half-open lips. 'Everybody says they look as if they're sleeping.' Milla looks at me. 'But they don't.'

'No,' I answer. 'They don't.'

'Robert was different.' She smiles all of a sudden. 'You should have met him. There was something gentle about him, even his breathing was always so calm, so relaxed, even when Camilla was ill and we had to help her.'

'Did you know her well?'

'No. But he brought her to Tjøme a few times in the beginning. We ate together, chatted a bit, but she got tired very quickly; she was depressed, and eventually Robert stopped bringing her with—'

'Was that after the two of you had started sleeping together?'

I notice her sharp intake of breath, as she straightens up ever so slightly, about to say something, but then suddenly crumples again. 'It wasn't like that, not behind Camilla's back. He had moved out, he … It just happened a couple of times. We had some kind of immediate connection. But it happened, and we handled it like adults. There was nothing wrong in it, but all the same it shouldn't have happened.'

'And Joachim?'

'He didn't need to know about it.'

'But he knows, now?'

'Yes. I told him later. After the funeral.'

'And?'

'Nothing. He sulked for a few days, and then it was over.' Her gaze is harder now. 'It's not the first time. Joachim knows who I am, what I've been through, and has found his way of dealing with it.'

'Crab fishing?'

Milla draws her coat more snugly around her neck as she turns to go. 'Come on,' she says.

Milla's apartment is on the top floor. The interior decor is minimalistic, bordering on sterile. Above a seating area, there are four large windows that let in the light from the sky above, giving a sense of sitting on a rooftop. Milla goes out to the kitchen and returns with a bottle of wine and two glasses. 'I thought we should get to know each other better,' she says as she pours the wine into our glasses. 'Now that you know what we're really up to.'

'Tell me about the rape.'

'Straight to the point, I see.' Milla raises her glass in a cold-blooded toast. I return the gesture and taste the wine.

'I'd just landed a job as a hairdresser in Drammen. I was out celebrating with some friends. I didn't notice that someone was following me until all of a sudden I felt a blow to my head. When I came to, I was lying on the ground in an alleyway. A man was on top of me and another one was holding my hands.' She looks down and lets her eyes run over her body. 'I remember closing my eyes, and I kept them closed the whole time until the pressure on my arms, on my body and my crotch disappeared. When I finally opened them again, they were gone, and it was nearly daylight outside. Soon a car stopped nearby, and then another. Faces appeared, more and more of them crowding around me. In the end a policeman arrived and crouched down beside me. He asked me something, then he covered me with his jacket and asked the faces to move back so that there were just the two of us there until the ambulance came.' At last Milla looks up at me again, pours more wine into her glass and puts it to her lips. 'That was how I met Iver, and then Kenny.'

'Did they find the culprits?'

'Would that have changed anything?' Milla asks softly as she looks at me through veiled eyes. 'I tried, Thorkild,' she begins, pouring more wine into her glass. 'Tried to be a mother to her for three years before I gave her up. After all, half of her came from me, but in the end I couldn't live with the other half in such close proximity. After the birth, no, after the rape, all through my pregnancy and afterwards I was a different person from the one I am today.'

'In what way?'

Milla tosses her hair back and drinks more wine. 'Pills, wine, one or two, maybe three unsuccessful suicide attempts. It wasn't until I gave her away, started to write and found August Mugabe that I saw a way out, no, *through* it all.' She gives me a fleeting glance before grasping the wine glass again. 'There were moments with Olivia when I felt that if I didn't get her away from me, then I'd take it out on her.'

She gives me a lopsided smile while she fiddles with the glass, running a finger round the rim and closing her eyes almost completely. Once again she shakes her head, as if to chase these images back down into the darkness. 'Maybe I'd already begun to do that,' she says quietly. 'Maybe that was why.' She nods to herself, at the same time continuing the finger dance on top of the wine glass. 'Yes, I think so.' Finally, she opens her eyes: 'Do you think she remembers it? That she still remembers what I was like, even now?'

'I've no idea,' I reply. It occurs to me that she's alternating between naked honesty and defensive barriers, sometimes in the course of one and the same sentence: her eyes are swing doors. The only thing I haven't made up my mind about is whether she is controlling these doors

herself, or if they are controlling her. Opening and exposing her innermost being against her will, just like mine do.

'Later, it got easier. I moved here to Oslo, took up writing, found ways of keeping her and the incident at arm's
length. August Mugabe came into my life, became a sort of
substitute, someone to carry my pain, someone I could exist
through, and with. Until that was no longer enough, until
missing the part of me that was her became too intense, and
I realised it was time to confront what had happened, face
to face, and to beg for forgiveness. See if something good
might come of it after all.'

'Why me?' I ask after a lengthy pause during which
neither of us utters a word. 'Of all the people you could
have hired to help you, why me in particular?'

Milla pours more wine into her glass. 'It was my grief
therapist who mentioned you, she said she knew a psychiatrist in Stavanger who worked with you. I felt something,
deep down inside, when she talked about you. Something
that said you were the one who would find her. A premoni-
tion, if you like.' Milla gives a brief burst of brittle laughter
and tosses her head again. 'Do you believe in such things?'

'Maybe,' I answer, turning away from her. 'What did Iver
and Kenny have to say when you told them that you'd hired
me to help you?'

'Iver didn't like it. He told me about what had happened
between you and that girl in Stavanger. Said you were sick
and unreliable, but I—'

'He's right,' I break in. 'I am sick.'

'You have an injury, don't you?' Her eyes search mine,
as if trying to force back the intimacy of a moment ago.
'Following a suicide attempt?'

'Yes,' I finally respond. 'The first one.'

'What happened?'

'Lack of oxygen to the brain. When you hang yourself, the oxygen supply to the brain is cut off. I hung from that rope for so long that there was damage to the amygdala; that's the part of the brain that disseminates sense impressions. Sometimes I experience things, people, a smell, or entire events, being there, taking place right before my eyes, but they're not genuine, it's just the brain injury that's fooling around with me.'

'Do you take medication?'

'Lots, but never enough.'

'Oh?'

'It's been difficult,' I begin awkwardly, 'to find the right balance.'

'What do you take?'

'Cipralex.'

'Happy pills?'

I nod my head.

'You're right,' Milla tells me. 'They don't work. I began to go to the grief therapist after I'd given up Olivia. She referred me to a pain clinic here in Oslo that was able to help me at last.' Milla's fingers play on the wine glass as she watches me. The smile doesn't completely fade until she finally stops fidgeting and puts the glass down on the table. 'Have you heard of Somadril?'

'No.' I can hear sporadic raindrops tapping on the skylights above us.

'They work, Thorkild,' Milla says, picking up a remote control that she uses to dim the lights in the ceiling so that the darkness outside blends into the gloom in the room.

'The product was actually taken off the market in 2008, but I'm part of a powerful support group and my grief therapist, Dr Aune, helps us with prescriptions. I might be able to ask her to let Ulf know about the clinic?'

'Ulf's not in the mood these days to discuss alternatives to the happy pills.'

'I see,' Milla replies. 'Maybe I can help you all the same, once we're better acquainted?'

'Yes, maybe,' I say. The pads of my fingers are moist when I touch the damaged side of my face. 'It's late,' I tell her, getting to my feet.

'You can stay here,' Milla says.

'I don't think so,' I answer. 'I've booked a hotel room nearby.'

'Well,' she begins, snatching at some strands of hair that have fallen into her eyes. 'I'm pleased we've had a chance to talk, just the two of us, and that you're happy to continue with the assignment.' She leans back on the sofa and smiles wearily. 'Very pleased,' she emphasises.

I stop in the doorway between the living room and hallway. 'I find out secrets, Milla. That's what I do. Yours, Joachim's, Kenny and Iver's, Robert's, Siv and Olivia's – all of them.'

'I know,' she says.

'You're going to hate me.'

'No,' Milla says, leaning forward now. Her face is grey in the murk.

'Yes, you will,' I insist, signalling that she should remain seated. 'Sooner or later you're all going to hate me.'

'Why?'

'Because,' I sigh audibly as I lean my head against the door frame, 'once I make a start, I won't be able to stop.'

The last part of the sentence is meant chiefly as a warning to myself.

CHAPTER 23

I can only just see him through the trees. Behind him cars are whizzing by in both directions. Siv is squatting down right beside me, with her trousers round her knees.

'Do you have any paper?' she asks when she's finished.

'No,' I answer.

She gives me a look of despair.

'What?' I ask her, making a face. 'I don't have any. Use some moss or something.'

'Yuck,' Siv says, scouring the ground around her before glancing up at me again. 'That's disgusting.'

'Your sleeve, then.'

'No!' she protests.

'Your fingers?'

'Stop,' Siv gasps, suppressing laughter as she struggles to avoid losing her balance and toppling over. 'I don't want pee on my fingers.'

'You should have thought of that before you came out here. You could have gone to the loo at the café in Drammen or waited till we get to Tønsberg.'

Siv leans against a tree trunk as she stares through the bushes towards the car parked with its engine running up there on the road. 'Can't you ask him?'

'Ask him yourself.'

'No!' Siv tries to grab my sweater with one hand without falling over. 'I'm butt naked, for God's sake.'

'Poor you,' I laugh, and step back so she can't catch hold of me.

'Olivia,' Siv whimpers as she clutches her trousers and the tree trunk at the same time.

Suddenly we hear the car door opening and spot the driver moving round to the front. He stands at the road verge. 'Is everything all right down there?' he shouts above the noise of the traffic.

'No,' I reply and at the same moment, Siv finally grabs hold of my sweater and pulls me towards her. 'She needs something to dry herself with.'

The driver nods before disappearing into the car. When he emerges again, he has a travel pack of tissues in his hand. He turns for a second towards the traffic behind him before starting to make his way towards the woods where we are waiting.

CHAPTER 24

A hazy light breaks through the wispiest of clouds in the dark sky to strike the topmost windows of the buildings on one side of the street. I walk slowly towards the place where Milla found Robert and hunker down, checking that I'm alone, before I stretch out flat on the ground.

The paving stones are cold – it's almost like lying on a slab of ice. The chill beneath me stings my cheek, slicing through the damaged tissue and making my sinuses throb with pain. I remain there until I hear a car approaching. 'Worth nothing dead,' I murmur to myself before struggling to my feet.

I hurry into the side street and start walking towards Grünerløkka. Something draws me to Milla, I think as I follow the route to the hotel on my mobile. We've both confronted the abyss, inhabited it and had to crawl our way up out of it again. That means we know too much about ourselves. The only thing I'm not yet completely sure of is whether that's the only reason I'm drawn to her, or whether there's something else as well.

All of a sudden I'm aware of a loud noise ahead of me, and when I look up, I'm staring right into the front of a car. The bumper hits my side and sends me rolling over the bonnet and car roof before I crash on to the tarmac.

I lie there gasping for air while I wait for the pain to kick in. The car has stopped about fifteen to twenty metres away and the driver is turning round, with the front now facing the spot where I'm sprawled on the road. The engine roars as it revs up and the car accelerates straight towards me.

I know I don't have time to get up before it runs me over. Instead I stretch out and roll on to the pavement, where I press my head and body close to the hard, cold surface. The car swings around to point directly at me and one front wheel mounts the kerb before the metal monster is upon me.

I feel nothing, noticing only that I'm being dragged across the road beneath the car, while I cradle my head in my hands and do my best to protect myself.

The car stops abruptly with me wedged tight underneath. The engine growls above my head and I smell oil and fuel. The driver reverses so that I'm lying in the middle of the road again. I screw up my eyes and wait for another onslaught, but nothing happens. The car sits with its engine idling a few metres behind me before finally reversing to speed away down a side street.

I remain prostrate, motionless, until someone comes running over and attempts to force my body on to its side.

'Are you OK?' I hear a voice ask, but don't dare to open my eyes or make any effort to answer. Soon I can make out more voices and eventually I also hear the sound of sirens somewhere out there in the cool spring air. An icy wind stings the skin on my face and I curl into a foetal position to shut it out.

'What happened?' another voice asks.

'He was run over,' someone else says.

'Someone tried to kill him,' a third voice answers and at that moment I feel two cold fingers on my carotid artery. The blare of the sirens is making my ears ring.

The very next minute another vehicle stops nearby, several doors are opened, and new people arrive to stand beside me. Someone lifts me up carefully from the cold ground and on to a stretcher that is trundled into the ambulance.

CHAPTER 25

'You were lucky,' the doctor tells me when he finally enters the room I've been installed in after the obligatory examinations. 'Apart from a few scratches and torn clothes we've found no sign of either fractures or internal injuries. How are you feeling?'

'I'm in pain,' I say.

'Where?'

'Everywhere.'

'You obviously banged your head, so we'll keep you here for observation until tomorrow, just to make sure that no swelling or suchlike develops.'

'That's fine, but then I'm going to need something for the pain. OxyContin, or maybe OxyNorm instead?'

'We don't administer that kind of pain relief here. You can have some Paracet or Ibux if you need it.'

'Forget it,' I answer grumpily and lie back in the bed.

'By the way, there are two police officers waiting to talk to you. Do you want me to ask them to wait until you're feeling better, or shall we—'

'Just send them in.'

'OK.' He backs out to the door and waves to someone outside. 'A nurse will come in afterwards to take your blood pressure and check that everything's satisfactory. I can ask him to bring a couple of Paracet in case ...'

I nod my head as I struggle to put on my tarmac-coloured shirt. My ruined jacket is draped on a nearby chair and I can see only one shoe on the floor beside it.

'Where's my other shoe?' I ask.

The doctor shrugs. 'Could it have fallen off in the accident?' He gives a crooked smile before leaving just as a man and woman, both in police uniform, step inside.

'How are you doing?' the policewoman asks, once they've closed the door behind them. The woman does the talking while the man clutches a notepad and pen.

'Just another sun-drenched day in paradise,' I reply before leaning forward in an effort to see if the other shoe might have fallen under the bed. It feels as if my head is going to explode and I give up the search.

'Thorkild Aske,' the woman says. 'Is that you?'

'Correct,' I groan.

'Can you tell us what happened?'

'I was walking, and then I was flying through the air, and then I was dragged across the tarmac.'

'Do you know who was driving?'

I shrug my shoulders.

'No thoughts?'

'Yes, one or two from time to time, but I don't know who it was. I didn't see the driver. It was a black Audi estate car, but I didn't see the registration number. Any witnesses?' I ask, as he makes notes and she watches.

'Yes,' the policewoman replies.

'And?'

'The make of car is confirmed.'

'The driver?'

Neither of them says anything.

'What are you working on, Aske?' the man with the note-pad and pen finally asks me.

'Aha. You think this might have something to do with my job?'

'What do you think?' the policewoman asks.

'I'm unemployed,' I tell them.

'Married?'

'Divorced.'

'Is there anyone you know who might ...'

'Consider murdering me?'

They both nod.

'Obviously,' I answer. 'But I've no idea who or why.'

'OK. Is there anything else you'd like to ...'

'Not now,' I say, closing my eyes. 'No more for now. I'm exhausted.'

I can hear the door opening and closing before the foot-steps ebb away and silence takes over. I lie like that for a few minutes and then open my eyes. 'Rise and shine, sunbeam,' I tell myself, hauling myself up in the bed. I grit my teeth when my head begins to pound from the sudden movement. I bend over the side of the bed, still searching for the other shoe, but I can't find it. Then I sit up, grab my jacket and fish out my mobile phone.

'Hi, Thorkild,' Ulf grunts testily when he answers. 'How's life with the cultural elite?'

'Oh, top notch! I really needed to get out of the bedsit and away from Stavanger. Loads of people, exciting expe-riences and lots of traffic. I think Oslo is bound to become my second home.'

'What do you want?'

'Are you smoking, Ulf? It sounds as if you—'

'No, I'm not bloody smoking. You know that.'

'OK, keep your hair on, I believe you.' I know he's standing firm. I can hear it in the restlessness in his voice. But I like to ask all the same. To remind him that he's not smoking, and in that way let him know I'm still missing my pills.

'What are you doing?'

'I'm lying in bed thinking about Milla's research assignment,' I tell him. 'About whether I should continue with it.'

'Do you want to come home?'

'No, but there are a couple of things …'

'We're not changing your medication regime,' Ulf answers peevishly.

'Why not?'

'Come home and I'll tell you again, preferably while I drive you out to that candle factory.'

'You know what? The worst thing is that I don't even believe such a thing as a job-centre-supported candle-making factory exists. That's just something you're using against me to punish me because you're no longer smoking.'

'Come home and then we'll see,' Ulf responds, goading me. 'You've searched for the abyss for a long time now, Thorkild, and that's where you'll find it. Down in the depths of the job-centre-subsidised vats of candle wax out at Auglendsmyrå.'

'What if something happened to me? If, for instance, I should end up having an accident and dying?'

'Dying?' All at once Ulf's voice has taken on a different undertone. More wary. 'What do you mean?'

'People do have accidents, people do die.'

'People do die, yes,' Ulf replies. 'Some even try to hurry the process along. What is it you're actually wondering?'

'If something were to happen to me, I'm just wondering, what would become of my body? Where would I be buried?'

This conversation has spun completely out of control, and I do my best to find my way back to what I actually wanted to find out.

'Are you asking me where you'll be buried when you die, Thorkild?'

'Yes.'

'Why?'

'It's not what you're thinking. I'm absolutely fine. But this work for Milla, people who just vanish into thin air, that's got me thinking.'

'Thinking of where you'll be buried?'

'I don't know, that's the point. I don't really belong to any particular place, and ...'

'What about Tananger?'

'No, Ulf. This doesn't revolve around Frei.'

'Everything revolves around Frei,' Ulf counters.

'No, no, it ...'

'OK. What if I have you cremated and put the container of Aske's ashes on the mantelpiece here at home as a reminder of my greatest professional setback, with a plaque in memory of the only patient it was never possible to help, someone there was no fucking way to hammer as much as a single scrap of sense into?'

'You know what, Ulf? I'm phoning you as a friend. If I were thinking of taking my own life, then I wouldn't have called. This is something else, and if you're going to be so fucking mean that you can't be bothered helping me, then we'll just let it drop. We'll talk when I get home. Bye.'

I hang up. Ulf isn't thinking clearly. If I travel home to Stavanger now, there's nothing waiting there for me apart from more happy pills that contain no happiness and fresh aims and objectives on the road to complete freedom from drug addiction. All I can hope for is that this conversation is yet another burden that brings him another step closer to the Marlboro packet again out of sheer frustration, or at least to make him more willing to have a rational discussion about my medicine situation once I'm finished with this case.

I take a deep breath and ring him back.

'It's me,' I say when Ulf finally answers.

'I know,' he tells me. He sounds calmer as well. Almost too calm; Marlboro calm.

'This case,' I begin.

'Yes?'

'It's not a case, not the way we thought.'

'What do you mean?'

'It's not research, Ulf. We're looking for Milla's daughter.'

'Milla Lind doesn't have a daughter.'

'Yes, she does. She was raped when she was a teenager, and later the child was taken away because of her mental state. That was why she hired Riverholt. To find Olivia. One week after they located her, Olivia and her pal ran away from a residential children's home. Milla and a couple of friends of hers in the police force are searching for her now. They want me to help them.'

Ulf is silent, and a lengthy pause ensues, during which I wait, unsure whether an outburst is brewing or whether he is just going to order me home. 'Mugabe also had a daughter,' he says in the end.

'What?'

'August Mugabe, the protagonist in Milla's book series. He had a daughter when he was young, long before he met Gjertrud. The child's mother wouldn't have anything to do with Mugabe, and even denied him access to his daughter, but August followed her from the sidelines, dreamt about her and fantasised about what it would be like to be a father. The girl disappeared around the time that August met Gjertrud. I've always thought she might have had something to do with the girl's disappearance.'

'So, should I continue, then?'

Another silence. It sounds as if Ulf is giving this some thought, not about whether I ought to continue, but about what this new information might mean for Milla's literary universe and the characters within it. 'So, you're searching for Milla's daughter?' he says at last. 'You, Milla and a couple of police officers, who know who you are? Or were? And they're happy to have you on their team?'

'At least one of them is,' I reply.

'Well, you're not the easiest person to like. One out of two I'd say was surprisingly good in your case. Especially given that they're in the police force.'

'So you want me to go on with it?' I've made up my mind not to tell him any more, about all the shady business surrounding my predecessor's death and my own hit-and-run.

'And all that stuff about where you'll be buried when you die, where did that come from?'

'Even though I'm unwell, I'm surely allowed scope for reflection when something breaks the surface? I thought you considered that sort of thing to be progress?'

'Yes, that's fine,' Ulf ultimately concedes. It sounds almost as if the answer comes as a surprise to him too. 'As long as things don't escalate. Then you have to give me a call. You will, won't you?'

'Of course,' I agree, and ring off. I put on my trousers, and my jacket even though it's practically torn in two down the back after my journey along the tarmac beneath the car, and then my one shoe. Raking my fingers through my hair, I set off out of the room in search of the exit.

The corridor outside is deserted. I hear someone moaning in one of the other reception rooms and hurry towards the open door. Inside, I see a doctor and nurse stooped over a bed in which a man is lying. It looks as if they're cutting up one of his trouser legs.

My breathing is laboured and I try to focus on both my respiration and my vision. I follow the wall to a notice pointing to the exit. A couple of poor souls are seated in a waiting room – their evening has also taken an unexpected, unfortunate turn. They both stare at me when I appear in the doorway but quickly turn away again, possibly in fright, when they see that I'm not the duty doctor.

The woman behind the window in reception looks up from her computer screen just as I pass by. 'Hello! I see this isn't the Kon-Tiki Museum,' I say, giving her a sheepish smile before slipping out of the door and breaking into a sprint towards the taxi stand.

It crosses my mind that in fact I have no choice when I finally settle inside a taxi and ask the driver to take me to the hotel. It's time for me to muster some courage and take things seriously. I have to talk to someone as soon as daylight breaks, before I meet up with Milla and the rest of the gang. And there's only one person in the whole world I can speak to about this, only one person who can help.

'He won't like it, though,' I murmur. I lean back in the taxi seat and close my eyes. 'He's going to be furious, in fact.'

CHAPTER 26

At the crack of dawn I leave my hotel room in Grünerløkka and go in search of a chemist's, as well as a shop where I can buy a new jacket and shoes. For financial reasons, my choice comes down to the nearby Fretex charity shop. The woman behind the counter is almost ecstatic when she tells me that my purchase can be considered a triple bonus: one vintage sheepskin gents jacket from the seventies and a pair of matching shoes unlike anything anyone else is wearing, for an unbeatable price. On top of all that, I've just contributed to saving the environment.

When I get back to my hotel room, I strip off and head straight for the shower. Afterwards I stand in front of the mirror. The lines on the damaged side of my face grow fainter every day, and my hair is greyish-brown, with split ends, like on a cast-off toothbrush. I take out a new sticking plaster from the chemist's bag and start to cover the scrapes and scratches from the night's turmoil. Then I leave the bathroom and sit down on my bed. Cold drops of water drip from my hair and run down my bare back.

I breathe evenly, and the muscles in my neck and chest relax a little, easing the ache in my cheek. As I massage my temples, I press my fingers gingerly into the bridge of my nose and my lips. I continue to apply pressure, but the shudders of pain this causes don't convey any answers, no moment of clarity or any sign whatsoever of what action I should take. In the end I give up, pack up my belongings and go down to reception to order a taxi to Grønlandsleiret 44, where the Oslo police headquarters are located.

The police station houses several police departments, including the top brass, the main switchboard and the Emergency Squad. On my way in I pass various police and Delta personnel who all squint inquisitively in my direction without uttering a word. In reception, I give my name and identify the person I've come to see. The man behind the counter answers with a suspicious look followed by a lengthy, extremely telling silence until I'm finally shown into an empty waiting room.

Forty minutes later the door crashes open as if the entire forced-entry team are standing outside waiting to let the itch in their biceps subside. A towering, close-cropped, muscle-bound hunk of a man strides in through the doorway.

'Well, hello, old chap,' I say meekly, getting to my feet as Gunnar Ore positions himself immediately in front of me with his fists clenched on his hips.

'What are you up to?' my former boss in Internal Affairs growls at me. 'You must be the stupidest person on God's good earth to think you can come here and—'

'Robert Riverholt,' I venture before Ore has time to talk himself into a bout of hysteria.

'What?' He takes a step back, as if the name has knocked him off balance.

'Did you know him? I know he worked in this building.'

'I didn't know him. Didn't he pack it in and transfer to an easy billet in the private sector?' Gunnar Ore remains on his feet, glaring at me as he considers this. 'Why are you asking?' he finally demands.

'No, wait,' he goes on before I have a chance to answer. 'You've taken over that easy billet of his, and have only just learned that he got a bullet in the back of his head last autumn, and now you're here because you're scared the same thing will happen to you? Ha ha ha. Don't tell me it's true, Thorkild.' Gunnar Ore bursts into loud laughter. 'Please, oh my God, Thorkild. That's the funniest thing I've heard all day.'

'People say it was his wife who shot him,' I say while Gunnar continues to laugh.

'Was it?' he gasps. 'Well, maybe he was a scumbag. What the fuck do I know? Never mind, thanks for the chat, Thorkild. It was certainly refreshing.' He turns on his heel to leave.

'You're right,' I shout after him.

Gunnar stops, hesitating at the open door. 'Right about what?'

'Right that I took over his job. I'm a consultant to the author Milla Lind and I need to know more about Riverholt.'

Gunnar Ore turns around and moves back to face me. 'Why? You just said he was shot by his wife.'

'Could you get me the case documents?'

'Why?' he repeats. 'What is it you're looking for?'

'I don't know,' I answer. 'He was working on a misper case when he was shot.'

'Why?' Ore reiterates more sternly.

'I just wanted—'

'Come off it, Aske.' Ore is now right in my face. 'Say it! I know you want to.'

'OK,' I sigh, exhaling noisily. 'There's something here that doesn't add up.'

'There, you see,' he says, with a smile, now standing beside the bookshelves that cover half of one wall in the waiting room. 'Was that so difficult?'

I shake my head. 'Can you help me?'

'Certainly,' Ore volunteers. 'That's the least I can do for you.'

'Are you kidding?'

'Why would I do that? After all, everyone knows that you're the joker between the two of us.'

'OK,' I reply in a faltering voice. 'Thanks.'

'I *like* helping you, Thorkild. Despite looking like a social dropout, your weakness and the fact that you're incapable of looking after yourself mentally and physically, you used to be a competent police officer. So, if you come to me, despite your many promises about never showing your face to me again, and especially here at my workplace, to talk about a case that involves a former policeman, a colleague who was shot down in broad daylight, then I want to know more. To know what it is you're searching for, and what you've found.'

Dragging a chair across the floor, Gunnar straddles it and nods at the adjacent three-seater sofa. 'So, when the case has been observed and analysed, what are you left with?'

'That's the thing. I haven't seen the case files yet,' I tell him as I sit down. 'I don't know anything other than what I've been told.'

'OK.' Ore nods his head. 'What is it that jars?'

'The emotional background. It doesn't fit with the chain of events. Riverholt's wife had motor neurone disease; she was ill and knew she was going to die. She and Robert were in the process of divorcing. She couldn't live without him, or die alone, everyone tells me, so she took a pistol and shot him in the back of the head in broad daylight before leaving the crime scene and finding a quiet car park near the lake at Maridalsvannet, where she took her own life.'

'An execution and a suicide,' Ore mutters as he bites the inside of his cheek. 'And what does the emotional background tell you?'

'He was shot from behind in the middle of the street. It's either a cold, professional hit or a cowardly, impersonal ambush.'

'And?'

'She left him, got in her car and shot herself.'

'She hated him.'

'Everyone says she loved him and couldn't live or die without him.'

'Then they were wrong.'

'OK, let's follow that thread. She hated him. He was a scumbag who left her, and she wanted to take him with her to the other side. So, where's the confrontation?'

'She was acting on impulse?'

'The only thing that seems impulsive here is this car park where she took her own life.'

Ore nods. 'Is that all?'

'Riverholt was working on a case, a so-called missing person ...'

'What case?'

'A disappearance last autumn. Milla Lind, the writer, is conducting research into her final book about August—'

'Mugabe, yes. Do you know how it ends?'

'What? No.'

'OK, go on.'

'Someone tried to run me over with a car last night. Twice.'

Ore studies the sticking plasters and scratches on my face while his jaws grind like millstones. 'So that's *not* how you usually look?' he says sarcastically, crossing his arms.

'Well,' I begin, but can't think of anything amusing to say.

'OK, then,' Ore finally says as he stands up. 'Let me do some checking up on these goings-on when I get time. You can't have the Riverholt case papers – the police don't dish these things out to just anybody, you know.' He nods in my direction, as if to emphasise that I'm a classic example of 'just anybody'. 'But I'll read them, do some investigating, and call you to let you know what I think when I'm done.'

'Thanks,' I say, stretching out my hand. 'By the way, how is ...'

Gunnar gives me an icy look without reciprocating the gesture. Then he turns on his heel and leaves without another word.

CHAPTER 27

A woman is standing outside the police station. Beautiful, slim and just as elegantly dressed as the first time I saw her when I was enlisted for military service at Haakonsvern more than twenty years ago. My ex-wife Ann-Mari has always preferred the suburban housewife look. Clothes, hairstyle, manicure, make-up, every detail a perfect fit. All she lacked was the right man to complement her flawless appearance. I have a feeling that Gunnar Ore is a considerably better match than I ever was.

'Hi,' I say when she approaches me. Ann-Mari stops right in front of me, and we end up a bit too close to each other. She smells fresh, of mango or something like it. She's two years younger than me, but looks several decades better. It's only in her eyes that I see everything she tries to cover up and gloss over. It's become attached to her irises and given them the cold metallic lustre that I recognise as soon as our eyes lock.

'What are you doing here?' she asks, searching for cigarettes in her handbag. Finally, she finds the pack and lights a fag while turning her body a few degrees to one side.

'Oh, didn't you know I was in the big city?'

'How would I know that?'

'Whatever,' I say. 'Just had to have a word with Gunnar about a case.'

'A case? Are you back in the police?'

'No. You know I'm not.'

Nodding, she blows the cigarette smoke away from us.

'What about you?' I ask.

'Gunnar and I are getting married.' The restless slight swaying of her hips that she has been doing since she lit the cigarette, stops abruptly. 'In Paris, this summer.'

'Oh, congratulations,' I reply, struggling to seem both taken aback and happy at the same time. 'You deserve it.'

'Deserve?' She tilts her head to one side. 'Why do I deserve it?'

'I just mean that you deserve to be ...'

'Happy?' She gives a lopsided smile.

'Stop,' I tell her before she has a chance to continue.

'But I have stopped,' Ann-Mari ripostes, unruffled. 'I've stopped blaming you and myself, stopped being sorry, even when I have to hear from other people about how you're running around in the north of Norway searching for a new way to die as soon as your last attempt proved unsuccessful. I've stopped everything, Thorkild, everything. Apart from one thing. Only one thing. So don't come here and ask me to stop, because you don't know, you've really got no idea about how many times I've had to stop in the years since you left.'

Ann-Mari puts the cigarette back in her mouth. 'You look old,' she tells me as her eyes drift over the sticking plasters on the bridge of my nose and ear before they come to a halt at the finishing touch in my damaged face. 'That scar doesn't suit you.'

'I *am* old,' I say. 'It's just that you keep yourself in such good nick that the contrast is dramatic.'

'What?' Ann-Mari says with a crooked smile. 'Do you think I'm attractive?'

'Well, you are,' I admit, but immediately regret the abject compliment we both know is given only in an effort to return the conversation to a superficial level again.

'Just as attractive as *her*?' Ann-Mari is still smiling. 'As that girl, Frei?'

'Don't …'

'No, Thorkild. I've already said I'm not going to stop. I love you, and you can't take that from me. I deserve to love you, someone who doesn't want me, someone who makes me feel so fucking terrible even when he's miles away. Who'd rather be with a corpse than anywhere near me. You are *my* Frei, Thorkild. My punishment.'

I'm at a loss for words, so we just stand there until she's finished her cigarette. Ann-Mari tosses the smoking filter on the ground before leaning across to kiss me on the cheek where the scar has converged into a hard, star-shaped lump. 'You'll just have to live with that,' she says, patting my chest gingerly before heading for the police station entrance.

Chapter 28

Milla opens the door to her apartment in a pair of black trousers and a beige chiffon blouse. 'What happened to your face?' Her appearance today is warmer, softer, making her seem slim rather than too skinny.

'I fell,' I tell her, running my fingers over the plaster on my nose. 'While shaving.'

Milla smiles broadly. 'Idiot!' She goes on looking at me, until finally she lets me in. She waits in the hallway while I take off my new-old shoes and the vintage sheepskin jacket that's already making me itchy, even though it's on top of my other clothes. 'Joachim and Iver are waiting in the living room. Kenny's coming later. He had to go out on a call.'

Iver is sitting in a living-room chair with a cup in his hand and Joachim is standing at the kitchen island reading a newspaper. Iver puts his cup down on the coffee table when he catches sight of me.

'What happened?' he asks, getting to his feet.

'Thorkild says he fell,' Milla answers. 'While he was shaving.'

'Really?' Iver stands immediately in front of me and Joachim stares inquisitively at us from the kitchen.

'I was run over,' I tell them. 'Last night, after I left Milla's apartment.'

'W-what?' Milla asks. 'Was it an accident, or …'

'Difficult to say,' I begin, taking a seat. 'I was knocked down on the footpath a block or two from here, and then the driver stopped, turned the car and ran over me again.'

'B-but …' Milla stutters.

Joachim has put down his newspaper and comes to join us.

'I've also had a word with a friend of mine,' I continue.

'About what?' Milla asks. 'About us?'

'No, not about us,' I reply. 'About Robert.'

'Who have you spoken to?' Iver asks.

'Gunnar Ore.'

'Ore?' Iver shakes his head, sounding discouraged. 'Isn't he in Delta, the Emergency Squad? What would he have to do with …'

'Ore was my boss in Internal Affairs,' I tell him. 'He can help.'

'With what?' Iver continues. 'What is it you think Ore can—'

'What I think,' I interrupt calmly just as Joachim puts his arms around Milla's waist and pulls her towards him, 'is that I'd like to see Robert Riverholt's mobile log and all the emails he sent and received in the period before he was killed. Also, I'd really like to hear exactly what it was he was doing in the days before he died.' I take a deep breath before I add: 'And I could really do with a cup of coffee, black and strong.'

Iver remains standing in front of me for a while until he finally shakes his head and moves across to the kitchen island. He pours coffee into his cup and slumps down into the chair beside me.

'Thorkild,' he says. 'This thing with Robert.' He leans towards me. 'Phone lists, emails, how do you think we'll get hold of that kind of stuff? We can't just—'

'I suppose you're monitoring Olivia and Siv's mobile phones?'

'Yes, but …'

'That means you have a friend in Telenor who lends a hand with that sort of thing, doesn't it?'

Iver doesn't respond. Joachim has released Milla. He walks over to the kitchen island, takes a new cup from one of the cupboards, pours in some coffee and approaches me with it. 'Here,' he murmurs, before moving to stand beside Milla again.

'Who arranged access?' I ask, after thanking Joachim for the coffee.

'Runa,' Iver answers reluctantly. He knows what my previous colleagues in Internal Affairs would say about their activities. 'That's the police station's contact person in the phone company. Her name is Runa.'

'Then you'll call her?'

'Yes,' Iver answers.

'Now?'

Iver looks at me for a long time until at last he nods and gets to his feet. He takes his mobile and goes out into the hallway.

'What on earth are you up to?' Milla asks while Iver speaks on the phone.

'The "what-if game",' I reply, forcing a smile.

'What's that?' Joachim asks.

'What if what happened to me last night is connected to my taking over from Robert?' I say. 'What if Robert had found something that he didn't tell you about? What if he wasn't shot by his ex-wife, but was killed because he was searching for Olivia? And last but not least: what if Olivia and Siv didn't travel to Ibiza like they did the year before? What if something has happened to them, something beyond your control?'

Joachim's glance alternates between me and the hallway where Iver is talking on the phone. Milla does not say anything, but simply stares at me.

'Tell me about your dream scenario.' I see I've scared her, and make up my mind to try to force her to focus on Olivia. 'The best outcome this can have.'

Milla hesitates for a moment as she gives this some thought. 'That I find her, Olivia, alive. That I get to tell her who I am, and why I did what I did.' I can see her grow calmer, her pulse rate dropping as she speaks. Joachim puts one hand round her waist and brushes her hair back from her eyes. 'That in time we can get to know each other, maybe even at some point be mother and daughter …'

'What's the worst?'

'That,' she finally answers. All the colour has left her face and she wears the same expression as when I saw her from between the trees in her study with Joachim.

'What do you mean?'

'What you just described in your scenario,' Milla replies huskily and squeezes Joachim's hand in hers. Iver returns from the hallway with his mobile in his hand.

'Anything to report?' I ask and move to get up from the chair.

'One number,' Iver answers, indicating that I should remain seated. 'There's one number Robert rang in the days before he died, one that stands out.'

'And that is?'

'The number of a local police station in Orkdal. The policeman up there was in a meeting, but received a message to call back as soon as it was over. The person I spoke to could nonetheless confirm that they had an ongoing case at that particular time.' He takes a deep breath before ploughing on: 'A body found during excavation work prior to installing a charging station for electric cars.' Iver's voice falters before he adds: 'Of a young woman.'

'No.' Milla turns away from us, burying her face in the crook of Joachim's neck and repeating the same word over and over again: 'No, no, no.'

Chapter 29

I can see the last rays of the autumn sun between the branches above us. I'm freezing, and the wind stings when it buffets my face. Siv is lying just in front of me on the cold ground. Her mouth is half open and a few strands of blonde hair touch her lips, but they don't move. Her hair and cold eyes bring to mind one of the social workers, the one that always used to ask those stupid questions during our interviews when she would look intently at me, as if she was trying to force her way in behind my eyes. 'Do you still think about her, Olivia? What would you like to tell her about yourself?'

I never answered, just shrugged and let my gaze follow the electric cables in her office from one point to the next. How the hell could I explain to her what it meant to lose the person who brought out the sun and chased away the clouds? She would never have understood if I'd told her that you've become a ghost that melts away, fading more and more each time I summon you from deep down inside me. And that if I don't find you soon, you'll disappear entirely from my memories, too.

'Siv,' I whisper as I reach out my hand to her face, running my fingertips over her mouth. It looks as if she is sleeping

with her eyes open, an everlasting, dreamless sleep. 'Please, Siv. You must wake up.'

Eyes closed, I continue fondling her face with my fingertips and try to conjure you up again one last time. Mum, this wasn't how this day was supposed to end.

PART III

THE ONES WHO NEVER COME BACK

CHAPTER 30

None of us says anything as we sit around the coffee table in the living room of Milla's apartment, waiting. When Iver's mobile finally starts to ring, all four of us get to our feet. Iver clears his throat and puts the phone to his ear. 'You had a case,' he begins once he's introduced himself and explained what this is all about, 'last autumn. I understand it had to do with finding a woman's body.'

'What are they saying?' Joachim asks impatiently, tightly squeezing Milla's hand.

'So you remember the conversation with Robert Riverholt?' Iver half turns his face away from us as he speaks. 'And you're certain it had to do with this particular case?'

'Is it Olivia?' Milla asks. Joachim releases her hand and puts his arm around her waist, as if he's afraid she'll fall.

'OK,' Iver says, sending a worried look in their direction. 'Do you know who she is?'

'Iver,' Milla repeats. Her voice is harder now, closer to breaking point. 'Is it Olivia?'

Iver puts a hand over his mobile. 'It's not her,' he hisses before returning to the phone conversation.

'So who is it?' Milla pulls herself free from Joachim's grip and stares tearfully at Iver. 'Siv?'

'No. A local girl.' Iver continues speaking and finally says thanks. After he has hung up, he takes a step forward to stand between us. 'Liv Dagny Wold,' he tells us, clearing his throat, 'left her home on the morning of 20 September last year and was found dead three weeks later. She'd a history of depression and instability. During the time prior to her disappearance, she told her sister that she was thinking of committing suicide because her daughter had been taken from her by the child welfare services and placed with a foster family because of her mother's mental condition. The corpse was found when excavation work was carried out at one of the charging stations for electric cars at a campsite. It's a definite case of suicide.'

'A suicide?' I ask, taken aback. 'Why would Robert phone to get details of a suicide?'

Iver shrugs. 'No idea.'

'Did you look at other misper cases around the same time that Siv and Olivia disappeared?' My eyes follow Iver as he leaves our circle and returns to his chair and his cup of coffee.

'We've gone through all the misper cases from last year until the time of Robert's death.' Taking a swig of the cold coffee, he makes a face and winces as he swallows. 'But there's nothing, nothing that sticks out. I mean, bloody hell, this is a suicide without a shred of doubt, so what on earth would it have to do with anything? If we're going to start examining every single tragedy that takes place in this country, then we'll—'

'OK, OK,' I say. 'Had the body in Orkdal been identified at the time Robert phoned there?'

'Yes.'

I fling out my arms in a gesture of resignation. 'Then why did he phone them?'

'A red herring.' Standing up again, Iver crosses to the kitchen island and switches on the electric kettle. 'This is a red herring that's taking us away from our task. It's completely—'

'What if it isn't?' I interrupt.

Iver glares at me. 'So you're keen to go to Orkdal?'

'Yes,' I say.

'Then you're just as desperate as Robert was,' he replies grouchily, clutching his coffee cup. 'And you?' Now he turns to Milla, still sitting close to Joachim, looking at me, her gaze roaming over my face, eyes, the scar on my cheek and lips, as if she's searching for a way into my head, into my thoughts.

Finally, she turns to face Iver and says: 'What if?'

'Christ,' Iver groans, taking out his mobile. 'What happened to Kenny?' He scrolls through his contact list and puts his phone to his ear.

'This is grasping at straws, Milla,' I tell her while Iver talks on the phone.

'It's *something*, at least,' she responds, turning towards Joachim. 'Don't you agree?'

'I suppose so,' Joachim answers hesitatingly. 'After all there must have been a reason for Robert to contact them about that case.'

'Are you sure?' I ask. 'Things are going to be considerably more difficult from here on in. These are real people, real dead people we're talking about. It has an effect on you, when you let dead people get so close to you.'

'Joachim's right,' Milla replies, forcing what might pass in other circumstances for a smile. 'We must.'

'A suicide,' I sigh, rubbing my hands over my face while Joachim follows Milla into the bathroom. 'Why did it have to be a suicide?'

CHAPTER 31

The light in Siv's eyes is now just a vague glint far inside her pupils. Her eye make-up has run, forming dribbling lines on her nose and cheekbones. Even her hair has lost its sheen and now seems almost white and skin-toned.

Somewhere nearby I can hear him digging, breathing heavily each time he sinks the spade into the cold earth. I daren't look and just lie there listening while I keep my eyes trained on Siv's face. Suddenly he tosses the spade aside, brushing soil from his clothes, and moves towards us. He doesn't even look at me, simply crouches down at our feet, filling his lungs with air as he grabs hold of Siv's legs.

Her body gives a sudden jolt as he starts to drag it, until her face slides away from mine.

Chapter 32

Robert fills my thoughts while I sit on the bed inside my hotel room, taking my evening medication. The pills taste foul, and the gelatine attaches itself to my tongue, making it difficult to swallow. This is not how happiness is meant to taste.

In the end, Robert must have been desperate. Desperate to find something to progress the case further. Why else would he investigate a suicide in another part of the country? I lie down on the bed and turn my face to the wall.

Actually, I should have told Ulf I'd been knocked down. I could also have added that the necessity for something effective had grown stronger – it has been allowed to crouch down there in my diaphragm taking sustenance for a long time now, and I can feel the most delicate area of my skull again. I've already started visualising the beginning of such a conversation when the phone rings, but I don't recognise the number.

'Thorkild, it's me.' Her breathing is laboured, as if even speaking is an effort. 'Ann-Mari.'

'What do you want?'

'To chat.' She lets out a forced burst of nervous laughter.

'You can't call me, Ann-Mari.'

'Why not?'

'You know.'

'Can we meet, then?'

'No.'

'Why are you so cold? More than twenty years together, sleeping in the same bed, doesn't even earn me a meeting with you? Can you at least tell me why? What is it I've done that I deserve so little?'

'You haven't done anything, you know that.'

'But all the same you won't even see me? Talk?'

'You shouldn't have phoned,' I repeat and hang up abruptly. Ann-Mari phones back almost at once. When she rings for the third time, I switch off my mobile. Just hearing her voice makes my head tingle, the head I've tried to keep intact ever since I returned home to Stavanger from the north of Norway, and I'm not up to this on top of everything else. I can't talk about what has been when it's difficult enough to live with what is now.

It occurs to me when I turn my face back to the wall and pull the quilt up over my head that Robert and I also have this in common. A dysfunctional relationship with the women in our lives. I notice that every time I think of Robert Riverholt I want to know more about him; whether his activities in the time before he was killed showed him at his best or whether Robert had reached rock bottom. Whether what happened to him was unavoidable, a storm that had brewed over a period of time and simply had to cause the devastation that sent him sprawling on the tarmac. I need to know if that bullet was fired because he was searching or because he was running away from something.

When I finally manage to break free from this flight of fancy, I notice that my whole body is shaking.

CHAPTER 33

During the plane trip to Trondheim airport, I picture various scenarios in which the metallic bird either explodes or plunges like a blazing bullet to the earth. Time passes slowly when you hate flying, but in the end we land anyway and emerge into the cold spring air of Trøndelag where a hire car is waiting.

The local police station in Orkdal shares a building with a dentist's surgery. The police chief welcomes us with a cup of steaming hot coffee and shows us into her office. The wall beside her desk includes a cork notice board; the rest is covered in fibreglass wallpaper.

She gives me a brief nod and puts her coffee cup down on the untidy desk, where Post-it notes are dotted around the keyboard and the computer screen. 'Ingeborg Larsen,' she introduces herself, her eyes on Milla, as she reaches out to shake hands.

Putting her handbag on her lap, Milla sits down facing Ingeborg while I have to move to a smaller table to fetch a chair for myself.

Ingeborg gazes at Milla. 'I have to admit that I told my daughter you were coming here today. The first thing she wanted me to do was to ask when your next book is coming out.'

'Oh,' Milla replies in a friendly tone, 'does she read my books?'

'Of course. All three of us do. Even my husband is totally hooked on the August Mugabe series, and we've been waiting impatiently for the next one.'

Milla snatches at a lock of hair.

'None of us wants the series to end, though,' Ingeborg goes on. 'We'd really like to know how things are going with August and his wife, Gjertrud.' She tightens her grip on her coffee cup. 'Is she going to succeed this time, or will they maybe make up, August and Gjertrud, despite all that has happened? You know, we've had quite a few discussions about it at home.' All of a sudden she gives a loud laugh. 'Yes, I told my husband that before he knew it, I might even be in the next book!'

'What can you tell us about the missing person case?' I ask, in an attempt to speed up the meeting and make some progress. The mere idea of being so far north makes me feel jumpy and filled with the urge to turn southwards again as soon as possible. 'Preferably from the moment the call came in until where we are now.'

Ingeborg puts down her cup and produces a ring binder. She withdraws an Excel spreadsheet and hands it over to me. On it are a name, case number and a few key words.

'It was her sister who reported her missing. As soon as we received the report, a search was organised. We also set up a Facebook group, but that brought no results. The body was later found when they moved a charging station for electric cars.' Leaning towards us, she indicates a red circle on the search map. 'There.'

'Cause of death?'

'An overdose. Several blister packs of pills were also found in her jacket.'

'Tell us about the discovery site.'

'At the time she disappeared, a new charging station was being built for electric vehicles, and we assume she toppled into the ditch and was then unable to find her way out of it again. It rained heavily – we think that's the reason the diggers didn't see her body when they filled in the hole again. It was sheer chance that she was found so soon. A water pipe had sprung a leak and had to be replaced. That was when it was decided that the whole charging station should be shifted.'

'Do you have photographs?'

Ingeborg looks at me and then at Milla, who seems distant and unwell as she sits peering at the search map and the Excel sheet with key words about the victim.

'Yes, of course, but I don't know if Milla should see them. Time, water, damp and suchlike, they do things to a human body ...'

'Aske is a former policeman,' Milla says without looking up from the search map. 'Show him the pictures.'

Ingeborg nods her head before finally opening a brown envelope and handing me photos from the discovery site. In the first of these I see only a ditch and the arm of a digging machine, a pile of soil and a few technicians standing in a circle around the ditch. Then the whole torso is unearthed and the back of a human head becomes visible, along with the washed-out denim jacket she'd been wearing at the bottom of the pit. She is lying on her stomach with one hand at her ear. A measuring stick is placed beside her hand

and I can see that she is holding a mobile phone, as if she is speaking to someone on the phone.

'As you know,' I begin, 'we're here because you received a call from one of Milla's friends, Robert Riverholt.'

Ingeborg nods again. 'We saw it on the news, of course, that he was shot by his ex-wife. Terrible business.'

'What did he want?'

'Liv had just been found; he said he'd seen it on TV. He told me he was working on some missing person cases from the same time frame and that he wanted to make enquiries about the case and the discovery of Liv's body.'

'Some?' I ask. 'Not just one?'

Ingeborg folds her hands on the desk. 'He said some. In any case, I told him that the final post mortem report had just come through and that its conclusion was that we were dealing with a personal tragedy, a suicide.'

'He called you again two days later?'

'Correct.'

'Why? If the investigation had already been wrapped up as a case of suicide?'

'I don't know, I wasn't in. He told the receptionist that he would phone back.' She shakes her head. 'Terrible business.'

'Thanks,' I say, getting up to leave. This meeting has not gone as I'd anticipated.

Ingeborg gives me a hearty handshake before turning to face Milla. 'Sorry,' she says, producing a book from one of the desk drawers. 'You couldn't sign this for me before you go?'

CHAPTER 34

'I just don't understand what Robert was up to,' I say as the plane fills with passengers. 'Why was he so interested in this case out of them all, why a suicide? And not least, why did he call back, when he had already received confirmation that this was a tragic case of suicide?'

'What I can't fathom,' Milla begins speaking as the plane judders before reversing, 'is why no one found her before they filled in the hole again.'

'The police chief said it had been raining heavily; the water would have gathered at the bottom, and soil or clay could also have slid down on top of her,' I answer just as a voice tells us over the intercom that the air stewardesses are ready to show us how to don a life jacket high above the clouds. 'It wouldn't have been so unusual.'

'Then there's the phone,' Milla goes on, growing enthusiastic. 'It's awful to think that the last thing she did was try to call someone from down there in that hole. Maybe she felt regret and wanted to ring for help?'

'The other thing I don't understand,' I mumble absent-mindedly, with my eyes fixed on the stewardess who is pointing out the emergency exits in front of us, 'is why Robert told the police that he was calling because he was looking into several missing person cases and not just one.'

'Siv *and* Olivia,' Milla answers.

'But that's still one case, not several.'

'Maybe her memory was faulty.'

'Maybe.'

Milla leans in to me with a crooked smile. 'What if?' she asks.

I return her smile. 'Aha!' I laugh. 'You mean what if he'd found something?'

'Yes.' Milla comes closer. 'It feels as if we're doing real police work at last.' She winks. 'Just as Robert and I were doing.' Her eyes are cast down now, moving away from my face to the side window. 'And this time we won't give up until we've found her,' she says softly to the grey weather outside. 'This time we won't give up …'

Milla continues to sit there with her cheek resting on the back of the seat as she stares dreamily out through the plane window. From time to time she snatches brief glances at me. There *is* something about her eyes, I haven't quite managed to put into words what it actually is until now, but when she looks at me for long enough, it's as if some of the colour in her pupils begins to trickle out, turning into a deep, dark oil. It meanders through the air towards my face, covering my scars and making the hardest tissue soft again, altering the lack of symmetry.

'What is it?' Once again she is looking straight at me.

'I was just thinking.' I blink hard and push back into the seat. It strikes me that either it's my brain injury that is playing yet another of its mean tricks, or else it's just that something happens to anyone who comes as close to her as I am right now.

Milla places one hand on the armrest between us. 'What were you thinking about?'

149

'Whether Robert really found something,' I begin. 'After all, Liv was found near a campsite with her mobile phone to her ear. It looked as if she was calling someone.'

'Yes?'

'Well, if I were Robert, and had a friend in the Telenor phone company, I think I would have liked to know who it was she was trying to phone.'

Milla lets go of the armrest and sits up straight as the plane finally reaches the runway. 'We must tell Kenny and Iver when we get back.'

'By the way, there's one more thing,' I say, checking the seat belt one more time while the engines rumble outside and rain and sleet pepper the aircraft. 'She was lying on her stomach.'

'What do you mean?'

'When you fall, or launch yourself from somewhere, a natural spinal reflex causes you to turn on to your back as soon as you've landed. If you survive the fall, that is. I'm thinking, if she was wanting to call someone, wouldn't she have turned on to her back first?'

Milla leans her head to one side. 'Was that what you did?' she asks. 'Turned on to your back?'

'Yes,' I reply and at that same moment our bodies are yanked back in our seats as the plane accelerates. 'Both times.'

Chapter 35

He stops at the edge of the grave, lets go of Siv's feet and jumps down. I can see him taking hold of her lifeless body and dragging it down into the hole. I keep my eyes almost completely closed, so that I can only just catch sight of him when he climbs out of the pit again.

I hold my breath when he stands up and starts to walk towards me. He crouches down and picks up my mobile phone that is lying on the ground beside my feet, looks at it, drawing his fingers over the touchscreen before dropping it into his shirt pocket. I shut my eyes firmly and in the next moment I feel his fingers around my ankles before he starts dragging me.

Everything is totally silent – sounds and smells, even the hard ground beneath me fails to reach where I am now, in this tiny corner of my innermost being. The place I found on the back seat of the car that drove me away from you, Mum. In fact, I think I've been there ever since then, and that without you I shrink into myself, becoming smaller and smaller, a black, almost invisible dot held captive in a prison of flesh, bones and tissue.

CHAPTER 36

As soon as the plane lands at Gardermoen airport, we contact Iver to tell him about our meeting with the police chief in Orkdal and ask him to get in touch with Runa at Telenor in order to requisition Liv Dagny Wold's phone records. Afterwards we take the airport train to Oslo and head for Milla's apartment in St Hanshaugen where Joachim is waiting.

'How was the trip?' he asks, setting out coffee and buttered bread rolls.

Milla shakes her head as she carries her travel bag into the bedroom. 'I'm going for a shower,' she says when she reappears. 'We can go out and eat later.'

I settle down on one of the chairs with a cup of coffee. The last few days have taught me that it's not travel I find taxing, it's the breaks in between, moments such as this that make me feel restless and out of sorts because I don't have the means to take away the craving in my diaphragm.

'Did you find out anything new up there? About Olivia?' Joachim quizzes me after Milla has gone for a shower.

'Zilch.'

He pours coffee into his cup and sits down in the chair next to mine. 'Just another dead end?'

'Maybe not.'

'Oh?'

'We'll have to wait and see what Iver finds out.'

'Milla doesn't tell me much about what you're doing.' Leaning forward, Joachim picks up the tray of bread rolls and offers it to me.

'As you know, we're following a lead that Robert had embarked on before he was shot,' I tell him as I help myself. Joachim gives a satisfied smile and replaces the tray on the table. 'A suicide in Orkdal.'

'What does that have to do with Siv and Olivia? I thought they'd run away to Spain.'

I glance in the direction of the bathroom door before leaning towards Joachim, close enough to trigger his masculine fear of physical contact, though I see he doesn't dare to move or change position. 'No,' I hiss. 'Olivia and Siv got into an unknown car. That was the last time anyone heard anything of them. What do you think that means?' I wink and then slump back into the chair.

'They're dead,' Joachim stammers. 'You think they're dead?'

I nod. 'So did Robert,' I add. 'That's why he'd started to root around in other missing persons cases.'

'B-but, I don't understand.'

'I think they were abducted by a serial killer. Robert was then killed when the murderer realised someone was on his trail. And now, now we're the ones he's after.'

'What?!' Joachim stares at me with his mouth half open.

'Thorkild, that's not funny.' Milla is standing in the bathroom doorway, wearing a dressing gown and with a towel around her head.

'What?' Joachim repeats, looking from me to Milla and back again.

'He's pulling your leg,' Milla says. 'Don't you see that?'

'Why?' Joachim demands once Milla has disappeared into the bedroom. 'Do you think this is funny?'

'Yes,' I answer. 'I think it's funny that you run around here like a nineteen-fifties housewife, baking bread rolls, grinding your own coffee and almost throttling your partner when you fuck her. I think Robert did the same.'

'You'd better watch your mouth,' Joachim says, springing to his feet.

'When the cat's away, the mice will play,' I tell him, humming to myself as I watch him, half-standing, half-sitting, with his hands on the chair back. Joachim's cheeks have taken on a reddish sheen. It looks as if he hasn't made up his mind whether it's a good idea to stand up, but nor does he want to sit back down again.

'You're sick in the head,' he finally says in Swedish, flopping back down into the chair.

'Yes, I certainly am,' I mutter as Milla emerges from the bedroom. 'And you're not the man you make yourself out to be either.'

'Are you two still larking about?' Milla crosses to the fridge and takes out a bottle of Farris mineral water.

'Not at all,' I reply, rising from the chair. 'We're just getting to know each other a bit better.' Then I look at Joachim once more. He's still clutching the armrests on the chair. 'Thanks for the rolls and butter, pal.' I reach out my hand.

Joachim stares at my outstretched hand before finally swallowing, getting to his feet and grasping it. 'Thank *you*.' He then heads straight for the bedroom.

'Why are you making fun of him?' Milla asks, moving forward to sit down beside me.

'Call it a natural consequence of the direction we're taking, by linking Robert's death to the investigation of Siv and Olivia's disappearance. It forces me to take a closer look at the men in the circles surrounding you, Robert and Olivia.'

'And you thought you'd start with Joachim?' Milla gives a brief burst of bitter laughter. 'Good God, you've seen him, you couldn't meet a kinder person. Besides, no one has supported me more in this than he has. Joachim was delighted, as I was, when Robert told us he'd found Olivia, and he was totally crushed when she went missing.'

'All I'm saying is that there's a gap between the baker-cum-housewife and the man I saw with his hands around your throat that first night at Tjøme. I just wanted to get a glimpse of what exists inside that space.'

Milla unscrews the lid of the bottle and takes a drink. 'You know I'm the one who asks him to do that?' She returns the water to the table before picking up one of Joachim's bread rolls. 'If it had been up to Joachim, we'd do it in the missionary position with the lights off,' she laughs, running a finger over her lips. 'Do you think it's strange?'

'No,' I answer.

'How do *you* do it, then? With a woman.' Again she smiles as her eyes dance over my face. 'How do *you* like to do it?'

'I'm impotent.'

'Sure?' she teases.

'Pretty sure.'

'Has it been long since the last time?'

'When the baby Jesus lay on the straw in the crib.'

'Why?'

'Because,' I reply, shifting in my seat as Milla leans closer.

'What?' She laughs and places a tentative hand on my thigh. 'Am I making you feel uncomfortable?'

'I'm always uncomfortable.'

'Not at all,' she says, with a gentle squeeze on my thigh muscle. 'Now you're lying.'

I'm about to say something when Joachim re-emerges from the bedroom. He has changed his clothes and is carrying a suitcase in one hand. 'I'm off to the summer house now,' he says, adopting a stance on the floor in front of us.

'Aren't you going to come out with us to eat first?' Milla asks without releasing her grip on my thigh.

'No,' he answers in a surly tone. 'I want to go home.'

'Joachim,' I say, rising to my feet so that Milla is forced to let me go. 'Listen, I didn't mean to wind you up.' I hold out my hand. 'Sorry, pal. OK?'

Joachim looks at my hand before finally taking it. 'OK,' he says, with a sigh of relief.

'Then you'll give me a call?' Milla gets up and looks at Joachim as she drinks more mineral water.

'What?'

'When you get there. To the summer house?'

'Yes, of course. I ...'

'Brilliant.' Milla walks across to the fridge and replaces the Farris bottle. 'Remember to water the flowers. The last time I was away, you forgot to do that.'

Joachim gives me a cold stare before lifting the suitcase and making his exit.

CHAPTER 37

Milla and I make our way to a restaurant with harsh light-ing and shiny hard chairs not far from her apartment. It occurs to me, as we sit there facing each other, each with a lager as we wait for our food, that the research assignment hadn't been the real reason for me agreeing to meet Milla when Ulf first mentioned her. On the contrary, it had been his threats of having to make candles at the job centre's behest. It had been the yearning to change the state of things, to put an end to the dead time, the vacuum in which I'm caught. A longing that no investigation or mountain of Cipralex would be able to alleviate.

'Who are you really, Thorkild?' Milla asks, before ordering another round of lagers. 'Who are you when you're not running around helping crime writers to put right old mistakes?'

'Just someone who sits in my bedsit and daydreams about everything that's never going to happen,' I answer, touching my cheek at the same time. 'Every day's a party.'

'Are you always so cynical?' Milla chuckles, holding the dew-fresh beer bottle up to her mouth. Her eyes have taken on a slightly hazy sheen that suits her. Her features all soften and it makes her more attractive, but not in a sexual way.

'My father called me a sarcastic cynic the last time we met,' I reply when a waiter arrives with our food. Milla has ordered a salad. I ordered a fish dish even though I don't like the idea of fast food. The conversation isn't flowing as it should, but we make an effort nonetheless. We're searching for something to talk about that doesn't have anything to do with death or missing persons. We land on the next best thing: family and the past.

'When was that?'

'Twenty-seven years ago.'

'He was right.'

'Yes.' I pick at the fish, pulling the meat from the bones and dipping it into the sauce, trying to hide it between the slice of lemon and the salad leaves. 'That one time. Not about anything else.'

'Is he still alive?'

'I think so. He's a marine biologist and eco-activist at home in Iceland.'

'There were times,' she spears some salad leaves with her fork and lets them slide in between her lips, chewing and swallowing with more lager, 'when I couldn't even face going in there. I heard her sobbing and crying in her cot, but I still couldn't get up off the sofa. The very thought of having to lift her up and hold her close filled me with terror and disgust. I hated myself because I felt like that, but at the same time I was petrified that I would see him in her, or smell him on her when I held her in my arms. Sometimes I could sit on the floor and study every single movement of hers, watch every single expression as she played in a world of her own, just to try to recognise what was mine and not his.'

'I think you did the right thing,' I tell her, putting my knife and fork down on the table.

'And now?' Her voice is breaking, muffling the words and making them brittle.

'I think you're doing the right thing again now, Milla,' I say.

'Thanks.' She takes a deep breath before starting to eat again.

'What did Joachim say when you told him you wanted to try to find her?'

'He was pleased. He said he'd always wanted a daughter. At first he was keen to adopt, but I couldn't face the thought of that. Not when I already had Olivia. So, when I told him that I wanted to find her, he encouraged me and even began to plan her bedroom, a TV room and family holidays to the east and west of Norway.'

'And what about Iver and Kenny?'

'It was a bit more difficult for them,' Milla tells me, and just then I notice a female figure standing in the rain outside the restaurant.

'What do you mean?' The woman is on the other side of the street as cars and passers-by rush past. There's something familiar about her, her shape, and the way she stands. I've seen her before.

'Because of their work,' Milla goes on. 'As you know, it's only children who have the right to take the initiative to find their parents once they've reached the age of eighteen. Olivia wasn't yet sixteen. Iver felt I should hold off, wait and see, but I didn't want to do that. He was the one who put me in touch with Robert, who'd quit the police and started up on his own.'

Once again my gaze wanders past Milla's face out through the restaurant window. She's no longer there; the woman in the rain is gone.

'I've been thinking,' Milla says, 'about what we discussed that first evening in my apartment.'

'Oh?' I mutter, fiddling with the label on the lager bottle.

'You told me that your happy pills didn't work, and that your psychiatrist wasn't in the mood to consider other alternatives. I told you about the time after Olivia, about Dr Aune's pain management clinic and about Somadril.'

'Yes.' I let go the paper label and push the bottle away. 'You told me that the product had been taken off the market in 2008.'

'The support group I'm part of helps. It's for former patients and health personnel. Dr Aune leads it.' Milla puts down her fork and reaches out her hand. 'You're so kind,' she says, 'and I'd really like to help you, the way you're helping me.'

'What do you mean?'

'Come back with me to my apartment,' she says, squeezing my hand harder. 'Would you like to do that?'

I glance out of the window again. Maybe she was never there. Maybe it was just my head injury that had decided to play yet another prank on old Aske. Or else it was a warning, a sign that something was soon going to put an end to the dead time and lead me out of the vacuum once and for all.

'Yes, Milla,' I finally respond, grabbing hold of my lager bottle again. 'I'd really like that.'

CHAPTER 38

It's nine o'clock by the time we return to Milla's apartment. She makes straight for the kitchen to get a bottle of wine and two glasses. She staggers across the room, placing the wine glasses on the coffee table and sinking down into the chair beside me with the bottle on her lap.

'Phew,' she sighs, waving a hand in front of her face. 'I can't tolerate anything these days,' she says. 'A couple of beers and I'm all over the place.' She puts a hand to her face and watches me through her fingers. 'I've got something else for you,' she tells me.

'What?'

'Mr Blue.' She opens her palm and holds it out to me.

'What's that?' I ask, grabbing the blue, diamond-shaped pill.

Closing her eyes, Milla turns her face aside, down towards one shoulder. 'I just told you.' Her eyelids slide shut, as if she's about to fall asleep. 'It's Mr Blue.'

'Viagra?'

She nods slowly.

'What?' My eyes look from Mr Blue to Milla, lying with her eyes closed and her hands on her stomach on the chair beside me.

'This first, and then you'll get the others afterwards.'

'The others? Do you have more than Somadril?'

'Somadril and OxyContin. The one doesn't work without the other.' Milla pats her chest before blinking her eyes. 'Have you taken it?'

'Yes,' I say, swallowing.

'Excellent,' Milla purrs, 'then it's just a matter of waiting.'

'How long?'

'Twenty to thirty minutes, it all depends.'

'Is it Joachim's?' I ask her, slumping into the chair.

'No,' Milla giggles, shaking her head. 'Joachim's is ramrod stiff without it.' She reaches out her hand, takes hold of mine and draws it to her chest. 'Come here,' she says, tugging me towards her. 'You have to search, my friend. Full body search, or whatever it's called, I can't remember …'

'I can't feel anything yet, I don't think …'

'Come on, Thorkild. I want you to touch me. Don't hold back. If you have to rip off my clothes to get it up, then go ahead. Go on, be a man.'

Rising gingerly from the chair, I take a step forward and lean over her. My movements feel mechanical, like a robot afforded a fleeting moment of self-awareness. All the same, an ache in my groin hints at some sign of life down there, and the way my mouth is watering reminds me that I haven't been so near to oxycodone for nearly six months. I don't know if it's the effect of Mr Blue or the craving for painkillers that is driving me forward. Maybe it's a combination of the two that is making me stretch out my hands to caress the pockets on her sweater, clumsily and awkwardly. Milla opens her eyes. 'No,' she tells me. Her breath is moist and smells of alcohol. 'Not there.' She reaches her arms above her head and thrusts out her chest.

I run my fingers along one arm, squeezing the soft material of her cardigan gently as I slide my hands from her wrist down towards her armpit.

'Warmer,' Milla murmurs, closing her eyes again.

I repeat the procedure with her other arm before squatting down in front of her and carefully stroking her side with my fingers, from the armpit to the waist on both sides, and further down over her hips. There's now no longer any doubt that Mr Blue has caused something to happen down below either. All at once I feel dizzy, as if all the blood in my body is heading in the same direction.

'Don't stop,' she whispers as I hesitate in confusion, wondering whether I should go on or risk losing what I need.

I move up again and lean over her. Milla reaches out her hands and I carefully lift the edges of her cardigan aside to expose her dress. Her chest heaves when I open the top button.

'Warmer,' she laughs.

I open another button, and then yet another.

'It opens at the back,' Milla tells me, leaning her upper body to one side so that I can open the fastener on her bra.

A small transparent zip bag falls from one cup and disappears down into her dress. I undo another two buttons and find it at her navel. Inside are four yellow pills.

'The oxies?' I ask, snatching the zip bag, opening it and taking out two of the pills to swallow. My breathing is more irregular, more intense now – I'm a hunter on the trail of my prey, a prey with a beating, capsule-shaped heart.

'What do you think?' Milla opens her legs cautiously and places my hand on one of her breasts before it moves on, following the curves towards her navel and her crotch.

The next bag falls to the floor as I pull off her knickers. I rush to open it too, tossing down the oxies and stuffing both of the bags with the rest of the pills in my shirt pocket.

Milla pulls her dress up to her waist and holds her arms out to me. 'Now you can finish what you've started, Thorkild.'

It feels as if my whole body is boiling now. I wipe my forehead with my arm before opening my belt and yanking it from my trousers, lifting up her legs and throwing them over my shoulders. Then I strip off the rest of my clothes, take hold of her hips and plunge inside as she pushes against me.

CHAPTER 39

Oxycodone is a river. And if you fill that river with carisoprodol, the river turns into a stream of pure, pain-free happiness. Everything is different under water. The first thing that strikes me is that benevolence does not accompany you on this side of the surface. Fish do not love other fish. The fish's parental love ebbs out once its offspring have grown and learn to manage on their own. One day it's all over, the ties are severed, despite all that has been. They are just two strangers, two of many fish. Maybe that's the way it should have been with Frei and me as well. We should have ebbed out and slid away from each other long ago.

I can see myself in the surface, smooth as glass; I am colourless, ethereal. I want to stretch out my hand to touch the reflection when I catch sight of a figure in front of me, dressed in a dark raincoat, drifting out into the middle of my river.

'Frei?' I notice how the currents pull our bodies towards each other. 'Was it you I saw out in the rain?'

There is no riverbed beneath us, and far above I see the sky, bright blue, just as blue as the water, and everything merges into one, everything becomes a sky. Soon I'm caught up in the maelstrom that surrounds the body and am pulled closer. I reach out my hand to touch the face inside the rain hood as we spin in a circle around each other.

'Frei,' I gasp. Air bubbles shoot out from my mouth when I see that the current is drawing us away from each other. 'Wait, I just want to see you, to look at your face one last time.' Immediately the hair is pulled back from the face and the rain hood glides away. It isn't Frei floating life-lessly around in front of me with wide-open eyes, dark tar running like tears down her cheeks and dissolving into the water of the river.

'Olivia?' I begin to manoeuvre my arms and legs to make my escape. The next minute I open my eyes. 'Christ,' I sigh, pulling the blanket over my face. I'd taken too many pills – I'd been too eager and had fallen asleep. It was only a dream. A fucking dream.

I lie beneath the blanket, re-running the previous evening in my head until my mobile phone gives two short peeps. I draw the blanket away from my face and see that Milla is sleeping beside me. It's not that I feel regret, or shame at sleeping with my employer in exchange for pills. The train of shame left this station a long time ago. But all the same, I should have known better. I turn and retrieve my phone from the bedside table.

A text message from a number I don't recognise: *I should have run over you one more time.*

Use a gun, I write back, sitting up in the bed.

He knew, says the message that ticks in before I get the chance to put down my phone again. *For one whole second before I pulled the trigger, he knew what was going to happen.*

The phone is switched off when I ring the number.

CHAPTER 40

I can't sleep after I receive these text messages. Milla is lying on her front beside me in the bed with her face turned towards me. Her quilt has slid down to the small of her back, and I turn on to my side, facing her, and run my hand down her back, letting it hover just above her skin until my hand starts to shake from the effort.

I stare at my hand lying there, resting on her back, aware of the trembling in my fingertips and the heat sucked in through my pores, surging up through my arm. Soon my fingers are twitching, and I see them move, caressing the smooth back, first in static, clumsy spasms, then in waves, up and down her spinal column to her shoulder blades, into her hair and down again, over her sides to the small of her back and then up again.

My eyes follow my dancing fingers and my body feels paralysed, as if my fingers are moving in a new, exotic way I've never experienced before. Doris said that it wasn't dangerous to fantasise as long as the fantasy gives me something, and doesn't harm me or anyone else. So why am I so afraid? Is it because I can't even stand the thought of another person getting close to me after Frei, for fear of uncovering the inadequacy that prances like blood- and disease-filled fleas on my damaged face? 'You'll never understand, Milla,'

I tell her softly, putting an end to the dance of my fingers on her back, 'what I'm like.'

'Mmmm,' Milla purrs before opening her eyes, breaking into a smile as she looks at me. She turns on to her side, yawns and pulls the quilt up to her chin. 'Are you OK?'

'Weird dream,' I answer, stretching out on my back with the healthy side of my face towards her.

'Oh? Do tell!'

I shake my head and reach out to the bedside table for my mobile phone. 'Someone sent me text messages last night.'

'Who?' She sits up in the bed.

I locate the exchange of messages and hand her the phone.

'B-but,' Milla gasps, putting her hand to her mouth after reading them. 'That … that's Olivia's number!' She stares transfixed at my phone. 'These messages were sent from Olivia's mobile.' She stops for a second, before directing her gaze straight at me. 'I don't understand, Thorkild … What does this mean? Why should Olivia send you a message and say that she killed Robert, that she …'

'This doesn't bode well, Milla,' I say, shaking my head. 'It doesn't look good at all.'

'But she's alive, isn't she! That's Olivia's number, don't you hear me?' Milla stares at me as if I were an alien from another planet. 'She's alive, Thorkild, she—'

'I don't think it was Olivia who sent me those messages,' I tell her, sitting up in the bed.

'What? Yes, yes, it's her mobile.' She points frantically at my mobile screen. 'That's definitely Olivia's number, Thorkild. She … she …' Milla is still pressing her fingertips hard on the screen as she fights her tears.

'Read the content of those texts, Milla,' I say. 'The person who sent me these wants me to know that he's the one who killed Robert, and who tried to kill me. There are only two reasons why someone would send me these, and one is that it actually is him and that he is telling the truth, the other is that it's been sent by someone who wants me to believe that it's the truth. All the same, though, we can't get away from the fact that the person in question has Olivia's mobile phone. He or she knows that I exist and that I've taken over the job that Robert Riverholt had before me. But at the same time he's telling us something else as well, that we're on the trail of something. Perhaps he didn't think of it when he sent me the messages, but he's actually told us that what we're doing now is working and that the trail Olivia left behind is not as cold as we'd first imagined.'

Milla sits staring at my mobile screen long after it has gone black. 'What shall we do?' she finally asks.

'We'll know more the next time this person gets in touch,' I tell her, clambering out of bed. 'In the meantime we wait.'

She clutches the quilt and follows me with her gaze. 'Do you think they'll make contact again?'

'Absolutely. Several more messages will come as long as we continue with what we're doing. But we have to be careful, Milla. Fucking careful.'

'I don't want anything to happen to you.' Her eyes have again taken on that warm brown glow that I've begun to like so much. Milla reaches out to me, grasps my hand and tries to pull me towards her. 'Thorkild, I …'

'I've told you before.' I struggle out of her grasp. 'I'm not Robert.'

Chapter 41

Iver and Kenny turn up at Milla's apartment just after half past four. They both seem out of breath, as if they've exhausted themselves talking on the trip from Drammen. Joachim is also there. He had appeared an hour ahead of them with a bundle of weekly magazines he said he wanted to deliver to Milla.

'Liv Dagny Wold.' Iver hesitates before continuing: 'A number of incoming calls from friends and family who were trying to get in touch with her in the weeks after her disappearance. But these tail off, grow fewer and more sporadic gradually as time goes by and hope diminishes. As it always does,' he goes on calmly.

'So, she didn't make any outgoing calls?' I ask, disappointed.

'No. Her mobile wasn't used after she went missing. But I thought I should be thorough and check the incoming calls too.' He smiles and takes a swig of the coffee that Kenny has served up. 'There are four incoming calls from the same number that stand out. These went straight to voicemail because the mobile batteries had already lost their charge some time before. No message was left on any of those occasions.'

'Who owns the mobile?' I ask.

'The number's no longer in use. The subscription was cancelled in the middle of October last year. The owner was Jonas Eklund, who was then a twenty-four-year-old man from Stockholm in Sweden.' Iver breathes loudly and his eyes look harder now. Darker, as the eyes of a policeman usually turn when he knows that something is not going to end well. 'I've spoken to Eklund's mother and to Liv's sister in Orkdal.'

'And?'

'They've no connection to each other. The Eklund family don't know anyone in Norway, and Liv's sister in Orkdal has never heard of them.'

'So the calls were in error?'

Once again Iver pauses for effect. 'As I said, Jonas's parents told me they don't know anyone in Norway …'

'And what about Jonas?' My patience is running out now. 'Did he know Liv?'

'That's difficult to tell,' Iver goes on.

'Haven't you spoken to him?'

'No. No one has since last autumn.'

'What do you mean?'

'He's dead,' Iver finally answers.

'Dead?'

'Jonas left Stockholm late last summer with his girlfriend and travelled north. Their bodies were found in some woods beside a campsite outside Umeå in October a few weeks later. The newspapers called it a suicide pact.'

'A suicide pact?'

'Exactly,' Iver replies before going on to add: 'Wasn't Liv also found near a campsite?'

171

'Yes, she was,' I tell him. 'So this boy phoned Liv in Orkdal several times and then took his own life along with his girlfriend's? How?'

'Well, this is where things start to get more interesting,' Iver tells me. 'All four calls from Jonas Eklund's mobile appear to have been made after he and his girlfriend were already dead.'

'What?' I groan. 'How on earth?'

'Kenny has spoken to the boy's mother,' Iver goes on. 'She says that her son took his girlfriend and headed north to escape from a bad crowd they'd fallen in with. They kept in touch by phone at first, and then he suddenly stopped answering when she called him. Now we know why.'

'But it can't have been him,' Milla interjects. 'Someone else must have been using his phone.'

'Yes!' Iver and Kenny answer in chorus. 'But there's more.' Iver opens a plastic bag he had set down between his legs and takes out a folder. 'I've had the case papers sent over from the police in Umeå.' He hands me the folder. 'You can see for yourself.'

'What am I looking for?' I ask, as I start to leaf through the documents.

'You'll soon see it,' Iver replies. I notice that his hand is shaking when he takes hold of his coffee cup again.

'Yes,' Kenny agrees grimly, nodding at the crime scene photographs. 'You can't miss it.'

I pick up a sheaf of photos and begin to thumb through them. In the first image there are two bodies only just visible beneath a thin layer of leaves and grass. Jonas Eklund is lying on his back with his face upturned and his arms by his side. His torso is bare and you can see the open wounds on both of his wrists. They resemble ravines in his dry skin. His skin is yellow and adheres to his skull in a way that reminds you of a mummy from ancient Egyptian excavations.

'Personal belongings?' I ask, turning to Kenny.

'No,' he says.

'None at all?'

I move on to the next picture which is of a girl lying on her stomach – her face is hidden by all her hair and she is holding one hand up under her tangled locks, while the other is stretched out along her body so that her fingertips brush against her boyfriend's hand.

'Have you found it?' Kenny leans towards me and looks at the photo I have in my hand, on which they've turned the girl on to her back and placed her body on a sheet of white plastic.

'What's this?' I point to the hand half-hidden in her hair.

'They believe she regretted what she'd done and may have tried to call for help,' Kenny says, clutching his coffee cup and giving Milla an appraising look. 'But it was too late.'

'It's the same,' I hiss, staring at Kenny. 'Isn't it? It's exactly the same as with Liv in Orkdal.'

'What?' Now Milla approaches us and hunkers down beside me. 'Thorkild?' she asks softly, placing a tentative hand on my thigh. 'What's the same?'

I put the photo on the table between us and point. 'Look at the way she's lying,' I say. 'With the phone to her ear as if she's dialled the number and is just waiting for someone to answer at the other end.'

'True enough,' Kenny says, with a slight shake of the head. 'Suicide cases, they always make everything far more difficult.'

'This is no suicide pact,' I insist as I stare at the photograph in front of us. 'No more than Liv's falling into a ditch was suicide. It's been staged. They were laid out like that. Someone has placed them there after they had died. Shit,' I groan, holding my head in my hands. 'We were right. Robert wasn't digging around in a random suicide in Orkdal when he was shot, he was on the trail of a series of crimes. Murders.'

CHAPTER 42

He drags my body all the way to the edge of the grave before stopping and walking around to stand beside me. He crouches down, grabs hold of my shoulder and hip and swings me up on to my side and shoves me down into the hole in the ground where Siv is lying. I land with my face on her chest.

I can only just make him out, standing over us with my mobile phone in his hand as he looks around, listening intently. I struggle to breathe through Siv's clothing without moving so much as a muscle. The very next moment, he jumps down into the grave and starts to pat our jacket and trouser pockets until he finally climbs back out of the hole again.

He picks up the spade from the middle of a heap of fresh soil, pulls it out and stabs it fiercely into the pile of earth. My body is tense and I have to screw my eyes up tight and press my face harder into Siv's chest to prevent myself from screaming when the first crumbs of earth start to rain down over us.

CHAPTER 43

'Eklund's mobile was used to ring numbers in several countries in the same period of time, right up until his body and that of his girlfriend were found and the subscription was cancelled,' Iver tells us. Joachim is sitting close to Milla, flipping carefully through the crime scene photos from the Eklund case, looking aghast, while Kenny paces restlessly back and forth across the floor. 'As I said, Runa is checking all of these just now, in order to have an overview of the movements of whoever had Eklund's mobile phone. But there was one more number on that list, another Norwegian number, that was called repeatedly.'

'Let me guess,' I say. 'Yet another suicide?'

'No,' Iver shakes his head. 'Have any of you heard of Solveig Borg?'

No one answers.

'Solveig Borg was a Norwegian folk singer,' Iver goes on. 'In fact, I think I've seen her on TV. Anyway, she died after a long illness at home in her bed on 12 August last year. She was fairly well known. Came originally from the south of Norway, but lived with her son in Molde.'

'Natural causes,' I comment. 'So what's the connection?'

'Her son,' Iver answers. 'Svein Borg. He was reported missing by his workmates a fortnight later, almost a month before Liv disappeared in Orkdal. Molde and Orkdal are only three hours' drive from each other. It was assumed that Borg had gone to St Petersburg after his mother's death to trace his father. No one has heard from him since.'

'So, we have another one,' I sigh. 'What the hell are we getting mixed up in here?'

Kenny is still pacing to and fro beneath the sunlight flooding through the roof windows in Milla's apartment. 'Aske's right, this is starting to look more and more like a serial killer on the loose, but there's still nothing to link these misper cases to Siv and Olivia's disappearance.'

'Yes, there is,' I answer, fishing out my mobile phone from my trouser pocket. I scroll through to the text messages I'd received the previous night and show them to Iver and Kenny.

'What?' Iver stares at the screen before turning his gaze on me. 'I don't understand …'

'It was sent from Olivia's mobile,' I tell him. 'The sender takes the blame for Riverholt's killing and the attack on me, and he's in possession of Olivia's mobile phone.'

'That can't be true,' Kenny says. 'Someone's messing around with us. That's the only possible explanation.'

'But all the same, we can't escape the fact that he has Olivia's mobile,' I insist. 'And now we also know that someone used Eklund's phone after he and his girlfriend were dead. I don't have to tell you what lies at the end of that line of reasoning.'

'OK,' Kenny says, scratching his head. 'Let's try to get an overview of the scope of things here. Look for concrete proof that this is what we think it is, before we choose what to do going forward.'

'Agreed,' I say.

'So, what do you suggest?' Iver asks.

'We have to search for more similarities between the cases,' I begin. 'But first and foremost, we have to prove that these really are murder cases and not suicides.'

'Autopsy reports?' Iver, leaning back in his chair, rubs his fingers together. 'There must be something there to prove that.'

I nod, but Kenny shakes his head, discouraged. 'It's a fucking mess.'

'We have to get Runa in Telenor to monitor the mobile traffic on Olivia's phone,' Iver suggests. 'If you receive further messages, we might be able to trace the number as well—'

'No,' I break in. 'I'll deal with that part myself.'

'What do you mean?'

'The messages were sent to me personally. I plan to handle them in my own way for the time being. In the meantime, I suggest we continue along this line and see where it leads,' I say. 'You can take care of the autopsy reports in the two cases in which we have dead bodies, and go through each and every one of the numbers that were phoned from Eklund's mobile.'

'And you? Kenny demands. 'What do you intend to do?'

'We.' I turn to Milla. 'Milla and I have to go to Molde to find someone who can tell us more about Svein Borg's disappearance. If it fits in with the others, then he's the first one who went missing. That could give us some idea of where all this really begins.'

Chapter 44

Molde has too much sea in front of it. It's too open, exposed, and the cold air has too easy a passage between the buildings. Iver has arranged a meeting for us in a café in the town centre with Inspector Øyvind Strand, who is going to tell us about the Svein Borg case.

'Svein Borg,' Øyvind Strand opens the conversation. He's around my age with thin, cropped hair that's greying at the sides and rusty-brown on top. He has ordered a slice of cream gateau. 'I actually mostly felt sorry for him,' he tells us as he dives into his cake.

'What do you mean?' As for myself, I've bought a croissant with cheese and ham, simply in order to have something to chew on between my slurps of coffee. Milla sits beside me staring moodily into her cup as Øyvind speaks. It looks as if she's already started to notice the gravity of this new direction the investigation has led us into. From experience I know that sometimes it's safer to stay in a place where the possibilities are still open, where you can hide behind false hopes and dreams as Siv's mother has done. For her, Siv is always going to be in Ibiza, just a phone conversation away.

'Well,' Øyvind Strand scrapes the last remnants of cream from his plate and then licks the spoon, 'this conflict between him and his mother's family in the south of Norway, after

Solveig Borg passed away. A quarrel about the rights to her life's work; the whole sorry business ended up in court in the end. Borg lost, and then he packed his belongings and left. He was a nice bloke, even though I only got to know him a little.'

'You met him, then?'

'Yes.' He turns away, looking longingly at the cake counter before dropping his spoon and grabbing his coffee cup. 'In connection with the criminal complaint.' He puts his cup down on the table again and scratches his forehead as he studies Milla's face, even though she refuses to look up.

'What criminal complaint?'

'Oh yes, they lodged a complaint.' When he digs his nails harder into his forehead, some thin flakes of dandruff fall on to the plate in front of him. 'His mother's family. For desecration of a grave, I think it was. They were of the opinion that he had raked around in his mother's grave and destroyed something, so I had to talk to him, and then he told me all about the disagreement, that his mother actually hadn't wanted to be buried, that he had asked for permission to scatter her ashes, but that the family, who I understand are deeply Christian, had put up a fight and forced through a decision that she should be transported to her home community on the south coast and buried beside her parents. They also denied permission when Borg and the record company wanted to issue a memorial recording of his mother's songs. Quite a commotion, in fact. I understand why he left.'

'Was there anything to indicate that his departure wasn't voluntary?'

'No, on the contrary. We spoke to some of his workmates, and they thought Borg had gone to Russia to try to locate his father. He'd even packed all his belongings, cancelled his phone subscription, electricity, water and suchlike before he left. Later it was also confirmed.'

'What was?'

Once again, he turns towards the cake counter as he stamps his feet impatiently, making his knees hit the underside of the table. 'That he'd gone to Russia,' he finally says.

'I see?'

'Well, he's serving a prison sentence in a labour camp in Arkhangelsk. I think it had to do with some drunken escapades in St Petersburg, I don't really remember. Anyway, a guy from the Norwegian embassy in Moscow was sent to confirm it. Borg didn't want any assistance, but all the same. At least it allowed us to close the case on this side. Borg is alive, maybe not in the best of health; you hear a few stories about prison conditions in other countries, but no matter. He's alive.'

'When did you find this out?'

'Just before last Christmas.'

'Are you sure it's him?' I ask. 'That it really is Borg who's incarcerated in that prison?'

'What do you mean?'

'That it's him, and not some other guy who's passed himself off as Borg?'

'I don't understand?' Øyvind Strand smiles uncertainly in Milla's direction although she gives no response in return. 'What are you getting at?'

All of a sudden, I can feel my mobile vibrate in my jacket pocket. 'Sorry. Back soon.'

I take my phone and step outside the café.

'It's me,' Iver says. 'Have you discovered anything else?'

'Yes,' I tell him. 'This isn't a missing person case. Borg's alive and kicking.'

'Alive! Then—'

'What about you?' I interrupt. 'Any news from your end?'

'I've got the autopsy reports.'

'And?'

'Have you heard of potassium chloride B?'

'No.'

'It's an infusion solution. Used in infusion bags for slow intravenous administration. Usually on elderly patients suffering from dehydration.'

'I see.'

'An overdose of potassium chloride B results in elevated potassium levels in the blood and can lead to disturbance of heart rhythm and even heart attack. It can also induce paralysis and confusion.'

'Can't you just tell me what you know?' I demand irritably, while I try to shield my face from the wind.

'Liv in Orkdal had high levels of potassium chloride B in her blood, according to the toxicology report.' He pauses. 'As did the two bodies in Sweden, but here comes the sting in the tail – they could of course have done it themselves, independently of each other, taken their own lives as the post mortem reports concluded. But potassium chloride B isn't something you have lying around at home, and it's not something that people have access to. It's more likely and normal for people to take an overdose of pills. Whereas, as I said, this is an infusion liquid, and no hypodermics were found at either of the discovery sites. So …'

'Someone else must have administered the injections.'

'It appears so.'

'These cases,' I groan, 'it looks as if they're as we feared.'

'Yes,' Iver answers before adding: 'Have you spoken to her about it? It's really time to tell Milla that we can no longer expect to find Olivia alive. That we're now searching for a dead body.'

Through the café window I can see Inspector Strand standing at the cake counter with a plate in his hand. Milla is sitting on her own at the table, fiddling with her hair. 'I think she already knows that,' I murmur as I hang up.

CHAPTER 45

He stops after a few turns of the spade. I can't see him from where I lie with my face pressed against Siv's chest at the bottom of the grave, but I can feel him, every single movement, hear his breathing, how it gets rougher and heavier while he labours, until it suddenly goes quiet when he stops and listens.

Twigs snap on the ground as he skirts around the grave to move between the trees a short distance away. If I were strong enough, I would climb out of this hole, taking Siv with me and run away, but my body refuses to obey, and instead I ease one hand in under Siv's jacket and draw her lifeless body closer to mine. The next minute, the shadow is back, above the grave pit, like a mountain wall that blocks the sun.

Then he starts digging again.

CHAPTER 46

I hang about outside the café long after my conversation with Iver has finished, letting the wind do its worst with my body while I try to locate the sea and the chill between the buildings. I'm at a loss; it's as if at some time in the past few days I've stumbled into a holy mess impossible to find my way out of again.

'Aske,' a voice speaks just beside me. I turn to see that it's Inspector Strand, holding a white paper bag that I presume contains more cake. 'Lovely to meet up with you,' he says, stretching out his hand. 'If there's nothing else ...'

'A pleasure,' I reply distractedly, still keeping the view of the sea in the corner of my eye. 'Thanks for your help.'

Øyvind Strand turns and waves to Milla in the café, who forces a smile before lowering her head to the table again. Then he leaves.

I hover outside for a few more minutes until I finally take a deep breath and return to Milla.

'I just spoke to Iver on the phone,' I tell her when I sit down. She hasn't touched either her coffee topped with white froth or her croissant. Instead, she's picking off little flakes that she crumbles through her fingers and drizzles on to her plate.

'What did he say?' she asks softly when she finally looks up at me.

'I think we can now say with reasonable certainty that we're investigating a series of murders, in extremely unusual circumstances. That also means …'

'No …' Squeezing her eyelids shut, Milla gives a faint smile. 'Don't say it,' she says, sotto voce. 'Not yet. I have a picture of her deep down inside me from the day when Robert and I went to her school. I haven't seen her so clearly for ages. I recognised her at once.' Milla continues to destroy the croissant with her fingers. 'There was something about the way she walked, how she put her hand to her face, to her hair when she talked. She was standing so far away, of course, but all the same, I recognised her right away.'

'Do you think she might have spotted you too?'

'No. We stayed in Robert's car.'

'Maybe someone else?'

'What are you suggesting? Do you think Olivia ran away because she found out that her mother was looking for her? That she hates me so much for what I did?'

'No, I'm not saying that, all I'm saying is that I don't like this kind of coincidence. Also, I'm saying that what we're doing now is going to cost you dear, Milla. I'm trying to find out what could have made her and Siv leave a week after you and Robert located her, and we can't avoid that question either.'

'Christ!' Her eyes are suddenly wide open. 'What have I done?'

'Milla,' I reach for her hand.

'No, no.' She pulls her hand away and continues to stare at me as if I were a ghost from the past. 'What have I done, Thorkild?' she exclaims. 'What on earth have I done?'

CHAPTER 47

'There's no longer any doubt,' I begin once we're back in Oslo, meeting up with Iver and Kenny outside Milla's apartment in St Hanshaugen. They're leaning against a patrol car, each nursing a cup of coffee from Deli de Luca, waiting for us. Kenny is still wearing police uniform, while Iver is dressed in civvies. 'We've got ourselves mixed up in a serial killer case.'

'Aske's right,' Iver answers as we make our way towards the entrance. Milla appears to be in a brighter mood now that we've returned to Oslo, even though she still has a faraway look, isn't talking much, and is keeping herself in the background. 'The cause of death in the two cases in which bodies have been found was the injection of a solution of potassium chloride B. No injection paraphernalia was found at the discovery sites, indicating that these actually aren't missing person cases at all but killings, perpetrated by the same murderer. A serial killer. The fact that Liv in Orkdal and Eklund's girlfriend both had their mobile phones placed at their ears as if they were filled with regret and trying to call for help, reinforces that theory.'

'I don't think they were placed like that to allow them to phone out,' I tell him. 'I think they were arranged like that so that someone could call them.'

'Why? They were dead, weren't they?'

'All the same,' I reply, as we stop outside the apartment block entrance. 'Serial killers who arrange their crime scenes usually do so in order to fulfil a fantasy, recreate an earlier act, or change something they hadn't managed to achieve before. The bodies they use are simply stage props in their own illusion.'

'So he calls ... to speak to them?'

'I don't know.'

'A serial killing case,' Iver sighs, turning towards the corner of the street, where Robert was shot. 'What the hell was it you got yourself mixed up in, Robert?'

'I've encountered this kind of thing before,' I say while we all stand staring at the same spot on the pavement at the corner of the street. 'When I was travelling around American prisons interviewing policemen who had committed crimes. These people, they ...'

Iver leans towards the door. 'Yes?' he asks.

'Most serial attackers are feeding their need for control and power, compensating for the reality in which they feel themselves to be powerless. The rest of us develop mechanisms to handle and even channel our feelings of frustration, anger and pain, at an early age. But some people never manage that, and the only way they find to deal with it is by manipulating, controlling and dominating others. We're working on the assumption that our perpetrator doesn't know his victims, that he neutralises them by using a hypodermic syringe, not just one person but two at the same time, and uses the bodies to satisfy some kind of fantasy image. Nothing points to a uniform motive of revenge on individuals either, but rather random people who fulfil some kind of fantasy harboured by the attacker. He arranges their bodies after they're dead, and there's only one special type of serial killer who does that. We ought to find potassium chloride B in the later victims too. But then we come to the problem.'

'What's that?'

'Something changes with Riverholt and his ex-wife. He becomes more daring, more reckless. It's not exactly abnormal for serial killers to develop and evolve but all the same, it's a conspicuous change of pattern.'

'Serial killer, my God,' Kenny groans, shaking his head in despair. 'Can you hear how insane this sounds? Am I the only one who ...'

'A series of crimes with the same perpetrator, Kenny,' I tell him. 'That's all. And if we follow the timeline of the missing person cases, then it starts with Svein Borg's disappearance at the end of August. Borg is the first victim, then Siv and Olivia three weeks later, then Liv in Orkdal four days afterwards, before we get to Sweden two days after that again with Eklund and his girlfriend. That makes six disappearances and three dead bodies in one month. If we include Robert and Camilla, then we're up to ...'

'Why is Borg included?' Kenny breaks in. 'After all, we know for a fact that he's in prison somewhere in Russia. Shouldn't we concentrate on the cases in which ...'

'Because his mother's mobile number is on that list, and because Borg was reported missing, even though we now believe he's still alive.'

'Believe?'

'We haven't had confirmation that it is in fact Borg in that prison camp. We have to talk to him, ask why his mother's number is on that list.'

'Then you're wanting to go to Arkhangelsk,' Iver concludes.

'Yes,' I answer, with a smile. I'm not sure if I'm smiling because of the look Milla sends me, or because I know that the change I've been wanting for so long has already begun.

CHAPTER 48

I leave the group outside Milla's apartment and take a taxi back to my hotel in Grünerløkka. When I arrive, I look up the phone number for Dr Ohlenborg, the man who ran the course I took in Miami while still employed by Internal Affairs. Ohlenborg is an expert in interview techniques and the profiling of serial killers. We travelled around together, visiting American prisons for almost a whole year until he took ill. The last time I saw him was nearly five years ago and he was in his late eighties then. I don't even know if he's still on the planet, to be honest, but there's no one else I know who can help me with what we're facing right now.

'Mr Aske. It's been a while.' Dr Ohlenborg's voice is soft, almost feminine, and with a faint lisp. 'I heard you weren't doing so well?'

'I've been ill,' I tell him as I pace to and fro in my hotel room.

'And in jail too,' he adds. 'What happened?'

'I met a girl,' I reply. I've drawn all the curtains and switched off the lights. In the chilly gloom I catch a glimpse of my face in the mirror by the door. The scars on my face are gone, my hair is smoother and the grey has disappeared. My eyes glint in the darkness, an animal spark that makes me turn away in disgust. I sit down on the edge of the bed, with my back turned as my fingers slide over my mouth, up to the scar on my cheek. 'I fucked things up,' I mutter.

Dr Ohlenborg hesitates and it's not until I hear him breathing that I'm reminded of his age and picture in my mind's eye how poorly he was when we parted in the private clinic in Miami. How drained we both were after more than nine months spent with serial criminals behind closed doors. 'You didn't strike me as the type,' he says finally.

'I need some help,' I tell him. 'With a case.'

'Oh?'

'Unknown suspect. Serial killer. Several victims.' I tell him about Borg, Siv and Olivia, Liv in Orkdal, the couple in Umeå, about the women found with their mobile phones at their ear, as if they were in the middle of a phone call when they died, and that they have all been initially assumed to be cases of suicide. I pass on the information about the potassium chloride B, about my predecessor Robert and his ex-wife and their presumed murder/suicide.

'This sounds totally fantastic,' Dr Ohlenborg says when I've finished.

'Can you help us?'

'*Of course*. But I need the case documents, witness statements, crime scene photographs – the whole package. Write down what you know or have observed so far. Map of the discovery sites, no, forget that, co-ordinates will do, and then I can see for myself. And all translated into English, if you don't mind.'

'Certainly.' All at once I notice that my entire body is trembling, shaking, and I'm in a cold sweat. 'But it might take some time, we don't even have an overview of all these—'

'Send me the paperwork, Aske. As fast as you can.'

'There's more,' I say as he's about to ring off.

'What?'

I tell him about the incident when someone tried to run me over.

'After that I got a text message from the mobile phone belonging to one of the missing girls. The sender wrote that he or she was the person behind it and also admitted responsibility for my predecessor's murder.'

'Well,' Ohlenborg comments, 'you know what they say: murderers don't call, and the ones who call don't kill.'

'I know that. But do they use text messages?'

'OK. Send me the text messages too, and I'll have a look at them and give you a profile of the sender if I can manage that. And a note of your own involvement in the case, from day one. And also of your predecessor, Mr Riverholt.'

I hang up and slump back on to the bed, curling into a ball, closing my eyes and trying to shut the door on the memories that have once again started to swim around inside me. Old memories of an earlier edition of myself, yet another version that didn't endure life in this bag of bones, with these knuckles and behind this face. The time I spent with Dr Ohlenborg destroyed me and I brought this destruction home with me to Norway to share with the people around me. I can't let that happen again.

CHAPTER 49

The plane lands at Talagi airport, eleven kilometres from Arkhangelsk, just after half past three the following day. It's raining outside. Milla and I find seats on the train that takes us to a bleak little station where we have to show the special passport Iver has obtained for us, allowing us to travel so close to the main headquarters of the Russian nuclear submarine base.

A guard dressed in an Arctic-coloured camouflage uniform and fur hat helps Milla and me off the train. Snow is still lying, making the branches on the spruce trees stoop towards the ground. The guard leads the way to a cross between a taxi and a minibus that he informs us will convey us to the camp.

IK-28 is a Russian concentration camp in Konoshky district in the northern part of the Arkhangelsk region. The camp is one of a number of Gulag camps set up in the 1930s and situated on a high plain surrounded by three circuits of wooden and barbed-wire fences. Inside, we can see rectangular timber buildings and barracks divided into zones separated by more barbed-wire fences.

Another guard standing in front of an entrance checks our special permission before entering a booth to make a phone call and then exiting again.

'This way,' he says while another guard on the inside unlocks the gate.

The camp seems empty, with no one to be seen apart from one or two curious faces at the windows of the largest building in the centre of the enclosure.

'Where are the prisoners?' I ask, while the guard kicks snow off his shoes before knocking on the door of yet another guard post that seems to be an extension to the main building.

'Forest brigade,' the guard replies.

'What?'

'They're working,' he answers. 'Out in the forest. With timber. It's only the ones who are sick and the ones who work in the kitchen who are inside just now.'

A heavily built man in his fifties sticks his head out from the guard post to scrutinise Milla and me. He is wearing nothing but a singlet on his upper body, and a fur hat on his head.

'Wait,' he says before closing the door. When he finally emerges, he has put on the same Arctic-coloured uniform as the first guard.

'Visit?' he queries, zipping up his jacket.

'Svein Borg,' I respond. 'The Norwegian.'

'Ah,' the commander grunts and holds out a wrinkled hand. 'Special permission?'

We show him our passports and he studies them carefully while speaking to the guard in Russian, in words of one syllable. 'OK,' he finally tells us. 'Come with me.'

The guard who brought us takes his leave of the commander and returns to his post. We follow the commander to the main entrance door.

'You can wait in the refectory until the prisoners come back for dinner. Are you hungry?'

'I'm not,' Milla answers. Her lips are greyish, as if she is freezing to death, even though it's barely two degrees Celsius outside.

'Coffee?' I ask when we enter the dining room, an oblong space with cold blue and white painted concrete walls and furnished with only wooden benches and long brown dining tables.

The commander nods and shouts something in Russian. Eventually a young, bare-chested man with cropped hair emerges from what looks like the kitchen with two mugs. The aroma of freshly baked bread percolates into the room.

The commander pushes one mug across to me and then removes his cap and puts it down beside him on the table. 'Great weather,' he says, gesturing towards a very small, dirty window.

'Yes, isn't it,' I reply, looking across at Milla, who still has nothing much to say. She seems off-colour, and completely out of her element. I think the feeling that this is not going to end the way she has always imagined has begun to grip her.

'We don't have many foreigners come to visit our prisoners,' the commander says, blowing on his coffee.

'Are there many foreign prisoners here?' I ask him to keep the conversation going.

'Four Scandinavians, but only one Norwegian. They work well, no nonsense. And they can stand the cold, you know.'

'How long has Borg been here?'

The commander shrugs. 'Three or four months. He was transferred here before last Christmas.'

'What's he serving time for?'

'Seven years hard labour for assaulting a policeman in St Petersburg. He probably had too much to drink and took it into his head to create some mischief.' He laughs and drinks from his mug. 'Russian vodka, you see. Not everyone can hold it so well.'

'Has he had any other visitors since he came here?'

The commander shakes his head. 'The Norwegian mainly keeps himself to himself. Hard worker. Tidy cell. Good hygiene. We moved him into the timber brigade in January. He asked for it himself. Said he liked working outside. Most of them whinge and complain the minute it gets a bit cold, but he's not like that. He says it reminds him of home.' The commander shakes his head. 'Norwegians are crazy. They enjoy being outdoors.'

He drinks more coffee. From time to time he sends fleeting, inquisitive looks in Milla's direction. 'By the way, what do you want from him?'

'He was reported missing by one of his workmates when he left Norway last autumn,' Milla tells him. She finally seems ready to take part in the conversation. 'No one knew he was here. We're researching some missing person cases from last year in connection with a crime novel I'm working on, and—'

The commander puts down his mug and opens his eyes wide. 'Karin Fossum?'

'No,' Milla blushes. 'Milla Lind.'

'Oh,' the commander grunts, sounding disappointed, and picks up his mug again. 'Never heard of you.'

'I don't want to stay here any longer,' Milla murmurs in my ear when the commander gets to his feet and walks across to the window.

'A brief chat, and then we'll be finished,' I say. 'If it really is Borg, I think we can cross him off our list.'

'Come and see,' the commander beckons us to the window, pointing. 'Here they are.'

We lean towards the filthy glass and see a column of four rows approach the entrance gate. They are all dressed in thick jackets and fur hats. No one utters a word; they just stare straight ahead into the back of the man in front while the guard at the gate opens up.

Gradually, as they approach the refectory, the group splits up; some take off their caps and rub their fingers, while others stop at the entrance to light up a cigarette. The door to the kitchen opens and the same young bare-chested prisoner in a white hat starts to carry out aluminium pans of various shapes and sizes and set them down on the tables.

The commander crosses to the table, picks up his cap and puts it on. 'Come with me,' he says. 'It's best if we go. It can get a bit noisy in here until they get their food down. They don't have much time until they have to go back out again. We'll go to the library. I'll bring the Norwegian to you after he's eaten.'

On the way out we pass a group of men on their way in to eat. They walk in single file, caps in their hands. They all look curiously at Milla as they pass by. The commander stops at the door to stand beside a burly man who is a whole head taller than him. The man remains standing motionless in front of him with his eyes down.

'Here,' the commander says, pointing at us. 'You have visitors.'

The man glances up from the floor and gives Milla and me a fleeting look before his eyes are cast down again. He mutters something in Russian and the commander nods. Then he claps the man on the shoulder and steps aside so that the row of men can continue. As he walks past us, our eyes meet again for a second. It's the same person as in the photographs, there's no doubt about that.

Svein Borg smiles. Only faintly, a childish, awkward smile, and then he is gone.

CHAPTER 50

IK-28's library is the greyest, saddest place I've ever clapped eyes on. It makes you think of the inside of a house left open for decades so that the weather, wind and hungry wolves have been given free rein.

At first glance, Svein Borg strikes me as a handsome man when he comes in to take a seat opposite Milla and me between the shelves of brown book spines. However, on closer inspection I can see that his hairline is half a centimetre too low on his forehead, his eyes are not so gentle and his teeth are yellower than the first impression had led me to believe.

'Hi,' Svein Borg says, stretching out a hand to Milla, who shakes it warmly. Then he gives me a peremptory hand-shake before clasping his hands in front of him on the table. 'You're from Norway, I hear?'

'Yes,' Milla confirms. 'I'm a writer conducting research for a new book. A crime novel about people who go missing.'

'And what about you?' He is looking at me.

'I'm helping Milla with the book,' I answer.

Svein Borg fixes his eyes on Milla again. 'August Mugabe,' he says, smiling. 'That was his name, your crime hero, wasn't it?'

'Yes.' Milla brightens up. 'Have you read any of my books?'

'My Mum loved books, and I used to read to her when she became ill. I remember yours. Mugabe was the one whose wife tried to kill him, isn't that right?'

'I'm working on the final book now,' Milla tells him. 'That's why …'

'Are you giving up writing, then?'

'Not at all, just about August.'

'Why is that?' The tone of his voice is calm, effortless, but lacks many of the traditional west-Norwegian phonological features I'd expect of a Molde man.

'All things have to come to an end, isn't that what we say?' Milla adjusts a few locks of hair and leans closer to the table.

'Where do you actually come from?' I ask him.

'Molde,' Borg replies.

'Lived there all your life?'

'No, we lived on the south coast with Mum's family for a while, but I was actually born in the north of Norway, even though I don't remember …'

'The north of Norway?' I say, taken aback.

Borg and Milla both look at me in amazement. 'What?' Borg demands. 'Is there something wrong with the north?'

'Yes,' I answer just as the pain in the punctured palm of my hand starts to throb. 'The place is cursed.'

'Cursed?'

'Thorkild worked on a case up there,' Milla says quickly, without taking her eyes off Borg. 'Apparently it didn't go too well.'

'A case? Are you a detective?'

'Sort of,' I reply. 'I find people. Dead people.'

Svein Borg looks at me without saying anything until he finally turns back to Milla. 'So, you've travelled all this way to ask me how I ended up here of all places?'

'If that's OK with you, yes,' Milla continues.

'According to the Russian writer and historian, Aleksandr Solzhenitsyn, an arrest is an instantaneous, compelling change, subversion, transposition from one state to another,' Svein Borg tells us.

Milla nods eagerly. 'Was that how it was for you?'

'No. It was expected. I lost my grip after my mother died.' He smiles shyly before adding: 'She was also a well-known artist, like yourself.'

'Solveig Borg. She was a folk singer, wasn't she?'

Svein Borg nods his head. 'They called her "Teeny" because she was so small and slim, like a doll. But her voice was as big as a fortress.' He gives a nervous laugh. 'Mum never liked her nickname.'

'You had a close and harmonious relationship, then?'

'Yes. There were only the two of us when I was growing up. She used to take me with her when she went on tour, even though I was a tiny tot.'

'I've heard one of her records,' Milla says.

'What do you think?' Once again the smile is there, reserved, as if he doesn't dare to give it full force, either because he's embarrassed by the state of his teeth or because he simply doesn't want to.

'Beautiful,' Milla replies. 'I think the record was one of her last, because she was singing about paradise.'

'Mum was ill when she made that recording. We had to arrange for a studio in our apartment because she no longer felt able to go out. She knew it was going to be her last record.'

'Was she religious?' I ask.

'Religious,' Svein Borg seems to taste the word on his lips as he goes on looking at Milla. 'Not devout, like the rest of her family, but religious, yes. Religious in her adoration of Norwegian nature, mountains, fjords and people. But towards the end I think she probably began to think more and more about what would come afterwards.'

'Was it after she died that you left?' Milla asks tentatively.

'Yes.' The smile is suddenly gone. 'Her sister's family insisted on Mum being buried in the south of Norway, even though I knew she despised both the place and her relatives after the way they'd treated her when she got pregnant and had a child outside marriage.'

'What happened?' Milla asks.

'They hired a lawyer to rake in what they could of the rights to her life's work, and in the end I gave up and made myself scarce.'

'To find your father? Here in Russia?'

'Mum met a man in St Petersburg when she was abroad on her first tour, a young Russian medical student who came to her concert.' He laughs again. 'They had a passionate night, as she called it, and she left Russia with me aboard. Her family wanted her to give me away, but Mum refused point blank.'

'A strong woman,' Milla says, nodding, as if to emphasise what she'd just said.

'Yes, she certainly was,' Svein Borg agrees. 'But I shouldn't have left. I didn't find a single trace of my father. All I had was a first name and a job title, Mum said I didn't need to know anything more about him, that we were enough, just the two of us. When she died I thought I needed something more, but there was nothing more to be found, so I just stayed on here, waiting for something to turn up, while I drank and wandered around in the city. Nothing happened, so I drank some more, and one day I got involved in an argument with a police officer, and decided to force some kind of change in my life by myself. Maybe I wanted them to shoot me so that we could meet again.'

'So sad,' Milla sighs.

'Do you have children?' Svein Borg asks her.

'A daughter.'

'Are you close?'

'No,' she says, her eyes boring into Borg's. 'I don't even know where she is.'

'She went missing,' I tell him. 'Around the same time as you. Milla isn't just writing a book about people who go missing. She's also searching for her own daughter.'

'I'm sorry,' Svein Borg says, reaching out a hand to Milla. 'I'm really sorry.'

Milla takes hold of his hand and squeezes it.

'When do you get out of here?' I ask as Milla and Svein Borg sit in silence, looking at each other.

'In six years, four months and seven, no, six days.'

'What will you do then?' Milla asks him.

'Go home to Norway. There's nothing for me here in Russia.'

'Did you travel directly to Russia when you left Norway?'

'Yes, more or less.'

'We thought you were dead,' I tell him.

Svein Borg gives a lopsided smile. 'Oh?'

'That was why we came,' I continue. 'To see if you were … you. And yes, indeed, you are,' I add.

'I don't follow,' Svein Borg says, still looking at Milla.

'Do you have a mobile phone?' I ask.

'No, it's not allowed. Anyway, I cancelled my subscription when I left. Wanted to get rid of the past and start a new life.'

'How did your mother die, Svein?' I probe.

'What?'

'Sorry,' I give a Gallic shrug and smile disarmingly. 'I don't mean to be nosy, but …'

'Well,' Borg clears his throat. 'She was ill. You could almost see her fading away, day by day, hour by hour. She passed away in her sleep at home.'

'Were you there?' Milla asks. 'Were you with her?'

'Yes,' Borg answers. 'The whole time. Right to the end. There were just the two of us.'

'Have you ever been to Orkdal?' I ask.

Borg clears his throat again. 'No, sadly.'

'Or fortunately?'

'Er, I guess so.' He forces another closed smile.

'As I said, I don't mean to seem too inquisitive, but I do like to find out about things. Apologies if you feel my questions are too intrusive.'

'No, not at all. I was only wondering …'

'Thanks,' I say, rising from the chair. 'For agreeing to talk to us.'

'Why were you so rude?' Milla asks me when we are finally outside the gate, walking towards our waiting taxi-bus.

'I found his lies tiresome.'

'Lies?'

'Everyone tells lies.' I pull up the zip of my jacket as the cold spring air hits me outside the wooden barriers. 'What is of interest to folk like me is therefore not whether some-one is lying, but how they lie and, not least, what they're not telling me.'

'So what was it that Svein Borg wasn't telling us?'

'Lots of things. The most interesting, though, was what he said about his mobile phone.'

'His mobile?'

'He said he'd cancelled his account, that he wanted to put the past behind him. Why didn't he tell us that he'd kept his mother's mobile?'

'How do you know that?'

'She died on 12 August. Nevertheless, her mobile was receiving calls right up until October of last year.'

'Maybe someone else had taken over the account? A family member, perhaps?'

'He said it himself, there were only the two of them.'

'So, what is it you're saying?'

'That we have to find out,' I reply.

CHAPTER 51

'I liked him.' The train has just started to move off and Milla is sitting on the lower bunk in the cramped sleeping compartment, unbuttoning her blouse. I can still feel the taste of Mr Blue on my tongue. 'Even though you didn't. He had a sort of open honesty about him that made it easy to identify with him.'

'All the prisons in the world are full to the brim with people who would have you believe they're behind lock and key only because of an unmitigated spate of bad luck and sheer chance.'

'I think you're jealous.' Milla inclines her torso forward and unhooks the clasp on her bra.

'Aggression, hostility and antipathy are characteristics that are easy to relate to, easy to accept in an inmate. And I'm not saying that everyone incarcerated in prison is guilty. I'm just saying that criminals with the ability to conceal, charm and manipulate are more dangerous than the ones who boil over with testosterone and aggression. They are—'

'Are you going to get undressed?' Milla puts her bra down on the bed and leans back with her hands cradling her breasts.

It is snowing. The train rattles through a flat, bare winter landscape that for some reason makes me think of reindeer, Christmas and multi-coloured wrapping paper.

'All I'm saying is that Svein Borg is not in there because he's unlucky, no matter what he says. But at least we do know that Borg is Borg, and that he was in St Petersburg at the time Robert and Camilla were killed.'

Milla sits up again when I make no move to get undressed. She grabs hold of my trouser belt and drags me towards her. 'His story belongs in a book,' she says, as she tears off my belt and opens my trousers. 'It's raw and painful and I think lots of readers will be able to identify with it.'

'But you're right about one thing,' I mumble. Milla nods in the direction of my shirt and gestures that it has to come off too.

'And that is?'

'That Svein Borg is interesting.'

'In what way?'

'I want to know more about him.'

'Such as what?'

'About him and his mother, about what he got up to after he left Norway.' I strip off my shirt and T-shirt and stand in front of Milla, who's waiting impatiently with her arms crossed.

'I still think you're jealous.' Milla clambers on top of me as soon as I lie down on the bunk bed. 'Was what you were doing in there what they call profiling?'

'No,' I groan, while Milla tries to massage my cock until it's hard enough for her to sit on. 'I'm just inquisitive by nature.' I regard what we're doing now as some kind of trade-off, sex for intimacy. A temporary solution to a greater underlying problem. Something that can't develop, that I'll relinquish when I travel home to Stavanger. I don't want to go down into that trench again, not after Ann-Mari, and I can't because of Frei. It would never work with the three of us.

'But you can do it?' Milla runs her fingers over my chest as she moves slowly on top of me. 'Profiling, I mean?'

'Yes,' I groan again, taking hold of her wrists, using my fingers to stroke her forearms, up and down. 'I learned something about it during my stay in the States.'

And even though I had managed to let go of Frei, to get well, had left Stavanger and let her stay behind there, so what? Ulf would have called it progress, definite progress, the fact that I could even play out such scenarios in my head with a living, breathing woman sitting astride me. He might even go so far as to suggest that I should acquire a hamster, a small animal that I could feed and take for walks, construct a ten-step therapy ladder on which the final goal is that Thorkild Aske should once again understand how healthy human beings practise committed relationships with one another.

'Then, if you were to make a profile,' Milla continues, dragging me back to the train carriage and the sex act. 'What would you have said about the person we're looking for?'

'UNS ...' I gasp, opening my eyes again. 'UNSUB.'

'What?'

'We call them *Unknown Subject of an Investigation*. UNSUB.'

'Tell me.' She's moving faster now. 'I want to know more.'

It feels as if the blood vessels in my cock are going to burst. 'Our friend,' I moan, blinking hard to push the image of Ulf and the imaginary therapy hamster away from my retina. 'He has a certain understanding of how he should behave in order to get close to the people he kills. You don't just stick a syringe full of potassium chloride B into a stranger anywhere. It means he's someone who is able to achieve that either through his physical appearance or a feigned personality that evokes sympathy or empathy in the people he meets. We can't exclude the possibility that he knew them already, but I think that's a bit doubtful given the geographical distances between the victims.'

'So it's a man?' Milla presses her hands down on my stomach muscles.

'Definitely a man.'

'What else?'

'The arrangement of the corpses suggests that the victims are faceless, sexless pieces in a larger plan, his fantasy, at least up until the killing of Robert and his ex-wife and the attack on me. The motivation there appears entirely different. There's no staging or intimacy in the picture then. Quite the opposite.'

'Anything more?' Her hip thrusts have increased in tempo and intensity.

'Since the MO in these two specific cases shows no sign of sexual undertones or motivation, the profiling is more complex than for instance with a straightforward violent rape or a robbery and murder.'

'Tell me more,' Milla pants. 'Tell me more!'

I grab hold of her hips to hold on until the ride is over. 'Since there are no outward signs of violence in either the case of Liv in Orkdal or the couple in Umeå, it means … it means that the attacks were quick as a flash, so that they could be neutralised as fast as possible.'

Milla digs her nails into the flesh of my gut as her pubic muscles contract. 'I'm coming now. Now ...'

CHAPTER 52

We are back in Arkhangelsk in less than an hour. Outside, the snow has vanished to be replaced by slush, rain and bare trees interspersed with looming tower blocks and grey warehouses. Milla is asleep while I sit at the train window, enjoying the after-effects of the pills she gave me following our antics in bed.

Sometimes the drowsiness that comes when the effects of the medicine are on the wane is better than the peak. Everything moves a few milliseconds more slowly than usual, you have more time to digest impressions and reflect on them, and at the same time your body is not screaming for an altered state of mind. You know it's coming, but you have time, time for every single moment between now and then. It dawns on me that this is yet another train of thought I can nourish and present to Ulf when I return to Stavanger.

I'm about to pick up my mobile to jot down some well-chosen key words when the phone rings.

'Hello, Iver,' I answer as the train rolls past several tall buildings surrounded by leafless trees and remnants of snow discoloured by exhaust fumes.

'Where are you?'

'On our way to the airport at Arkhangelsk. We're finished with Borg.'

'How was he?'

'Milla liked him.'

'And you?'

'Not particularly. But we've spoken to him and confirmed that it really is him.'

'I've found something,' Iver tells me before I have a chance to continue. He seems on edge. 'No,' he says, finally releasing his breath. 'No, Aske, I really think we've found him, by God.'

'Him? What do you mean?'

'While you were paying a visit to Borg in Arkhangelsk, I've been doing some further checks on the owners of those other numbers that were called from Jonas Eklund's mobile phone after he died. It took a while because the numbers belonged to different countries – Finland, Estonia and Russia – and most of the numbers were no longer in use. Up till now we've managed to identify the owners of four of the numbers that were called in the relevant time period, that is the time following Jonas Eklund's death. The subscribers are all either dead or reported missing in their home countries. Three of the cases are still open misper enquiries with no body found, but there is one case in St Petersburg in which we do have a body.'

'St Petersburg?' I ask in surprise.

'I've received the case documents from Russia. There was never any discussion about a suicide – the woman was attacked and killed in a park on the fringes of the city last October. But the best thing about it is that they have the man who killed her in custody. He was arrested a few days after the murder. And he has confessed, not only to that attack, but also to four others.'

'Any of ours?'

'No, unfortunately, just Russians in the St Petersburg area. Thorkild, I think we're on to a breakthrough here. I've told them about the cases we're investigating, and that the trail has led us to Russia and St Petersburg.'

'Is it Borg?' I ask, with a fleeting glance in the direction of Milla, still fast asleep.

'No. A Russian. Mikhall Nikov.'

'Where is he?'

Iver gives me the details of the case and directions to where we need to go. Behind me I can hear Milla stretch and yawn. 'We'll talk later, Iver,' I round off. 'I'll call you when we get there.'

I hang up and turn to face Milla. Blinking away sleep, she reaches a hand out to me. 'Thorkild,' she whispers. 'Come here.'

I set my mobile down on the bedside table and get to my feet. The train has begun to slow down and I can make out the contours of the big city in the distance under a grey dome of exhaust fumes and rain clouds.

'Will we soon be there?'

'Soon,' I reply, starting to put on my clothes. 'Iver phoned. He's found something.'

'What?'

'One of the numbers on Eklund's mobile is linked to yet another murder case, and they've arrested the perpetrator. He'll send over the documents by email.' I stop getting dressed. Her eyes are already filling up with that darkness again, heavy clouds that spread over the irises and dampen the colour play inside. 'Milla, I think we've got him.'

'Where is he?' Her fingers touch her cheek and ear, searching for a few strands of hair to catch hold of.

I perch on the edge of the bed. 'Have you heard of the Black Dolphin?'

CHAPTER 53

The plane lands at Sheremetyevo International Airport outside Moscow just after half past seven in the evening. The airport is a modern concrete and glass construction reminiscent of the drab square buildings from the communist era. We intend to stay in Moscow until Iver has organised entry permits for us both, when we can take the long trip to Orenburg and the prison known as the Black Dolphin.

It is raining outside. We take a taxi from the airport to a hotel in the city centre. A grey carpet of rain and fog covers the city and hangs heavily between the tallest skyscrapers.

'About tomorrow,' I begin, crossing to the window and drawing the curtain aside. Milla is lying on the bed, watching me as I speak. Our hotel room hovers high above Moscow city centre and beneath us I can see the streetlights and neon signs reflected in the water of the river. 'I was thinking of dividing the conversation with Mikhall Nikov into two phases. In the first of these I'll try to find out if he has ever been to Norway and whether he has anything to do with Siv and Olivia's disappearance. If that turns out to be true, then I can undertake the second part on my own. OK?'

'Come here,' Milla says softly, running her fingers over the animal print bedcover. Two blister packs of OxyContin and Somadril are lying beside her. I've discovered that the reason I no longer see her black mood so clearly is not that she has accepted what most probably awaits her at the end of this road we have embarked upon, but because she has increased her dose of pills since we left Molde. I can see it in her eyes when I'm close enough, notice it when she is sitting on top of me, stroking my face with her fingers and rocking her hips. She has begun to pay the price it costs to be close to someone like me for more than a short time.

Dropping the curtain, I move across to her and sit down at the edge of the bed. 'Are these for me?'

Milla nods.

'Thanks,' I say, covering the packs with my hand.

'Mugabe has met a woman.' Milla grips my hand and leans towards me. 'I'd like to give August hope,' she goes on. 'While he's searching for his daughter, while Gjertrud is planning her final move at the kitchen worktop, I want him to glimpse a way out. A happy ending.' She squeezes my hand. 'Do you believe in happy endings?'

'Milla.' I make a move to stand up, but she tightens her grasp on my hand and pulls me towards her. I can't bring myself to tell her that all hope of a happy ending disappeared at the same moment I received that text message from Olivia's mobile.

'Do you?' At last she releases my hand and starts to run her fingers through my hair.

'Define happy,' I tell her, choosing instead to run through the seconds at the end of that rope in the prison showers when Frei came back, rather than explain to her what was really going through my mind. Soon I can feel the tingling

217

of the water on my bare skin as my throat contracts with the pressure from the rope, and I squeeze harder and harder on the blister packs in my hand. 'It means different things to different people.'

'Please,' Milla purrs as she caresses my hair and face. 'Can't you just say that you do?'

'Ulf believes I don't really want to die, but that the fantasy appears because I've limited my existence so much that I can't see another way out. That the fantasy makes me create a place where only one fact remains: making amends to a person who is already dead.'

She lets go of my hair and turns over on to her back. 'Are you saying that I'm like you? That the two of us, Olivia and us, are merely an illusion?'

'The two of us?' I ask, taken aback.

'Yes.'

'What about Joachim?'

Milla shakes her head. She sits up, clambers out of bed and crosses to the window. 'Look at the lights,' she says, gazing at the city down below. 'So beautiful.' She smiles. 'Don't you agree?'

I get to my feet and follow her. 'Milla.' I put my hands gingerly on her shoulders. 'The two of us, I don't think …'

'Anyway, you're wrong,' she insists. 'I'm not like you, I'm not fooling myself the way you are.' Finally, she turns around. 'In fact, I'm glad.'

'Glad?'

'Tomorrow we might meet the man who took Olivia.' She leans gently towards my chest without our bodies making contact. 'No matter what happens in that prison, I'm going to take her with me when we leave. She will no longer be his because I intend to take her home with me again. That's what I was left with after Robert went away. I must take back what belongs to me.'

'Robert didn't go away,' I tell her. 'He was killed.'

Milla turns all the way round. She leans her back against me with her eyes staring out through the window at the river and the big ice floes, stained with exhaust fumes, jostling on their way through the city with the meltwater. The grey weather, the yellow and purple coloured lights from windows, street lamps and neon signs make me think of sci-fi films with soulless humanoids in a world that no longer makes any impression. Not unlike how things will turn out for the two of us if I let this continue. Milla needs someone to love, before it is too late for her as well.

CHAPTER 54

The earth presses down on us from every direction. I push my body into Siv's. Her jacket is covering my face, so that I can still breathe without choking. Her body already feels as cold as the earth that blankets us.

I keep my mouth closed while I breathe through my nose. I know it won't be long until the air is all used up. Nevertheless, I refuse to give up. Something inside me screams that this darkness is nothing compared to what I saw in your eyes that day they came to fetch me, insisting that the cold that cuts into my face, neck and hands cannot be measured against what I felt when they led me out of our home. Claiming that the pain and sorrow beating in my heart just now is a pale imitation of the visceral torment I felt when they placed me in the back seat of that car and drove me away from you.

Is it you I hear talking to me now, Mum?

CHAPTER 55

The first thing we notice as we draw near is the noise of the dogs. Rough growling that echoes between the buildings inside the gate. The sky is deep blue with dark clouds suspended above the forest. The Black Dolphin is one of the oldest prisons in Russia, built to house life prisoners at some time in the eighteenth century. The name comes from a sculpture of a black dolphin that can just be made out through the main gate. The buildings resemble building blocks in solid colours surrounded by barbed-wire fences.

'Mikhall Nikov,' I say while we sit in the back of the taxi-bus, waiting to be allowed in, 'is fifty-seven years of age and worked as a welder until he lost his job in the early noughties. He comes from Peterhof on the south coast of the Gulf of Finland, not far from St Petersburg, and was arrested last October. He was found guilty of killing four women and two men.' I glance impatiently at the guard who has stopped to talk to another guard at the gate. 'All in the St Petersburg area.'

'Do you think he'll want to talk to us?' Milla asks. The skin on her face has taken on that fixed shape, hiding the muscles below and the feelings that govern them – it's only when we're together, on our own, that the mask slips.

'Yes,' I answer. 'People usually become talkative in places like this. Besides, the inmates here have nothing to lose. They know they're never going to leave the Black Dolphin.'

When the guard finally opens the gate and lets us in, we are escorted through the open yard to an administration building in the middle of the camp. Inside, a man with thick black hair, dressed in a camouflage uniform, is waiting. He introduces himself as the camp's head guard. 'Don't touch the dogs,' he instructs us in English. 'Don't touch the prisoner. Don't step over the green line on the floor on the way in or when you're making your way through the corridors. Don't speak to anyone other than the man you've come here to meet. And remember,' he repeats at the end, 'don't touch the dogs.'

'Mikhall is serving his time in solitary confinement,' he tells us as we approach the end of a long corridor on the building's first floor. In front of us we see something that looks like a phone box built of plexiglass and corrugated iron with a door on one side and two wooden chairs beside it. A phone from the fifties is attached to the corrugated iron and we can see through the glass that another one is hung on the other side too. 'Stay here while the guards fetch him. Don't say or do anything until Mikhall is installed in the interview room.'

'What a place,' I say, blowing on my hands. The temperature in here can't be more than ten degrees Celsius. I pull out one of the wooden chairs and sit down. After a while the head guard returns, with a guard following behind with a dog, as well as a guard holding the hands of a man who is walking in an ingenious way on the other side of the green line on the floor. Doubled over, his head is cast down and his hands are locked in handcuffs behind his back. The prisoner is wearing a black and white striped hat on his head, the same colour as the prison uniform, and he has black slippers on his feet. When they come close to us, the head guard barks a brief command and the prisoner stops with his head on the wall while the guard opens the door into the phone box. When he has done so, the prisoner is led in and set down on a stool before the door is closed again.

'OK,' the head guard tells us. 'He's ready now.'

Mikhall Nikov is slim and sinewy with hollow cheeks. He sits in the phone box looking out at us expectantly through the plexiglass before picking up the phone.

'Mikhall Nikov?' I ask when I lift the telephone receiver on this side and raise it to my ear.

Smiling shyly with toothless gums, his answer is a brief nod. His eyes are grey, inquisitive, and his gaze is almost childlike as it alternates between the two of us outside the plexiglass. He brings to mind a child desperate for attention.

'Do you speak English?'

Mikhall shrugs. 'A little.'

'We're here to ask you some questions,' I go on. 'We're from Norway.'

'Oh,' he answers, with a smile. 'Then I know why you're here.'

'Do you?'

Mikhall treats us to his toothless smile again. 'Yes, I do.'

'Have you been there?'

Once again he smiles without saying anything.

'Tell me about the woman in the park.'

Mikhall nods apathetically as he moistens his narrow lips.

'Ask him about Olivia,' Milla interrupts. 'I want to hear what he knows about Olivia. Whether he's done anything to her.'

Mikhall follows our conversation with curiosity without moving a single facial muscle. He leans forward to the plexiglass. 'I used to drink after I lost my job,' he eventually begins. 'A lot of vodka, too much. The first girl I killed, I don't remember so well, other than that I needed money and I stabbed her with a knife. Then I killed two brothers in a fight at home in their apartment. I don't remember what it was about, but I woke up on the floor, covered in blood. I took the microwave oven and bolted. The ones that happened later, I remember even less about them.'

I nod my head as he relates his story.

'But the woman in the park. I do remember her.' His eyes have taken on a sheen that had been absent earlier. As if talking about the past takes him to a different place from where we are now. 'We'd been drinking heavily for a couple of days and decided to go out to buy some meat and make ourselves something to eat.'

'We?'

'I had made a new friend who was staying with me for a while. We ended up in a bar,' he continues. 'After we had spent all our money on vodka, we made up our minds to rob someone so that we could buy meat and more vodka. We left the bar and started to wander the streets searching for someone to rob. In the end we spotted a woman walking on her own in a recreation area and followed her. I remember it was warm outside, even though it was autumn. The trees in the park still hadn't dropped their leaves.'

Mikhall speaks slowly, repeating some of his words two or three times followed by a nod, as if to check that we understand what he means. 'I grabbed the woman by the arm,' he goes on. 'My friend began to search her clothes for money or something we could sell. I held my hand over her mouth so that she wouldn't scream. I must have been holding her too tight, because all of a sudden she stopped struggling and just collapsed. We took what we found in her pockets, but there were only a few roubles. Then we dragged her down into a ditch where we covered her body with branches and twigs and whatever leaves we could gather.'

'Tell me more about your friend.'

'We just called him *Nesti*, because of his size. It wasn't until we were finished and were heading off that I noticed he was standing beside the corpse doing something to her. At first I thought he wanted to have his way with her, or else he'd found something we could sell, but when I approached him I saw that he had taken out her mobile and written a number into his own phone. Then he put the mobile in her hand and placed it beside her ear. I said we could sell the mobile, but he just brushed me off. He was a big guy, and I didn't want any trouble now that we had some money, so I just let it be. When we got home to my apartment with the meat and the vodka, I asked him why he'd left the phone like that, and what he wanted with her number.'

Mikhall's eyes suddenly narrow, as if the situation is still puzzling him. 'He said that he did it so they could keep in touch.'

'Who was he?' I ask. A spot somewhere between my neck and shoulders has started to tingle, itch, the way it does when I sense a connection in something I've been turning over in my mind for a long time.

Mikhall gives a crooked smile as he leans back on his stool. 'He was like you,' he says quietly, breathing out heavily through his nose. 'Norvezhskiy.'

'What does he mean?' Milla asks nervously, looking from me to the guard.

'He says he was Norwegian,' I reply before addressing myself again to Mikhall. 'Do you know his name?'

Mikhall smiles and shakes his head.

'Where is he now?'

'I don't know. I was arrested a few days later for the murders of the two brothers, and since then I haven't heard from him.'

'Is there anything else you can tell us about him?'

Mikhall shrugs. Once again the smile is there. 'We met in a park a week earlier. He had nowhere to live, so I let him stay with me for a few roubles. I know that he was in St Petersburg to search for his father.'

'Shit,' I curse, and spring up from my seat before Mikhall has time to complete his sentence. I give a sign to the head guard that we're through.

'We have to go back to Arkhangelsk,' I tell Milla.

Chapter 56

Iver picks up the phone after the first ring. 'Hello,' he growls. 'How did it go?'

'It's Borg,' I puff as we scurry through the arrivals hall at Sheremetyevo International Airport towards the gate for the next flight to take us back to Arkhangelsk.

'What?'

'Borg is the man we've been searching for all this time. Everything fits. Christ, Iver ...' I stop while Milla takes her place in the queue of passengers at the check-in desk, 'we've got him.'

'What about Siv and Olivia? Do they also fit into—'

'Yes. Borg was in Norway when they went missing. We just have to find a way to persuade him to talk. When we were there, he didn't strike me as the type who liked to talk about himself. But maybe that will change when I tell him we've met his drinking buddy, Mikhall.'

'You have to get him to talk, Thorkild. Get him to tell us everything.'

'Yes,' I agree. The queue has moved on and people are gathering in a semicircle around the desk. 'But there's one problem,' I add after a pause.

'Oh?'

'Robert and Camilla. The car that knocked me down. Borg was in Russia when Robert and Camilla were killed, and he can't have had anything to do with the murder attempt on me either, unless he has a partner helping him.'

Iver hesitates. 'Could he have?'

'What?'

'Does he have such a partner?'

'I've no idea,' I reply. 'I haven't even had time to think it out properly.'

'We have time, Thorkild,' Iver tells me. 'Borg is in prison. He's not going anywhere. Besides, we mustn't regard it as a setback if it turns out that Robert's death doesn't have anything to do with this after all.'

'You're right,' I admit, pivoting round. I can't see Milla among the jam-packed crowd at our check-in desk.

'Thorkild?' Iver asks over the phone. 'Are you still there?'

'Wait a minute.' I press the mobile to my chest as I approach the huddle of passengers.

At last I catch sight of Milla leaning over the desk, talking to the check-in official who is gesticulating and shaking his head while attempting to answer everyone in turn. Eventually she forces her way out of the queue again and heads towards me.

'What's going on?' I ask when she reaches me.

'All travel permits to Arkhangelsk for foreigners are temporarily withdrawn.'

'What? Why?'

'There's a major police operation underway there.' She falters and takes a deep breath before continuing: 'They're searching for a prisoner who's escaped from one of the work camps in the area.'

At that moment a familiar face appears on all the TV monitors. The rolling text beneath is in Russian initially and then changes to English.

'Bloody hell,' I hiss, putting the phone back to my ear. 'Iver? Are you still there?'

'I'm here,' he answers. 'Has something happened?'

'Yes,' I groan, leaning back against a pillar. 'Svein Borg has escaped.'

CHAPTER 57

The return flight to Norway passes in silence. Milla sits by the window staring out into the distance while I struggle to keep my disappointment in check with the help of her pills. At Gardermoen airport an attractive young woman approaches and stands immediately in front of me once we've collected our luggage. She gives a cold smile and points to a bench where a well-groomed young man, dressed in a uniform identical to hers, is waiting.

'Hi,' the man greets us when we reach him. 'Home again after your holiday?'

'What?'

'Have you been on holiday?' he rephrases his question.

'No,' I answer.

'Where have you been, then?'

'In Russia,' I reply.

'Do you have anything to declare to customs?'

'Customs?'

'Can we have a look at your luggage?'

'Why?'

Bending down, the man lifts my suitcase, places it on a nearby table and opens the zip.

'Is it because I'm black?' I demand, as he rummages through my clothes.

The man smiles to himself as he starts to place my belongings, layer by layer, on the bench. 'Have you been away long?' he enquires.

'No,' I tell him.

'What's this?' he asks when he finds the two blister packs of OxyContin and Somadril that Milla gave me in Moscow.

'Pills,' I say.

'Where did you get them?' He puts the packs down on the bench between my clothes and the suitcase. Then he picks up a phallus-shaped gizmo that he uses to scan my clothing and the suitcase lining.

'I was given them,' I answer when the man hands the phallus-like device to the woman, who takes it over to a machine and slots it in.

'By whom?' the man demands on the woman's return. She shakes her head.

'A doctor,' I lie. I've no idea whether Milla has a prescription for these and no desire to put my new pill supplier in an awkward position.

'Can I see the prescription?'

'I'm not a drug addict,' I insist. 'I'm ill.'

'I didn't say you were,' he answers obligingly. 'All the same, without a valid prescription we can't—'

'Thorkild?' I hear Milla break in behind me.

'Listen, you can't just take vital medication from people, what kind of bloody cock-eyed setup is this you're running here, pal!'

'There's no need to ...'

'What? Get excited? Blow my top? What the fuck do you mean by that?' I feel my heart thumping harder and harder in my aching body, and my pulse rate soars. 'You

can't take my medicines, do you understand? I'll die without them.'

'If you need prescription pills, then it's only a matter of
visiting your GP to get a new script. What we can't do is to
let in medicines bought abroad without a valid prescription. It …'

'I can't go to a fucking GP, you damned idiot,' I bark at
him. 'He doesn't know that I've got them!'

'OK, OK.' The customs official raises a hand, as if to
manually adjust my temper. At the same time, an older man
in identical uniform approaches us wearing an even colder
fake-friendly smile. Whispering something to his colleague,
he stands by his side with his hands folded in front of his
belt and his gaze directed straight at me.

'What if you just come along with us,' he says. 'Into a
more private room where we can …'

'Go to hell,' I snarl. 'I can see what you are, pal, you're
the group's serial sodomite, aren't you? I can smell the shit
under your nails all the way from here. The least excuse for
some finger fucking, eh? Well, you can just fuck right off …'

I don't get the chance to say anything further: the man
and woman have taken a few hurried steps on either side
of me. They grab hold of me in a friendly but firm fashion,
taking one arm each, and start to escort me towards a door
further back. Out of the corner of my eye I can see Milla
saying something. It looks as if she has dissolved into tears
and is asking something over and over again, but I don't
know how to answer her.

Part IV

THE ONES WHO LOVE

CHAPTER 58

Once I've finished with the customs manual's multitude of stages involved in a full internal and external body search, I re-emerge into the arrivals hall to search for Milla. While I stand there, a text message ticks in on my mobile that leaves no doubt as to why I was the lucky person selected for special attention. The message is from my former boss in Internal Affairs, Gunnar Ore, and reads as follows: *When you've finished with customs, come straight to police headquarters.*

'You shitty, vindictive—'

'Save yourself the trouble.' Gunnar lets me into his office at Grønlandsleiret 44. He indicates a chair in front of his desk and then sits down on the correct side. 'You can stand if you prefer,' he adds with a grin on his thin lips. 'If you've got a sore backside.' He laughs and shakes his head.

'They confiscated my medicines.'

'If I know you, you'll get some more PDQ.'

'Why haven't you phoned me?'

'I sent you a message, didn't I?' Gunnar slaps the palm of his hand down on a bundle of papers on his desk. 'Robert Riverholt,' he says. 'Did you know that Camilla, Robert's ex-wife, followed him one night a few weeks before he died?'

'No,' I reply. 'But it no longer matters. We no longer believe his death has anything to do with the case we're working on.'

'Sure?'

'What do you mean?'

'As I told you,' Gunnar continues with a note of triumph, as is his habit when he knows something we don't, 'Robert had almost reached home when he caught sight of her car. It was idling a short distance away. It was dark outside, he couldn't see any driver, but he recognised her car. All of a sudden she accelerated and came racing towards him, but then it seemed as if she changed her mind, because the car braked abruptly and then turned and disappeared down a side street.'

'So she killed him,' I conclude, crossing the room to stand by one of the windows. I pull up the venetian blinds and look out. The sun is shining over Botsparken and from where I stand the green trees might almost fool you into thinking that summer had already arrived, but I know that if you step outside and walk right up to them, you'll see that the green hue is not leaves but the green slimy algae that consumes city trees.

'He had mentioned it to a former colleague here at HQ, and when he was shot, some importance was attached to the episode as yet another confirmation of the course of events,' Gunnar tells me when I turn around. 'But,' he presses his lips tightly together and a gleam appears in his eye, 'no one went to the bother of checking the incident, they just noted it as hard fact. On the other hand, I like to check things,' he goes on when I turn away from his triumphant face yet again. 'And what I discovered, simply by leafing through the case documents and making a few phone calls, was that Camilla Riverholt couldn't have been driving her car that night.'

I stare out at the algae-coated park and the buildings beyond. 'She was in hospital,' Gunnar goes on. 'She'd been poorly all day, dizzy, nauseous and had difficulty walking unaided. She rang her GP in the morning, then turned up at the doctor's surgery at 11.30, and was referred to hospital for tests and kept in overnight.'

I squeeze the blind cord harder, stretching it out as if it were a noose, before letting go. The venetian blinds plummet down the glass, smack the window ledge and shut off all the outside light. 'Are you thinking of telling me how she got to the doctor's as well?' I ask in annoyance, turning to face him again.

'She was driven there. I have a statement from her GP who remembers that he asked her whether they should book some transport for her, but Camilla replied that she had a driver. I've gone on to speak to all her friends, and none of them drove her that day. Also, a neighbour was able to tell me that Camilla Riverholt had a friend who picked up her post and drove her around in those last few weeks.'

'Male or female?'

'Male, she thinks. The woman is old and called the person in question her beau, though she couldn't confirm that it was a man she had seen.'

'It could have been Robert she saw.'

'Yes. But all the same that doesn't explain who was driving Camilla's car that night outside Robert's house, the person he thought had tried to run him over. By the way, was it a man or a woman who tried to kill you?'

'I didn't see the driver. I've received some text messages from someone who claims to be the person who knocked me down.' Producing my mobile, I hand it to Gunnar and show him the texts.

'Ah,' Gunnar says, skimming the contents. 'Yet another member of your fan club.'

'Were toxicology tests taken from Robert's wife?' I ask when he has finished and is leaning back in his chair again.

'Why?' Clasping his hands behind his neck, he stretches his ribcage and smiles. 'She had a big hole in her head.'

'Did she?' Gunnar can play this game till the cows come home and the end of time. Every conversation with Gunnar Ore progresses like a standard interview with a suspect. It starts with him giving you something, information that cheers you up and makes you believe you're both on the same side. It's not until you're approaching the end of the conversation that you realise you've been led through this labyrinth of emotions and impressions by his expert hand. And then it's too late, as I experienced at the customs post at Gardermoen airport a few hours earlier. All you can do is to bend over with your trousers round your knees, grab your buttocks and admit that the game is up.

He prolongs his smile, revelling in making me wait. 'No,' he says finally, leaning forward across the desk again. 'Unfortunately.'

'Would you consider conducting an exhumation?'

'Doubtful.'

'Why not?'

'Come off it, Thorkild. We still have no similarities between Riverholt's death and these missing person cases you're rooting around in. You haven't even found anything to link Milla's daughter to Svein Borg.'

'Then you know about Borg too.' I nod slowly as I walk back to my side of the desk and sit down. This is not going to end until he has told me what he wants me to know, in his own peculiar fashion. 'Tell me, how long have you known Kenny? Because he's the one who's been keeping you informed about us, isn't he?'

'Kenneth Abrahamsen, hmm, no, I don't know him at all. But Iver tells me he's a decent chap.'

'So you've been talking to Iver. Great.'

'And now Borg's on the run, and Thorkild Aske and his gang of good Samaritans are thinking of jumping on the bandwagon.'

I shrug. 'I'd like to talk to him again. Before the Russians shoot him.'

'Well,' Gunnar begins, 'this is where things become a bit difficult. You're not allowed to search for killers, are you?'

'No.' I know what's coming now, this part of the conversation is what I call the weigh-in, which is when Gunnar takes everything you are, the sum total of your actions, and places them on an invisible scale in front of you, weighs it all up and tells you what he sees. In the old days, in an interrogation room, it was almost amusing to witness him doing it to others. With the passage of time I've learned it's not so funny when you're the one standing on the scales.

'It's the police who hunt down murderers.'

'Yes,' I sigh.

He nods his head. 'And you're no longer a police officer, are you?' Gunnar really enjoys hammering it in.

I shake my head. 'No.'

'No. So I've advised the local police in Orkdal and our colleagues in Sweden of the coincidence. I've sent back the new information in the Riverholt case to the people who dealt with it first. They'll decide what's to be done, whether the case should be reopened or not. Maybe they'll contact you if they find anything of interest, maybe they'll want to know if you believe someone has good reason to wish you harm, and so on. You can give them the list, however long it is at present, tell them about the text messages, and then the professionals can take it from there. OK?'

'What car are you driving these days?' I ask, mostly to annoy him and disrupt the flow of the conversation.

'An Audi.' Gunnar gives me a quizzical look. 'Why do you ask? Do you think I was the one who knocked you down? Well, that's sweet.'

'By the way, I met Ann-Mari,' I continue unabashed. 'Just outside here.' I start to rise from my seat and point outside as if for emphasis before subsiding into the chair again. 'The same day I was mowed down. She phoned me too, and I also think I spotted her outside a restaurant here in town, she was standing there in the rain dressed in a rain-coat and just staring in at me.' I notice how his jaw muscles tense beneath the skin as I speak. A vein has started to pulse in the middle of his forehead. 'She doesn't have a licence, does she? I know she didn't have when we were married, but now that we can say with some certainty that it wasn't Borg who ran me down ...'

'No,' Gunnar replies, sounding irritated. He doesn't like personal questions and hates it when he feels compelled to answer them. 'She doesn't have a licence.'

'And you're sure she doesn't drive a car?'

'Ask her.'

'No, no, no. I'm no longer a policeman, so I'll just have to mention it with reference to that list your pals are going to ask about. And then we'll all get to know about those letters she sent me when I was inside.'

'She's stopped all that now,' Gunnar tells me.

'I only mention it,' I add, 'since you brought it up.'

'Listen.' Gunnar Ore leans forward, placing the palms of his hands on top of the piles of paperwork on the desk in front of him. He's done answering questions, and it's time to give in. 'Instead you can search for the crime queen's lost daughter, write a book and play at policemen, if that's what she's paying you for. What I'm saying is just that you shouldn't forget which side you're on.' He presses his palms harder on the papers and leans in even closer. 'And by that I mean you mustn't start believing you're a police officer again, the way you did up in Tromsø last year.'

'Fine, boss,' I say, with a hint of defiance. 'I'll be careful.'

'I'm no longer your boss.' Leaning back, he releases his grip on the documents and folders, clasps his hands in his lap and rocks gently on his office chair. 'That would require you still to be a police officer, and I'm telling you you're not. You were lucky to escape from that case in the north of Norway with your life intact, and now you're at it again, almost killed in a hit-and-run, and drugged to the hilt with all kinds of medicines.' He nods in the direction of my sheepskin jacket. 'Dressed like a hippy, stinking to the high heavens and looking more damn dead than alive. Christ, you're no longer fit for this world. Look in the mirror, man, and get yourself on to the first plane back to Stavanger. You're drowning again, everyone can see it except for you. I'll personally keep an eye on this Riverholt investigation. The police are going to take over these misper cases and follow whatever clues are to be found in them. If, contrary to all expectation, Milla's daughter turns up somewhere along the line, then I'll let you know and you can come back to be informed of where her body can be collected. OK?'

'You're right,' I tell him, brushing down my jacket sleeves. I run my hand through my hair in a vain attempt to stop it sticking straight up and out at the sides. 'Of course you're right.' I get to my feet, lean across the desk and hold out my hand. 'Thanks for the chat, pal. I needed that. Really. From the bottom of my heart. Thank you.'

Gunnar Ore doesn't move a muscle. He goes on sitting in his chair without making a move to take my outstretched hand.

'Well, bye then,' I continue babbling as I back out towards the door. 'A brand new shiny day awaits you out there, boss. Rainbows, nursery rhymes and cherubs that drive taxis. Thanks, o master. Thanks for all you've given me.'

I dash out of the office before he decides that what poor Aske needs now is a lesson in manners.

CHAPTER 59

Dr Ohlenborg used to say that the person in charge of an interview should act as an observer in the conversation he is directing. He called it being the water in an aquarium. You are invisible, but fill the space all the same, while the fish swim around and do what they usually do. Gunnar Ore doesn't succeed in becoming the water, that's not enough for him. The alpha male in him doesn't permit that. He yearns to show you that he already knows everything, and this leads him to drum it into you sooner or later. The danger is that you risk telling the person on the other side of the desk something they didn't know. In the urge to dominate and excel, you sometimes end up sharing information instead of gathering it. All of us do it on our bad days, but Gunnar Ore should have known better.

All the same, I don't exclude the possibility that Gunnar is handing me this knowledge and applying so much pressure to make sure I'll give up and go home – something he knows I'm never going to do – exactly because he wants me to continue, that this is his way of telling me I have to find the right perspective, regard the cases as separate, deal with them one at a time, until we can finally find the connection. So I decide to start at one end in order to eliminate possible red herrings. First of all: my own hit-and-run.

The house Gunnar shares with my ex-wife, Ann-Mari, is a white-painted villa in Gyldenløves gate, Frogner. I knew that Gunnar's parents were loaded, just not to *that* extent. The villa facing me is not the kind of place you can afford on a police officer's salary.

I follow the gravel driveway up to the entrance and ring the doorbell.

'Thorkild?' Ann-Mari is wearing a V-necked white top and white trousers. Her make-up is so discreet that it looks as if she doesn't wear any at all, a skill I remember took an eternity to achieve.

'Come in.' She turns and ambles barefoot through the bright hallway.

I step inside and close the door. The hallway and living room are furnished with pale surfaces; every piece of furniture has obviously been chosen for visual appearance rather than utility. Ann-Mari has taken a seat on a grey, curved sofa with buttons sewn into the fabric. Her legs are tucked up under her and she is holding a steaming mug in her hands. I get the feeling she's been waiting for me.

'You don't look well,' she says, blowing gingerly into her mug.

'I don't feel well,' I answer. 'Your future husband saw to it that the customs officers at Gardermoen deprived me of my medicines and gave me a thorough health check into the bargain.'

'Do you need anything?' She puts her mug back down on the coffee table.

'What do you have?'

'Valium. And Imovane, if you need something to help you sleep. I can make up the bed in the guest room.'

'That's not necessary ...' I don't get as far as finishing the sentence before she's jumped to her feet and left the room. Soon she returns with an almost half-full blister pack and a tall glass of water with ice cubes in it. She places the glass and the pack on the table beside me.

'I've put more water in the kettle,' she says. 'You should have a shower too.' She nods towards the door she has just come through. 'Gunnar probably has some clothes you can borrow while I wash yours. His shaving gear is in the cupboard under the wash basin on the left.'

'Does he know I'm here?' I ask, popping out the rest of the pills from the pack and washing them down with the ice-cold water.

'Of course.' Ann-Mari picks up her mug again and cradles it in her hands. 'He phoned a little while ago.'

'What did he say?'

'That you would call round.' Ann-Mari shrugs her shoulders. 'To ask me something.'

'Someone tried to kill me,' I begin, but I already realise I've made a mistake.

'And you came here to ask if it was me who did it?'

'I saw you, Ann-Mari. Outside the restaurant.'

'Who was she?'

'Milla Lind. I'm working for her.'

'Are you sleeping with her?'

'No,' I lie.

Ann-Mari folds her arms across her breasts. 'So, you've come all this way to ask me about something. Well, don't give up now; you've almost reached your goal.' Her eyes are grey, her voice soft, controlled; she's practically whispering, as if this is the only way she can manage to say what she has to, without the mask slipping. 'Ask me,' she goes on. 'I want you to ask me what you came here for.'

'Was it you?' I ask, in an undertone.

'Scumbag!' She throws one of the sofa cushions across the table. It hits the glass of water and knocks it over. The water spills, dripping down from the edge, over my trousers and gathers in a puddle around my feet on the floor.

'Sorry,' I tell her, standing up to leave.

'No!' Ann-Mari springs up from the sofa and moves towards me. 'Don't go. Stay.' She puts a hand on my chest. 'You can have more,' she says, letting her gaze fall on the empty blister pack on the table. 'I have more, plenty more. You can have them, all of them.'

'Do you have oxies?' I no longer have a conscience, that's the problem. Life is simple for people who simply use others.

She shakes her head before taking half a step closer. 'But I can get some. You can stay here, sleep in the guest room, and I'll have them for you by tomorrow morning.'

The Valium will help – I already feel calmer, sleepy, but it's not enough. Without the oxies I'm only half a human being. And I want to be whole again. 'OK. I'll stay until Gunnar comes.'

'Take a shower,' Ann-Mari insists, giving a lopsided smile before taking a step back. She points to the door at the opposite end of the living room. 'I'll bring you a towel and some clothes.'

The bathroom is completely white. Double wash basins, white wall tiles and a solid marble floor. I wait until Ann-Mari has arrived with the clothes and towel, and then I take two more Valium, strip off and step into the shower. I realise I should have turned around at the door and not looked back. Ann-Mari is going to do everything she can to make sure I stay, and I do stay, for her pills. I'm at a loss to understand why she has so many, but I'm not going to ask, either. All of a sudden it strikes me that Ulf is right: I can't manage to divvy things up, to balance my substance abuse. Abuse. Christ, I even used his word for it. Pill addict. So infinitely tragic. No, tragicomic. I'm a tragicomic pill addict. I let the insults rain down, accompanied by the sound of the constant flow from the shower head and the wall fan until I regain my equanimity. I blame it on the Valium; on their own they're not good enough, it's not the pills, it's the balance, as I've said so many times before. Benzodiazepines without opiates are poison, absurd downward adjustment of the register of senses and the pain in my body. That's why I have to stay, stay here until my ex-wife comes back with the oxycodone. She wants to help me, and I need all the help I can get. Yes, that's it. That's the truth.

I turn off the shower, dry myself and drape the towel around my waist, cross to the basin and crouch down to search for Gunnar's electric shaver.

'Everything OK?' Ann-Mari is suddenly standing in the doorway. Her gaze sweeps over my face before continuing down across my shoulders and chest. 'What's that?' She is pointing at the scar where Harvey's harpoon hit me.

'A few more scratches on the varnish,' I reply. 'Where's the shaver?'

'He doesn't use a shaver.' Ann-Mari closes the door behind her and approaches me. Shaking her head, she forces a smile. 'He uses a razor.'

'Of course.' I step aside as Ann-Mari squats down in front of me. Gunnar Ore is of course one of those men of steel who regard shaving with a regular razor as a lost art, a counter demonstration against the electric castration society has forced upon the alpha male.

'Here you are.' She stands upright with a new razor and a can of blue gel. 'Sit down.'

'I can manage by myself,' I tell her, stretching out my hand to take the shaving paraphernalia from her.

'No,' she pulls them away. 'I'll do it.'

'Fine.' I sit down on the chair and thrust out my chin. 'Be careful around the scar,' I tell her.

'Yes, Thorkild.' Her eyes follow the movements of her fingers as she paints the blue foam on my face. Only now do I see that she has taken off her bra underneath her top before coming in, so that her breasts are visible below when she leans in towards me.

'When is Gunnar coming back?' I ask, reaching out my hand to look at my watch lying beside the basin. I don't want him to pop his head around the bathroom door while I sit here coated in his blue shaving foam, with his towel around my waist, his freshly-laundered clothes neatly folded on the floor and his wife-to-be leaning over me without a bra.

'He won't be back until tomorrow.'

'What?'

'I called him while you were in the shower and said you were going to stay the night. He's going to his parents' house in Nesodden.' She opens the pack and rinses the razor under the tap. Then she makes a start on the healthy side of my face.

'Why?'

She hunkers down with one hand resting easily on my thigh. 'You know why,' she says, returning to her task and raking away the grey, variegated stubble from my damaged face. She glides the razor up and down over my chin and throat, slowly, almost mechanically, with her other hand remaining on my thigh. 'So we can have a little chat.'

I shake my head and am about to say something when Ann-Mari takes hold of my chin. 'Sit still,' she tells me, rinsing the razor. 'I'll soon be finished.'

I spread my arms in resignation. 'OK then.'

'Excellent.' She gives a burst of laughter, stops shaving, rinses the razor again and continues, drawing the blade slowly around the edges of the scar, following the line of the wound all the way down to my upper lip, first on one side, then the other. 'That's settled, then. You're staying.'

CHAPTER 60

'Do you think I would have been a good mother?' Ann-Mari is perched on the edge of the bed while I stand by the window peering out into the darkness. The wind tugs at the trees in the garden, the rose bushes have begun to flower, and the grass is green. It is already summer in Ann-Mari and Gunnar Ore's garden. 'If we'd had children together?'

'Of course,' I answer, unwilling to start a quarrel that might disturb my Valium high.

'Tell me about Frei.' I see Ann-Mari beckon me to her in the reflection on the windowpane.

'No,' I answer, keeping my back turned.

'Why not?'

'Because.'

'Do you hate me?'

'No.'

'But you don't love me any more.'

I don't reply.

'Did you ever?'

'You know I did.'

'But not now.'

'No.'

'When did you stop? Was it when you found out that I couldn't have children?'

At last she gets her own way and I turn to face her. She is lying in the bed with the quilt over her. 'I don't want to argue.'

'But don't you want to sleep with me either?' She opens the quilt to let me in.

'No.'

'Am I too old for you? Was that why? Is it just young girls like Frei that get it up for you?'

'Christ,' I groan, crossing the room to sit down on the edge of the bed. 'Frei's dead. It wasn't that either, it was something entirely different. I ...'

'Love?' The word becomes a wet whip as it leaves her lips. Ann-Mari gasps for air and her chest tenses. 'Worth dying for? Hanging yourself for? I'd really like to have met her, so that I could fathom what she had to have that effect on you. Gunnar said you were a wreck when he visited you in hospital after you'd killed her.'

'I didn't kill her. It was an accident,' I say.

'So you hanged yourself in the prison shower block after-wards because you couldn't live without her?'

'I don't know.'

'But when you learned that I couldn't have children, you just left. It made no impression on you that your wife, who had shared the longest part of life with you, who loved you, completely, had half her female parts cut out, depriving her of the one thing ...' She can't bear to continue. Instead she draws the quilt up to her neck and presses it against her chin.

She does this because she wants me to punish her, to say something that will tear her up the way the surgeons did when they removed her uterus and tumours. But I can't bring myself to do it. Instead I crawl into the bed and lie close beside her.

'Do you know why I still love you?' Ann-Mari asks in a low voice with her head resting against mine.

'Self-harm?' Her face is so close that I can feel her breath tickling my nose.

'You couldn't do anything about what happened to me,' she begins. 'That I was destroyed inside and couldn't have children. But you felt guilty all the same. I even played on that guilt, helped you to reinforce it, made sure you never lost it, because that was easier. And you just took it, carried the torment for us both, deep down inside. Because that's the kind of man you are.'

'I just made myself scarce.'

'You had to go. We couldn't stand it any longer. It took time for me to accept that. But when I finally came here, I knew I had to go on loving you, because one day you would come back.'

'Ann-Mari,' I whisper. 'I'm not back.'

'You are,' she insists. 'You're here. Right now. At this very moment you're back. You're lying here in bed with me, after all, aren't you? I know you are, because in my dreams you're always younger, not as rusty and grey-haired.'

We laugh, and she snuggles closer to my face.

'I should never have come,' I tell her, struggling to extricate myself.

Ann-Mari clutches my hand and places it on her stomach, on top of her scar. 'But you did.'

Wriggling on to her side, she grabs me around the waist and pulls me closer. Her lips make me think about rain, warm drops that tap and tickle when they first hit my face, rain that increases in strength and intensity, that traps you within a shimmering, sparkling cascade of water. Rain that burns.

Chapter 61

It is light outside when I wake. The sun is shining in through the bedroom window, catching me on the back of my head and the damaged side of my face. I gingerly inch my way out of the quilt and plant my feet on the floor by the bed as I survey the room. Only now do I feel the pain.

I raise my forearm and stretch it out in front of me. The incision runs from my wrist almost all the way up to my elbow. My body is crimson from the chest down. The quilt covers and sheet are also clogged with dried blood. Very soon I also become aware of the smell of it. It brings to mind the barn belonging to one of our neighbours in Iceland in the autumn when he slaughtered lambs, a sweet, metallic odour that is difficult to purge from your tongue once it has set in.

I grab hold of the pillow on my side – it, too, is splashed with blood – to tear out the filling and rip the pillowcase along the seams before wrapping it carefully around my arm now that it has started bleeding again.

Ann-Mari is lying on her stomach with one arm outstretched to where I had been lying. Her face is turned towards me. Her eyes are open and the sun is shining on her hair, giving it a peculiar tinge.

'Ann-Mari?' Her wrist is cold and withered, with a deep transverse incision. 'What have you done?'

I skirt around to the other side of the bed, but slip in the blood pooled on the floor and take a tumble. When I finally scramble up again, I dash out to the bathroom. The wound on my arm has started to bleed profusely. I yank off the pillowcase and rinse my arm in the basin before finding a towel to bundle around the cut. Then I locate my mobile and call for an ambulance and the police. I return to the bedroom and sit down on the edge of the bed beside Ann-Mari's lifeless body.

I dial Gunnar Ore's number.

CHAPTER 62

Some people are condemned to failure. Whatever they do, no matter what direction they turn, the fires of hell are staring straight into the whites of their eyes. If they win the lottery, they get face cancer the very next day. Some of them are just chosen to live like that, no one knows why, that's just the way it is. We should be forced to walk carrying a warning triangle.

I am seated on a chair in Gunnar and Ann-Mari's living room, draped in a blanket; people are moving in and out of the bedroom and house. One of the paramedics has cleaned the wound on my arm and bandaged it. He says it will need stitches.

Gunnar says nothing while the police and paramedics are busy. He merely hovers in the background with his arms crossed, his jaws working furiously. When they are ready to move Ann-Mari's body out of the bed, he turns away. Very soon a policeman approaches and asks me to follow them.

They drive me to Accident and Emergency, where the wound is stitched while the two police officers stand watch in the doorway.

'It's not as easy as you'd think,' the doctor who stitches me up tells me, 'to pierce the artery even if you make a deep incision. The smaller veins in the arm bleed a lot first, but they soon dry up and form a scab. We see it fairly often.' He puts down the sewing implements and turns to look for a compress.

'I wasn't the one who did it,' I answer.

'I see,' he says, sounding apathetic. He opens the compress and starts to wind the bandage around the wound. When he's finished, he gets to his feet and nods to the policemen, as if to say: 'Good enough. He's ready.' Then he departs.

The bare cell in Majorstua police station is like every other bare cell. A concrete coffin, just as colourless and cold as I am on the inside. Even the smell in here is oppressive and sweaty, and turns my thoughts to everything that is wrong with the life I'm leading. I've no idea why Ann-Mari did this, whether it was planned or an impulsive act. Whether it was meant as a punishment, or whether she'd just discovered at that very moment that her life was as good or bloody awful as it was ever going to be. Some days are just like that and it's difficult to resist when the urge first takes hold of you.

I realise that I'm furious with her as I lie here on the bunk, staring up at the coffin ceiling, an unfair, egotistical rage that wells up inside me. I'm incensed because she stole my tactic and yet again found a way to force herself inside my head. That place was reserved for Frei and me. I remain lying like that, running through the gamut of emotions until someone comes to the door and opens it up.

'Come with me,' the police officer says, summoning me towards him.

'Where are we going?' Another officer appears at his back. He does not say anything and just looks straight through me.

'Come on,' the first officer insists.

They escort me, one on either side, along the corridor and out into the foyer. 'No,' one of them says when I start to make my way up the stairs to the offices and interview rooms. 'We're going down.'

'Down?'

'The garage.' I stop and make a move to turn around, but I'm pushed carefully but firmly onwards. 'We're driving you to Grønlandsleiret. Somebody there wants to talk to you.'

I stop again. This time they don't succeed in shoving me on. I turn on my heel. 'You know he's going to kill me?'

The two men smile, not convincingly, but with a certain empathy. Either because they know what I'm saying is true, and they like the idea, or because they couldn't care less as long as they deliver the package Gunnar Ore is desperate to tear the wrapping off and beat to a pulp until all his rage is burned away.

CHAPTER 63

It is dark outside when we arrive at Grønlandsleiret 44. Gunnar is waiting at the entrance. 'Come on,' he says, waving away the police escort and ushering me up through the floors to his office, where he points to his chair and tells me to sit down.

Gritting his teeth, Gunnar stands with his back to the wall. 'Did you sleep with her?' His eyes are narrowed, his gaze intense, as if he is struggling not to explode too soon.

'No,' I lie.

'Really?' He takes a deep breath and folds his arms on his chest.

'Gunnar,' I venture. 'I didn't know she could—'

'Shut up, you idiot. She wasn't the one who did it.'

'Yes, she did. She gave me pills.'

I curl up in the chair when Gunnar approaches me and leans over the desk. 'Did you see the phone?' he asks.

'What?'

'Her mobile, did you see it?'

'What …' I stutter. 'What do you mean?'

'She was holding her mobile in her hand.'

'W-what?'

'Maybe this will help.' Gunnar opens the screen on his laptop before retreating back to the wall again.

'What's this?' On the computer screen, I'm looking at a picture of the main entrance of their house. Someone is standing on the doorstep, and in the doorway I can only just make out Ann-Mari's face. In the top left-hand corner I can see a digital clock showing the time as 16.23 the previous day.

'That's you,' Gunnar tells me. 'When you arrived yesterday.' He clenches his teeth. 'Press "play".'

The image divides in two: one part is from the same camera above the front entrance and the other is at the back. It is dark outside and it is now 02.16 at night.

After about thirty seconds a dark figure appears at the outer edge of the screen. He stops a few metres from the rear entrance before moving towards the door and touching it. Then he goes across to the nearest window, cups his hands on the glass and peers inside. Then he disappears out of the picture. After about a minute he reappears on-screen, this time at the front of the house.

Stunned, I stare at Gunnar and then back at the screen as the figure starts to approach the front door. He lingers there for almost a whole minute, almost directly beneath the camera, so that we can see him from above, looking down. In the end he opens the door and goes inside.

Gunnar comes over to the screen and fast-forwards almost forty minutes before standing up again and returning to the wall. 'Watch it now,' he commands.

Immediately afterwards, the figure comes out again. The door closes, he stops on the steps for a second, and then he runs down the gravel driveway and out of the picture.

'B-but, how on earth?' I finally blurt out.

'How could someone have come in and murdered a woman lying right beside you, and ripped a nine-centimetre-long gash in your arm without you noticing anything?'

I hold my face in both hands and dig my nails into the tissue of my cheek, pressing and pressing, so hard that the pain makes tears trickle out of my eyes. 'It's impossible,' I insist. 'It's out of the question. I thought, I thought she'd ...'

'Done it herself?'

'Why didn't you come home?' I demand. 'What the fuck's wrong with you, Gunnar? If you'd just come home and thrown me out, like any man would and should have done, then, then ...'

'No!' Gunnar raises his hand and balls it into a fist, his whole arm shaking as he presses his fingers into the palm of his hand. 'Don't, Thorkild! Put a lid on it, or else I'll kill you. Do you hear me?'

At last the muscles in his face relax. It's as if his entire face crumples, and he turns his back on me, pressing his head against the wall, bumping his head harder and harder against the plaster.

I don't dare approach him, and just sit there without moving an inch, watching helplessly as he attacks the wall with his hands and head. Soon the thuds grow fewer; he has worn himself out, and in the end he just stands there with his back to me, clawing at the wall as he sobs and gasps for air.

'We have to stand together,' he hisses into the wall. 'Until we find this bastard ...'

His head moves slowly from side to side. 'She was a wreck, Thorkild. When you packed your bags and headed for the States. I should have kept my distance – after all, she was a colleague's ex-wife – but it happened anyway. Then I felt guilty, and let you get away with far too much when you came back again. I saw that you weren't yourself, I know what you'd done over there, all the interviews, conversations with serial killers, rapists and the rest of the world's scum. I should never have sent you to Stavanger that time. Maybe I did it for egotistical reasons, to keep you away from Ann-Mari and me and what we had found together. But we were to be married this summer. And before we did, I wanted to be sure of where you both stood.' Once again he presses his face into the wall as he runs his big fists along the tattered wallpaper.

Neither of us speaks for a long time. I sit looking at the computer screen and the camera images from the exterior of their house. The film keeps running, even though everything is at a standstill. Only the leaves on the trees behind the villa tremble at the edge of the picture. The on-screen clock has passed three a.m. Ann-Mari is already dead at this point in time, while I lie there in the bed beside her, dreaming of Frei. I'm always close by when the women in my life die. The bird of ill omen that comes fluttering into their lives at the decisive moment.

Gunnar turns round, dries his face on his shirt and crosses the room to sit in the chair opposite me.

'What is it you want me to do?' I ask. 'Go home to Stavanger? If you ask me to, then I'll do it. Tell me what you want me to do. I ...'

'Get out,' he says at last. 'I don't want to see anything more of you, right now. I'll phone when I'm ready.'

'So, you don't want me to go back to Stava—'

'No. We'll work together now,' he says finally. 'Riverholt's ex-wife will have to be exhumed, Borg and these misper cases, the whole shitstorm will have to be gone through with a magnifying glass. And when we find him ...' He clenches his fists so that the muscles and blood vessels expand all the way up to his forehead. 'But not yet. I'm not ready. I need to get all this hatred out of my system first, or else I'll end up taking it out on you.'

'I—'

'Go,' he seethes. 'Just get up and go, Aske. Before I lose control.'

CHAPTER 64

I leave Gunnar's office and walk along Grønlandsleiret towards Platous gate and Norbygata. I'm unable to gather my thoughts, and my gaze jumps from brick and metal buildings to leafless city trees planted in hard tarmac gardens and car headlamps that slice across the terrain with a cold white light when I look at them for too long. I don't know whether it's the raw evening air or the cold inside me that makes me shiver. The stitches on my forearm sting, the wound throbs, and the compress makes me itch even more than the sheepskin jacket.

I continue my journey up Nylandsveien, cross the River Aker at Hausmanns Bridge and walk on towards St Hanshaugen and Milla's apartment. I need her; no, I need her pills, now, and I don't want to be alone when they kick in.

It dawns on me that I've made the same mistake that Robert did. I've let myself be blinded by Milla's sense of loss and failed to see the danger signals when they appeared. Like Robert, I chose to bring the case into the home of someone dear to me. To Ann-Mari. The only difference is that I'm still here with yet another scar that will heal, while Robert is lying beneath the ground with a bullet in the back of his head. The scarred egotist, wrapped in the skin of dead lambs, wearing another man's shoes. This can't go on.

It is Kenny who opens the door when I arrive forty-five minutes later. I'm sticky with perspiration and exhausted by the barrage of thoughts that has dogged my footsteps all the way here. I need to abandon this overloaded ship as soon as possible before it sinks.

'Thorkild?' His face stiffens abruptly before he forces out a version of a welcoming expression, though his eyes don't entirely go along with the gesture. 'So it's you.' He puts a hairy arm on my shoulder and draws me inside. 'Milla!' he shouts. 'We can call off the search. Here he is.'

'Thorkild?' Milla enters the hallway with a glass of wine in one hand and a cigarette in the other. Her eyes are blank and she staggers slightly, using the doorframe for support. 'Where have you been? We've been expecting you.'

'At the police station, in a cell,' I reply, struggling to regain control of my breathing. My body screams out for stimulants and my head is buzzing. I've no intention of telling them about Ann-Mari. That can wait. Until later, and until I've spoken to Gunnar again.

'Yes, I heard the customs officers at Gardermoen got hold of you,' Kenny chuckles, flopping down on the sofa. Milla perches on the armrest beside him. The room smells stuffy, reeking of smoke and booze. The lights are dimmed, with only moonlight filtering through the roof windows.

'Some wine?' Milla asks, pouring a glass for me.

'And a drop more,' I reply.

She points as she takes a drag of her cigarette. 'The kitchen worktop.'

'What happened to your arm?' Kenny asks as I cross to the kitchen island and pick up what I've come here for.

'Later,' I answer, swallowing the pills she's given me. 'No news of Borg?'

'Iver's in touch with the Russians,' Kenny explains. 'He's also come across yet another misper case here in Norway he thinks may be of interest to us.'

'Woman or couple?' I suck in my cheeks in an attempt to generate enough spit to swallow.

'Neither. Olaf Lund, a retired head teacher aged eighty-seven, who left the nursing home in Svolvær where he was living on 18 September last year. It's presumed that he had a bad turn or fell into the sea. His body was never found.'

'The north of Norway?' I ask, looking at Kenny. The mere mention of the place makes my hand and chest throb.

'Correct. Is there something wrong with the north of Norway?'

I shake my head and ball my fist as I take a deep breath in through my nose. 'What's the connection?'

'The mobile phone belonging to Borg's mother,' Kenny answers. 'Looks as if it was connected to a base station up there at the same time as the man disappeared.'

'When are you thinking of telling us about your arm?' Milla asks.

'Later,' I reply dully. I can already feel it, the warm cloud seeping in through my ears, nose and eye sockets. The cloud that promises to put a lid on everything if only I give it enough nourishment.

'OK.' Milla nods. 'Let's forget everything for one evening and just have a good time together.'

'Yes, let's.' I notice that my voice is already becoming slurred. The timbre of it reminds me of the sound of a machine working outside in a field in summer, or the outboard motor on a boat moving out to draw nets early in the morning before the sun is up. The drug-induced high fills my memory banks with false childhood memories of summer, the calm blue sea and meadows dotted with grazing animals, sounds suggestive of growing up in Iceland. When I'm sober, the landscape is desolate, grey and ochre-yellow, lava stones and dark hollows teeming with the faces of the departed. I should have told Ulf about this as well. Told him that the brain injury has destroyed my memories, and that only a fine-tuned combination of benzodiazepines and opiates can crack the code.

In between times, the image of Ann-Mari appears, and sometimes her face merges into another one further in, and she and Frei meld into another face comprising features of them both. Other times she is too close, so close that I can feel the rain hammering on my skin and her breath blowing cold fire on my cheeks.

Milla says something to Kenny while I sit in the chair watching them through half-open eyes. I don't catch what it is, but I see Kenny move across to the kitchen island where he starts to rummage around in the drawers. Eventually he returns with a cigarette that he lights up, taking a deep, long drag before handing it on to me.

Taking it, I look up at the roof lights as I inhale, coughing and spluttering before trying again. If only I can just keep my eyes fixed up there, focusing on the one insignificant light among all the other lights, I think.

'An innocent fag,' Kenny says when it's his turn again. 'We can make a toast to that, can't we?' He inhales and passes the joint on to Milla.

'Yes, cheers,' I answer dreamily. 'To Frann-Mari.'

'Who?'

'Frei and Ann-Mari,' I explain. 'Frann-Mari.'

'Christ,' Kenny gasps. 'Yes, here's to them too.'

'To Olivia,' says Milla, who has slumped deeper down on the sofa, where she sits clutching a wool blanket she has wrapped around herself.

'To Robert,' I say, raising my hand to the stars.

'Yes, cheers to Robert fucking Riverholt,' Kenny chants, rocking his body from side to side. 'The best of the very best.'

Milla grabs the wine Kenny has on his lap and drinks straight from the bottle. 'To August Mugabe. I would never have survived without you!' she shouts, passing the bottle back.

Kenny takes it and is about to raise it to his mouth when he lets it slip and the wine spills down his crotch. 'No,' he wails, finally catching hold of the neck of the bottle. He lifts it up in the air between us. 'To the police chief,' he yells. 'Cheers to that fucker.' He thrusts the neck of the bottle into his mouth and takes a swig. While he's drinking, his body tilts to one side and he finally crashes into Milla. He yanks the bottle out of his mouth and pushes it over to me while Milla struggles to right him again.

'To Frann-Mari,' I say.

'You've already toasted them,' Kenny slurs.

'I know that,' I reply, hoisting the bottle up again.

'You can't toast the same people over and over again,' Kenny says. 'We don't have enough wine for that kind of nonsense.' He reaches out to the table and lifts one of the bottles sitting there. 'To the King,' he bellows. He tries to drink from the bottle but discovers that it's empty. 'Bloody hell,' he says in an undertone, returning it to the table before deciding to lift and examine each and every one of the bottles there.

'I know,' I whisper.

Kenny leans forward and gives me a nudge. 'To the King, for Christ's sake,' he says, rejoicing when he finally finds one. The bottle contains nothing but dregs and Milla's fag ends and, as he pours them into his mouth, they rain down over his face while he sways from side to side.

I've already burst out laughing by the time Kenny wriggles on to his side, spluttering and choking. I realise I can't stop laughing – the laughter fills my diaphragm with an intensity that makes it difficult to breathe. I'm laughing so hard that my eyes fill with tears, and it feels as if I'm about to boil over. The light outside Milla's roof windows has started to pulsate, rocking on the sea of the sky, dipping in and out of the darkness, as if it's sitting somewhere up there with a pocket torch, trying to make contact with me.

'To the Crown Prince,' Kenny jeers, wiping his face with Milla's blanket.

I gasp as I struggle to concentrate on the light signals out in the darkness. My mouth fills with a sticky white froth just as stomach cramps creep up from my diaphragm to my chest and throat. Suddenly I notice that I've started shaking, jerky convulsions that course through me as I clutch the chair fabric with my fingers, searching for something to hold on to.

'You're wasted, man.' Kenny is struggling to stay on his feet. 'I think it's time to get you to bed.' He grabs my arms and starts to haul me out of the chair.

'Don't you see it?' I say, pointing at the sky. 'Up there? It's them!'

'Who?' Milla asks, canting her head to one side and looking up at the window.

'Them,' I repeat. 'The dead. Frei, Ann-Mari, Robert or Olivia, I don't know, I can't decipher the signal.'

'OK, OK.' Kenny tightens his grip on my arm and takes a deep breath. 'That's enough now, Thorkild. No more nonsense.'

'No, wait,' I insist, resisting fiercely while Kenny tugs at my arm.

He musters his strength, and in the end manages to haul me out of the chair before dragging me into one of the bedrooms and depositing me on the bed. 'Sleep, pal,' he slurs before grabbing the door handle for support on the way out.

CHAPTER 65

I'm left stretched out on the bed where Kenny dropped me, with my eyes closed, trying to recreate the light signals in the sky within me. I can't do it. I decide to call Gunnar, to beg for forgiveness, and to tell him about the light signals. Maybe he can help me decipher them.

While I lie there like this, all of a sudden my mobile rings. As I cast around under the quilt searching for it, I notice that the room has started to vibrate. I lie down flat on the bed, trying to hold on tight, but the more effort I make, the more difficult it becomes to breathe. In the end I catch sight of the phone and lift it up to my face. The display tells me that it's an unknown number.

'Yes?' I slur. 'Who am I speaking to?'

There is silence at the other end, nothing but the sound of a bus rumbling along and someone's laboured breathing into the microphone.

'Who are you?' a subdued voice asks as the rumbling of the nearby bus grows louder.

'Thorkild,' I answer, struggling to find a way out of the quilt. 'Thorkild Aske. Don't you know who you're calling?'

'Are you kind?'

'Kind?' I stop and take a breath: 'No, certainly not,' I laugh. 'I'm the very worst. You wouldn't like to meet me.'

A lengthy pause ensues, during which I can hear a bus door open while the engine continues to rumble. Then I can hear the breathing into the microphone again. 'You have to stop,' she says.

'What do I have to stop?' I ask. There is something about the voice, the tone and the fear it carries that makes me lie completely still beneath the quilt and listen closely. It sounds as if the mobile is scraping against fabric while a male voice speaks in the background, followed by more crackling from the material before her voice is there again. 'You have to stop searching.'

'Olivia?' I ask in amazement from beneath the quilt. 'But aren't you dead?'

'You have to stop,' she repeats.

'Stop? What do you mean?'

'Promise me. If you really are a kind person, then you have to promise me that you won't go on searching.'

'Why?'

Another lengthy pause follows and I can still hear her breathing through the receiver and the rumbling of the bus. 'Because,' she finally says, 'he's going to find me.'

I remain there underneath the quilt, staring at the mobile screen for a long time after she has hung up. *Unknown caller*. Even after I've let the screen go black and turned it on again, it appears on the list of calls.

'Milla!' I start to tear off the quilt to get out of the bed. 'Milla! Kenny! Help!' I shout, once I'm finally free. I haul myself halfway up in the bed and manage to keep my balance for a few short seconds until I start to lurch to one side and bang into the wall, head first.

'Milla!' I scream at the top of my voice before my body begins to thrash around, shaking with convulsions. I gasp for air and throw up between the contractions.

Suddenly the door is flung open and Kenny comes running in. He's naked, and his hairy beer belly protrudes like a drum skin above his sex organs, and his face is scarlet with sweat. He drops to his knees in front of me and his partially erect cock ends up hanging right in front of my face.

'It was her,' I moan when I catch sight of Milla in the doorway. She has a blanket wound around her. Her face is white and her curly hair is sticking out in all directions. 'It was …'

'What is it?' Milla asks, afraid, as she clings to the blanket.

'Her,' I groan, struggling to release myself from Kenny's clutches so that I can locate my mobile and show her the call.

'Phone for an ambulance,' Kenny orders when he turns breathlessly to her. 'He's choking.'

Kenny rolls my body over into a stable side position and I end up face to face with his penis again. It has shrunk and is disappearing into the thicket of grey-black pubic hair. I try to catch my breath one last time, to gather enough air to talk, but my windpipe is blocked. The air stops in my throat and the next minute everything is grey and black.

CHAPTER 66

He stops before coming all the way forward. Siv is still squatting after her pee break, holding on to her jeans and my jacket sleeve as she bends over.

'Did you say she needs paper?' he asks. 'To wipe herself?'

'Yes,' I answer, standing between him and Siv.

He gives a crooked smile and shakes his head. 'Here.' He tosses a packet of tissues over to me. Then he turns around and starts to head back to the car up on the motorway. 'We'll soon be in Tønsberg,' I hear him say. 'It's not far from there.'

'We're coming!' I shout back, picking up the tissues and handing the pack to Siv.

'Embaaarrassing.' Siv tears open the cellophane, wipes herself with a tissue and throws away the paper and the rest of the pack. She gets dressed and pokes me in the back as she passes.

'You're unbelievable,' I say, following behind her.

'Do you think they know we've gone?' she asks as we scramble up the slope to the motorway where he is waiting at the car.

I look at my watch. It's only a few hours since we left the bus bay, since that first and last day began. 'No,' I tell her. 'Unless they've phoned from school to say we haven't turned up.'

'Have you decided what you're going to say when you meet her?'

'Yes,' I reply, stopping at the car door.

'What?'

'Mum, here I am. It's me, Olivia.'

CHAPTER 67

All hospitals are the same. After my suicide attempt in Stavanger prison, I learned that the first thing to strike you when you wake is the feeling that nothing has changed. Not for even a millisecond do your body and soul let you believe that anything is different. You are you, just with larger cracks in your shell and more unwanted baggage floating around inside your nut.

'We gave him Anexate. It reverses the effect of the pills.' The doctor lifts one of my eyelids and blinds me with a bright light from a mini pocket torch. 'There,' she says. 'He's awake.'

'Thorkild.' Milla is standing beside the doctor, holding my hand. 'Why?'

'Why what?' I ask, trying to swallow, but my mouth is a desert.

I let go of Milla's hand and haul myself up into a sitting position. My body aches, but no more than usual on bad days.

'You scared us.' Kenny appears from behind the doctor's back.

The medic turns to face Kenny. 'He can stay here for a while longer, but the effect of the antidote is rapid, so he should really be OK pretty soon.' She has another look at me and then nods, giving a poorly hidden half-smile. She turns to Kenny. 'I understand that you'll pass on the information to the appropriate people? I don't think he should be left alone now, not at first anyway.'

'I need something,' I whisper, stretching out my hand to her as the memories, the ones I had managed to pack away so well, start to jostle their way out, pestering me for their rightful command over my memory banks. 'For the pain.'

'We can give you some Nozinan, that should …'

'No,' I argue. 'Nozinan doesn't work. Diazepam or Sobril. Or OxyNorm, at the very least. You have to give me something. Something that works.'

She studies me as she mulls this over.

'I need them,' I wheedle.

'Sorry,' she replies, before turning on her heel and leaving.

'Benzodiazepine poisoning.' Kenny shakes his head. 'Fuck, I thought you'd had a heart attack.'

'What's the time?' I ask.

'Two a.m.,' Kenny informs me. 'You were out for only an hour. It's actually incredible how effective that stuff they gave you is.'

I peer over the edge of the bed for my shoes. They always take your shoes from you in hospitals, I don't know why.

'Listen,' Kenny says, taking a step towards the bed. 'Thorkild, I think it's best that we take a break from this. It's cost a lot, and we've made great progress, but I think I'm speaking for all of us when I say that this is all coming to grief.'

'I got a phone call yesterday,' I venture, fishing out my mobile. I see there's a new message from Gunnar Ore, but I hop over it and locate the call log. 'While you were … in the other room.'

'Who from?' Milla takes a step closer.

'I think it was Olivia,' I reply.

'What?!' Milla freezes. She must have taken the time to apply make-up and tidy her hair while they were waiting for the ambulance.

'Are you kidding?' Kenny looks just as unkempt as when he came dashing to my rescue in his birthday suit.

'No,' I answer, holding my mobile up to them. 'Unknown caller, lasted for two minutes and eighteen seconds. I thought at first it was the pills talking, the brain injury playing a trick on me, but ...'

'What did she say?' Milla steps even closer.

'She begged me to stop.'

'Stop?' Kenny shakes his head in confusion, waggling the dark curls at the sides of his head. 'Stop what?'

'Searching for her.'

'Why? Why doesn't she want to meet me? Does she hate me so much that—'

'No. No, Milla,' I say, hoisting myself further up in the bed. 'It's more than that, much more, she says she's in danger—'

'Danger? From whom?'

'I don't know. She didn't say ...'

'Does it have something to do with what happened to you?' Milla points a trembling finger at the bandage on my forearm. 'I want to know what happened, Thorkild, are you in danger too? Is there someone who ... who ...'

'No, Milla. I'll explain about that too, but not now. I just need some time alone first,' I tell her. 'I'll phone you as soon as I'm ready.'

'No!' Milla grabs hold of my hand and starts to tug at it, as if to haul me out of the bed. 'No, you have to come now.

We need to call Iver, get him to trace the number … I have to talk to her, I have to tell …'

I try to wriggle out of her grasp. 'I'll come tomorrow,' I say, 'as soon as I can.'

All at once she stops, gives up the fight and looks resigned. 'Robert said the very same thing,' she whimpers, and the tears start to roll, past her mouth and down her neck.

'I'm not Robert,' I tell her. 'I've told you that before.'

'No, no, no.' Milla propels herself forward and clutches my arm again. 'You're lying,' she sobs, 'you haven't spoken to her at all, you—'

'Milla,' Kenny breaks in to place a restraining hand on her shoulder. 'Please. This has gone far enough.'

'No, no!' Milla cries as Kenny begins to pull her towards the door.

As soon as they're outside and the door slides shut, I take out my mobile and read the message from Gunnar Ore. *It's time.*

I push the quilt aside and sit up. Then I get up and take my phone with me into the bathroom. He's right, I think as I start to unpick the bandage from my arm. It's time.

PART V

THE ONES WHO PLAY GAMES

CHAPTER 68

'Did you get the email I sent you yesterday?' I ask, as I examine the angry red scar on my forearm in the hospital bathroom. I switch on the speaker and turn on the water.

'Condolences, Thorkild,' Dr Ohlenborg says. His lisp always becomes more pronounced when he lowers his voice. 'Your friend, Gunnar Ore, told me you sustained quite an injury.'

'When did you speak to Gunnar?' I move my forearm under the water and grit my teeth when it hits the wound.

'Not long ago. Your phone was turned off and I needed the crime scene photos from the attack on you and Ann-Mari. Listen, Thorkild, you should have told me that your ex-wife was Ore's current partner.'

'Apologies,' I groan as the water flows over my arm. 'Have you found out anything?'

'One or two things,' he says. 'It's not so easy, really, when you're not on the scene yourself. However, the first homicides have almost a touch of religiosity about them, something you usually find with serial killers who operate in hospitals or other institutions where they kill elderly patients, people with some kind of God complex. They have taken on the task of deciding on life or death, and they often use poison as their preferred signature.'

'What can you tell me about Borg that I can use?'

'I've drawn up a list,' Ohlenborg tells me. 'About them.'

'Them?'

'We know that there are two people operating here, Thorkild. Not only because Borg was behind bars in Russia when someone tried to run you over, but it's also absolutely clear when you start going through the cases, one by one, and look at the modus operandi, the victimology, examine the crime scenes and so on. I'd really hoped you would have spotted that earlier yourself.'

Turning off the water, I use a towel to dab carefully around the scab, and can hear Dr Ohlenborg rustling papers at the other end.

'Let's take Borg first,' he begins after a pause. 'There, we have a face and a background for our profile. Borg has a certain understanding of how to react when encountering his victims to avoid scaring them off, that indicates intelligence, even though the arranging of the bodies, the mobile held to the ear and the subsequent phone calls are evidence of a man living out a fantasy that other people would define as the actions of a madman. Borg is probably a man it is easy to underestimate, and that's something he knows how to make use of. I understood from your email that you yourself more or less made the same mistake when you met him.'

'Tell me about him,' I urge, casting around for somewhere to dispose of the bloody towel.

'The use of a hypodermic to attack the victims and leave them paralysed for a moment might indicate that he has a fear of confrontation. There's no sexual factor. The fact that both sexes are involved also indicates that the victims are faceless, asexual pawns in a greater plan, similarly the arrangement of the corpses. The killings are part of a fantasy: he has a project, and it's not until we completely understand what this project involves, what the endgame is, that we can predict what he is going to do with any certainty. But we know that loss of work or of someone close are typical actuating factors for men like Borg. The frequency also suggests that there's something urgent about the project, though I can't tell what, maybe Borg himself has planned how this was all meant to end. By the way, it wouldn't surprise me if Borg was actively responsible for his mother's death. I would also like to know more about what it was Borg did at her grave.'

'Can you tell me something about what he'll do now that he's on the run?'

'I'm pretty certain that the project both begins and ends with his mother.'

I take out a fresh compress and apply it carefully to my wound before starting to wrap a new bandage around it. 'And what about Borg's friend?'

'This is where the water gets muddied. Men like Borg usually work alone, but in extreme circumstances they can cooperate with others, as long as this cooperation is to their benefit and that of the project. We know that Borg worked with this Mikhall Nikov in Russia. In cases involving two killers, usually one is dominant, an organised killer who plans the crimes and leaves few clues behind. He is always prepared and chooses his victims on the basis of fixed criteria. As far as Borg is concerned, we know that this involves so-called high-risk individuals, people on the run. Nikov is a typical partner in such cases, a disorganised opportunist, something the crime scene in St Petersburg clearly demonstrates. But the person behind the first attack on you, and who killed the Riverholt couple, doesn't fit that profile.'

'What can you say about him?'

'He has an entirely different approach. Intelligent, impulsive. He plans, but also has the ability to change those plans along the way. A risk-seeker. Kills exclusively for his own gain, and has a personal connection to the victims. He's dynamic and develops gradually as he becomes more secure, more experienced.'

'Male or female?'

'More likely to be a male. I've outlined a few key words for a profile: adult male, either married or with a partner in a problematic relationship, or divorced. Above average IQ, with a job in which he is used to taking responsibility. Self-assured, direct approach. Well versed in police routines. Could even be a police officer himself, either currently or in the past.'

'What?' I collapse down on to the toilet seat. 'What did you say?'

'I'm afraid I can't exclude that possibility, taking the circumstances into account.'

I turn my head to the mobile phone beside the wash basin. 'So which of those two was it who attacked me and murdered Ann-Mari?'

'Well, I would have said Borg because of the arranging of the mobile phone beside Ann-Mari's ear, even if you don't find potassium chloride B at your ex-wife's post mortem. But the crime scene, in her home, that's a high-risk setting, there's a lot that could go wrong there, and to that extent it's more like Borg's friend's MO.'

'She called me,' I tell him: 'Olivia. Last night. Or at least, I think it was her. She asked me to stop searching for her and told me she was in danger.'

'Hm, very interesting.' Ohlenborg smacks his lips as he gives this some thought. 'It makes you wonder what it is she knows or has seen that's of such consequence that the people who are searching for her have to die? That's the lead I would have followed, but it also brings me on to my next concern.'

'And what's that?'

'The text message.'

'I thought you said that—'

'I was wrong. What I'm trying to say, Thorkild, is that the person in question must be somewhere close to you, that's the only explanation. And I don't need to tell you what that means for your own personal safety. I'd like to tell you to give this case a body swerve, to hand it over to the police and get as far away from it as you possibly can, but I can't do that.'

'Bloody hell, man,' I groan. 'So what can I do?'

'That, Thorkild, is the simplest question of them all. Stay alive, find Olivia and solve the case.' Dr Ohlenborg laughs a bright, almost childlike laugh that ends in a fit of coughing. 'And call me when you know more.'

Chapter 69

I leave the hospital and take a taxi back to the hotel in Grünerløkka. As soon as I enter the room, I call Gunnar Ore. 'Gunnar,' I venture before he has time to say anything, 'Olivia's alive, she phoned me last night. I'm sure it was her.'

'What?'

'I've also spoken to Ohlenborg. There are two of them, Gunnar. We're searching for two perpetrators who are working together. Ohlenborg says we can't exclude the possibility that the person in question is someone in my close circle of friends, maybe even a policeman.'

Silence.

'Gunnar,' I whisper when he fails to respond. 'I'm so tired, I need ...'

'What?' he asks coldly. 'Some pills?'

' ... Yes.'

'And after that? What happens then? Do you take more pills, gulp down glass after glass until you finally succeed in what you go around daydreaming about?'

'No. I won't do that. I won't leave, not ... like that.'

'I don't believe you.'

'Come on, Gunnar. Please. I know that Ann-Mari had pills. Loads of them.'

'The funeral's in two days' time. You'll come, and until then you're going to help me find them, both of them. I'll give you what you need into the bargain. OK?'

'Will you?' I blurt out. 'Do you want me to come over? I just need a few, a handful to get me through the next few days. Maybe I can borrow—'

'No.'

'No? What do you mean? You just said—'

'What's the plan?' he asks, unruffled. 'What do we do now? With what we know. With all the shit you've dragged with you into town and into my home.'

'I ...' I look around the sterile hotel room, searching for something to focus on, something to remove the craving from my guts and take away this feeling of total helplessness, 'I don't know.'

'Then think, man. Use what little brains you haven't boiled away in self-pity and drug abuse, and come up with a strategy. At one time you were able to do that.'

I can't think of anything. I'm all alone in this room. 'I can't, I need—'

'No, Thorkild. No plan of action, no pills.'

I clench my fists and gnaw at them, biting as I screw up my eyes. 'We have to start at the beginning,' I say when I finally let go. 'With Borg's beginnings, that's what we know most about. I need to go to the south coast.'

'Why?'

'The timeline.'

'What about it?'

'Borg's mother dies in August last year. I think that's the actuating factor. We also know that Borg ends up in a distressing court action with the family in the south of Norway both about inheritance and about where his mother should be buried. This culminates in Borg travelling south and for some reason vandalising his mother's grave. Then he returns home, where the police confront him with this vandalism, and tell him that his relatives have reported him. Borg takes off. No, first he hides away somewhere in Norway for almost a whole month, before setting out on a killing spree en route to St Petersburg, where he tries to locate his father.'

'OK. That's a start. And Borg's friend, what about him?'

I start to walk around in a circle, forcing the urge to flee down into my diaphragm, dragging the remnants, something to hold on to that can be arranged into some sort of system that will persuade Gunnar to let me into my deceased ex-wife's medicine cabinet. I'm without honour, don't possess a shred of self-respect and have taught myself how to stand and walk minus a backbone. 'He made a mistake, no, the same mistake, twice. I'm still alive. He's going to want to put that right as soon as he can.'

'We have to change the terms,' Gunnar points out. 'Let him get the sense that we're working against him, from all quarters, tightening the net. That should force him out of his comfort zone and into open terrain. Where we can see him.'

'Agreed.'

'How, though?' Gunnar insists.

'We have to create the impression that it's a team, a working group of competent investigators who are now on the move and on his tail. He's afraid, maybe even panic-stricken right now because I survived. And that's good, for us. It's going to force him to contact me again, or to close in on me. That's a good thing, that's what we want. But it's not without risk. Our friend is too close, he knows what we know, and I don't know how. We must put a trace on his mobile phone before he gets in touch with me again.'

'OK,' Gunnar agrees, while I struggle to retain control, breathe, think and not feel. 'But I want you with me all the way, Thorkild. Do you hear?'

'Not without medication. It's impossible.'

'Afterwards. I'll sort it. Just keep a clear head. So, what do we do now?'

'OK. OK. I'll get the gang to meet in Tjøme later on today,' I say. 'I want to see how they react under pressure, one by one. But you have to get people working on the other cases. All the misper cases, Riverholt, everything. Each and every one has to be gone through with a fine-tooth comb. And don't be afraid to let everyone involved know what they're looking into, in all these cases apart from one.'

'Ann-Mari?'

'Yes. Close the door on that one.'

Gunnar is breathing more easily now. He recognises the strategy. 'How?'

'Pull a few strings – you have a lot of them – and insist on full confidentiality regarding information from the investigators in charge of the case. Internally too.'

'Information and manipulation, eh? Split the troops, a good idea. Is there anything further you need before we swing into action?'

'Yes.' I stop in the middle of the room. 'You have to contact someone for me.'

'Who?'

'Ulf. My psychiatrist in Stavanger.'

'Why?'

'He's going to find out, will want to know, what I'm up to, and when he does, he's going to insist that I come home to Stavanger. As we both know, that's no longer an option.'

'What do you want me to do?'

'Call him, say that I'm helping you, tell him I'm well, that I look well, and that you need my help for a while longer.'

'Are you, though?' Gunnar finally asks.

'What? Well? No. I've got a brain injury and I dream of dying.'

'Fine. I'm coming over. Where are you?'

I give him the address of the hotel. 'And remember,' I say as he's about to ring off. 'I need—'

'Ann-Mari's pills?' His tone of voice has altered. The contempt is there again, that cold, hard contempt that he brought with him into my cell that first day after Frei.

'Yes. I saw she had a whole—'

'Do you see what you do to people?' Gunnar asks calmly. 'I, who had promised myself that I would never give you as much as a single fucking fluoride tablet, am now going to bring my dead fiancée's medicines and give them to the man who shared a bed with her on the last night she spent on earth. That's the coercion tactics you had in mind to use on me? Is that how far you've sunk? Tell me it's not true, that it was all a joke, please.'

'No,' I answer coldly. Once again, I've begun to wander restlessly around the hotel room. 'I need them.'

'Christ,' I hear Gunnar say under his breath.

'Gunnar? I have to have them. You understand that, don't you?'

*

Gunnar turns up an hour later. He doesn't bring any pills and laughs cruelly when I ask about them, shaking his head even though I'm aching all over. He crosses his arms and glares at me when I start to pace restlessly to and fro across the floor. Nevertheless, he stays, and we end up spending more time together than we've done in ages.

For long periods we almost manage to forget. The case and the planning erases everything: Ann-Mari is still there, both at home in our apartment in Bergen and in the villa she and Gunnar shared in Gyldenløves gate, at one and the same time. Other moments are worse: the conversation stagnates, we are stuck, we raise our voices, hurl insults and accusations and threaten to throttle each other. Then we start all over again, encircling each other until we find the flow zone.

'When this is over, Thorkild,' Gunnar announces in the doorway as he leaves. I've already promised to follow the plan and refuse to give in to the weakness raging within me, at least until Gunnar and the perpetrator who entered his house and killed Ann-Mari are standing face to face. 'When this is over, you can have her whole collection. Every pack, every single fucking tablet. The whole bloody pharmacy. OK?'

'Promise?' I ask, digging my fingers into my cheek to enhance the pain.

He shakes his head ever so slightly, biting back the abusive words that are no doubt welling up inside him, and gives a brief nod. 'Yes. You can finally have the party you want so much, on my account. I promise you that.'

Then he shuts the door and leaves.

Chapter 70

Siv fell asleep in the back seat of the car before we reached Tønsberg. I can see her in the rear-view mirror, lying there clutching her mobile while a gentle hum comes from her nose when she breathes in. The sunlight feels stronger here, and I notice I have tears in my eyes if I look at her for too long.

'This road leads to Verdens Ende.' He points straight ahead when we arrive at a spot where the road divides in two.

'Verdens Ende?' I dry my eyes and turn to face him.

The driver looks at me as he drums his fingers on the steering wheel. 'Have you been there?' he asks.

'No,' I say, shaking my head. 'I've never been there before.'

'Will we be there soon?' Siv twists around on the back seat, yawning and hauling herself up into a sitting position.

'It's not far now,' the driver tells her, watching her in the rear-view mirror. 'Nearly there.'

The landscape is flat, green and yellow meadows beneath fluffy white clouds. You would almost think that autumn hadn't reached here yet. From time to time I can make out the sea between white-painted houses, surrounded by trees and rocky hillocks. Siv sits bolt upright and presses her face against the side window when the driver flicks on his indicator and turns into a driveway leading up to a massive house encircled by a garden and tall trees. 'Does she really live here?' she gasps, taking a photo with her mobile.

'Yes,' the driver says, parking in front of the entrance. 'Welcome to Verdens Ende.'

CHAPTER 71

Milla, Joachim, Iver and Kenny are sitting on a bench beside the bus stop in Tjøme town centre. They're all eating ice cream and wave when they catch sight of me.

'There you are,' Milla says, giving me a hug after I've shaken hands with the men in the group. She grips my shoulders and looks me in the eye. 'Feeling better?'

'Yes.'

'Sure?'

I nod. 'Absolutely.'

'Brilliant.' She turns to Joachim, who still hasn't finished his ice cream. He tosses the rest of it in the rubbish bin and takes out his car keys.

'What happened to your arm?' Joachim asks as we walk to the car. I've rolled up my shirt sleeves so that the bandage is visible.

'I fell,' I answer, getting into the car. 'While I was out fishing.'

'Oh? So you like to fish? We've a boat out at the summer house, maybe you'd like—'

'He's lying,' Milla says, sending me a look filled with disappointment and curiosity. 'Thorkild doesn't go fishing.'

Joachim gives us both a quizzical look in the rear-view mirror.

'She's right,' I reply. 'Sorry.'

'So ...'

'He won't tell you,' Milla says. 'Will you?'

'No,' I answer, turning towards Kenny who is sitting staring out of the side window. It's time to put the plan Gunnar and I have hatched into operation. 'When did you get here?'

'An hour ago.'

'You should have phoned me first,' I tell him.

'Oh?' Kenny turns away from the window.

'Two's company, three's a crowd, that sort of thing.'

'What do you mean?'

'I'm saying you should have stayed in Drammen. I need you there.'

'You need me?' I can see Kenny's cheeks flush. 'What the hell are you saying?' He raises his voice, looking alternately at me and Milla.

'Listen, pal. Olivia's alive, and Robert was killed. This isn't a game, this is deadly serious.'

'What?' Joachim gasps so loudly that he almost steers the car right into the ditch.

'She's alive,' I repeat. 'Haven't they told you that?'

Joachim stares at Milla. 'Milla?'

'Thorkild claims she phoned him yesterday,' Kenny replies grumpily.

'I don't understand,' Joachim stammers. 'What do you mean?'

'She's alive,' Milla answers calmly, even though the tone of her voice tells me she's far from calm. 'Olivia's alive, and Thorkild's going to find her.'

'How ...' Joachim stutters, unable to formulate a sentence. 'Where ...'

Gunnar and I agreed that the only way forward is to divide and rule, push them all away from me and fragment the information flow to such a degree that our friend is forced out of his shell.

'Milla?' Kenny is still staring at Milla. 'Don't you have anything to say about this?'

Milla is waiting for me to say something further. In the end she nods her head and addresses herself to Kenny: 'I think we should do as Thorkild says. He was the one she phoned.'

'So,' I begin, 'we're talking about a series of murders. That starts with Svein Borg, and continues northwards to Sør-Trøndelag, through Umeå in Sweden and on to Russia until it culminates in the killing of Robert and his ex-wife last autumn. After that, nothing happens until I enter the picture just over a week ago.'

'Nothing,' Kenny sniffs, tapping his fingernails on the side window in irritation.

'Milla hires Robert Riverholt to help her find her daughter, Olivia. One week after she's found, she disappears. The police believe she and her friend have run away from the children's home where they were living to go to Ibiza. The morning they went missing, they were observed getting into an unknown car at the bus stop outside the home. Since then no one has seen or heard from them.'

'We know that,' Kenny says.

'Correct,' I answer.

'Just not why.'

'That's coming.'

'OK.' Kenny throws out his arms in resignation.

'Robert, Kenny and Milla travel to Spain to search for Olivia without finding any trace. One week after they come home, Robert is apparently shot by his ex-wife outside Milla's apartment in Oslo. Robert's ex-wife then seems to have driven away and shot herself in her car. We know now that Robert's ex-wife wasn't in any fit state to drive a car at that time, and possibly her illness was so far advanced that she wouldn't even have been able to pull the trigger on a revolver. We also know that in the final period before her death, she was driven to and from hospital by an unidentified person in her own car. The same car that Robert himself had told the police had been parked outside his home a few weeks before he was shot and that had made an attempt to run him down. This episode was first assumed to reinforce the theory that his ex-wife was the one who had shot Robert because she couldn't live without him. That she was tailing him in the period before the killing.'

Everyone in the car is silent while I speak.

'I was hired to take over from Robert in the search for Olivia.' I start to roll my shirt sleeve further up my arm so that the entire bandage is exposed. 'Immediately after I took over, I was knocked down twice outside Milla's apartment, and when we came back from Arkhangelsk, another attempt was made to send me over to the happy hunting grounds. Someone broke into my ex-wife's house, slashed both her wrists, held her mobile phone up to her ear and sliced my arm open from the wrist to the elbow.'

'What?' Iver gasps. Kenny stares at my arm as I loosen the tape and lift off the whole bandage to expose the wound and stitches.

'If things had gone according to plan, it would also have looked like a suicide pact, or possibly a murder/suicide. So,' I continue, before replacing the bandage on the wound and fastening the tape again, 'Borg's disappearance marks the start of this entire case, and the investigation conducted by Milla and Robert marks the start of something else. It now looks as if Borg, who is on the run himself at the moment, isn't working alone. Borg was in Russia when the Riverholts were killed, and was in prison when the attempt was made to run me over.'

'We have to stop,' Kenny comments. 'This is too big for us. Christ, look at yourself, you can't do it, we can't risk …'

'Gunnar Ore has established an investigation task force. We can't touch the Riverholt murders,' I point out. 'We can't investigate the part of the case that has to do with what happened to my ex-wife and me either. We can't dabble our fingers into any of that stuff: I've received a clear message to that effect. Also, I've been instructed to keep Ore updated about everything we do, and we have to comply with that. But we can still go on looking for Olivia. That case is still yours, Iver, isn't it?'

'Yes, that's our case,' he agrees.

'Exactly. So Milla and I will travel south to talk to Borg's family as soon as this meeting is over. Iver, you keep in touch with the Russians in case any news of Borg turns up.'

'And me?' Kenny asks crossly. 'What will I do?'

'You go home,' I instruct him as Joachim flicks on the indicators, turns up the driveway and parks in front of the stone steps leading up to the Swiss-style villa at Verdens Ende.

CHAPTER 72

Mum's garden is green, pleasant and warm, just as I'd imagined it would be. It's only on the side facing the sea that the leaves on the trees have begun to change colour to orange and red.

'Is anybody home?' I ask, stepping out of his car. I stop at the foot of the stone steps in front of the entrance. Siv is still standing beside the car, her face turned up to the sky, where the clouds are dissipating.

'No,' he answers. 'She'll come soon.' He takes a step up and stands on the first tread. 'Come on,' he says. 'Do you want to see inside?'

I turn to face Siv. She nods eagerly and we climb the steps, hovering behind him while he keys in a code on the door lock.

'Take your shoes with you,' he tells us as he opens the door. The house looks so bright and cosy from where I stand. A number of jackets are hanging in the hallway, with her shoes in a neat row underneath.

'Does she live here on her own?' Siv asks, advancing cautiously through the hallway to a living room with white curtains and windows filled with flowers and ornaments, all bathed in sunlight.

'No,' he replies, closing the door carefully behind him.

'Does she have children?' I ask, looking inquisitively at him. 'Apart from me?'

He smiles and shakes his head. 'No, none.'

'Why not?' Siv is standing in the middle of the dining room, gazing around in every direction. She keeps a tight hold on her shoes and her mobile phone.

'Well, she has you,' he answers without looking at Siv.

'She didn't want me,' I blurt out.

'Everyone makes mistakes,' he says, pointing into the kitchen. 'Come on, let me show you her study.'

I follow Siv through the living room to the kitchen, where I can see several bottles of wine on a worktop beside a glass door that leads out to an enormous terrace. I stop at the kitchen worktop and turn to face him.

'Is she really searching for me?'

'Yes,' he replies.

'And she really wants me to come and live here?'

He nods. 'Yes.'

'With her?'

'With us,' he whispers, placing his hand lightly on my shoulder.

CHAPTER 73

Iver is ensconced on the terrace talking to Joachim in the spring sunshine while Kenny has disappeared further into the garden. Through the open door leading into the study, I see Milla sitting on her own in front of the computer screen. I take a beer with me from the fridge and go through the garden to the boathouse. Kenny is seated at the far edge of the rocks, staring out over the sea.

'Hi,' I say, taking a seat beside him.

Kenny nods and makes a grunting noise.

'Are you looking forward to summer?'

He shakes his head as he accepts the bottle of beer I've brought.

'Well?' Kenny takes the bottle and has a swig before passing it back to me. 'What are you doing?'

'What do you mean?'

'Go home, we no longer need you, all that stuff there? I've known Milla for two decades, and ...'

'Dividing the troops,' I reply while my gaze dances over the surface of the sea. I roll my shirt sleeves all the way up to the elbow. The bandage is still white, and the wound is no longer bleeding.

'I understand that much. Why?'

'If you ignore Olivia and these missing person cases, what are we left with?'

'Milla,' Kenny answers, snatching the beer bottle back again.

'Yes. It's almost as if we're working on two different cases here. One is the misper case and the other concerns people who help Milla to find Olivia. They die.'

'So you're sending me back to Drammen for my own protection? Christ, how noble of you.' He turns partially towards me and raises a pointed finger between us. 'Let me tell you something, Aske. I've been in the police for thirty years, and I ...'

'You're not really going back to Drammen,' I say, retrieving the bottle of beer.

'Sorry?'

'You're going to the north of Norway.'

'What?'

'The north of Norway. Arctic tundra, jagged mountains, claustrophobic fjords with tiny islands populated exclusively by seagulls and sheep. Have you ever been there?'

'What?' Kenny repeats. 'Yes, I've been there. What on earth ...'

'Milla and I are heading south, while Iver is staying in Drammen to find out more about the time Svein Borg spent in Russia. There's only one case outstanding.'

'The old man in the north of Norway?'

'Correct.'

'Why?'

'Borg told me he was born up there. Besides, there's something wrong with our timeline. Borg was in hiding for nearly a month before he embarked on his killing spree.

We have to find out why, and where he was. We know that Borg took Eklund's mobile when he killed him and his girlfriend in Sweden. He used this mobile to phone Liv in Orkdal and the later victims, right up until the bodies of Eklund and his girlfriend were found and his parents cancelled his subscription. But Iver said this mobile was also used to call Borg's mother's phone. This means it wasn't Borg himself who had his mother's phone. The call was traced to a base station outside Svolvær. So who was Borg calling?'

'Oh, now I get it.' Kenny takes back the bottle and drains the rest of the contents. He tosses the empty bottle out to sea, where it disappears into the silvery shimmer before the spout pops up again. It bobs up and down as it drifts away. 'You're not separating us to protect us – you're splitting up the flow of information. Ha ha ha. You think one of us is feeding the killer with information. No, no.' He stops and looks at me again. 'It's even worse than that, isn't it? Yes, by God, I'm so stupid.' He taps his head. 'You think he's here, among us, don't you?'

'No,' I reply.

'Yes, you do, that's exactly what you think. Shit, you believe he's one of us.'

'You and Iver were in Drammen. Milla and Joachim were here at the summer house when Ann-Mari was murdered.'

'So you've checked up on all of us?'

'Of course. Gunnar Ore had your mobile phone logs examined. So ...' I shrug.

'You cynical fucker,' he laughs, clapping his hands derisively.

'Of course, it only means that the mobile traffic shows where the phone apparatus was located, not the person who owns it.'

'Obviously,' Kenny agrees. 'But you and this guy Ore are setting a trap, aren't you?'

'Yep.' I put my hand on the bandage and squeeze. It doesn't feel as painful as pinching my damaged cheek, but the pain helps all the same, keeps the cravings at bay. It will soon be twenty-four hours since the last time I had a top-up, and my body has started to let me know. 'You can all pack this in whenever you like,' I go on, 'it's only Milla and I who can't give up.'

'Fuck,' Kenny sighs. 'Fuck, fuck, fuck.'

'So, are you with us?'

'I haven't been to the north of Norway since my national service.'

'I hate that place,' I tell him.

Kenny shakes his head.

'You're a competent policeman, Kenny. Maybe you'll find something up there.'

'And no one's to know anything?'

'Just me. Switch off your mobile and keep it switched off, use the hotel landline or buy a pay-as-you-go card.'

'Why? No, wait, now I see. Everybody has a friend in Telenor?'

I nod. 'Are you in?'

He spreads out his arms in resignation. 'I need more lager.' He gets to his feet and slopes back to the house.

CHAPTER 74

Siv stops at the grove of trees between the garden and the boathouse. She sends a fleeting glance towards the terrace where he stands watching us, before turning to face me again, opening her jacket and flashing a broad smile. 'Want some?'

'Where did you get that from?' I ask, as she brandishes a bottle of wine.

'From the kitchen worktop,' she says, ambling away.

'You shouldn't have taken it.' I look at the sea beyond the smooth coastal rocks, the water flat calm, the sun glittering on the surface, making you want to dive right in, even though it's late autumn by now.

'They have loads. Your mum must be rolling in money. She'll not miss it.' She bites the plastic around the neck and spits it out. 'Screw top,' she says with a smile. 'Peachy.'

We pass the boathouse and sit down on the rocks, all the way out on the edge. Siv unscrews the lid and guzzles some wine before handing it to me. 'Here,' she says, pulling a face as she uses her hand to give her lips a quick wipe.

The wine tastes foul. I take a gulp and return the bottle to Siv.

'Do you think you're going to live here?' she asks, taking another drink.

'I could stay here forever,' I answer, lying back on the smooth rocks. 'It's so lovely.'

'You must be really happy,' Siv says, clamping the bottle between her legs before taking off her jacket, 'having a mother who lives in a place like this. Look, damn it,' she closes her eyes and stretches out her arms on either side. 'Think of the parties we could have here.'

'Yes,' I mumble to myself, turning on to my stomach so that I can see all the way up to the house between the trees. 'Lucky.' The word almost sticks in my throat. It's not one I can ever remember using about myself before. Lucky is a word that's foreign to me, one I've thought about other people, one I can feel smarting inside me whenever I pass grown-ups and children spending time together, families out in restaurants, or look inside cars lined up outside our school after the last lesson of the day.

'Come on.' Siv puts the bottle of wine down on the rocks in front of me. She tears off her blouse and starts to unbutton her jeans. 'I want to swim.' Hesitating, she looks at me, laughing. 'No, we both have to go in for a swim.'

I turn my gaze back to the woods and the house on the other side. 'Lucky,' I murmur, pressing my chin down against my hands on the warm, smooth rock. 'Yes, I really am.'

CHAPTER 75

I stay down there on the rocks after Kenny has left. In front of me, the sun sparkles on the sea in silver and blue while the trees behind me creak in the wind.

'There you are.' Joachim appears close by. 'Aren't you cold?'

'Yes,' I admit.

'Then come on up with me.'

'Soon.' I watch the sunlight as it drifts away from the rocks and draws back out to sea where the water is darker and more turbulent.

Joachim stands behind me. 'Did you really talk to her? To Olivia?'

'Yes.'

'Where was she?'

I shrug.

'Are you sure it was her?'

'No.'

'What did she say?'

'She asked me to stop looking for her.'

Joachim comes nearer, his shadow sliding up along my arm before he comes to a halt. 'Why?'

'She was scared, scared that someone would find her.'

'Who?'

'I don't know,' I sigh, glancing up at him. 'What do you think?'

'Milla,' he says, settling on the rock beside me. 'I thought she'd be happy to hear that Olivia was alive, but it seems as if …'

'Do you have children, Joachim? From a previous relationship, or …'

'No. I wouldn't mind being a father,' he admits, digging his fingers into the stone. 'A little boy or girl I could take out in a boat on days like this. I was pleased when Milla told me she had a daughter, and even happier when she said she wanted to find her and that we would be a family.'

'And if she doesn't come back?'

With a shake of the head he turns away, letting his eyes wander out across the water to the islands in the far distance.

'You could adopt, couldn't you?'

'Yes,' he says. 'We could.'

'But?'

'Well, I don't know.' Joachim gets to his feet and brushes his clothes clean.

'I have to take Milla away with me again,' I tell him. 'To the south coast. Preferably today. Can you arrange it?'

He nods his head. 'This Svein Borg? Is that why?'

'Yes, we have to talk to his relatives. They live outside Kristiansand.'

'Do you think he's the one who took Olivia?'

I look at him without answering.

'I'll give you a hand,' he agrees. 'But not until you come back to the house with me. I've done some baking – fresh bread rolls. My grandmother's recipe.'

'I'll come in a bit,' I reply. 'I just want to sit here a while longer.'

Chapter 76

The water feels warm against my skin, even though the sun has left the rocky shore and hangs low on the horizon.

'Are you cold?' Siv appears a few metres away from me; the sun is shining on the back of her head and her features are in shadow.

'No,' I tell her, plunging into the water and caressing the surface with my fingertips. 'No, I'm not cold.'

'I feel sick,' Siv says, swimming towards me.

'Well, you drank nearly the whole bottle,' I reproach her when she comes all the way up to me and flings her arms around me. I let my hands sink down beneath the water until they are touching her back. Her skin is cold gooseflesh.

'Come on,' I say, releasing her. 'Let's swim back.'

'No,' Siv says, twisting her lower lip as she grips my neck tightly. 'I don't want to. I want to stay here.'

On land, a figure emerges from the woods, heading for the rocky shore. Siv kisses me hard on the forehead before grabbing my shoulders, bracing herself, and ducking my head under the water. When I come up again, she's already several lengths ahead of me, heading back to shore. The figure stands down at the water's edge, with two towels draped over his arm. Siv stands up as soon as the water is shallow enough, crosses her arms over her breasts and turns towards me. She mutters something through clenched teeth and waves to me as she stands there with her back to him.

'Come on,' he calls out, placing the towels on the rocks behind Siv. 'Time to get out.'

CHAPTER 77

When I return to the main building, Milla is sitting on her own in front of her laptop at the kitchen table, writing.

'Joachim is organising the tickets,' I tell her, taking a seat opposite her. 'We're planning on leaving today if he can arrange that.'

'Excellent.' Milla closes the laptop lid and tilts her head to one side as she looks at me. 'Excellent.'

Joachim sets down the basket of bread rolls in front of us on the table. He's about to pick one up with a pair of tongs and drop it on Milla's tea plate, but she shakes her head.

'She always gets restless when there's a lot of stress,' Joachim comments, offering the roll to me. I want to refuse, but instead I hold out my plate and force a smile that cheers him up.

'Brilliant,' I answer, struggling to produce enough saliva to swallow.

'It was originally my great-grandmother, Alva Marie, who—'

'Joachim,' Milla breaks in, touching her forehead. 'Can't you just go and organise the tickets?'

'But—'

'Please?' She turns towards him, laying a hand on his arm. 'Then I'll be sure everything will go smoothly.'

'OK, OK,' Joachim smiles before taking off his apron and leaving us.

'I've heard the story of those fucking bread rolls at least a hundred times before,' Milla tells me once Joachim has gone.

'Are you sure you're ready?' I ask her. 'After everything that's happened, it's maybe best that I travel alone. You and Joachim, you should—'

'I can't stand being here,' she says.

'Milla?' All of a sudden Joachim has appeared at the door again. His cheeks are flushed. 'What do you mean you can't stand being here? Is it something I—'

'Nothing,' Milla sighs. 'There's nothing you need reproach yourself about.'

'B-but …'

Milla gives a frigid smile. 'Relax, sweetheart. I'll be back. Thorkild will look after me in the meantime.'

'Will he?' Joachim's face has crumpled. His cheeks are red and his mouth narrow. 'The way Robert used to look after you?'

'Calm down.'

'Calm down? How can you—'

'You don't have children, Joachim, do you?' Milla snaps. 'No, but I have a girl who was taken away from me, who is out there somewhere, terrified, and I don't even know how I can …'

'Sorry, Milla,' Joachim says. 'I only meant—'

'I understand perfectly well what you meant. And none of us here is interested in hearing that right now. Weren't you supposed to be arranging the flight tickets?'

'Yes, yes, but—'

'Well, do that, then. OK?'

Crestfallen, Joachim turns around and sidles off to the study, while Milla turns to me once more. 'I don't know what's wrong with you, Thorkild,' she sighs, tearing a chunk of one of Joachim's bread rolls without eating it.

I reach out a hand to hers. 'Are you sure you don't want to stay here? This phone call from Olivia and everything else that's happened, I appreciate it might be too much for you.'

'It's not that.' She drops the roll and squeezes my hand. 'It's this house,' she says softly. 'There's something here that makes me feel ill, turns my insides upside down, and makes me want to leave the minute I set foot inside the door. Do you understand?' She squeezes my hand more tightly. 'There's something wrong with this house. It's felt like this ever since Olivia disappeared. I've told myself that it's me, because I'd come so close to her before losing her again, but now I know, at last I know that it's not me.' She goes on squeezing my hand really hard while looking around the room. 'It's this place.'

CHAPTER 78

Milla and I arrive in Kristiansand late that evening. Svein Borg's aunt lives with her family just over an hour's drive west on the E39, not far from the headquarters of a prominent Norwegian missionary organisation.

'I'm going for a shower,' Milla says when we enter our hotel room.

'Do you have anything to help me come down?' I start to unbutton my shirt. 'I—'

'I didn't bring anything with me,' Milla says.

'What?' My insides freeze. 'What do you mean?'

'It's not on, not while I know she's out there somewhere. I need to keep a clear head until she comes home again. That would be best, Thorkild, for both of us.' Milla goes on undressing until she is standing, totally naked, in front of me. Then she slips past me. Pausing at the bathroom door, she turns around. 'Are you coming?'

'Soon,' I whisper, crossing to the window and opening it wide. Milla has changed since I told her about Olivia and the phone call. Joachim is right: she *is* different. I think Kenny has noticed it too. It's crystal clear that she's not as helpless, not as dependent on others as she used to be. She still needs help from us to find Olivia, but this strength, this tenacity of purpose, is also an indication that she's not going to need any of us afterwards. I open one of the dusty curtains and peer out at the town. Down by the sea, eider ducks are swimming in pairs beyond the harbour wall. It crosses my mind that they must have felt like this, all the men in her life, even that first time, when Robert came waltzing in and located Olivia right under their noses.

I wait at the window, watching the seabirds flocking on a tiny island further out. From time to time I hear a cry for freedom out there, while others spiral upwards, their wings flapping in beautiful strokes as they chase higher and higher into the bright evening sky. While I stand there gazing out at the birds and the sea as the last rays of sun permeate the blue distance, my mobile rings. It's Kenny.

'Where are you?' I ask.

'In a hotel room in Svolvær. Fuck, hotel rooms are exorbitant up here.'

'You'll get your reward in heaven,' I reply.

Kenny mutters something I don't catch before clearing his throat and continuing: 'I've been to the police station here and spoken to Johanne Rikhardsen, the officer responsible for the case of the missing head teacher. I've also taken a trip out to the care home where Lund was living before he disappeared.'

'What did you find out?'

'Olaf Lund, retired head teacher, aged 87. Not seen since 18 September last year. Presumably took ill or had an accident. His body has never been found.'

'We already knew that.'

'Yes.'

'Anything else?'

'No. Can I leave now? I'm missing Drammen.'

'No one misses Drammen.'

'I do.'

'Didn't you find out anything else?'

'There is one thing,' Kenny says. 'You said that Borg had told you he was born up here somewhere.'

'Correct.'

'I was sitting here with time on my hands and googled his mother's name, Solveig Borg.'

'And?'

'There's nothing much about her on Wikipedia, but they do list all her recordings, prizes and so on. She was quite famous in her day.'

'Just let me know when you're ready to get to the point. We've got all night.'

'Her recordings comprise mostly folk songs with lyrics about nature: "The Blue Sea", "Lilies", "Watch the Sun Go Down over Gråtinden", and suchlike. But the last recording is different, it reeks of religion. "Meet Me in Paradise", and the song is all ...'

'I know. Apparently, she found her way back to God at the end. It's not unusual.'

'OK, but there's something about one of the old records, it turns out there's a mountain up here called Gråtinden. In fact, it's located not far from where I am right now.'

'So Borg *does* have a connection to the place. Well done, Kenny. But we need more than that. He must know someone up there, we need a person, something specific.'

'Yes, boss.' Kenny hesitates for a second before speaking again: 'How are things going at your end?'

'With Milla?'

'Yes.'

'I'm sleeping with her in return for pills. Or, I was. Now I'm just sleeping with her.'

'Why are you telling me that?'

'So that you know.'

Kenny falls silent for a moment or two. 'Bastard,' he mutters, disconnecting the call.

I continue to stand at the window long after Kenny has rung off. In the end I close the window and draw the curtains. Heading for the bathroom door, I can hear the shower running. It sounds as if she is crying in there. I wait for a long time before opening the door and stepping inside.

'Why did you actually hire Robert to find her?' I ask, crossing to the shower. Milla turns her back on me and buries her face in the shower spray. 'After such a long time?'

'Because I need her,' she answers.

'For what?'

Finally, she wheels around, the water streaming down her hair, face and chest as she takes a step towards the glass.

'I want a child.'

'Olivia's no longer a child.'

'She's mine. I want her back.'

'And afterwards, once he found her? What then?'

'What do you mean?'

'Was it to be you, Olivia and Joachim? Or you, Olivia and Robert?'

She doesn't say anything, just looks at me through the steam in the shower.

'What? Kenny? Iver?'

Milla runs her fingers along the glass shower wall. 'Olivia and me,' she says at last, under her breath.

'And now?'

She smiles faintly, and I can see how the water divides into two rivulets when it reaches her lips, finding new routes over her face. Milla takes a step back to where the spray is at its most intense and turns her head away.

CHAPTER 79

'About time,' I mumble when the text message finally ticks in, early next morning. Milla is still asleep in bed beside me. It's light outside, I've hardly slept all night, and the craving for pills has started to become unbearable. I'm perspiring, even when I'm cold. The message reads: *She didn't even shed a tear.*

Crawling out of bed, I head for the bathroom to phone Gunnar Ore. 'He's just sent me a text,' I tell him. 'Can you trace it?'

It sounds as if Gunnar has just woken. 'What?' He fills his lungs and exhales loudly. 'What did you say?'

'Our friend, he's been online. Are you ready?'

'Yes, yes, wait a minute.'

'Where are you?'

'At home. I fell asleep on a chair in the bedroom. I can't bring myself to lie on the bed.'

'So you're all set?'

'Yes, yes, give me a few seconds. Is he online now?'

'I don't know, I was just about to send a message in return. Let's hope he answers.'

'OK. Speak later.'

I sit down on the toilet seat and locate the message. *Who?* I write, and fire off the message at once.

After a few minutes, the mobile peeps. *I sat on the edge of the bed watching you. Long after she had bled to death. Why did you just lie there?*

What were you thinking of? I ask in the hope that I can keep the conversation going long enough for Ore's boys to trace the mobile's location. *While you were doing that?*

You don't want to know.

Yes I do, I tap in, adding: *You interest me.*

Almost thirty seconds go by before the mobile peeps again. *In what way?*

The way you manage to fuck things up. This is the third time.

When there is no further response, I key in Gunnar's number again. 'Did you trace him, then?'

'Yes, our people are on their way to check out the area. It's in a residential district here in Oslo. In the west end. They'll have to go from house to house, so it'll take some time.'

'OK, call me when you've got something.'

After I've hung up, I leave the bathroom. Milla has woken up. Blinking, she turns towards me.

'I dreamt about you,' she says. She still hasn't fully opened her eyes and is lying on her side with the quilt pulled up to her neck.

'What did you dream?'

'You were someone else. Some kind of creature that was going to kill me.' She tightens her grip on the quilt and shivers. 'God, how you scared me.'

'That's the price of stopping,' I answer, balancing on the edge of the bed as I button my shirt. 'The body doesn't like to do without.'

'We can manage it, Thorkild.' She puts her hand on mine. 'Together.' She pulls my hand towards her and I topple backwards and lie with my face beside hers. The bed suddenly feels cold, hard and cold like the paving stones outside her apartment, like the bunk in a bare cell, or the interior of a coffin.

'Come on,' I tell her. 'We have to go. We've a long drive ahead of us.'

CHAPTER 80

'Do you believe in God?' Svein Borg's aunt asks, after admitting us to her home. The house is near the road beside a church and Gunnhild Borg is a little grey mouse of a woman with pepper and salt hair pulled back in a bun. Her eyelids are heavy and her lips narrow and dry.

'I believe in hell on earth,' I answer as we sit down on the verandah that affords a view of the church and the rows of gravestones immediately beside the cluster of houses. The village is surrounded by irregular, tree-clad hilltops with a small community centre in its midst. Here on the south coast, it is still summer. The trees are green, the grass fresh, and the garden crammed with colour from the plants and flowers.

Gunnhild gazes at Milla for a long time before turning around and heading into the kitchen. When she returns, she is carrying a jug of fruit squash and three plastic beakers.

'So, you're from the police?' she asks, pouring squash into the beakers.

'Yes,' I lie. We can see her husband seated in a rocking chair in the living room, where he is reading the newspaper with the radio on in the background. 'Tell me about your sister, Solveig. She was a folk singer, wasn't she?'

'She chose a different path,' Gunnhild answers, sitting down.

'She got pregnant,' I go on. 'Outside marriage?'

'Yes.'

'And the boy's father? I heard he was Russian?'

She rolls her eyes and shakes her head. 'That was what was said, yes.'

'What do you mean?'

'There were rumours,' she says, 'that she was living with a married man up north, who kept her as his mistress somewhere in the mountains. I think the story about this grand doctor in St Petersburg was just something she made up to suck up to our mother and father so that they would give her money for that so-called singing career of hers.'

'Did she get some?'

'Money? Ha! No, actually she didn't.'

'Whereabouts up north did she live?'

'She worked as a temp teacher in Lofoten somewhere.'

'When?'

'In the late sixties.'

'And her son, Svein, did you ever meet him?'

'She came here, dragging him along with her, when he was just a little boy, after the romance with the married man had come to an end.'

'They lived here?'

'Yes. In our mother and father's house for six months or so, until Father died. Then she packed her belongings, left Mother and passed all the work to me. After everything they had done for her.'

'What was he like? Svein, as a youngster?'

'He ran around, tied to her apron strings, from morning till night. Couldn't even sleep in his own room. Trailed after her the whole time. Didn't like to share his mother's attention with anyone, and she was weak, wasn't up to disciplining him.'

'You were involved in a legal dispute with Svein Borg concerning the rights to your sister's inheritance?'

'We thought it was only right and proper that my sister's music should die and be buried with her. But that man couldn't even find space in his heart to do that.'

'He came here, do you remember?' we hear the man in the living room pipe up.

Borg's aunt gives a heavy sigh as she makes the sign of the cross. 'Yes, imagine. Not even his mother's grave was sacred to that boy.'

'What do you mean?'

'Well, he stole her gravestone.'

'Pardon?'

'It was the pastor who came and told us. That Solveig's gravestone was gone, and that someone had been rooting around in the earth there. All the flowers and … and …' She gasps for air and stares in consternation at the cloudless sky above us.

'How do you know it was him?'

'Who else would it have been?' Borg's aunt asks indignantly.

I quickly take a gulp of the sour squash and force a smile. 'Mmm,' I say, drinking some more. 'What I mean is that from the police point of view, definite observations are always important, even though you know,' and here I put my hand on my heart, 'in your own heart of hearts. What is right and what is wrong.'

Gunnhild takes a deep breath. 'Yes, yes,' she says, nodding.

'Well, he wanted her to be cremated,' we hear her husband pronounce from the adjacent room. We can also hear a sermon about the symbiosis between salvation and financial gifts on the radio.

'Yes, just think,' she says, shaking her head, looking vexed. 'That his own mother should be burned, and the ashes scattered at the foot of some mountain or other. On top of all that, he was impudent enough to call here after all we've been through. Oh, sweet Jesus,' she frets.

'Did he call?' I ask in surprise.

'Yesterday. I thought that was why you were here, to—'

'Yesterday? Where from?'

'I don't know. He said he wanted to talk to my husband—'

At last her husband folds up his newspaper and turns down the volume on the radio. 'He wanted to talk about his mother,' he says, 'and about heaven and paradise.'

'Aren't they the same?' I glance at Milla and she shrugs.

'*Truly I tell you*,' Borg's uncle intones, kicking his rocking chair into life, '*today you will be with Me in Paradise*, as Jesus said to the repentant criminal on the cross by his side.' He kicks harder so that the rocking chair swings faster to and fro, while he clings to the armrests.

'But the paradise that Jesus promised is outside heaven,' Gunnhild tells us, nodding to her husband, who adds:

'God wants his children to come with him into the New Jerusalem where he has his throne, and longs to live there with us for all eternity. But it is up to us, it is the weight of our belief that decides on which level our final resting place will be.'

'So Svein wants to know whether his mother is in heaven or in paradise,' I conclude, turning to Svein's uncle in the living room. 'What answer did you give him?'

He gazes at me for a long time while his body swings back and forth with the rocking chair. 'That Solveig died before she received salvation,' he finally admits. 'Therefore, it is up to Our Lord to decide whether her final place will be in heaven or in paradise outside.'

'He's scared,' Borg's aunt interjects.

'Scared of what?' I ask.

'Of being alone.' Borg's uncle goes on: 'Svein knows he won't be admitted to heaven, because people who never develop their belief into anything larger than a mustard seed while they live on earth will at best have to spend the after-life in paradise without ever being admitted into heaven.'

'Solveig told us, didn't she, that he had changed after he got ill again.' Gunnhild folds her hands on the table between us and her eyes dart from me to the beaker of squash.

'Ill?' I clench my teeth and take a deep breath before taking another swig of the bitter liquid. 'Is he ill?'

'Yes. Svein developed a brain tumour when he was younger.' She hurries to pour more squash into my beaker before continuing: 'It was removed in an operation, and he got better. Solveig told me when she phoned that Svein had deteriorated again, that she had taken him to a doctor who had discovered new tumours. The cancer had spread.'

'I said to him when he phoned that he should ask for salvation too, and be cured in the kingdom of God as long as he first proved himself worthy of God's justice,' the uncle says from the living room.

'Cured?'

'The fire of God's Holy Spirit can burn the cancer away, just as it can with bacteria and viruses. Even though the nerves or cells and tissue are dead, they can be restored if they are kept in God's place.'

'What answer did he give to that?'

'He said he first had to know where she was,' he replies before adding with a sigh: 'It's perhaps the best that can be hoped for in the circumstances.'

'What?'

He gives a reverent smile. 'That he be allowed to meet her again.'

'In paradise?' I ask.

His wife clasps her hands and nods her head.

'But not in heaven?'

Gunnhild Borg continues to smile while she clamps her hands more tightly together. 'No. Not in heaven.'

In the living room, her husband has resumed reading the newspaper, turned up the volume on the radio and applied more acceleration to the rocking chair.

CHAPTER 81

Kenny calls while Milla and I are waiting at the airport in Kristiansand. It sounds as if he has just woken up, even though it's mid-afternoon.

'Have you discovered anything further?'

'Yep,' Kenny replies, sounding pleased with himself.

'Oh?'

'Borg's mother lived in the north of Norway when she was young. She had a boyfriend there, and they say that's where she was living when she fell pregnant.'

'I know,' I answer. 'We've just spoken to Borg's aunt. Now I know why his project is so urgent. Borg is ill and doesn't have long to live. Come home. We need to talk. I think Borg may have managed somehow to find his way back to Norway, and we have to—'

'I'm not in Svolvær,' Kenny tells me. Milla is sitting on a bench some distance away, working on her laptop. From time to time our eyes meet during my conversation with Kenny. She gives a lopsided smile and cants her head as she looks at me, waiting for a reaction. 'I'm in Oslo,' Kenny goes on, just as I turn away from Milla and start to walk towards a row of windows overlooking a business park.

'What? Why?'

'I thought I should meet up with you here when you and Milla come back. I need to talk to her, and she's not answering her phone, so I—'

'Idiot,' I snarl. 'Where?'

'The Brun bar.'

'So you're waiting there for Milla? To talk about the two of you? To tell her that Iver and you knew about Olivia long before she disappeared, long before Milla decided to start searching for her again?'

'How—'

'It was you and Karin who went to Ibiza to bring them back the first time, wasn't it?'

'I didn't know it was her,' Kenny sighs. 'They were short-staffed. Hønefoss is a small department.'

'So, you lied to me. You knew about Olivia a whole year before she went missing. Are you one of those flies in the police soup, Kenny? Are you one of the individuals I need to start looking at more closely now?'

'No. I didn't know it was Milla's daughter when Karin and I went to Ibiza to pick the girls up the year before, it was just two kids who had run away from the children's home: that kind of case happens all the time.'

'Did you tell Robert?'

'Yes,' he finally admits.

'When?'

'While he, Milla and I were in Ibiza searching for Siv and Olivia, a week before he died.'

'Not right away, then?'

Another lengthy pause before he answers: 'No.'

'And now you have it in mind to tell Milla this. To open up and ask for forgiveness, am I right?'

'Yes,' he sighs. 'You're right.'

'What did Robert say when you told him this?'

'Iver thought we shouldn't say anything, that it would just make things go from bad to worse, and that it might even be a good idea for Robert to start with a blank sheet.' His heavy sigh sounds loud in my ear. 'See how he got on.'

Kenny falls silent again and all I can hear is his harsh, jagged breath in the receiver, as well as muffled voices from the customers around him. 'But I didn't tell him everything.'

'What do you mean?'

'What?'

'What was it you didn't tell Robert?'

'Oh, that, yes.' Suddenly he is laughing to himself. 'I said we were keeping an eye on her, checking that she was doing well, without getting directly involved. But Iver went further than that. When the missing person report came in and we realised it was Olivia, we panicked. Iver tasked the whole force with finding her. We were given responsibility for looking for the girls in the circles best known to us: among the town's sex workers, junkies, down-and-outs, alcoholics and problem kids. We knew that Olivia's friend was well acquainted with that environment.'

'What was it you found out?'

'A girl we spoke to told us that they often came across Olivia and Siv at a shopping mall after school, and all of a sudden they had loads of money. She'd asked them why they had so much cash and Olivia had answered that she had a new uncle.'

'An uncle? I don't understand?'

'Iver gave her money.'

I get to my feet. 'Are you sure?'

'Who else? It was only the two of us who knew about Olivia.'

'Did you confront him with this?'

'Yes, but he denied it. Of course he denied it.' He sighs. 'It doesn't matter now. The only thing left is the showdown. Get the shit on the table and face the consequences. Who knows, maybe Milla will be understanding about it.' The final sentence is formulated as a question. 'That we did it for her. That we were looking after things.'

'Go to Milla's apartment, Kenny.'

'Why?'

'Go to the apartment. I'll come this evening. Can you do that?'

'Where are you going?'

'To talk to Iver. I need help from you both to find out what Robert did with the information you gave him in Spain.'

'OK.' Kenny hiccups, and I can hear a chair scraping across the floor. 'It's time to pack it in, anyway.'

'Do you have a key?'

'Yes. Milla gave me one the last time we were there.'

After I've rounded off the phone conversation with Kenny, I go back to Milla.

'Was that Kenny?' She puts down her laptop and looks up at me.

'Yes,' I reply, taking a seat beside her.

'Where is he?'

'He's waiting for you in Oslo.'

'Me? What do you mean?

'Kenny wants to talk to you. I told him about us.'

'Us? What do you mean?'

'That we're sleeping together.'

'Why?'

'I thought he needed to know that.'

'Because?'

'Because of the way he looks at you.'

'*Does* he look at me?' The corners of Milla's mouth curl upwards into a vague smile.

'Yes. He says he'll wait for you so that you can talk. I don't want you to meet him before I've had a chance to speak to him.'

Milla folds her hands on her laptop. 'It was a mistake,' she says. 'What happened between Kenny and me.'

'We all do that sort of thing,' I answer.

Milla refuses to relinquish eye contact. 'Do you think *this* is a mistake too?'

'You know it is.'

'How can you be so cold?'

'We're nearing the end, Milla,' I tell her. It's time to get it over and done with; I've been dreading this ever since we were in Moscow. 'Don't you see it?'

'So you've started preparing yourself for the end, getting ready to leave?'

'In actual fact, I was never here, Milla.'

'You bastard.' She sniffs, then stands up and makes for the gate.

CHAPTER 82

Milla and I have barely exchanged a single word on the flight home. Maybe it's OK: after all, we're moving into a new phase of both the investigation and our relationship, one in which all the secrets will have to be on the table. I can see Joachim standing beneath an arrivals sign, scanning the row of passengers en route to the baggage carousel. When he catches sight of us he waves, shuffling his feet impatiently as he waits for Milla to spot him. Milla doesn't seem to notice him – instead she comes to a sudden stop in front of the baggage belt and grabs my arm.

'Come with me to Tjøme,' she says, just as Joachim starts to move towards us.

'No.'

'You can have more pills,' she whispers. 'I promise. We don't need to—'

'I need to go to Drammen to speak to Iver.'

'No.' She squeezes my arm harder, trying to drag me towards her. 'I don't want you to go. I'm going to tell Joachim everything. I want the two of us to—'

I stop. 'Don't mess about, Milla. We—'

'No, no, I'm not messing about!' she shouts, making the people around us stop and dart curious looks in our direction. 'I want you to stay with me. I've paid for you to be here and help me. You can't go until Olivia—'

'I'll be back,' I finally tell her, at the same moment that Joachim appears beside us.

'When?' Milla turns her back on Joachim, who has made a move to hug her. He is left standing with his hands held out in thin air.

'Soon.'

'No,' Milla insists. 'I want to know when you're coming.'

'OK. Tomorrow. Kenny's in your apartment, and I'm going to meet him there if that's OK with you. Then we'll both come tomorrow morning. Agreed?'

'Promise?'

'Yes.'

I nod to Joachim, who makes another attempt to embrace Milla, again without success, and I set off towards the escalator for the airport train that will take me to Drammen.

CHAPTER 83

The carriage I'm sitting in is half-full. Gunnar Ore answers the phone at the first ring. 'What?' he growls.

I turn my face away from the other passengers and watch the rain-soaked landscape flit by. 'Have you made any progress on tracing the mobile?'

'Well, this is starting to become a clusterfuck of undreamt-of proportions. We had to go from door to door all day long, and it wasn't until we were almost finished and ready to give up that it struck me.'

'What?'

'That I was familiar with the area.'

The raindrops buffeting the window form long streaks as the train picks up speed. 'What do you mean?' I ask, running my fingers over the inside of the glass.

'It's an apartment in Eilert Sundts gate. We found the mobile too. On the kitchen table.'

'Who lives there?'

'Don't you remember?'

'No.'

'The apartment's empty. The previous owners died last autumn in the midst of a bitter divorce. Ring any bells?'

'Can't you just spell it out for me?' I say impatiently. I'm not ready for another round in Gunnar's labyrinth.

'Camilla and Robert Riverholt. It was their apartment.'

'What! Who lives there now?'

'No one. The apartment is still exactly as it was when they died. According to the lawyer in charge of the administration of the estate, the heirs have still not wound things up.'

'And you found the mobile there?'

'Yes, bloody hell. In the kitchen! We're taking it with us to see if there's anything useful on it. And by the way, Ann-Mari's funeral's tomorrow. Are you coming?'

'Yes, I'm coming. I'll come back as soon as I've finished in Drammen,' I tell him. 'First I just have to talk to Iver in private.'

'Is that a good idea? After all, we don't know—'

'Iver is the second in command at the police station in Drammen. If I end up in a rubbish container or at the bottom of the Drammen Fjord, he knows who'll come knocking on his door.'

'OK, but be careful.'

'Hold on a second,' I say, as he is about to hang up. I turn away from the rain and the buildings outside as the train starts to slow down, back to my fellow passengers in the compartment. They all look like sleeping mannequins. All at once I feel dead tired, absolutely exhausted. 'I—'

'Wait,' Gunnar says. His voice is lowered now. 'Just wait. Bottle it up. The two of us won't be able to rest until we've found them and I've throttled the last oxygen—'

'You can't kill—'

'Really?' Suddenly he is laughing. 'Are you going to stop me, then?'

I don't want to end the conversation with a lie, so I ring off.

CHAPTER 84

I stop beside a sofa in the living room. A nearby window is open and outside I can hear the trees sway and Siv laughing out on the terrace. I've always liked the wind, when it rushes through the treetops and makes the branches shake and creak like dancing green giants. I don't know why, because I have no memories of us being anywhere like that.

I pick up one of the cushions on the sofa and carefully press my face into it. There's a smell inside it, deep down in the fabric, that I've known before. I sensed it at once when I came here but it is stronger here than in the rest of the house. Mum, I think it's of you.

'What are you up to?' Siv asks, laughing. Her voice always sounds different when she's been drinking. Her hips tilt more, as if she can't find the right way to stand.

'Nothing.' I take the cushion away from my face and replace it on the sofa.

'You were sniffing it.'

'No.'

'Yes, you were!' she screeches, laughing, as she rocks her hips back and forth.

'So what,' I answer, and turn to leave.

'Hey!' Siv comes over and grabs me by the shoulders. 'Where are you going?'

'To the bathroom, I've got a pain in my stomach.'

'Are you drunk?'

'No, but you are.'

'Fine,' Siv says, hiccupping as she staggers from side to side, still keeping a tight grip on my shoulders. Her eyes have a glassy sheen, and lipstick or wine has discoloured her front teeth. 'Then I'll go outside and ask if the old man wants to dance.' She sways slightly before finally releasing me and whirling around, laughing, until in the end she runs back into the kitchen, heading for the glass door that leads out on to the terrace.

CHAPTER 85

'Come in,' Iver says when at last I'm standing outside his house in Austad, Drammen. 'I've made some meat broth and all that travelling must have made you hungry.'

On the way to the kitchen I notice a series of pictures of Iver and a woman. The photos cover a period of several decades and the last one is of the two of them on a holiday abroad.

'Your wife?' I ask as I sit down at the table.

'Ex-wife,' Iver answers, pouring me a glass of beer. 'We divorced in 2006. She couldn't cope with my job.'

'It usually ends that way,' I say, without asking why he has kept all the pictures displayed on the wall.

'Where's Milla?' Iver lifts the casserole lid and ladles some broth for us both. He's wearing a blue shirt and jeans, both of which I seem to recall from one of the photographs.

'She went to Tjøme with Joachim.'

'Well,' Iver begins, blowing on the spoonful of vegetables, salt beef and stock. 'That's maybe for the best right now.'

'Yes.'

'As you know,' he says, quickly tasting the soup and swallowing it down with some beer, 'Milla and I go back a long time.' He puts on a smile. 'She's even hinted that Mugabe is partly based on me, though I struggle to see the similarity myself.'

'In the book she's working on now, it looks as if I've usurped that place,' I reply.

'Oh?' As Iver looks up from his soup spoon, his eyes take on an intense glow. The next minute it's gone and the muscles around his eyes relax. Some people are smarter than others at hiding what they don't want their sidekicks to see.

'It's obviously part of her writing process,' I continue, 'to adapt the main character in the book according to whoever she's sleeping with at any particular time. I expect there are aspects of Kenny and Robert in him as well.'

'It was only a couple of times, many years ago,' Iver tells me, 'but it ended as quickly as it had begun.'

'And your wife found out and insisted on a divorce?'

'Quite the cynic, aren't you?' He puts down his spoon and takes hold of his beer glass. 'As I said, it's a long time ago now and doesn't have much to do with anything.'

'Shall we talk about Olivia, then?' I suggest in an effort to get things moving.

Iver takes a deep breath and nods glumly as he caresses his glass. 'I've been thinking,' he says.

'That's known to be helpful,' I reply.

'If Borg really is working with someone …'

'Then we're all in danger?'

He nods gravely. 'There's something I haven't told you,' he says, with a deep sigh. 'That I should perhaps …'

'It's about time, yes.'

'We should have told you at once.'

'That you and Kenny knew about Olivia long before Milla hired Robert to find her daughter? Yes, you should have told me that right away. And Milla.'

'Did Kenny tell you?'

'I think also that you knew the day would come,' I go on without answering his question, 'when Milla would want to ask you for help in tracing her daughter. I think that was why you persuaded her to hire Robert too, so that you and Kenny could avoid having to tell her that you'd known about Olivia all along.'

'What could we do?' Iver sighs, hardening his grip on the beer glass. 'We weren't supposed to know.'

'No, you weren't supposed to know.'

'Kenny's struggling with all this now,' Iver tells me. 'I don't know if he can manage to keep it together for much longer.'

'Did you ever meet her?'

'What?'

'Did you ever meet Olivia before she went missing?'

'No, I ...' He takes a deep breath and reaches out for the beer glass again, as if it were an oxygen tank. 'It was really by chance that we found her. You see, Kenny went to Ibiza with Karin when the girls ran away the previous year, and when Milla began to talk about finding her ... After that we watched over her for a bit, saw to it that she was OK, if that's what you want to know. But we kept our distance and we never spoke to her.'

'You and Kenny?'

'Yes. But we hadn't seen her for the past six months because it looked as if everything was going well once they came back from Ibiza, and we were reluctant to get too involved. Listen, where are you actually going with all of this?'

'I'm just saying that I find it difficult to imagine two teenage girls getting into Borg's car. I think it's more likely that a girl like Olivia would get into the car of someone who said he knew her mother, her biological mother. Someone who might have contacted her in advance and said he would introduce her if she'd like that. Or a police officer?'

'So you think *I* did something to her? Why? Christ, man. You're off your head!'

'Kenny tells me you gave her money.'

'He's lying!' Iver says, grabbing his jacket from the chair back. 'Bloody idiot,' he snarls, producing his car keys. 'We're going to clear this up once and for all. Get into the car. I'm driving.'

Chapter 86

The bathroom is bigger than my whole room. There are two wash basins, a shower on one side and a bath on the other. Closing the door, I walk across to the mirror and pull my hair back from my face. I turn on the tap, wait until it is hot enough, and then stick my fingers under the water and let it run over my hands all the way up to my forearms before I splash the water on my face.

Outside I can hear Siv laughing, or singing, I'm not sure. I turn off the tap and dry my face and hands with the towel. I sit down on the toilet seat. Again I hear Siv's voice. She's louder now, shouting something out there. I listen as my gaze dances over the floor, the walls, the elegant bath. In the mirror I see only the top of my head, my hair and part of my forehead. I look so small, as if I'm a child again and can't reach higher than the basin. All at once I feel a stab of pain in my stomach, and I feel my mouth fill with bile. I get down on my knees and open the seat lid just in time before throwing up.

The bowl fills with wine-coloured water, I gasp for air and vomit again. When my stomach is finally empty, I get up and go back to the basin, turn on the water again and fill my mouth, spit and rinse. My body stiffens when I hear Siv's voice for a third time. There's something different about it now. It's not just her usual drunken racket now – it's more of a concentrated outburst, the kind you make when you're afraid.

CHAPTER 87

'Do you have a key?' Iver asks, once we've parked in front of Milla's apartment in St Hanshaugen.

I shake my head. 'Kenny said *he* had one.'

'Let's just go up.' Iver gives the street corner a fleeting glance before pulling his jacket lapels more tightly around his neck and heading for the lift.

'It's locked,' he says as we stand outside the door to Milla's top-floor apartment. He rings the doorbell, though we can't hear anyone inside.

I take out my mobile and call Milla. Joachim answers. 'What is it?' he asks. 'Milla's sleeping.'

'Has Kenny phoned?'

'Yes, earlier. I told him Milla was asleep. She's exhausted after all the travelling. He was in her apartment in Oslo.'

'We're there now. The door's locked.'

'Have you tried phoning him?'

'His mobile's switched off.'

'He's probably fast asleep in there. He sounded drunk over the phone. I said to him that—'

'Wake her.'

'Can't it wait, I—'

'Wake her!'

'OK, then.' I hear Joachim open a door. 'Darling,' he murmurs. 'Darling, they want to talk to you again.'

I hear tired grunts from the bed and then Joachim's voice returns. 'She's taken some pills, I—'

'Christ, man. Can't you just give her a shake?'

'Milla? Milla, please. They need to speak to you.'

Once again, I hear Milla groan and mumble something before it goes quiet again.

'It's impossible,' Joachim whispers after a lengthy silence. 'I can't.'

Iver takes the phone from me and puts it to his ear. 'Iver here,' he says brusquely. 'Do you have a key for the Oslo apartment?'

He waits for a few seconds and then nods to himself. 'Brilliant! Then bring it here right away. OK?'

He hangs up and returns the mobile to me. 'The wimp's coming with a key. We'll wait here in the meantime.'

CHAPTER 88

Two hours later, Joachim arrives. We hear him in the hall-way below before he jogs up the stairs.

'There's a lift here,' Iver comments crossly when he finally turns up.

'I don't like confined spaces,' Joachim replies, rattling the bunch of keys. 'We should have installed a code lock so you don't need a key, but after what happened to Robert, we haven't really used the apartment much.'

Joachim unlocks the door and steps aside to let Iver and me in. 'Can I go now?' he asks. 'I don't want to leave Milla alone for so long, and—'

'Stay here,' Iver mutters as we reach the living room. Above our heads we see a rust-coloured moon wreathed in dark clouds shining down through the roof lights. There is a strong odour of cleaning chemicals, but also of something else, a faint hint of alcohol, exhaled intoxication hidden in the semi-darkness. Deep down inside I'm aware of a grow-ing revulsion, the same feeling I usually get when my body prepares me for a strong visual impression.

'Is there anybody here?' Joachim asks, standing partly hidden behind my back.

'I don't know,' Iver replies before flicking on the ceil-ing-light switch. He goes inside and takes up position in the middle of the room, looking around with a worried frown before continuing on into the other rooms.

A fine coating of soap and water still adheres to the living-room floor, making it slippery. 'Who has washed the floor?' I turn to face Joachim, still hovering in the doorway, clutching the bunch of keys.

He shrugs. 'We pay a company to do that.'

'In the evening?'

'No.' He hesitates. 'I don't think so.'

'Nobody here,' Iver tells us on his return. He sits down on the sofa, yawns and rubs his hands over his face. 'What do you think, Thorkild? Shall we wait?'

'No,' I reply, signalling to Joachim that I want the keys. 'Go home, I'll stay here overnight. I'll let you know if he turns up.'

The two men sigh before nodding briefly and leaving the apartment. I follow them out to the stairwell and wait at the top of the stairs until they've disappeared out of the front door and into their cars. Then I take out my mobile and call Gunnar Ore.

'What?' he grunts, sounding tired. 'It's almost midnight.'

'I'm in Milla's apartment,' I tell him. 'And I need help.'

'What on earth for?'

Again my eyes drift to the roof lights and the rust moon up there above the city. 'A crime scene investigation.'

Chapter 89

'What have you done?' I yell when I come out to the terrace. Siv is lying on the edge between the terrace and a rockery filled with flowers. Half of her body is prostrate on the wood, with one foot and arm dangling down into the flowerbed. It looks like wine, the liquid seeping out from under her hair, staining the planks and stones red, as if she has fallen and landed on a broken bottle.

'It was an accident,' he says, standing there with his hands hanging heavily at his sides. Her face is distorted, twisted into a strange angle at one side and her eyes blank, cold, like the glass in a mirror. 'We were dancing,' he sniffs as he sways from side to side. 'Just fooling around a bit, and then she slipped.' He looks at me. 'She slid, I ... I ...'

I crouch down in front of Siv, take hold of her shoulder and try to turn her round. As soon as I move her, the pool of blood begins to spread. 'We have to help her,' I sob, using my fingers to feel beneath her hair in search of the spot where the blood is coming from.

'Yes, yes,' he says, nodding, but without moving a muscle.

'So call for an ambulance, then!'

He says nothing, just stares blankly into the distance.

Chapter 90

'Right, I think we'll pack up now.' Gunnar's crew have worked through the entire night. The apartment has been gone through with a fine-tooth comb, but nothing noteworthy has turned up, apart from that we're pretty sure someone has recently been cleaning in here. When the company responsible for cleaning the apartment opens, we will at least get an answer as to whether it was their cleaner or someone else who can take the credit for that.

It's almost half past six in the morning and my whole body is screaming for sleep and painkillers. Nodding to the rest of the crime scene technicians, Gunnar hands me the apartment key and turns to face me again. 'You're coming with me. We have to get ready for the funeral. If we're lucky, you can maybe even get a couple of hours' shut-eye before we have to leave. God only knows, you look as if you need it.'

We leave Milla's apartment and venture out into the cold morning light. 'We have to check out Borg's apartment in Molde,' Gunnar tells me as we head for his car.

'It was sold.'

'Sold?'

'The apartment was included in the bankruptcy proceedings,' I tell him. 'By the way, Borg phoned his aunt and uncle on the south coast. He was trying to find out if his mother was waiting for him in heaven or in paradise.'

'Is there a difference?'

'Apparently so,' I answer.

'Bit of a character, eh? I'm already looking forward to meeting him.'

It occurs to me that it is difficult to tell where Gunnar's anger stops and his sorrow begins. 'Borg is ill,' I tell him. 'These murders, this project of his, I'm starting to understand more of what it's actually all about. His friend, on the other hand ...'

'What about him?'

'I'm struggling to comprehend what's at risk as far as he's concerned, why he has to clear us out of the way. Nor can I fathom what links him to Borg. I've tried over and over again, but there's nothing there. It's as if the two of them are completely separate, but nevertheless follow each other on a parallel course wherever we turn.'

'One will lead us to the other,' Gunnar grunts as I find Kenny's mobile number and call it. It's still switched off.

CHAPTER 91

The living-room floor in Gunnar's house is littered with boxes. 'Are you going to give them away?' I flop down on the sofa where I sat the last time I was here.

'They'll go in the attic for now,' Gunnar replies. 'It's her things, I don't know what to do with them.' He strips off his jacket and shirt and throws his clothes on the floor.

'Do you have,' I begin to ask, scanning the bare living room, 'what you promised me?'

'What?' He crosses his arms. 'Do I have what?'

'The pills? The ones I was to get, when—'

'Of course,' he answers, without taking his eyes off me.

'Can I ... see?'

Gunnar gives me a look of contempt and purses his lips. Eventually he disappears into the bedroom. 'Here,' he says when he returns with a shopping bag and tosses it on to the table in front of me. 'Ann-Mari's pills. Every single one of them.'

I grab the bottom of the bag and shake out the contents. The pill boxes cover the table as if they were Lego bricks emptied out by an overeager youngster. Imovane, Apodorm, Stesolid, Xanor, Sobril, Paralgin Forte, codeine, Tramadol, and oxies, a whole pile of oxies. 'So you didn't need to go to the doctor's,' I say to myself as I pick up a box of OxyContin.

'The prize waiting at the end of the run,' Gunnar says harshly as I stare longingly at the mountain of pills in front of me.

'Why did she have so many?' I balance an unopened box of OxyNorm in my hand, caressing the paper flaps with my thumb.

'She consulted doctors, new ones all the time; they prescribed a number of pills. Of all configurations and colours, but she didn't take them. Just stashed them away and went out and asked for more.'

'Why?'

'Maybe she knew all the time that you would come crashing in through the door one day and wanted to be prepared for that eventuality?'

'Gunnar,' I say, 'don't—'

'You can have one now,' he replies coldly. 'But no more than one.'

'What?' I stare at the box in my hand and feel the saliva secretion in my oral cavities working furiously.

'Come on,' he goads me. 'I know you want to. I can almost feel the craving all the way from here. Take one.'

'I'm not weak,' I insist, replacing the pill box on the table with the others.

'What are you, then?'

My gaze lingers on the pile of boxes in front of me. 'I'm ill,' I insist.

'Is there a difference?'

Gunnar continues to stand there, watching me, waiting for me to give in. I can see that he is itching to snatch up the pill boxes, to take them through to the bathroom and force me to watch as he empties every packet and capsule down into the toilet bowl before asking me scornfully if I still want them. He wants me to show him rock bottom, so that he can demonstrate his rage. I can't let that happen, not here. Not now.

'Yes.' I return the pills to the bag and push it towards him. 'There is a difference.'

'OK,' Gunnar says. 'So there is a difference.' He turns on his heel to go. 'Take a shower. It's only a few hours until the funeral starts. I'm going to grab forty winks.'

CHAPTER 92

I must have dropped off in the chair after I'd finished in the bathroom. The shopping bag of pills is gone from the table when I open my eyes.

'Are you ready?' Gunnar emerges from one room and goes into another. He has already put on a suit and is carrying a pair of shoes.

'Yes,' I answer, getting up from the chair. 'I'm ready.'

'So you didn't take a single one?' he asks, stifling what could have been a smile.

'Did you count them?'

'I have a suit you can borrow,' Gunnar replies. 'And shoes. They're laid out in the guest room.' He points towards the door next to the room where I last saw Ann-Mari.

'Fine.' I make a move, yawning and massaging my cheek and jaw as I struggle to remember whether I dreamt anything while I slept. 'Give me five minutes.'

'Do you think he might have come back to Norway?' Gunnar asks me when I emerge again. 'Svein Borg, do you think he could be in town?'

'I think he was on his way home to complete his project, yes. But I still don't know where home is, that's the problem.'

'And what about your friend Kenny? Any news of him?'

I glance at my mobile, but there are no new messages. 'No.'

'Maybe we should have posted a guard outside Milla's apartment in case he turns up again?'

'I don't think that will help,' I say, keying in Kenny's number. His mobile phone is still switched off.

'Oh? Why not?'

'Because,' I answer, tucking my phone back inside my jacket. 'I think Kenny's in trouble.'

CHAPTER 93

He still just stands there, in the middle of the terrace, staring at the woods. 'Don't you hear me?' I shout as I press my hands over the wound on Siv's head that won't stop bleeding. 'You have to do something!'

'Yes,' he mumbles and at the same time the fingers of one hand jerk, as if his body is suddenly coming back to life after being in a trance. At last he looks at me.

'Yes, I have to do something.' Then he takes an unsteady step forward, towards me.

I can see in his eyes that he isn't going to do what I'm asking him to. He has decided on something else. Something else entirely.

I want to let go of Siv, to stand up and take to my heels, but my legs refuse to cooperate. He walks all the way up to me and stands right in front of me. 'Please,' I whisper.

He smiles when he notices my tears, the tears I can no longer keep in check. He takes hold of my shoulders and drags me carefully away from Siv, laying me down on my back on the terrace. Then he sits on top of me and strokes the hair that is plastered to my cheek, smoothing it away from my face. 'Don't cry,' he says as his hands run over my lips. 'Don't cry, Olivia.' I feel his fingers continue down over my chin and gather around my neck. 'Please. It was just an accident.'

Chapter 94

'Listen,' Gunnar says, once we have left his villa and are driving to the church where the funeral is to take place, 'during the funeral, can't we just try to get through this ...' he bites his lower lip as he searches for the right words, 'and behave like men?'

'Big boys don't cry and all that jazz?'

Gunnar nods vigorously. 'Yes, yes, that's exactly what I mean. Not that there's anything wrong with it, but ...' He looks at me, for just a brief second, before turning away again. 'You get what I mean?'

'Yes, boss,' I reply. 'Sorrow with dignity.'

He nods again, squinting out at the traffic. 'Yes, precisely, I don't want to have to worry about you breaking down when ...' he bites harder on his lower lip, 'when they lower her coffin down ... down ...' He doesn't complete the sentence and merely blinks furiously, tightening his grip on the leather of the steering wheel.

'I'll behave myself, boss,' I assure him just as Gunnar turns into the car park outside the church.

Once parked, he switches off the engine. 'And another thing,' his voice has immediately returned to his familiar authoritative tone when he turns around in the seat, pointing a finger at me, 'how many times do I have to say that

I'm no longer your boss? I don't see why it has to be so damned difficult for you to—'

'What the hell is *he* doing here?' I ask when I catch sight of a towering figure enjoying a cigarette on the church steps, screwing up his eyes as he gazes at the spring sunshine.

'Who?' Gunnar lowers his finger and leans forward to peer out of the front windscreen.

'Ulf,' I reply, and at the same time, a red-haired woman in a dress with a shawl draped over her bare shoulders, appears behind his back, 'and his new girlfriend, Doris.'

Gunnar looks askance at me. 'Doris?'

'She's German.'

'Christ,' Gunnar answers, opening the car door. He rakes his fingers through his millimetre-length hair before we both leave the car and head for the church steps. When we arrive there, we stop in front of Ulf and Doris. Gunnar says hello and then excuses himself to go to see the pastor.

'Thorkild Aske.' Ulf blows his cigarette smoke straight into my face, all the while gazing at me with a mixture of disappointment and contempt, as if he has just caught me red-handed playing with a rubber duck in some inappropriate way. 'Did you think I wouldn't find out about this?'

'Yes,' I reply, nodding at Doris as I force out a smile.

'What happened?' Doris gives me a warm handshake.

'We don't know yet,' I reply.

'You look surprisingly well,' Ulf lies. 'The medicines I give you obviously work.'

'Yes, just as well as nicotine patches.'

'What?' Ulf pinches the cigarette and tosses it away. 'I'm not smoking, am I?'

I shake my head.

'Will you come home with us after the funeral?' Doris asks as Ulf fumbles to take another cigarette from the pack. As he lights it, his eyes squint at me through the cigarette smoke while he circles me like a hawk hovering over a dwarf hamster.

'Sorry, Doris,' I say, taking a step back as Ulf tears the glowing cigarette out of his mouth and takes a pace closer. 'Listen here, your—'

'Ulf, Ulf,' Doris says softly and puts a hand on his arm.

Ulf takes a deep drag of his smoke before looking at it, swearing and throwing it away. 'Afterwards, Thorkild.' He replaces his lighter in his jacket pocket. Then he turns and marches into the church.

'How did you find out?' I ask once Ulf has left.

'Gunnar Ore phoned,' Doris replies. 'He didn't want to say anything, but Ulf got the picture. They worry about you, Thorkild, both of them.'

'I can't go home yet,' I tell her, darting shifty looks at the people passing by. 'We haven't finished with the case.'

'Was this where you got married?' Doris looks at me. 'You and Ann-Mari?'

'No,' I answer. 'Her mother's buried in the graveyard here, though. She died when Ann-Mari was young. Cancer.'

'That's lovely,' she goes on.

'What?' I ask. 'What's lovely?'

She gazes at me for a few short seconds before answering: 'Coming home to Mother again.'

Something is on the tip of my tongue when a thought strikes me more forcefully than usual: 'Fuck,' I mumble, turning towards the church door.

Gunnar is sitting in the front pew. There is a space between him and his parents, who both look at me with a mixture of recognition and distrust. One is undoubtedly connected to the other. 'Sit down,' he whispers when I finally reach him. 'The service is about to begin.'

'The criminal complaint,' I mutter. 'When Svein Borg was reported by his mother's sister and her family for desecrating the grave and stealing his mother's gravestone.'

'Yes,' he murmurs just as the pastor appears in front of the podium beside the pulpit, behind Ann-Mari's coffin.

'And after his mother's death he was mixed up in some kind of legal wrangle. He applied to the authorities for her to be cremated, but his application was denied.'

'Yes.' Gunnar's eyes continue to follow the pastor. 'The deceased must have personally specified a wish for cremation and that the ashes be scattered to the winds, as they say. As far as I recall, that hadn't happened in Solveig Borg's case. Therefore, the application was turned down.'

'Where did he want to scatter the ashes, do you remember?'

Gunnar nods his head as the pastor ascends to the pulpit and gazes reverently out at the congregation. 'At the foot of a mountain,' he says softly.

'Where?' I demand impatiently.

He shrugs in irritation just as the pastor begins to speak. 'I don't remember,' he responds. 'We can look into it later.'

'Gråtinden? Do you remember if it was called Gråtinden?'

'I think it might have been. Why do you ask?'

I take a deep breath as the organ strikes up and the mourners begin to sing the first hymn. 'Then I think I know where Svein Borg is heading.'

Chapter 95

'What is it we're searching for?' Gunnar asks as we stand in front of the computer screen in his home office. The members of the funeral party who have returned for the reception are sitting in the living room, waiting for him to appear so that the coffee and cakes can be served.

'A mountain,' I say, stealing a glance at the window. On the steps below us, Ulf is standing smoking with Doris, ready to tell me that I must come home with them to Stavanger. 'And a cabin.'

'Gråtinden?'

I zoom in on the computer map and Gunnar leans in over the desk. 'There.' I point at a precipitous mountain ridge surrounded by other peaks and the sea.

Gunnar points at a dot beside a small lake at the foot of the mountain. 'What's that?'

'A plot of land in the wilderness.' I zoom in further. 'Gråtjønn, it's called.'

'Move.' Gunnar forces his way on to the chair. He copies the farm and title number and opens another computer program.

'Is it his?' I ask once Gunnar has finished his search and leans back in the chair.

'The owner of that parcel of land is Olaf Lund.'

'The missing head teacher.'

'There's a cabin on the property.' Gunnar looks up from the screen. His face takes on a hazy glow in the light of the pendant lamp.

'Borg's aunt said that Solveig was a married man's mistress while she was working in Lofoten in her younger days, and that he kept her in a cabin in the mountains.'

Chewing his cheeks, Gunnar zooms in closer to an area beneath a curved ridge. The place is dark, as if the mountain blocks the light from reaching the valley. 'Well, it's certainly in the middle of no man's land,' he mutters to himself.

'Sea and steep mountains,' I say. 'God, how I hate the sea and mountains.'

Gunnar leans back again and clasps his hands at the back of his neck. 'Can you tell me again why we should go up there?'

'Borg's project,' I reply. 'Svein Borg's mother died last summer. Borg then applied to the authorities for permission to scatter her ashes at the foot of that mountain, but his application was rejected. It all ended in a legal battle with the family, not only about the burial, but also about his mother's will. Borg lost again. Later that summer, Borg's aunt reported her nephew for desecration of the grave. Borg knows he will soon die. He has an inoperable brain tumour, but he's also afraid. Afraid of what awaits him on the other side. I don't think Borg travelled south just to steal his mother's gravestone and wreck the flowers. He went there to take her home.'

Gunnar cocks his head as he runs his fingers over his chin. 'What do you mean?'

'Solveig Borg had found her way back to God on her deathbed,' I reply. 'Her family are devout Christians – they believe in heaven and paradise.'

'And they're not the same?'

'No. There's a class distinction. Heaven is for those in first class, while paradise is in a way their version of economy class. Borg knows he can never enter heaven: his aunt has told him that ever since he was a little boy, but he might harbour some hope that he and his mother could meet in paradise instead.'

'Are you telling me what I think you are?' The finger dance on his chin has stopped. Gunnar crosses his arms on his chest. 'That Borg has ...'

'Yes, I think so.'

'OK,' Gunnar says, switching off the computer. 'Let's finish up here first.'

'Shit,' I groan, putting my head in my hands, as Gunnar gets to his feet and goes out to his guests again. 'Why does it have to be in the north of Norway?'

PART VI

THE ONES WHO KILL

Chapter 96

Northern Norway. Open harbours, dark fjord arms surrounded by cold, jagged mountain peaks that rise from the earth's crust, impaling the sky and shutting out the sunlight. The place is so dark and chilly even on a bright spring day such as this that I shiver as soon as the cabin crew open the door of the Widerøe plane, letting in the brisk Lofoten air.

'At last,' Gunnar Ore mutters, unfastening his seat belt and standing to put on his outdoor jacket while impatient northerners push past to get out of the aircraft as fast as possible.

Svolvær airport is a short runway almost entirely surrounded by sea, the contours of dark mountains and a deep blue horizon. Flying in brings a sense of landing on an aircraft carrier in a strange, uninhabited sea and mountain planet in the far reaches of the solar system, a planet so small that you can discern the curvature of the earth with the naked eye.

It starts to rain as soon as we leave the plane, and we jog to the entrance of the barracks building that is clearly the main air terminal. 'Hire a car!' Gunnar orders as we make our way to the baggage carousel in the arrivals hall.

'I can't,' I answer. 'Don't have a licence. Anyway, it doesn't look as if anything's open as late as this,' I go on, pointing at a row of darkened booths exhibiting the recognisable names of car hire companies.

'No, of course you don't,' he grunts in irritation, looking at his watch. It is half past seven in the evening. 'Well, get us a taxi, then. Can you manage that?'

'Are we going to try to find the cabin tonight?'

'No, of course not. I've no intention of wandering about in an unfamiliar mountain range in the middle of the night.'

'OK,' I answer, heading for the door. 'Up to you.'

We book into a hotel with a view of the sea and the little islands dotted around. I turn on the TV and tune in to a programme about people with no money. Just as the broadcast is interrupted by commercials, there is a knock at the door.

'I've spoken to someone up here about this place we want to find,' Gunnar tells me, once I've opened the door and let him in. 'The cabin is situated on the north side of Austvågøya, the island we're on now. We drive to a place called Sydalen, and from there we go on foot until we reach a fishing spot.'

'Do you have your service revolver?'

'I'm not on duty,' Gunnar replies.

'So, what if—'

'Is he that big?' Gunnar pulls a face. 'Don't you think the two of us will manage to take him on?'

'No.'

'Well, we'll take a few others with us,' he suggests. 'I'll call the police station tomorrow before we leave, if you like.'

'I certainly would.'

'OK.' Gunnar folds his hands as he impatiently paces the floor. 'OK, OK, OK.'

'I was thinking of hitting the hay now,' I tell him.

'Good idea,' he says, but goes on trotting to and fro while scanning the bare walls for something to fix his eye on.

'It still feels so unreal,' he tells me as I scrape out a single pathetic Cipralex from my pill box.

I stop and look at him. 'What does?'

'Everything. The two of us up here and her down there. Dead. I don't know quite what I'm supposed to feel, and whether what I'm feeling is right. I'm just going around waiting for it to hit me. Knock me for six ...' He stops beside the curtains and pulls them aside so that the lights reflected on the sea outside filter into the room. 'The way it did with you when Frei died.'

'Everyone's different,' I tell him.

'Are we?' He stands with his back turned, staring out at the dark sea. 'Or am I the only one who ...' At last he turns around. His face is greyer now, his jaw muscles tense, almost locked beneath the skin, and his teeth are tightly clenched. 'Maybe I didn't love her the way you did Frei, maybe—'

'Gunnar,' I begin. 'I'd reached breaking point even before Frei died. Besides, I scarcely knew her; it was more that I'd fallen in love with the idea of someone like her, who allowed me to be a different version of myself. This is something entirely unlike that. This,' I hold up the Cipralex between us, 'this is also an illusion that draws a veil over reality and turns days into nights and nights back into days again. That's all.'

'So why do you take them? Why are they so fucking important?'

'I need them so that I can be half myself and half not myself. But it's not a life, it's a waiting room.'

Gunnar crosses his arms. 'What are you waiting for?'

'You know, of course,' I reply calmly as I pop the solitary capsule into my mouth.

He shakes his head. 'Talking to you is the most fucking depressing thing I can think of.' Then he turns to the window again. 'I don't understand what she saw in you.'

'Who?'

'Ann-Mari.'

'She probably saw the same thing as I see when I'm wrapped up in the right pills, the ones you promised me,' I answer.

'And that is?'

'A way out.'

I see Gunnar's burly frame sway as he stands with his back to me. He is waiting for me to help him sink down into some kind of abyss where he can wallow in self-hatred and misery, acting the way he believes he should in order to prove to himself that he was capable of loving the way I did.

'From what?' he finally hisses. 'Me?'

Self-hatred does not suit Gunnar. He isn't able to manage it in the right way, and I don't propose to help him achieve that either. 'No,' I answer. 'From herself.'

'Why?' Gunnar turns again to face me. 'Why did she have to see you again after she'd met me, after you returned to Norway, after you killed that young girl in Stavanger, after your suicide attempts and your drug abuse? Why would she want to see someone like you, rather than me? Can you explain that to me, because I can't fathom it at all. Ann-Mari, Frei, Milla, what do women like that think they're going to find in you?'

'They know what they get.'

'And what's that?' he demands impatiently. He stands there staring at me with eyes steeped in contempt and genuine wonder at the same time.

'Someone who is going to hurt them, again and again, and betray them when they need me most. There's a security to be found in that knowledge, too. Knowing that, immediately. I'm a substitute for pain. For them as well as for you.'

'I can't bear to listen to you any more.' He makes for the door. 'You're off your head, man.'

'Tell that to Ulf,' I call after him. 'Tell him I'm sick, that you can see it clear as day.'

Gunnar slams the hotel-room door without another word. I am left sitting on the bed, waiting until I hear him let himself into his own room, and then I stand up and go to the window to draw the curtains. I turn back to the bed again, turn up the volume on the TV and wait. Wait for sleep, and for the faces hidden within it.

CHAPTER 97

I sit in a hire car outside the police station in Svolvær. Gunnar has gone inside to meet our guide, Johanne, a local police officer who is going to assist us. There is a fresh layer of new-fallen snow on the mountains, and the ochre-yellow grass from last summer gleams wet in the grey morning sun. While I wait, I key in Iver's number.

'Have you heard anything from Kenny?'

'Not a word,' Iver says. 'His mobile is still switched off. I don't like it,' he adds. 'Kenny's not the type to take off without a word.' He sighs. 'Where are you, by the way?'

'Ore and I have come to the north of Norway. Following the Borg trail. It looks as if it's going to lead us up into the mountains.'

'Is there anything I can help with?'

'Yes. There's a number I'd like you to check out, from the day when Siv and Olivia went missing until today's date. Can you do that?'

'What's the number?'

'I don't have the number,' I tell him as I catch sight of Gunnar and the policewoman who have emerged from the police station and are moving towards the car. 'Just a name.'

'OK,' Iver replies once I've given him the name. 'I'll see to that.'

'And keep it to yourself, Iver. Do you hear?'

'I promise. And listen, be careful, won't you?'

'Always,' I answer, ringing off.

'You need hiking gear,' Gunnar tells me when he and the policewoman reach the car.

'I only have this,' I reply, looking down at my sheepskin jacket and vintage shoes.

With a shake of his head, Gunnar disappears behind the hire car and opens the boot. He changes quickly before returning to settle into the driver's seat.

'The shortest route from here is to drive to Gimsøystraumen and then go on up to Sydalen. It's quite a distance to walk,' Johanne tells us from the back seat of the car, 'but as soon as we get there, it's a fabulous hunting ground.'

'The mother of the man we're searching for apparently lived up here for a while in the sixties and could possibly have had a relationship with the missing head teacher,' Gunnar tells us as we drive out of Svolvær town centre.

'Olaf Lund.' Johanne nods. About thirty, she has a broad-shouldered, muscular build and smooth, blonde hair pulled back in a ponytail, clear blue eyes and a pronounced jaw. She could have passed for Gunnar's daughter if she lost her regional dialect and put on a few more kilos. 'We even used divers to search the harbour for him, but without success.'

'What made you think he'd ended up in the sea?'

'Well,' Johanne says, gazing out of the side window, 'look around you. There aren't many places an old man can wind up out here. Either the sea or the mountains. These old men are fit and fast on their feet, but the mountains here …' Leaving the rest of the sentence to hang in the air, she shakes her head.

'Could he have made his way to the cabin?' I ask.

'To be honest,' Johanne says, 'we didn't even know he had a cabin. Olaf Lund, according to what we were told, had severe dementia, was dependent on nursing care and had lived in the nursing home for eight years. And as I said to your colleague who was here earlier in the week, Kenneth something or other, it's doubtful that Olaf Lund left the centre of Svolvær, unless he took a bus or was picked up by a car driver.'

'So you met Kenny?' I ask, turning to face her.

She nods. 'He told us you were working for a well-known Norwegian writer who was searching for her daughter, and that you'd eventually come upon a lead about something bigger that brought you here to the north of Norway. It sounds exciting,' she laughs. 'We don't get many cases of that nature up here, and it created quite a stir down in the police station. As I understand it, this whole business is a bit …' Johanne leans back in her seat, 'off the record, as we say up here.'

'Did he tell you anything else?'

'He told us about the woman you're working for, this writer. I got the feeling they had something going, if you know what I mean.'

Gunnar glances at me.

'What do you mean?' I ask her.

'Well, it was just something about the way he talked about her, that she was a touch …' Johanne clears her throat before she goes on, 'promiscuous, to use a more polite expression than he did.'

'What expression did *he* use?' I ask.

Johanne hesitates for a second or two. 'Whore,' she answers in the end.

'When was this?'

'Er, Monday, or Tuesday, I think it was. The night before he left. I was actually to have met up with him again the next day, but when I arrived at his hotel, they told me he'd checked out.'

'He's gone AWOL,' I reply.

'What?'

'He went missing after he got back to Oslo.'

'Has something happened to him?'

I shrug.

Johanne leans forward again. 'Could it have something to do with this case you're working on?'

'We must assume so,' I answer.

'Wow,' Johanne exclaims. 'He didn't do much when he was here apart from sit in his hotel room or the bar. I didn't think what he was doing was ...'

'Dangerous?' I ask. 'We're searching for a serial killer who's escaped from a prison camp in Russia, and we believe he's on his way here, to this cabin we're heading for now.'

'Bloody hell.' Johanne sighs. 'Maybe I should have asked the boss for permission to be armed, then?'

'Well,' Gunnar says with a faint smile on his thin lips, 'it's too late now.'

'What about the two of you?' Johanne's face appears in the rear-view mirror. 'Do *you* have permission to carry arms?'

'Nope.' Gunnar shakes his head. 'I'm just here on holiday.'

'And I'm not even in the police any longer,' I add.

We sit for a long time without uttering a word until Johanne suddenly leaps up from the back seat, grabs the backrests and points. 'Stop,' she shouts. It is raining outside and the clouds that have followed us all the way from Svolvær seem to be moving towards the same place as us.

'What is it?' Gunnar asks genially, glancing in the rear-view mirror. 'Do you want to turn back?'

'No,' Johanne replies, with a broad smile. 'We've arrived.'

CHAPTER 98

The stony terrain lies open to the sea and the north wind. Above us a jagged mountain peak divides the landscape in two.

'We go up here,' Johanne informs us, 'and follow the mountainside until we reach the plateau overlooking Sunndal Fjord. From there it's just a matter of starting to search. There are lots of little lakes there, but not so many cabins.'

'How long will it take?' Gunnar asks.

'One hour max to the top.' She gives a lopsided smile. 'As long as you can manage to keep up.'

I look back one last time before we start walking. The sea looks calm, but beneath the surface it pitches and rolls all the same. 'I'd prefer the mountains to the fjord,' I mutter to myself, and start to follow the path leading up from the car park, picking my way between boulders and birch woods.

By the time we've reached the foot of the mountain, I've thrown up three times. I'm chilled to the bone, my vintage shoes are soaked through and my sheepskin jacket seems to have shrunk in the rain. Gunnar and Johanne stand further up on the stones, waiting for me.

'I said you needed hiking gear,' Gunnar tells me crossly when I finally manage to drag myself up beside them. His face is glistening and his complexion has acquired a fresh, reddish tint. As for me, I feel closer to death than I have for a long time. I've lost all feeling in my face and am shivering like a wet dog. 'Here, you moron.' Gunnar wrestles his rucksack off and takes out an all-weather jacket that he tosses in my direction. 'At least get something on you before you freeze to death. It'll get colder further up.'

'It's only my face that's cold,' I insist, reluctantly grabbing the jacket and taking off the sheepskin jacket, sodden by now.

'Don't you have a pill for that too?' he says, looming over me from a boulder above my head with his hands on his hips.

'No,' I mutter, donning the jacket. 'I don't have any pills. You know that.'

'Shall we continue?' Johanne claps her hands and looks longingly up at the mountain.

'Yes,' I mumble, clutching my face in my fingers to reassure myself that it's still there. 'By all means. Let's not breathe too much.'

'Too much fresh air?' Johanne asks when we finally reach the plateau. She stands with her legs abnormally far apart and her hands on her hips, a sort of attempt at manspreading in the middle of the mountain range. The plateau extends only a few hundred metres. The landscape is stony, barren and flat. I lie down under one of the last rocks large enough to shelter beneath, and spread my sheepskin jacket over my all-weather jacket. My body is aching, not only with the craving for pills, but also in painful shudders that shoot through each and every one of my muscles.

'I need to rest,' I groan, pulling my feet closer to my body to protect them from the rain. The wind gusts straight in from the sea, making the moss on the ground bristle. Further inland, freezing fog hovers around a number of large snow-filled gullies that the sun has not yet melted. From time to time the ice-cold rain is replaced by sleet.

'Just let him lie there for a while,' Gunnar sniffs, standing with the map in his hand, surveying the plateau. 'At present Aske is pretty useless in all areas except for one.'

'Oh?' Johanne raises an eyebrow as she gravitates closer to Gunnar. 'What area is that?'

Gunnar grins. 'Tell her, Thorkild. Where would she not like to encounter you? Do you remember?'

'In an interview room,' I groan, struggling to keep my jaws from chattering. 'You wouldn't like to meet me in an interview room.'

'Smart boy,' Gunnar smiles before turning back to the map. 'At least you still remember who you are.'

Gunnar and Johanne glance alternately at the map and their surroundings before it finally seems as if they have agreed on a way forward. 'Come on, now,' Gunnar shouts as he sets off. 'Just a bit further. We'll put on some coffee when we find the cabin.'

We follow the plateau to a viewpoint where I'm again allowed to rest while Gunnar and Johanne consult the map.

'You can see the Laukvik islands out there.' Johanne points to a number of tiny islets and reefs out at the mouth of the fjord. Between the sea and us there is another lower plateau with woods and several mountain lakes of various sizes. We can also see the mouth of a river at the head of the fjord in front of us. 'It's now a nature reserve for wading

383

birds.' She turns her gaze down to the left of us, towards a small lake almost concealed by the birch trees at the back of the mountain. 'The cabin must be down there in the woods somewhere.'

'How do we get down there?' I ask.

'We have to tread carefully.' Johanne runs her fingers over her chin as she peers down the pebble-strewn scree on the mountainside.

'Why would someone want to build a cabin in an area like this?' Gunnar asks.

'Hunting, fishing in the fjord, the birds out on the islands. There are a few farms down there and further north on the peninsula between Nordpollen and the Sunnlands Fjord, but no one wants to live in these places any longer. In the past the boat was your car and the sea your motorway, but now people drive around in the mountains on ATVs.'

'Aha.' Gunnar nods thoughtfully in response to the policewoman's local history lesson.

'No, is that right?' I say grumpily to myself, following them down the slope to the scree. 'Would you believe it, they used boats. Well, I'm from Iceland, you silly goose, how do you think we got there? With paper aeroplanes?' I go on making fun of her as I totter down the stony ground until I suddenly come to an abrupt halt. 'All-terrain vehicles, you said?'

'What?' Johanne stops and turns to face me. 'What did you say?'

'All-terrain vehicles. You said that people drive ATVs here in the mountains.'

'Correct.'

'Are you telling me we could have driven up here too?'

With a smile, she shakes her head. 'It's illegal.'

'But we could have.'

'It's illegal.' She continues walking and addresses herself to Gunnar when he reaches her: 'The cultural landscape in the north of Norway is under attack. Drilling for oil, motor-homes and jet skis – if people don't make a stand soon, our grandchildren will inherit a black sea and beaches covered in the rusty skeletons of motorhomes with EU badges.'

'By the way, have I told you I hate the north of Norway?' I call out as I follow in their wake. 'Intensely and bitterly. One hour up here feels like a year. I hate this place from the depths of my being ...' In the end my outburst goes too far and I trip over a stone, slide and crash into their backs so that we all end up in danger of falling headlong down the stony scree to a certain death. After giving me a juicy mouthful, Gunnar forces me to keep my mouth firmly shut and walk between them for the rest of the way.

We finally emerge from the scree into a wood where the wind isn't quite so fierce and the rain doesn't sting quite so much. Through the branches we spot a dark little lake, which most of all resembles a tarn surrounded by rotten tree stumps and dead rushes. At the edge of the mountain-side we can also make out a small, red-painted cabin with the branches of a blown-down tree protruding from the roof.

CHAPTER 99

All of a sudden we are surrounded by silence, as if the mountain slope behind the cabin keeps the wind at bay. The ground is covered in a patchwork of coarse-grained slush. Spruce trees encircle the area, affording shelter from the wind as it gusts from the sea below.

'This must be it,' Johanne says. We move together towards the entrance. Several branches of the blown-down tree hang in front of the door.

'It doesn't look as if anyone has been here for some time,' I comment, disappointed.

The cabin has two small windows at the front, one on each side of the door. A row of fish tails is pinned up beside the entrance and to the right of the cabin, in between the spruce trees, there is an old outside privy with its door ajar. I catch sight of something just inside the door and break out of our trio to investigate more closely.

'Do you see something?' Gunnar calls out behind me as I struggle to open the door.

'Yes,' I groan, before finally succeeding in tearing the door open. 'A gravestone,' I announce, taking a step back as I stare at the stone block inside.

'A what?' Johanne asks, as she and Gunnar approach.

'*Solveig Borg*,' I read aloud. '*Born 6 July 1939, died 12 August 2016.*'

'*Meet Me in Paradise.*' Gunnar Ore completes the text.

'Why on earth?' Johanne asks before all three of us turn to face the cabin again.

I let go of the toilet door and walk towards the cabin. All at once it seems as if the trees lift their branches in unison to let the wind from the sea blow in. The cold penetrates my clothes and grips my face. 'Time to see what else he has hidden up here.'

The two front windows are closed and have heavy curtains behind them. We skirt round to the rear where there is another window, smaller than the ones at the front, but it is also closed. We walk back round and try the door again, but it's locked. 'Shall we break it open?' Johanne looks at Gunnar. 'Reasonable cause?'

'Wait.' I take a step back to gain a better view of the cabin and the blown-down tree protruding through the roof trusses. 'I've had a brainwave.'

I move towards one of the nearest spruce trees and start to climb up the branches. I've forgotten the cold and my wet clothes. Something else has taken over, a strong sense of disquiet about what awaits us inside; and at the same time an unhealthy dose of curiosity forces me forward. As soon as I reach high enough in the tree, I begin to edge my way forward along a thick branch until, in the end, I prepare to spring and jump across on to the cabin roof.

'The trunk has smashed through the roof,' I shout, peering over the edge at Gunnar and Johanne who are both waiting at the entrance. 'I'll see if I can get in from up here.'

Gunnar turns and casts a sceptical look at the boggy lake and then up at the sky above the mountain ridge. 'It looks as if the fog is closing in,' he says, pulling his zip all the way up to his chin.

I sit astride the tree trunk and press my head between the branches to peer inside. I start to remove some roofing felt in order to squeeze between the roof trusses. A few minutes later, I've created an opening large enough for me to slip in under the cabin roof.

I can smell the strong odour from inside the cabin, a combination of rotten wood, fabric, leftover food and something else, a less distinct smell that I nevertheless recognise from my years as a police officer. A smell you never forget, one that clings like wet ash to your skin and clothes, that becomes ingrained in your spine and lasts for days on end: the smell of death.

I rummage around in the roof insulation, searching for an access hatch to take me down, without finding anything. In the end I put my back to one of the roof trusses and press my feet against the underlay until it gives way. Carefully, I tear off the fibreglass insulation before giving the roof sheeting a couple of quick kicks to loosen it completely so that it topples down to the floor in the cabin below.

'I'm in!' I kneel, thrusting my head down to squint into the room. Below me, all is dark.

I remain suspended like that with my head between the roof tiles until I can hear Gunnar and Johanne's footsteps outside the door. The stale air, combined with the almost sweet stench of whatever has died down there, is more pungent now, almost overwhelming, so strong that for a moment I consider putting some of the fibreglass into my nostrils so that I can breathe. Finally, I decide to jump – I turn around to keep a tight hold on one of the trusses before dropping down.

CHAPTER 100

I hit the floor with a crash. The interior of the cabin is bathed in a deep reddish gloom. I can make out the outline of a fireplace, furniture and various ornaments on the walls.

'Hello?' I hear Johanne shout outside as she hammers on the door. 'Are you OK in there?'

'Yes,' I answer feebly. 'I can hear you.' I can't bring myself to shout, and I'm almost whispering as I haul myself up on to my knees with my eyes trained on the three-seater sofa. Maybe it's just the way the darkness has settled in the room, but it looks as if someone is sitting there, the shape of a head with a halo of short, curly hair, as if I've just tumbled into the living room of someone who prefers to enjoy cabin life in pitch darkness.

'I think there's someone in here,' I hear myself hiss as I crawl nearer.

'What?'

I clear my throat before getting to my feet and moving gingerly to the back of the sofa. 'I said, there's someone in here.'

Once again, loud knocking on the door. 'Open up, Thorkild!' this time it's Gunnar who is shouting.

'Wait,' I say in a low voice. 'I have to take a look.' I stand as if frozen to the spot as I stare at the back of the figure's head. After a while I take a step to one side to come in line with the sofa. 'My God,' I gasp when I finally skirt around it to view her from the front. She looks like a doll, no, not a doll, something else, an Egyptian mummy. Her mouth is open and the skin around the jaw has dried out completely and cracked open in the middle of the chin so that the lower jaw is hanging from the joints on the shrunken chest. She is wearing a dress, though it's impossible to make out the colour, and her hands are folded on her lap. I stand in the silence that vibrates in my ears, and simply stare, as if I'm peering through glass at a picture that captivates me, filling me with disgust and fascination at one and the same time.

I'm startled when the hammering on the door resumes again. I force my eyes away from the corpse on the sofa, stepping carefully back to the door between the seating area and the kitchenette, fumbling my hands along the wall until I can find the lock and open up.

'Be careful,' I say, letting Gunnar and Johanne in. Both screw up their noses before they take a deep breath and step inside the cabin. They stand transfixed in the doorway, staring at the back of the woman's head. While we stand there, the front door slides open, allowing light to penetrate into the room.

'Are there two of them?' Johanne asks when we catch sight of the other corpse slumped in the armchair opposite the body on the sofa. I cross the room and make for the sitting area again. The man in the armchair is wrapped in a blanket, his head falling forward so that only the top of his head is visible. In the centre of the skull I can see an oblong crater surrounded by wispy white tufts of hair.

'I assume that's the missing head teacher,' I say.

'So, you were right,' Gunnar replies, taking a step closer. 'He dug her up too.' The female body on the sofa has lost all of her aura and mystique now that the light has reached her. It is nothing but desiccated skin, cartilage and bone dressed up in human clothing.

'We have to call for help.' Johanne shakes her head, holding her hand in front of her mouth.

'Before he turns up,' I add.

Johanne stares at the corpses with her mouth half open. 'Do you really think the man is on his way here?'

'Yes.' I nod at the two bodies facing us. 'They're waiting here for him, don't you see that?'

'Thorkild,' Gunnar says. 'Don't—'

'No,' I interrupt, pointing at the table between the sofa and the armchair. 'Look, for God's sake.' In the centre of the table, beneath a fine layer of dust, there is a deck of cards. Also, on the table beside the corpse on the sofa, three cards are laid out and another three in front of the man in the armchair and yet another three on the empty chair beside him. 'He's even dealt out a new hand,' I go on. 'For when he gets back.'

'We have to get reinforcements here, ASAP,' Johanne urges.

'Johanne's right,' Gunnar tells me as we stand on the steps outside, all taking deep breaths of fresh air. 'This could get a bit hair-raising if we don't have more uniforms in place.' He fixes his gaze on the sky above where the fog has descended even closer down the hillside.

'If they can even manage to find their way here,' I say. Half of the mountain has disappeared into a grey and white bank of cloud.

'We might be able to requisition a helicopter,' Johanne says.

'A helicopter?' I ask, dismayed. 'Where on earth would a helicopter land? I mean, look around you. In this fog ...'

Gunnar presses his lips tightly together and turns to Johanne. 'Can you find your way back to the road again?'

'Yes,' she answers. 'I can go on down the scree here on the north side and follow the sea until I reach the road.'

'OK. Phone, and then go down and meet them at a suitable spot and make sure you find your way back here, if need be on foot if the weather doesn't change. Thorkild and I will stay here.'

'Sure?' Johanne grabs her mobile, keys in the number and puts the phone to her ear.

With a nod, Gunnar turns to me. 'I've changed my mind, Thorkild,' he says sharply while Johanne is speaking on the phone. 'I've no wish to meet Svein Borg up here in the mountains after all.' He turns to Johanne again. 'Get a patrol out here without delay. And ask them to arrange permission for guns as well. All officers must be armed.'

Chapter 101

'We can't wait out here until they arrive,' Gunnar says once Johanne has disappeared into the spruce trees en route to the north side of the mountain. 'Presuming you don't want to sit and freeze in the toilet.'

'We'll go inside,' I answer with reluctance.

'Did you see an electric cable anywhere, or a generator?' Gunnar asks when we've gone inside and closed the door behind us. He opens the curtains slightly to let in some light.

I shake my head.

'Have a look, see if there are any operational switches here. Although we can't put on any heating until the crime scene technicians arrive.' Gunnar steals a glance at the back of Solveig Borg's head and shudders. 'It's going to be dark soon, and I'm not very keen on spending the rest of the evening here in the pitch dark with you and these two.'

I move to the kitchenette where there is a tabletop cooker of the kind I have myself in my bedsit below the city bridge at home in Stavanger. It has two hot plates and sits on the worktop beside a coffee pot and a few unopened bags of ground coffee. I lean in closer until I find an electric socket. I plug in the cooker and turn on one of the hotplates.

'Did you find anything?' Gunnar approaches, shining a pocket torch on the cooker.

'There does seem to be electricity here, yes,' I reply, pointing to the red light on the cooker.

'Could we make some coffee, at least?' Gunnar plays the light over the interior walls of the cabin.

'If you fetch some water from the bog,' I tell him, handing him the coffee pot.

Gunnar gives a disgruntled groan as he grabs the pot and disappears out of the front door.

I follow him to wait in the doorway and catch sight of two light switches behind the curtains at one of the windows. I flick them on and soon a fluorescent tube above my head starts to flicker.

I stand surveying the room while I await Gunnar's return. There is a sideboard along the wall opposite the seating area, the shelves of which are crammed with ancient LP records and various crossword magazines. I see a record player on top with a single speaker beside it. At the far end of the room there is a small wood stove and behind the kitchenette I spot a door. I open it and find a tiny bedroom with a double bed that fills the whole space and a window with red curtains that are closed. The bed is unmade, as if the last person here just left it like that because he didn't intend to be away for long. The room smells stuffy and dank.

I hear Gunnar at the door and move to the sideboard with the record player while Gunnar puts on the water for coffee.

Hunkering down, I push the unattached plug into a socket at floor level. The speaker emits a faint crackle as the system fires up. I lift the stylus and place it on the first track of the record already on the turntable.

'What the hell are you up to?' Gunnar demands when the speaker begins to crackle noisily. Before long, a light female voice strikes up, followed by some hushed flute and guitar notes.

'It's her,' I tell him, holding the empty record sleeve in my hand, gazing at the childish drawing on the front. 'Solveig Borg. She's the singer.'

We both stand quietly, listening to her voice and the music, until I catch a glimpse of the hair on the woman on the sofa behind me. 'Maybe we shouldn't …' I say, and pick up the stylus.

'No.' Gunnar looks almost embarrassed as he stands there, his head turned away from the dead bodies. 'We shouldn't.'

'I need some fresh air,' I tell him, putting down the record sleeve. Gunnar removes the coffee pot from the hotplate.

'Good idea,' he replies, adding ground coffee to the pot.

Taking the coffee pot and two mugs outside, we sit down on the steps. It is now snowing heavily. The mountain above the cabin is blanketed in grey fog and the area around the bog is shrouded in a fine layer of fresh, wet snow.

'At least the wind's died down,' Gunnar comments.

'What time is it?' I blow on my coffee and let the hot steam waft over my face. I've almost forgotten how cold I am.

'Nearly four o'clock,' Gunnar answers.

'Maybe we should give her a call? Make sure she's got down safely?'

'Too soon,' Gunnar replies.

I let my gaze range over the landscape, taking in the black surface of the bog between the cabin and the foot of the mountain. It's as if the water in the bog has swallowed up the surrounding nuances of colour so that the entire area, the cabin, the mountain, the trees, the snow and the fog, all fade into the infinite darkness. 'All the same,' I say, hugging the coffee mug more tightly. 'It would be good to know.'

Gunnar puts his mug down on the step and takes his mobile from his inside pocket. 'Voicemail,' he finally tells me, hanging up. 'There's probably a poor signal further down the rocky slope. I was surprised that we managed to make a call out earlier.'

'I guess so.' I dart a glance at the snow-covered terrain and the bog. 'For sure.'

'What is it?'

'I'm freezing,' I answer.

'Shall we go back inside?'

'No, I'm not freezing in that way.' I stand up and take a few steps away from the cabin, peering up at the heavy cloud cover above us.

'Oh? Is there another way to be freezing, then?'

'Yes,' I mumble, stamping my feet to keep warm. 'There certainly is another way.'

Gunnar chuckles unconvincingly before falling silent once more. 'Tell me,' he says finally.

'It's difficult to explain,' I begin.

'Try me,' Gunnar says. 'We've more than enough time.'

'It's more as if your body's trying to wake you, to prepare you for something. I had the same feeling that last evening with Frei, before the crash, and the last time I was here in the north of Norway. As if I'm trying to step into something or other with my eyes closed and—'

A faint hum has started up somewhere nearby, a low, metallic noise that doesn't belong out here in the mountains. I stop and try to locate the sound.

'Are you going to answer?'

'What do you mean?' I ask.

'Your mobile,' he says. 'It's ringing. Aren't you going to answer it?'

I open my jacket and feel for my phone. 'It's not mine,' I tell him.

'Are you sure?'

'Yes, for Christ's sake, take a look!' I insist, yanking the phone from my pocket and showing him the black display.

We stare at each other for a few seconds before we both turn to the half-open cabin door.

CHAPTER 102

We rush back into the cabin and stop in the middle of the living room to listen out for the source of the ring tone.

'Where is it?'

'Sounds as if it's coming from the sofa,' I answer.

'Have a look,' Gunnar says, taking a step back.

I lean over the sofa towards Solveig Borg's body. Finally, I catch sight of a black charging lead protruding from between her fingers and stretching along her dress down to the floor and in under the curtain. The monotonous, metallic buzzing sound assails our ears.

'It's him,' Gunnar says. 'Answer it.'

I carefully take hold of the charger lead threaded through her fingers and tug at it without managing to extract it. Instead the corpse moves towards me along with the lead, and tilts to one side, as if the body were made of cardboard. Next I try to hold the lead tightly with one hand while I attempt to open her fingers with the other. The hand is cold and hard, and it's like grabbing a branch out in the woods. I struggle to twist one of my wrists as cautiously as I can while turning away from the desiccated face by my side and coax the lead out with my other hand in an effort to free the mobile phone.

A hollow click sounds when I finally manage to separate the fingers, and the call terminates, leaving the silence to settle around us again. I can see a black Doro mobile phone for seniors lying in the cadaver's lap, covered in a fine layer of dust, dried human tissue and flakes of skin. At last I manage to free the phone and rearrange the hand to the way it had been, and back off quickly with the mobile in my hand.

There are more than forty incoming calls. The first ones are from as far back as last summer, and then there's a break from October until only a few days ago when they resume.

'It's Borg,' I say. 'The last three are from the same mobile number. ET phone home.'

'What are you doing?' Gunnar asks as I'm about to press the call icon.

'Just one ring,' I say, holding up the phone. I let my thumb hover above the green call button and break into a wicked grin. 'Let's see how long he manages to wait before returning the call.'

'He won't buy it.'

'If only you knew,' I go on, 'the strength of the human desire to believe, sometimes. How intense your delusions can be, and how willing you can be to breathe life into them. Frei is dead, but all the same, not a single day goes by that I don't wake in the expectation that we'll soon meet again. Human beings *want* to believe.'

The wind has started to pick up again, and we can hear the trees creaking as it blows through the branches, stretching the outermost tips over the exterior cabin wall.

'OK. Go ahead.'

We both have our eyes fixed on the mobile display. I press the call button. A light immediately comes on in the display to indicate that the mobile is searching for a receiver. Half a second later we hear a long ring tone.

Gunnar sighs with relief when I hang up. 'Christ,' he groans. 'That was nerve-wracking.' He gives a hollow laugh. 'I'd really have liked to see Borg's face when it started ringing!' He laughs again, this time with greater conviction. 'The guy must have—'

All of a sudden he stops and takes two steps back towards the wall as he stares at the mobile phone, which has started to vibrate on the kitchen worktop.

CHAPTER 103

'Don't answer it,' Gunnar tells me. 'I … I've changed my mind. Don't answer.'

'Take it easy,' I say. 'We wanted him to call back. By the way, start walking around in here, don't say anything though, just walk, we need some acoustics, if you know what I mean.'

Gunnar nods.

'And also,' I add, 'turn on the record player.'

'What?' Gunnar looks at me in amazement.

'Turn it on,' I repeat, gesticulating towards the record player. 'Acoustics, Gunnar. Acoustics.' Then I pick up the phone and press the answer button. Out of the corner of my eye, I watch as Gunnar moves slowly towards the record player.

'Mum?'

I hold the mobile up to my ear as I stare at the back of Solveig Borg's head. She resembles a misplaced mannequin doll in the gloom that sucks in the light from the fluorescent tube on the ceiling. The next minute we can hear Solveig Borg's voice issue from the speaker:

'Tired feet cross the bare floor. Restless footsteps to the farthest door. I've wandered for so long, I'm so tired, I want to go home.'

'Mum?' His voice quivers; he sounds tearful, a mixture of imminent euphoria and relief at one and the same time. 'Mum. I've done something terribly wrong.'

Organ, flute and cello music builds up to the refrain: '*Meet me in Paradise, where no tears fall and longing turns to ice …*'

'Mum,' Svein Borg whispers for a third time. 'Please.'

The organ music and Solveig Borg's vocals ebb slowly away and soon only the cello and flute continue the melody, until in the end it fades to silence. Svein Borg is breathing heavily in the background.

Then he rings off.

CHAPTER 104

'Did he say anything?' Gunnar asks me. I stand looking around the cabin, letting my eyes wander over the walls, all the nooks and crannies, as I struggle to analyse my impressions of the mobile conversation with Svein Borg.

'Good God,' I say, with a shudder, and lay the phone down on the kitchen worktop. 'The guy gives me the shivers.'

'How long do you think he spent here with them before he took off?' Gunnar asks. 'There's food here, after all, rubbish, empty tins and newspapers left behind; it suggests he might have—'

'It's not just that,' I reply. 'Have you seen the bed in there? It's a double bed. I think they "lived together" up here.'

'For God's sake,' Gunnar spits out, shaking his head in despair. 'How can you "live together" with the dead body of your own mother?'

'They were together again,' I answer calmly. 'Just as they had always been. There's also a pile of used hypodermics and empty infusion bags of potassium chloride B on the floor. I think he went on caring for her while they lived here, that he dug up her body so that he could keep her here, together with him. In the same way that he went off to find his father, he needs someone to cling to, someone to share the misery of the world with him.'

'Why did he kill them, though, all those innocent people?'

'Maybe he phoned them, in the hope that one of them would pick up and give him the answer he was waiting for?'

'And that is?'

'That his mother really is in paradise, or whether there is in fact such a thing as paradise. I think Borg panicked when his aunt and uncle wanted to send up a bible preacher when his mother became ill to administer the last rites to her and the salvation of Jesus Christ. When he was little, Borg's aunt told him that children like him would never get into heaven. He didn't want his mother to go to heaven either, because then he wouldn't be able to meet her in paradise. Therefore, he killed her with an overdose of potassium chloride B before they were able to save her. Then he applied to have her ashes scattered up here, and when that wasn't successful, he dug her up from her grave anyway and brought her here to assure himself that they would both be together.'

'And the old man in the chair? Olaf Lund? What about him?'

'I think he may be his father.'

'Christ,' Gunnar groans. 'Why did he choose those other victims in particular?'

'Maybe he saw something in them, his own sorrow, and thought he would help them cross over into paradise, just like in his mother's song: *Paradise … where no tears fall and longing turns to ice.*'

Gunnar gives a crooked smile as he studies me with his eyes: 'Did she really sing that? *Where no tears fall and longing turns to ice?*'

'Yes,' I reply. 'We've played that song twice already since we arrived here.'

405

He goes on looking at me, all the while pressing his lips together, not hard, as he usually does, but in a different way, as if he's trying to suppress laughter.

'What is it?' I ask. 'Don't you believe me? Shall I put it on again?'

'Can't you just sing it for me instead?' Gunnar asks in jest.

'Scumbag,' I retaliate.

'Come on, Thorkild. Sing it, for God's sake. This place could do with a lift. The atmosphere's at rock bottom right now.' He gestures to the two seated shadows. 'Look, good grief, people are falling asleep!'

I shake my head in dismay, turning towards the sofa.

'Yes,' I tell him in the end. 'It's pretty dead in here.'

Finally, we both burst out laughing. An all-consuming eruption of laughter that makes my cheek throb as the tears roll down my face. All the anxiety, the disquiet at being here in this open coffin beneath the mountains, the craving for pills and rest, everything finally has an outlet.

We lurch across the room to the door, gasping and roaring with laughter like two drunken teenagers as we squeeze out together through the doorway and run out into the cold evening darkness.

'Oh my God,' Gunnar gasps. He bends over with his hands on his knees, fighting for breath. 'What the hell are we doing here? What?' He stands up straight and turns his gaze up to the skies, almost black now. 'This is madness, Thorkild. We can't stay here any longer; this place, it's not having a good effect on us.'

'I know,' I reply once I have wiped away my tears. Sporadic snowflakes are drifting down from the gloom and settling on the ground with all the others.

'Just imagine, living here with your dead mother.' Breathing heavily, Gunnar stands staring up at the sky above us. 'What would that do to you? How would it mess with your head?'

'For all we know, it was the best month he'd had in a long time,' I reply. 'Borg is a parasite, Gunnar, and he has no intention of letting go of his mother either in this life or the next.'

'I need a break.' His voice is gentler now, the timbre deeper, as if he needs to delve further down into his system to dredge up the words. 'When this is all over.'

'Yes,' I agree, closing my eyes. I look up at the clouds and feel the soft snowflakes touch my cheeks, forehead and lips. I squeeze my eyes shut and try to imagine that the snow-flakes are wet kisses, caresses from a loving ghost.

'At last,' I hear Gunnar say somewhere outside the bubble I've created around me.

'What is it?' I ask without opening my eyes.

'Don't you hear it?'

'What?'

Before he has a chance to respond, I hear it too, a faint rumble from further down the hillside. The noise made by a motorised vehicle firing on all cylinders through the demanding terrain. The next minute, a phone rings. I open my eyes and see Gunnar take out his mobile.

'It's Johanne,' he says, putting the phone to his ear. 'Hi, it's you,' Gunnar answers. 'We'd begun to think you'd got lost. Listen, I thought you didn't use ATVs up here, all that about destroying the cultural landscape?' His smile turns into a speechless frown and his expression darkens as he clamps the phone to his ear and stares out into thin air.

'What is it?' I ask, sotto voce.

'B-but …? So where are you?'

I take a step nearer. 'Gunnar?'

'And how long will that take?' Gunnar darts a worried glance in the direction of the spruce trees down below, where the sound of the vehicle is growing louder by the minute.

'What is it?' I walk across to Gunnar and stand directly in front of him.

'OK. Hurry.' Gunnar rounds off the call. 'Thorkild,' he says hoarsely. 'I think we're about to have a visitor up here …'

Chapter 105

The ATV stops somewhere below the spruce trees, and the engine is turned off. All at once it is quiet outside, and even the wind holds its breath. Gunnar and I remain standing outside the cabin, listening intently.

Gunnar tucks his mobile into his jacket pocket. I see how tense the muscles in his face, shoulders and chest have become. 'Into the cabin,' he says, breaking into a run.

I follow without a word.

'Lock the door,' he orders once we're inside. He shrugs off his jacket and rolls up his shirtsleeves as he stalks towards the kitchenette, then opens the drawers and roots around through them until he finds what he is looking for. 'Use this,' he says, handing me a small filleting knife.

'What about you?'

He replies through gritted teeth, 'I'll manage.'

Then he draws the curtains and switches off the ceiling light. 'There are only two ways in,' he continues while we stand there in the darkness. 'The front door, and the hole in the roof. Anyway, we'll be able to hear him in plenty of time. Remember that, Thorkild. We're the ones with the upper hand here. He should fear us, not the other way around.'

'I understand,' I say without conviction. 'We have the upper hand.'

'You take the door, and I'll guard the hole in the roof. OK?'

I swallow and nod.

'And not a word until he's inside the cabin. Use your knife if you have to. Got it?'

'Yes,' I reply. I stretch out a hand, fumbling my way across to the door, and stand beside it with my back to the wall.

First of all we hear nothing but the wind gusting through the trees outside and the branches scraping against the roofing felt. The chilly mountain air creeps through the hole, making my face and hands as cold as my insides. After a while another sound intrudes, wary steps tramping over the thin layer of snow on the ground outside, heading for the cabin.

The sound gets louder and louder until he sets foot on the decking outside the door. The boards creak faintly under the pressure of the heavy body before the noise stops. It feels as if I can hear his breath through the wall where he is standing right outside, ready to kick down the door and drag me out into the fog, while I stay quiet and force the sense of dread down into my guts.

He stands there for what feels like an eternity. My eyes have at last adjusted to the darkness, allowing me to see the door handle in front of me and the contours of the two seated bodies across the room. I don't want to look there, but my eyes are drawn to them against my will. Sometimes it seems as if they move, turn their heads a little, or are about to give a signal to warn the man outside of what awaits him in here. Then I blink quickly, over and over again, until the illusion is gone, and I try to keep my focus on the door handle.

Gunnar is standing only a few metres away from me, beside the bedroom door, half a metre from the hole in the ceiling. Suddenly I hear a faint sound nearby and see that the front door handle has started to turn. I tighten my grip on the knife and open and close my eyes to acclimatise my sight once again. When the door handle is depressed almost all the way down, it stops and then moves again, this time upwards. I think I hear footsteps retreating slowly, back down from the doorstep to the ground.

I want to approach Gunnar and tell him that Borg was at the door just now, but I'm scared to make a sound and so I don't move. Several minutes tick by until we hear him again. This time by the window immediately in front of the seating area. A dark shadow moves in towards the glass, as if he's pressing his face against the outside of the window-pane in an effort to peer inside.

I see Gunnar crouch down and draw back to the side-board where the record player is, concealing his shadow in case it's possible to see through the thick curtains.

Once again it sounds as if the wind outside has picked up. The cold air inside the cabin suddenly becomes even more bitter, and we can hear the sleet or rain tapping on the roof above us. The shadow at the window has gone, no footsteps, nothing apart from the two of us, the wind and weather. Nevertheless, I know he's there, somewhere directly outside. Either he knows we're here, or else he's uncertain, cautious. The very fact that he hasn't come barging in through the door wielding an axe or a scythe, but is investigating, calculating, tells me that Borg is far more painstaking than I had first thought.

411

I am startled by a movement and suddenly notice that Gunnar is squatting on the floor by my side. His face is hardly visible in the darkness, and only his eyes reflect any light.

'Where is he?' Gunnar whispers. 'I can't hear him any longer.'

'Me neither.'

'Could he have gone away?'

'Wouldn't we hear the engine fire up?'

'I suppose so.' Gunnar turns and creeps carefully across the floor, back to his original post.

He has just reached the other side of the room and is about to stand up when I catch sight of a movement immediately beside him. At first I think it is Borg making his way through the hole in the roof until I see the bedroom door slowly opening.

'Gunnar!' I call out before the door suddenly opens with a bang and hits him full force.

His head hits the wall with a hard thud before his body crashes to the floor, where he lies motionless. The next minute a huge figure towers in the doorway. Hesitating for only a moment, he then rushes into the room, heading straight for me. I try to say something, but don't get a chance before Svein Borg grabs hold of my neck and hoists me up against the wall. The next second his skull pounds into my face. At once I feel my features crumple and go numb just as blood fills my mouth and throat. Then Borg's head pulverises my face again. This time I feel nothing – all I see is a bright light that sears my eyes before I black out.

CHAPTER 106

I awake slowly, not suddenly with a start, but gradually, via tiny muscle contractions throughout my body, each one becoming increasingly intense, until finally they force me out of my comatose condition back to the cold, the dark and the rank smell of death and decay.

My face is turned to the floor. I breathe through my mouth, stagnant gulps down into my lungs. My nose feels blocked, or knocked out of position, giving me a retching sensation every time I try to inhale air through my nostrils.

I remain quiet on the floor as I wait. From time to time I attempt to move my fingers, to check whether I can wriggle my toes and turn my neck. Everything aches, and something tells me this is a good sign. In the end I open my eyes and look around. It is brighter inside the cabin now – the door is wide open. Outside, it is snowing, and the fog has crept all the way down to ground level. It hangs like a heavy curtain, as if the sky and earth have been pressed together since the last time I looked.

All is silent around me. I remember at once what happened before I was knocked out, and I push my head up to look for Gunnar. He's not here. I force my head further up, and catch sight of the filleting knife on the floor in front of me. I grit my teeth and try to haul myself forward to reach it but all of a sudden I hear footsteps outside.

I drop down to the floor again and hold my breath. Borg stops and stamps his feet to clear them of snow before entering the cabin to stand right beside where I am, stretched out on the floor. I hear his heavy breath, feel his close proximity, his shadow looming over me.

He stands there for a long time without a sound except for his heavy breathing. All at once I feel something wet and hard on the back of my head as my skull is pressed down and to one side. I blink furiously. Borg has put one foot on the back of my head and is pushing it down, slowly, but continually exerting more and more pressure.

My teeth are throbbing and it feels as if my cheek is going to explode as Borg gradually increases the pressure on the back of my head. All the same I don't let out a single sound. Instead I allow the pain to take control of my body, to fill every single chamber. It hurts so much and it feels as if my teeth are going to come loose and drop into my jawbone. My cheek stings, making me believe my whole cranium will explode at any minute. I know I won't be able to hold out much longer: my whole body is crying out to be released from this vice-like grip.

Just as I am about to scream with pain, Borg lets go and takes his foot away from my head. He stands over me for a long time, still without a sound. Then at last he turns on his heel and moves away. I hear him stop some distance off and then the speaker crackles on the record player and Solveig Borg's voice fills the room.

I lie motionless on the floor, battling to get my pulse rate down. Then I start to move my fingers, toes and neck once again to make sure everything is still in good working order.

I hear Borg shuffle the cards on the table and then deal them out. When another cold blast rushes in through the open door, I decide to open my eyes. The knife is gone, and Borg is sitting on the chair between the two corpses. He leans forward to the table, his elbows on his thighs, and holds a few cards up in front of his face. It looks as if he is deep in thought until at last he plays one card and picks up another.

'Your turn, Mum,' Svein Borg says impassively, before leaning across the table towards his mother's corpse and picking up her cards.

I lift one hand to my cheek, all the while keeping my eyes trained on the seating area. I run my fingertips gingerly over my face to wipe the blood from my eyes.

I raise my other hand too and place it palm down beside my face. I can see Borg put down another card and then lean back into his chair.

When the song's refrain strikes up, I press both palms forcefully down on the floor and haul my body carefully to one side, towards the open door, and then I stop and lie down quietly again.

'You have to pick up, Olaf,' I hear Borg mutter. He leans across the table again and gathers the cards into the middle before throwing them down in front of the shrunken body on his right-hand side. While he sits like that, I perform another rotation so that I'm now lying with my head facing almost directly towards the door.

When Borg again gets up to deal the cards for his mother, I drag myself closer to the exit with an extended arm movement. If he were to turn to the side now, he'd notice that I've moved.

I can no longer see him, the sofa back is in the way, but nevertheless I wait until the next song has begun. As soon as the melody increases in volume, I haul myself over the final stretch to the threshold. There, I rise to my knees, lift my head into the refreshing cold air outside and start to move on all fours, through the doorway and out into the snow.

CHAPTER 107

Outside, everything is shades of grey. Even the trees and mountains have been swallowed up by the fog. I see Borg's footprints in the snow at the bottom of the steps. Beside these tracks, a furrow on the ground leads away from the cabin.

As soon as I'm past the last window, I get to my feet, but have to crouch down again when the pain in my face makes me feel faint. I force my eyes open and clench my teeth harder, stagger up again and follow the tracks in the freshly fallen snow.

Eventually, as I put some distance between myself and the cabin, I catch sight of something far out in the bog that makes me gasp and gain momentum.

Gunnar is standing almost in the middle of the bog, but only his head and half of his chest are above water. It looks as if something below the surface is trying to drag him down into the depths, because the muscles in his face and neck are bulging and his skin is a patchwork of red and white from the cold.

'Help me,' he gasps in terror as soon as he spots me. His eyes are black and his breath is creating a frosty fog when he speaks. 'I can't hold out any more.'

'What's keeping you stuck?' I tear off my outdoor clothes and wade out into the ice-cold water that burns my skin.

'I d-don't know,' he groans, his teeth chattering, 'I came to when I landed in the water. Hurry up.' Gunnar stares into the fog between the tarn and the cabin. 'For God's sake, hurry.'

My body has already started shaking from the cold, and my teeth are knocking together. I take a deep breath and grab him with both hands – his body feels chilled, his skin is gooseflesh, as if I'm stretching out to grasp of a block of ice, while I struggle to feel my way forward beneath the water in order to locate his hands. They're tied together behind his back and I can feel something tugging on the rope at the other end.

'How in hell are you managing to stay upright?' I ask as I fumble with the knot.

'I can't do it,' Gunnar sobs, 'untie me, for God's sake.'

'It's too tight, I …' Once again I take a deep breath before diving below the water, catching hold of the rope and starting to follow it. After a couple of metres I reach a boulder beneath the water, or else it's bedrock I'm stand-ing on. The rope disappears over the edge, where the water is completely black and impenetrable. I crouch down, still holding the rope, dragging myself forward to the edge, and at the bottom I hit against something that feels like a metal frame. I try to lug this over the edge but soon give up. It's far too heavy.

'It's hanging beyond the edge,' I tell him when I break the surface. 'I'll never manage to pull it back up again.'

'Fuck,' Gunnar snarls, thrusting his body forward towards the land. 'I can't take it any more, I—'

'I'll try to untie the knot on the frame,' I tell him, holding the rope. 'Give me some slack when you feel me tug on it, just a little.'

'I'm going to drown,' he gasps.

'No, you're bloody not,' I answer, plunging in again. I find the rope, drag it with me down to the knot and start to work on it. My lungs feel as if they're going to explode as I'm doing so, my face is numb with the cold, but in the end I succeed in untying the first knot. Then I set about the next one and soon it is loose. I feel the rope finally let go and the frame plummets down into the murky depths. I swim back to Gunnar, grab him by the arm and start to drag him towards dry land, where we both collapse on to the snow.

I force myself up again. Only now do I realise that Gunnar is stark naked, and his clothes are floating among the reeds some distance away. I untie the rest of the rope before hauling him up into a sitting position and dressing him in my outdoor gear. Once that's done, I grab one arm and hoist him up and then begin to tow him towards the trees below.

As soon as we're under the canopy of trees, I stop to stretch Gunnar out on the ground. There's no snow here and the earth is blanketed in spruce needles and frozen sheep droppings. I squint out at the tarn and the cabin, both only just visible through the fog. All of a sudden I see a towering figure slip out through the mist heading straight for the water.

CHAPTER 108

Svein Borg is no more than thirty metres away. He stops at the water's edge and hunkers down as he stares into the water before him, as if he's struggling to see something beneath the surface. Gunnar is lying face down on terra firma, his breathing irregular, rasping, as if his system is still in shock after the time spent in the freezing water. I place my hand carefully over his mouth when his breathing grows too loud.

Suddenly Borg gets to his feet again. He turns, his gaze still focused on the ground.

'Christ,' I groan. 'The snow. He's following our tracks.' Next minute, Svein Borg looks up from the ground at last and fixes his eye on the spot where we are sheltering.

I grab hold of Gunnar and start to drag him further into the woods. The terrain slopes downwards, making it easier to bring him with me.

We continue down the slope towards a grey clearing ahead of us where the fog is dense. Behind us I can hear branches rustling. I am about to turn around when I slip on the steep terrain. Gunnar lets out a groan as his body hits the earth, falling heavily on his side and starting to roll. I cling to him as we tumble together down the slope. In the end we stop beside a heavy boulder covered in moss and snow.

I sit Gunnar up with his back to the stone. We've left the woods behind and the wind is blasting down the mountainside somewhere beyond the sea of fog. A broad gully of stones stretches out ahead of me.

I don't have the strength to drag Gunnar with me on to the scree, and the route back up again is no alternative. Instead I start to walk away from the boulder, away from Gunnar, in the direction of the piles of stones where the fog is thickest.

'Your father wasn't a Russian, was he?' I shout. 'It was Olaf who was your father, wasn't it?'

'So he said.' Svein Borg's voice sounds ghostly as it echoes from the woods somewhere above me. 'The day he came up to the cabin. I met him on the way and picked him up. He thought I was still a kid and started telling me about the time we lived here, when I was small. He said we'd had to keep it secret because he already had a wife.'

'I've spoken to your aunt and uncle,' I tell him, continuing to trudge through the stones, further away from Gunnar. 'They don't like you much.'

'Have you forgotten your friend?' Borg asks. I can hear that he's descended the slope, the sound of his voice is louder now. He's getting close.

'No. He's here, with me,' I reply, snaking my way across the stones to where I can hear the wind is strongest, towards the foot of the mountain. 'We're playing cards. I've just dealt out another round. Come and join us, pal.'

'I don't think he has much time left,' Svein Borg says. 'Maybe we should have called a doctor out here?'

'They're on their way,' I answer. 'With a helicopter and the full works.'

'In this weather?' He laughs. 'No, I doubt that.'

'Well, then, there's just the three of us.'

'Are you really not thinking of coming to his rescue?' Borg calls out, from the same spot as last time.

'No, I don't even like the guy. He used to be my boss.'

'Ha ha. Shall we count together, then? One, two, three and then I'll smash his skull with a stone?'

The game is up. He's not going to follow me down into the scree. 'No,' I finally respond from the place where I'm standing, between two boulders, listening intently. 'I'm coming.'

'Smart lad.'

'They're going to return her to the churchyard where she belongs,' I say, struggling to scramble back to where I'd set out from. 'A straight road to the Promised Land amidst the clouds. No one is going to remember her for anything other than the corpse her crazy son dug up from her final resting place, a shrivelled mummy found in a cabin in the mountains. Her songs, her voice, all of that will be forgotten.'

'They won't do that.'

'They will. I know them.'

'They can't.'

I come closer. Soon we are face to face again. I doubt whether my head will withstand another blow.

'They don't care.'

Nestled in the swirling fog, the boulder beside which I left Gunnar has come into view. 'Just go,' I say. 'Let my friend sleep, he needs the rest. Go. I won't follow you.'

'You saw her, you shouldn't have—'

'I'm not going to say anything,' I assure him and stop, looking for some sign of movement in the dense fog. 'Leave,' I shout at the top of my voice. 'Get away, save her before it's too late.'

No response. I stand there waiting, listening intently for several minutes before finally crawling the last few metres across.

Gunnar is still sitting where I left him. His body is almost white with the snow, and his skin is icy cold. He is motionless, beside the boulder, with his face turned down. 'Gunnar, can you hear me?'

He doesn't answer. I brush the snow from his wrist and press two fingers on his artery. His skin is so cold that I can't feel anything at all. I turn him over on to his side and put my ear to his mouth. A faint, moist exhalation strikes my cheek. I press my head to his chest and feel my own warmth increase when I hear his heart beat – slowly, softly, but it is beating.

I skirt around the boulder and explore the other side. 'Svein!' I shout hoarsely, but the only answer comes from the wind swirling down the mountainside. I start to pull some branches from the nearby spruce trees, as well as long strips of moss from the boulder, and carry them back to tuck around Gunnar's body. 'We'll have to wait here,' I tell him, before clasping his hand and squeezing it hard in mine. 'Just hold on until I've had some rest. We'll move on as soon as this fog lifts. OK?'

Gunnar moves his head a fraction, as if he's trying to say something, but then it drops to one side again. The next minute I hear a faint crack from the dry moss at the back of the boulder. When I stand up again, I see Svein Borg emerge from the fog to stand immediately in front of me.

Chapter 109

'So there you are,' Borg says, sounding pleased, when he catches sight of us. It looks as if he has grown a whole head taller since our last encounter.

'You couldn't just leave, then,' I sigh, shaking my head.

'No.'

'OK.' I pat Gunnar on the shoulder and straighten him up against the rock. 'I have to admit,' I begin, 'that I was wrong about one thing.' I brush moss, snow and dry grass off my wet clothes.

'What?' Svein Borg is standing only a few steps away from me with his hands hanging heavily at his sides.

'I said you were a wimp, not necessarily physically, but in the way you kill, your MO. You've certainly grown. In every sense.'

'Well,' the corners of his mouth stretch up slightly. 'You need to adapt in a Russian work camp. They think they can push Norwegians around in there.'

'I have to warn you. I'm pretty good at fighting.'

Svein Borg takes a step closer. 'You shouldn't have come here.'

'We took photos, too,' I tell him when he is about to take another step forward.

'What?' He stops, his eyes black, glinting in the damp fog. 'What did you say you did?'

'Pictures. For the investigation. For the newspapers. The whole shebang. After all, you're a serial killer, Svein. A lunatic with a head full of cancerous tumours who attacks and kills innocent people. We don't have many of them in this country. Who knows, maybe Milla will write a book about you after you're dead? No, not about you, but about me. The hero who caught Norway's most dangerous man in the mountains of Lofoten and returned his poor mother to Christian ground where she belongs. *The Doors to Paradise*, that could be the title – what do you think?'

Svein Borg's breathing has become more laboured now and his entire body is heaving as he stands there gulping down air, mustering strength for the imminent onslaught. Just as he takes the last step forward to smash my skull with his fists, but before he completes the move, I kick out with all my might at the knee bearing his weight.

A horrible crack splits the air when the blow strikes. Svein reaches out to grab me, with a look as black as tar, but I slip out of his range. Struggling to regain his balance, he wobbles as the foot of the leg I kicked teeters as if the knee muscles have been torn loose. I brace myself against the boulder and kick out again at the same target. This time the strike is emphatic, and his entire knee buckles and shifts to one side while Svein swings out with his arms, as if trying to gain a hold on the fog that envelops us.

'You shouldn't have come here,' I say before delivering a third kick, this time aiming for his stomach. Svein grunts as I land the blow. I back away towards the boulder once more to gain some traction and launch myself at him full force so that he falls back, down on to the stony ground, waving his arms impotently. He turns halfway around, trying to use his damaged leg to check his momentum, but it bends backwards instead, causing his speed to increase, and he shouts something inaudible as he disappears into the fog. When I hear his body hit the ground in the distance, I retreat to the boulder and lean heavily against it.

I stand like this, gasping for breath, aware of pain coursing through my body and adrenalin surging. I daren't leave the boulder and Gunnar. I simply stand there, listening and panting, listening and waiting.

Eventually I regain physical control. I'm breathing more easily, even though I daren't sit down or move from this spot. Everything has gone quiet. Only the soughing of the wind and Gunnar's jagged breathing at my feet disturbs the silence. Time passes, the wind picks up, and gusts hack through the dense fog, producing pockets of clear space in all the greyness, so that fragments of the landscape come into view. Soon I can also make out the sea and the highest mountain peaks on the other side. The fog is lifting.

I wait until the mist has become so sparse that I can see clearly in all directions. I move a couple of tentative paces forward to the stony scree in front of me. I stop after each step, listening and looking around. Then another step, until I reach the spot where I think Svein Borg must have landed. I clamber on to the largest boulder and peer over the edge.

There is no one to be seen.

I inch forward, peering behind every rock and precipice, but see no one. I creep further down, following a course several metres to either side, but still nothing.

Svein Borg is gone.

I stand there, in the midst of the rocky scree until finally I turn around, clambering back up to Gunnar and sit down by his side. 'Just a bit longer, Gunnar,' I whisper. 'They'll be here soon.'

CHAPTER 110

A noise startles me and I see that Gunnar has opened his eyes at last. 'Did you hear that?' I ask when our eyes meet.

Gunnar nods almost imperceptibly and moves his lower jaw slowly in a semicircle, raising his hand and running his fingers gingerly over his face. He stops at the dent in his forehead. 'Where are we?' he asks hoarsely, pressing the wound warily.

'Just below Svein Borg's cabin,' I answer, raising my head above the boulder to survey the landscape.

'And Borg?'

'No idea.'

'What actually happened?'

'Borg came out of the bedroom and slammed the door in your face. Then he rammed my face with his head.'

'How did we get away?'

'We ran.' I stand up straight when I hear the same noise again. The sound is coming from the woods above us. When I look out over the boulder, I catch a glimpse of three figures walking in through the trees. 'Here!' I shout, raising my hand to wave at them. As I wave, I accidentally touch my face. My nose feels like a wonky potato, and the skin beneath my eyes is rough and sticky. I use my tongue to ascertain that I've broken one of my front teeth.

A female voice yells something to the others, and all three set off towards us.

'At last,' I groan, holding my head in my hands.

'You look like shit,' Gunnar tells me when I drop down beside him and I use my fingers to make a cautious examination of my face. Gunnar shifts position just as I hear footsteps approaching.

It's still grey all around us, but the fog is higher now, enabling me to follow the scree all the way down to the fjord where I can see the waves turning white further out. The snow has gone, and somewhere behind the dissipating mist, sunlight has forced its way through to light up the stones on the slope beside us, making them glint and gleam.

'My God,' a nearby familiar voice exclaims. It's Johanne, wearing a red anorak and a sheepskin hat. She looks like one of these skiers you used to see in ancient Norwegian black and white films. 'You're alive!' She rushes forward and crouches down in front of us.

'Where's Borg?' I ask, as she and a policeman help me to stand up.

'He must have tried to get down off the mountain in the fog and taken a wrong turning. He and his ATV are stranded on the mountainside. It'll take four men to carry them down to the road. He's alive, but only just.'

'Them?' Gunnar asks. He had managed to struggle up by himself.

'It looks as if he has …' Johanne hesitates for a moment before continuing, 'his mother with him in the vehicle.'

Gunnar groans as he extends his arms and stands up straight. He rolls his neck, even though the movement causes him to grit his teeth. Then he scans his surroundings, first the men around us, then me, and finally his chest and legs.

'Where are my shoes?' he asks, gazing alternately at me and his own bare feet. 'And why aren't you wearing any warm clothing?'

'What happens in the mountains, pal,' I murmur as I gingerly press my tender, squashed nose again, 'stays in the mountains.'

'Oh, shut up.' He leans back against the boulder and turns his head up to the mountain ridge above us where the fog still wreathes the highest peaks.

CHAPTER 111

'The CT images show that you have a nasal fracture.'

'A what?' When I breathe, it sounds as if someone has filled my nose with paper or raisins.

'It's broken,' the ear, nose and throat specialist tells me, lifting a pocket mirror up to my face.

My nose is swollen, lopsided and blue. The blue tint also forms two semicircles beneath my eyes. The added colour and transformation of my features bring to mind a cave dweller suffering from rabies.

'Take it away,' I say, turning away from the mirror.

'We're going to have to perform a so-called septorhino-plasty, a surgical procedure to repair the nasal septum. We don't do that here. Anyway, you have to wait up to ten days until the swelling has gone down before you can be operated on. In the meantime, we'll put a splint on the bridge of your nose and bandage it with surgical gauze. It's important that you stay as quiet as possible during the next few days and take great care to make sure the injury is not exacerbated. If it starts bleeding, sit down and lean forward, breathing through your mouth to avoid the blood draining through your throat. I would also recommend that you visit a dentist as soon as possible to take care of that broken front tooth.'

'My whole face is sore,' I tell her.

'You'll be given a prescription for Paracet when you're discharged from here,' the doctor says before putting down the mirror and returning behind her desk. 'So I'll put on the splint right away. You'll be able to have the operation in Tromsø, if you live in this area. You'll be sent an appointment in the course—'

'Not Tromsø,' I reply. 'Stavanger. I'll be travelling back as soon as my friend is ready.'

The doctor nods as she writes something on her computer. 'That's fine. As soon as I've applied the splint, you'll be ready to leave. However, I'd like to draw your attention to the fact that if you fly in the next few days, you might experience an increase in the pain and possibly bleeding during certain parts of the flight, it can be—'

'I'll just have to put up with that – I'm not staying up here any longer than I have to.'

'It'll be fine, I'm sure.' She writes out the prescription and signs with a flourish. 'Then I'll go and find a splint for you and something to bandage it up. If you'll just wait here …' She stands up and leaves the room. While she is gone, I snatch the pocket mirror and hold it up to my face again.

'Fucking hell,' I groan, shuddering at the sight that confronts me. I quickly put the mirror back down on the desk. Gunnar is right – I look like shit.

'Ha ha ha!' Gunnar laughs and coughs in turn when I visit his room in the hospital in Svolvær, where he is under observation because of suspected concussion. 'What the hell is that?' he gasps, heaving himself up in his hospital bed.

'A splint,' I answer crossly as I sit down on the bedside chair. 'When are you getting out?'

'Today, as long as they don't find anything loose between my ears,' Gunnar replies. He lifts his hands from the quilt and holds them in front of his face, tenses and closes them as he studies his fingers and knuckles intently. 'Johanne popped in while you were downstairs getting your face plastered.'

'What did she say?'

'Borg is being transferred to Tromsø by helicopter later today. He's broken his spine, apparently, and damaged his knee.'

'And?'

'She said it was OK. We'll be allowed to speak to him first.'

'When?'

'She'll come and collect us.'

'So, we just have to sit here and wait?'

'Correct.' Gunnar sends me another look and bursts into peals of laughter again. 'Have you seen yourself in the mirror?'

'Yes.'

'And?' He goes on laughing.

I lean back in the chair and close my eyes. The next minute, Johanne and a colleague appear in the doorway dressed in full police uniform, their service weapons holstered at their hips.

'He's ready,' Johanne announces. 'Are you?'

I open my eyes and haul myself out of the chair. 'Yes,' I say, 'let's just get this over and done with.'

Gunnar is about to pull back the quilt, but Johanne gestures to indicate that this is not necessary. 'Sorry, pal,' she tells him. 'You've not been cleared for discharge by the doctors as yet.'

'What the ...' Gunnar says, struggling to get up. He almost succeeds but then loses his balance and flops back on to the bed, toppling on to his side. 'Fuck!' he roars with his head turned into the quilt. 'Fuck, fuck, f—'

'I'll take care of it,' I say, moving across to help him up. 'Relax, I'll be back as soon as we're done.'

Gunnar slaps my hand away and raises himself up in the bed without looking at me. Then he draws the quilt all the way up to his face and shuts his eyes. I turn to Johanne and the other officer, glance at Gunnar, and follow them along the corridor to the lift that will take us to the ward where Svein Borg awaits.

CHAPTER 112

Svein Borg is lying in a bed in the middle of a room, surrounded by beeping apparatus and cables. His whole body is encased in plaster and his face is turned up to the fluorescent light tubes on the ceiling. A police officer is guarding the door. He too has a holstered weapon and is in full uniform. With a nod to Johanne, he lets all three of us enter.

'Where's my mother?' Svein Borg asks when I approach the bed.

'In the mortuary,' I reply, dragging a chair across while Johanne and the two officers remain standing at the door, keeping their eyes fixed on us. 'They're going to send her back to the churchyard you dug her up from, I expect.'

'She hated that place. She got scared, towards the end, about what was going to happen.'

'What did you really intend to do with her up there? Burn her body and scatter the ashes?'

'In the end, yes,' Borg answers when we finally make eye contact. 'Did the other guy survive?' he asks. 'Your friend?'

'Yes.'

Svein Borg licks his lips as he stares up at the lights again. 'I should have killed you both inside the cabin,' he says.

'I guess so,' I reply.

'You had no business being up there. That place was just for us.'

'You and your mother and father?'

'Was he really my father?'

I shrug. 'What do you think?'

'I shattered his skull with the back of an axe.'

'Fathers and sons,' I comment.

'She shouldn't have lied to me, she should have told me the truth.'

'Mothers and sons.'

Svein Borg lies there without saying anything further. His gaze dances over the fluorescent tubes on the ceiling while his tongue protrudes between his lips. He is still massive, even in this wretched condition. 'They say I'm paralysed from the middle of my back down,' he tells me. 'But I think they're lying. I can't feel anything below my neck.'

His eyes blink rapidly when I get up from the chair again. I lean over him so that our eyes meet. 'Robert Riverholt,' I say. 'His ex-wife, Milla's daughter Olivia, her friend Siv and my ex-wife Ann-Mari. Kenneth Abrahamsen. You don't know who any of them are, do you?'

He looks at me for a long time, not closely, as he had when we met him in the work camp in Arkhangelsk, not dark and determined, as he was inside the cabin and outside in the fog on the mountainside. His eyes are more like the glass discs you paint irises and pupils on and insert into a doll's head. 'No,' he finally answers.

'You didn't know that Riverholt and Milla had started looking at old missing person cases before we came to see you in Russia and told you about it?'

'No.'

'You don't even know who my ex-wife is, or why I've acquired a new, elegant scar running up the inside of my forearm?'

'No.'

'You didn't plan your murders, choose the victims in advance, follow people, study them and get to know them before you killed them, did you?'

'I can tell you about them, if you want.'

'Another day.' I move away from his face and those damaged eyes and sit down on the chair again. I remain sitting there, deep in thought, stroking my fingers carefully over the gauze that holds the splint in place on the bridge of my nose.

'I died,' Borg begins speaking when I signal that I'm ready to leave, 'while I lay on the operating table having my brain tumour removed. In the middle of the operation I woke up and had the amazing sensation of floating. I still took in what was happening around me and watched the surgeons working. There was no white light, like my aunt had told me, no dead forefathers standing there waiting for me, just a red fire pressing against the windows of the operating theatre. I remember I called out, and I got angry because no one would answer or help me.' He looks at me. 'I told Mum when I woke up again. That I had seen the flames. Mum said it was only a dream, but I knew. And when I started to feel the swelling start to grow inside my head again, I knew that the time would soon be up.'

'Did you kill her?'

'Mum was afraid of dying.'

'And the others?'

'They were scared. I helped them. Helped them with the worst part.' His voice drops and his eyes follow mine like two magnets. 'You know too, don't you?'

'Know what?'

'That this life is not for you. I see it in your eyes, your yearning for something else. I would have helped you, too,' he says when I give no sign of answering him. 'Even after what you did to my mother. Even you.' He blinks, and it looks as if his eyes are shrouded in a smooth membrane. 'Do you think he has seen everything I've done for him, for them, and will let me in?'

'He?'

'God. Do you think he can really see everything, even what's hidden in your heart, that he understands?'

Svein Borg tries to twist his head round so that he can still see me when I rise from the chair and stand beside his bed, beyond his peripheral vision. 'No,' I tell him in the end. Then I turn on my heel and leave.

CHAPTER 113

Gunnar is perched on the edge of his bed, getting dressed, when I return to his room.

'What did he say?'

'He'll talk,' I reply, sitting down on the chair. 'I decided to let him wait for the proper interviews with the real police officers. All the same, I've established a strong enough relationship with him in case we need to speak to him another time.'

'Fine.' Gunnar pulls a face when he has to reach his arm back to put on his shirt. 'What now?'

I look at him and smile. The manoeuvre makes my whole face throb. 'The other case. Now that we finally know the extent of the Borg case, it's time to turn back to what set this whole thing in motion. Back to the beginning.'

'And what *is* the beginning?' Gunnar throws off the quilt and leans forward to a nearby chair, grabbing the trousers draped there, and puts them on. When he has done so, he tucks in his shirt, smoothing the front, back and sides with the palms of his hands before tightening his belt.

'When I spoke to Dr Ohlenborg,' I begin, while Gunnar crouches down cautiously to search for his shoes, 'he gave me his interpretation of Svein Borg and his project, and we assumed that Borg had worked alongside whoever killed Robert and attacked me. That they had a common interest in cooperating. But we were wrong, we fell into the same trap that Robert did, we began to widen the net, and that was how we came on to the trail of Svein Borg. Instead, we should have tightened the net and taken a closer look at what we had, what we already knew.'

'And that is?' Gunnar asks, once he's finally found his shoes. He sits up and puts them on.

'That Siv and Olivia got into a car with someone they knew, or at least thought they knew. That Robert was killed while he was searching for Milla's daughter. Dr Ohlenborg told me that the person we were looking for does what he does exclusively for self-preservation. He doesn't want anyone to know what he has done. Dr Ohlenborg also said that the killing of Robert and Camilla wasn't his first murder, that he must have begun elsewhere, when something went wrong, and that he'd had the opportunity to reflect on it. I asked Iver to get me an overview of the traffic on a mobile number and an email account while we've been up here. Now that I have that, there's someone I need to talk to ASAP.'

'Why?' Gunnar crosses to the wash basin to stand in front of the mirror.

'I made a major error when Olivia phoned,' I go on as he examines his face. 'I told the whole gang about the conversation. I don't think the person we're looking for knew that Olivia was still alive until she called me. And he's going to want to change that.'

At last Gunnar turns away from the mirror to face me again. 'How is that possible? How couldn't he have been aware of that?'

'That's what I have to ask the relevant party when we meet.'

'I see.' As he takes a deep breath, his shirt hugs his shoulders and chest. Then he blows out again and balls his fists. 'Where are we going, then? Who is it we need to talk to?'

'Not we, I. You're going home and waiting there till I phone. You have to be ready.'

'And you?'

'I'm going back to where it all began.'

Chapter 114

I wake with a violent jerk, as if a switch is flicked on all of a sudden. When I open my eyes, I am looking straight into Siv's face. Her mouth is half open and her blonde hair cascades over her lips, without moving. It's so hard to breathe, my throat and neck are throbbing, and the air feels like sand as it passes through my bronchial tubes.

I swallow more air and stretch out my hand to her face, searching for the same switch on her that had just activated me. 'Siv,' I whisper, 'Siv, please. You must wake up.'

I continue caressing her face with my fingertips until a nearby noise makes me stop and turn to ice again. I don't move, just lie there focusing on Siv's eyes while he continues to dig, on the vague glow in there that still resists the darkness.

Behind her I hear the sea, and I can just make out the boathouse and the sun between the trees. I remain lying there like this, imprisoned in my own body, until the turns of the shovel stop and the air is filled with the smell of cold, wet earth.

He doesn't even look at me when he moves across and squats down beside Siv's legs. Her body twitches as he starts to pull, until her face slides away from mine. I go on just lying there, staring vacantly through the trees towards the sea and the rocks as the wind tugs at the branches above us. I don't move as much as a muscle, not even when he has finished with Siv and comes back for me. I let his hard hands grab my shoulders and throw me down into the grave with Siv, without uttering a sound. I press my face against Siv's chest as the soil begins to rain down on us.

CHAPTER 115

Karin waits for me outside André's door after we've had a chat in her office. I've asked for permission to be alone this time too, and she reluctantly agreed to let me talk to him without either Kenny's or Iver's blessing when I explained what this was about.

'Hi, André,' I greet him after knocking on his door and opening it.

André is sitting at his desk like last time. He gives me a wary look before returning to his school books. 'Hi,' he mumbles.

'Do you remember me?' I cross to his bed and perch on the edge, behind his back.

'What happened to your nose?' André asks.

I run my fingers over the splint on my nose. 'I ended up face to face with a serial killer,' I answer. 'He didn't like it and decided to add some decorations to my mug.'

'A serial killer?' Finally, he turns around. 'What did he look like?'

'Big as a bear, angry as a bull. But I have a few tricks up my sleeve, too.'

'What—'

'I'm good at playing dead. And at delivering a kick in the balls.'

'Did you kick him in …'

I nod my head. 'Right in the crown jewels.'

'Why did he kill?'

'He thought he was helping them, and himself.'

'Was he the one who—'

'No, André. Now we've caught one of them. But there's another one. That's why I'm here.'

'I don't know anything,' he says, returning to the books on his desk again.

'When we in the police talk to a witness for the first time,' I begin, 'it's to obtain the person in question's account of how he's involved in an incident. What we do afterwards is to check whether anything in that account doesn't tally. If we find anything, we ask ourselves: why did the witness say this, and not that? What is the motivation? The next time we meet, we've found the answer as to why, and we can then confront the witness and give him a chance to tell us what we already know. This is the second time we've met, André. I'm here because I know why you said what you did the last time. I've got a printout of your mobile phone and email records, and I know too that you're a good lad who's doing it to protect a friend. Someone who's all alone.'

'He said he was going to take her to her mother.'

'He was lying,' I tell him. 'I don't lie.'

'He killed Siv,' André tells me in a whisper.

'Where is Olivia?'

He turns towards me again. 'Somewhere in Oslo. I think she's living in some sort of commune. We Skype.'

'Did she tell you what happened on the day she disappeared?'

'Yes.'

'Can you tell me?'

André clasps his hands and looks down at the floor. 'Yes.'

Chapter 116

I still feel the heat seeping out from Siv's chest as the cold earth presses down on all sides. I screw up my eyes and try to breathe in through her clothes. Maybe it's the absence of sound that finally tells me the coast is clear, that I don't need to wait any longer, or the tingling in my feet, the severe spasms and the increasing sense of panic that makes me start to move my body – first my fingers and toes, and I kick out, dislodging the cold earth and forcing it down between Siv and me.

I breathe through my nose to avoid throwing up, to avoid being suffocated. In the end I can no longer manage to hold the feeling of being drowned without water inside me and I swim through the chill earth up to the surface, towards the light.

I have the urge to scream as soon as I break through, to empty my lungs and fill them with fresh, healthy air, but I can't get a single sound out and I'm rooted to the spot as soon as I catch sight of him through the trees, standing up at the house.

He is on the terrace, swaying with his head bent down to the wooden planks where Siv lay only a short time ago. In the end he grabs hold of the glass door and disappears into the kitchen. I retch again and again until my stomach is empty and then I crawl out of the grave, using my fingers to rummage in the soil in order to conceal the vomit, and cover the hole again. Then I look back at the house one last time before I get to my feet and break into a run.

CHAPTER 117

'He took them to her mother's house in Tjøme. Said he would show them where she lived, and introduce them to her. Olivia told me she was in the bathroom when something happened to Siv. When she came out, Siv was lying on the ground outside on the terrace. Her head was bleeding. He said it had been an accident, and he put his hands around Olivia's neck, sobbing and crying all the time. When she next came to, she was lying beside Siv on the slope beneath the house, in the woods, and he was digging a grave nearby. He threw them down into it and filled the hole. But Olivia managed to climb out. She Skyped me a few days later and said she needed money and some of her clothes. I went into her room and collected a few of her things, and took them with me when I went to meet her. That's when she told me what had happened and insisted that we couldn't trust anyone and told me not to say anything to the police. Not a word.'

'And now? What's she doing now?'

'She says she's working, I think she ...'

'I see. You're worried about her, you're protecting her. But I have to find her, and I need your help to do that.'

'I told her about you too. Said you were looking for her, and that you seemed OK.'

'Yes, she phoned me. When did you last speak to her?'

'Yesterday. She was so happy. Said we would soon meet again.'

'What do you think she meant by that?'

'She'd just received an email from her mother and they were going to meet up today.'

CHAPTER 118

The leaves on the tallest trees were orange and red when Siv and I came here, nearly six months ago. The same trees have grown new leaves – it's spring now. There is a catch in my throat the moment I glimpse the house at the end of the driveway. Siv is still here, in the woods on the other side of your house, Mum.

I continue walking towards the stone steps that lead up to the front door. It's as if his fingers are closing around my neck again. But I don't stop, because I believe in you, Mum. The last six months have been the most difficult of all, and I've been so afraid that he might be there if I contacted you. Maybe he would hurt you too if he knew that I wasn't in the grave along with Siv, that I'd managed to escape.

I'd given up when I received that email from you. I was so tired of being scared, of being alone. But you wrote that you'd never give up searching for me until the two of us were reunited again. I wrote back to say that I would show you where he'd hidden Siv, and you told me we'd phone the police together, so that she'd be able to come home too.

I stop for a second on the bottom step: the wind blowing in from the sea gusts through the trees around the house, and all of a sudden I feel dizzy. Once again it's so difficult to breathe, once again his fingers are around my neck. But I swallow down the pain and force myself to ring the door-bell. Soon I hear your footsteps behind the door and see your shadow appear on the coloured glass.

Mum, are you just as excited as me?

CHAPTER 119

I park the car right beside the entrance and walk up to the house. I stop on the steps and listen, but can't hear anything. I stand there for a few moments without hearing a sound, so I put my hand on the doorknob and step inside.

The hallway and living room are flooded with sunlight. All I can hear is a faint hum from the fridge in the kitchen. A girl's red jacket is lying on the floor in the centre of the living room.

I pick up the jacket and carry it through to the kitchen. The oven is on and some kind of bread has been left to rise on the worktop. Apart from that, the house seems completely deserted.

Opening the terrace door, I venture outside and peer in through the glass door leading into Milla's study before I stop and focus my eyes on the woods, the boathouse and the rocks below, and catch sight of a man's figure.

I run down the terrace steps in the direction of the woods. It looks as if he's about to launch the boat. All at once I lose my footing, topple forward and hit the ground with a smack, knocking all the wind out of me. I open my eyes and see that I've landed in a freshly dug hole in the ground in the middle of the woods.

There is a rotten, acrid smell in the hole and I have to hold my nose as I struggle to scramble out. Not until I've hauled myself up to the edge do I notice a roll of black bin bags and silver gaffer tape, and when I peer down into the hole again, I spot the partly unearthed body of a young girl, lying on her side. Time has done its worst to erase the person she once was, but nevertheless I recognise the contours of Siv's face from photographs.

I rise to my full height, stand beside a tree trunk and keep a lookout towards the boathouse and shore. The figure down there has dragged the boat almost all the way down to the sea. A few metres further up, I see a man's body lying face down on the pebbles.

Continuing on to the perimeter of the woods, I slink around the boathouse through thick undergrowth and climb up on to the rocks on the other side.

'Hi, mate,' I call out once I reach the highest point on the rocks, immediately above the slipway. 'Are you planning to go fishing?'

CHAPTER 120

He stops and gazes at the rocks on which I'm standing, squinting in the cold spring twilight. 'W-what?' he says loudly, taking a few steps back to the boat, before clearing his throat, composing himself and repeating his question. 'What did you say?'

'I was wondering if you were going out fishing?' I say. 'Or is it crab pots you're after?'

'Think it's too early for crabs,' he replies, his fingers drumming impatiently on the gunwale of the boat.

'Are you thinking of taking Joachim out fishing with you, then?' I nod at the body on the ground in front of him. 'Are you planning to dump the girls' bodies out at the crab pots and throw Joachim in for good measure, making it look as if he fell in and drowned while he was getting rid of the bodies? A crafty plan, and almost a perfect scapegoat. Just one little flaw.'

'Oh?'

'Resources, motive and opportunity,' I answer. 'You know about those, don't you? Joachim has motive, that's true, opportunity, well, perhaps. But the resources to carry through what you've done? Come off it, Kenny, no one will buy that. You already knew Olivia, and you'd met the girls the year before when you and Karin went to Ibiza to bring them back the first time they ran away. They would have trusted you if you came up to them one day and told Olivia you'd found her mother and you wanted to take her home.'

His facial muscles twitch. 'It was an accident,' Kenny says, as his fingers clutch and let go of the gunwale. 'That wasn't what was supposed to happen. Siv got plastered: she stole a bottle of wine from the kitchen while I showed them around the house, and sneaked it down here. I made up my mind to bring them back again another day, but Siv fell,' he uses his finger to point, 'up there on the edge of the terrace while she was dancing and fooling around, and hit her head on a stone. What else could I do?'

'Why did you bring them here in the first place? What was your plan?'

'Why should Robert have the honour of bringing her home to Milla? I'd been there for her long before he even came on the scene. Why should he ...' he stops for breath. 'I told Iver over and over again after Milla started babbling about wanting to find her daughter, I said to him that we should tell her we already knew about Olivia, but he wouldn't hear of it, and then suddenly Milla turned up with Robert at the police station, telling us she'd hired him to find her.'

'And then it was too late. Your opportunity was gone.'

'Yes.'

'And now we're standing here. You and I.'

'You and I.'

'Where is she?'

He glances up towards the woods and the boathouse. 'You shouldn't have trusted me, when we sat here only a few days ago. Do you remember? I was the only person you trusted to travel up to the north of Norway to follow Svein Borg's trail.'

'No, Kenny. I sent you there to keep you away from the others. And because I knew you'd do your utmost to persuade us to continue on the track of Borg, as you've done the entire time. But I have to admit, when you faked your own mysterious disappearance in Milla's apartment, a crime scene lacking any evidence, I did begin to wonder if I had the right man in my sights. I expect you panicked when Olivia phoned me; you thought the game was up, and that was why you had to do a vanishing act?'

'I got a shock when you said she'd called you. Naturally I thought she was still where I had left her, as I'd thought the whole time since then. All the times I've walked over that grave since then. The idea never struck me that she might have ... I had to come out here, open up the grave and take a look, and yes, she really was alive. Who would have thought ...'

'What was it that made you change your mind? To change your plan?'

'Olivia,' he says. 'You're right, I thought of making myself scarce. I saw no other way out. But then my policeman's brain kicked in: if she really was alive, where had she been? I was aware that she knew I was a police officer, that she was scared and had no choice but to hide somewhere, but at the same time, she must have talked to someone and got help to keep herself under the radar for so long. And then there weren't so many alternatives: André, the school geek at the children's home where she lived, who couldn't hide that he was head over heels in love with her. Just the type I'd have phoned myself if I were in her situation.'

'So you got Runa to give you the mobile phone and email details, just as I did.'

'They'd been chatting. Skyping, too. Her email address was easy to find in his log, he's not exactly flush with friends. So I created a new email address, millalind@hotmail.com, and sent her an email, saying that I'd been searching for her, that I knew what had happened, and asking her to come home to me, so that I could help her and make all the dreadful things she'd been through go away and send that nasty man to jail. Ha ha ha, Christ Almighty, she answered only a few minutes later.'

'So you arranged to meet her here.'

'Just hung around the area until Milla disappeared back to her apartment in town, she can't stand more than a few days with Joachim before she needs to go back to the big city. I sent Olivia an email, said that the coast was clear and asked her to come as soon as she could.'

'But you needed Joachim here to get your plan to work.'

'He was in the kitchen baking bread when I came in. In a flowery apron and all that jazz. You should have heard that fucking Swedish housewife scream and shout when he realised what was going on. I dragged him down here, smashed his head on the gunwale and ...'

'You show real dedication. Even those pathetic text messages you sent me when you tried to play the part of Borg, and leaving the mobile in the Riverholts' apartment to give Borg the blame for those murders too. And then, despite all your hard work, Milla didn't want you. She would never leave Joachim. You, Iver, me, even Robert, we're all passengers in Milla's life, in at one stop and out at the next. The only man who had a seat for the whole journey was the guy lying dead at your feet. Even Robert would have understood that eventually, if you hadn't put that bullet in the back of his head.'

'Robert Riverholt,' Kenny fumes. 'You didn't know him. He was just like you, would never give up searching for the girls. Robert was the type that always had to give maximum effort, insisting that the sun had to shine on him and no one else.'

'So, you killed him because he no longer bought your story about Siv and Olivia having gone to Spain. And because you thought he was going to steal Milla away from you. That the battle was between the two of you rather than between you and Joachim.'

'Robert was a zero.'

'You took your time, you were a good boy and planned every step. You ingratiated yourself with Camilla, Robert's ex-wife, pretending to be her friend, picking up her mail and driving her around, while all the time you were planning how to kill him and give her the blame. It must have been difficult when you both sat in her car and she finally understood what you were going to do to her.'

Kenny closes his eyes and shakes his head. 'She was dying anyway,' he says when he opens them again. 'I did her a favour.'

'The same way that Borg did *his* victims a favour?'

'No,' Kenny bristles. 'I'm nothing like Svein Borg.'

'And Ann-Mari? What kind of favour were you doing her?'

Kenny laughs. 'Your ex-wife?'

'Yes.'

'Aske and his women,' Kenny snorts, full of contempt, as he glances at a fishing tool with a hook at one end lying in front of him inside the boat. 'How do you actually get these women to do everything for you? I went there to kill you. I stood for a long time at the bedside watching you both, watching her hold you close. You were totally out of it, half hanging out of the bed, drooling with your mouth open like a mental patient. Then she woke up.' All of a sudden Kenny bursts out laughing, as he grasps the fishing gaff and tightens his fingers around the pole. 'I grabbed her around the mouth and said that I was there to kill you. Said it was either you or her. She raised her hands and let me cut her, all without a squeak. I considered for a long time whether to keep my promise to her, but in the end I realised it just couldn't be done.'

When Kenny has finished telling me this, I let my eyes roam out over the sea to the floats marking the crab pots out there in the gloaming. 'Where is she?' I ask at last.

Kenny nods in the direction of the boathouse. 'In there,' he says.

'Is she dead?'

'You'll have to go and see,' he replies, leaning towards the gunwale with the gaff in his hand as his gaze follows me, waiting, measuring the distance between us, calculating the time before the next move.

'Soon,' I say, and at that moment I catch sight of another figure between the trees behind Kenny.

Kenny has let go of the gunwale. He stares at me as I move down from the rocks towards the boathouse, stopping a few metres in front of him and squinting one last time out at the sea before looking back at him. 'By the way, there's someone I'd like you to meet,' I tell him, nodding towards the person at his back.

Kenny wheels around and gazes at the figure looming behind him, sneaking out of the undergrowth. 'This is Gunnar Ore, my former boss in Internal Affairs,' I say, rushing past him as I head for the boathouse. 'Ann-Mari's fiancé. He wants to talk to you.'

Chapter 121

'Turn around,' Gunnar hisses as he passes me.

I grab the sleeve of his jacket to hold him back. 'I have to see if she's in the boathouse first.'

Gunnar tears himself free of my grip and heads towards Kenny. I sprint up to the open boathouse. In the middle of the floor I can see a tarpaulin rolled up and tied with rope. It looks as if something is wrapped up inside it.

I kneel down and start to tug and tear at the knots in the rope.

Meanwhile, I can see that Kenny is now standing on the other side of the boat. It looks as if they are playing tag, with Gunnar slowly chasing Kenny, who is about to be caught.

When at last I manage to untie the knots and open out the last folds of the tarpaulin, I see a young girl lying on her back in front of me. Her hands are bound, and she has tape across her mouth. Olivia's eyes shine with fright when they finally meet mine.

Gunnar turns to face me. 'All OK?' he asks.

'Yes,' I answer, hauling Olivia up into a sitting position. 'She's alive.'

Gunnar turns his attention back to Kenny, who has stopped his merry dance. I can see Kenny's grip on the fishing gaff tighten before he lunges at Gunnar.

Gunnar leans back slightly and uses his open hand to fend off the blow, yanking the pole out of Kenny's grasp and throwing it away across the pebbly shore. Then he plants a fist on Kenny's face and catches hold of him by the scruff of the neck before he can recover from the blow to his jaw. Then Gunnar starts to drag him.

'No,' Kenny gasps, grabbing hold of the gunwale with both hands. 'No, no, no.'

The sound of his wheezing breath reaches all the way up to the boathouse. Eventually, Gunnar releases his grip on Kenny's neck and takes a deep breath down into his lungs before seizing his feet.

Kenny hangs vertically in the air, struggling to hold on to the gunwale and screaming for help. In the end he can no longer hold on, and Gunnar starts to drag him down the slipway to the water, while Kenny feverishly tries to find something to grab hold of.

'Gunnar,' I call out when they reach the water's edge. 'You can't—'

'Turn away!' Gunnar barks without taking his eyes off Kenny. He stops on the shoreline and changes his hold, standing with his legs on either side of Kenny, and then begins to wade out into the sea. He paddles out, hauling Kenny behind him, until the water is up to his knees. 'Turn away, Thorkild,' he repeats as he takes another step forward. 'You don't want to see this.'

When he is far enough out, he forces Kenny's body under the water and straddles his back.

'Help,' Kenny gurgles as he flails about, trying to keep his head above water.

I grab hold of Olivia and turn her head into my chest, using my hands to cover her ears and forcing her to look away. In the background I can hear Gunnar intoning to himself, over and over again. 'Look away, Thorkild. This is not for your eyes.'

Chapter 122

I open my eyes again when he finally takes his hands from my face. He asks if I'll let him take me away from here. I nod and he lifts me up carefully and carries me through the woods, past the hole in the ground, towards the house. He goes round to the front, where he stops for a second to show the arriving police officers where they should head for. He doesn't let me go, not even when we reach the driveway. He asks me if I want to wait in his car, but I shake my head and cling to him, afraid to feel the ground beneath my feet.

Soon another car arrives and stops beside us. I see a man in the driving seat, and he comes out and says something before walking around the vehicle to open the passenger door.

I recognise your eyes at once: they haven't changed since the last time I saw you. They are exactly the same. You look so afraid, disheartened, just like me.

I slip out of his arms and into yours. I hug you tightly and turn my head so that I can see the whole of your face at last: 'Mum, here I am. It's me, Olivia.'

Epilogue

I think graveyards look their best at the crack of dawn, when the mist rises from the ground and restores colour to the plants, the grass and the city buildings. On this particular day, the streets are swept clean of the dust left by winter, and flower troughs are displayed on the balconies. The shoots in the gardens force spring to show through, even when it rains and the bleak weather refuses to release its grip.

I stop in front of the temporary wooden cross. Behind me I hear a car draw to a halt and the door open and slam again before hurried footsteps approach, crossing the gravel between the church and the graveyard where I stand.

'Been waiting long?'

'Just arrived,' I say. 'When did they let you out?'

'Immediately after they finished interviewing you,' Gunnar Ore replies, taking up position by my side. 'They obviously don't like you much. The officer in charge of the interviews was furious, to put it mildly. I think you've made a new enemy.'

'Tell him to join the queue.'

'Thanks,' Gunnar says, planting a fist on my shoulder. 'For not giving them anything.'

'Why should I?'

We stand there without a word as we both stare at the heap of earth in front of us.

'They're going to erect the gravestone some time this week,' Gunnar tells me before crouching down and struggling to find a suitable spot on the heap to place the flowers he's brought.

'Good,' I answer. 'How is Iver doing? Are they finished with him too?'

'Iver managed fine,' Gunnar says, nodding, as he gets up again and brushes the knees of his trousers. 'Are you coming back with me? We can have a coffee and—'

'Do you have them?'

'What?' Gunnar asks in a hushed voice.

'You know what.'

'Sure? I thought you no longer needed them?'

'No. You didn't.'

'OK,' Gunnar sighs. He slings a plastic bag down on the ground in front of Ann-Mari's grave. I bend down to retrieve it, open it up and look inside.

'Do you remember I thought she was the one who'd done it?' I begin, as my gaze roams over the packets and blister packs inside. 'That it was Ann-Mari who had used the knife on me and then herself?'

'Yes.'

'I was right about one thing, though, Gunnar,' I tell him, closing the bag before pivoting round to stand face to face.

Gunnar folds his hands over his chest. 'What?' he asks.

'It was a farewell. Ann-Mari wanted me to be there because she knew it was the very last time. Before the two of you got married.'

Gunnar nods fiercely and stares at his toecaps. 'What now?'

'Time to go home to Stavanger. There are people waiting for me.'

He looks up, first at the plastic bag, and then at me. 'Frei?'

'Frei is dead.'

'And Milla? Have you spoken to her since—'

'She has everything she needs now.'

'Are you going to be OK?'

I shrug. 'I've got a bag full of medicines and my winning ways. What could possibly go wrong?'

Gunnar blows on his hands and looks up at the sky. 'When are you leaving?'

'This afternoon.'

'Time for a coffee before you go?'

'I guess so,' I reply.

We turn around, leaving Ann-Mari's grave, and head for Gunnar's car. Above us the sun is breaking through the clouds. It shines down between the buildings enclosing the graveyard, making the streets of Oslo look sublime.

A NOTE ON THE AUTHOR

HEINE BAKKEID grew up in the rugged landscape of northern Norway. His Thorkild Aske series is highly acclaimed by critics in his home country, and has earned him a reputation as a virtuoso of darkly atmospheric suspense. *Scatter Her Ashes* is the second in the series, after *I Will Miss You Tomorrow.*

ANNE BRUCE graduated from Glasgow University with degrees in Norwegian and English. She lives in Scotland.

A NOTE ON THE TYPE

The text of this book is set in Linotype Sabon, a typeface named after the type founder, Jacques Sabon. It was designed by Jan Tschichold and jointly developed by Linotype, Monotype and Stempel in response to a need for a typeface to be available in identical form for mechanical hot metal composition and hand composition using foundry type.

Tschichold based his design for Sabon roman on a font engraved by Garamond, and Sabon italic on a font by Granjon. It was first used in 1966 and has proved an enduring modern classic.